When the man passed under a street light, McCleary noted his dark clothes, dark cap, his height, his build. Then the man glanced back, saw him, spun around, and ran. McCleary sprinted after him, the gun tight in his hand, his bare feet slapping the sidewalk, lawns, flowerbeds, curbs, asphalt.

The man dashed into an alley, stumbled, lurched forward again. His head jerked around; his cap flew off. His hair sailed around his head, a dark halo.

A WOMAN. JESUS. HE'S A WOMAN.

McCleary hurled himself at her, tackled her at the legs, and they both went down.

The air rushed out of her as they smacked the ground. . . .

Also by T.J. MacGregor
Published by Ballantine Books:

DARK FIELDS

KILL FLASH

DEATH SWEET

ON ICE

T. J. MacGREGOR

BALLANTINE BOOKS • NEW YORK

 Published in the United States of America by Ballantine Books, a division of Random House, Inc., New York, and simultaneously in Canada by Random House of Canada Limited, Toronto.

Library of Congress Catalog Card Number: 88-92192

ISBN 0-345-35045-6

Manufactured in the United States of America

First Edition: March 1989

For Linda Griffin,
who hasn't forgotten a thing
in twenty years

"Every man's memory is his private history."
—Aldous Huxley

"This is your house. On one side there is darkness. On one side there is light. . . ."
—Conrad Aiken

June 12

A DARK SILENCE, smooth as a pearl: he was hidden inside it.

If he breathed too hard, if he moved, the beast of pain would find him, seize him, rip him apart like a slab of old meat and spit out the grizzle. He remained utterly still. He tried to sink back into the cool, safe dark. But it no longer wanted him.

Several times before when the dark had released him, he'd surfaced so quickly the pain had found him, torn through him. He'd gripped the sides of his head, certain he was dying, and the dark had rescued him, pulled him back into itself again. But not this time. Now the dark shoved him away, up, up through silence, the smoothness, up faster and faster toward awareness, light, a voice. . . . The beast slammed into him, and the inside of his head exploded.

He gasped. His hands flew to his temples, pressing against them as if to contain the pain, to neutralize it somehow. But it swept through him in waves, a white-hot agony that scorched the inside of his eyes and nailed his lids shut against his cheeks. His ears rang. His flesh crawled. He sucked at the air and it whistled between his clenched teeth. He bolted forward on the bed, the pain blinding him. Hands grabbed his shoulders, restraining him. A voice hissed, "Hey, scumbag, hold on, just hold on. You're not going anywhere. I want answers, and I want them now."

He opened his mouth to speak, but nothing came out. He tried to focus his vision so he could see who the voice and the hands belonged to, but the room tilted and everything blurred. "My head," he rasped.

"You got worse problems than your head, scumbag. But here, hold this against it. It'll help." Something cool and damp pressed against the back of his head. A towel, a wet towel. He held it in place, and after a few moments the pain lessened. His vision began to clear.

The first thing he saw was a gray carpet against which his own feet looked abnormally white, bloodless, like marble. His toes were strange, pale worms that curled and uncurled, as if in an attempt to escape. His legs were bare. He had on nothing but underwear, and he shivered as a burst of cool air struck his spine.

"What's your name, scumbag?"

He drew his eyes slowly upward, to the Voice. The man was husky and broad-shouldered. He had pepper hair streaked with gray and a mean mouth that twitched with annoyance. He wore a brown uniform with a patch on the shoulder that said BROWARD COUNTY SHERIFF'S DEPARTMENT. His hand rested on a holstered gun. "Your name, pal, what's your name?" the cop snapped.

"I . . ." *Christ, what's my name?* He wiped the damp towel across his face and dropped it on the bed as his eyes flitted around the motel room, seeking something that would tell him where the room was or who he was. But the room revealed nothing. It could've been a motel room anywhere: a TV, a second double bed across from him, curtains drawn over the windows. "My, uh, name is . . ." He stammered, stopped, shook his head. "I . . . I don't know. It's . . ."

"Yeah, that's what I figured." The cop hooked his thumbs in his belt and hoisted his slacks as he strutted over to the other bed. He whipped the spread back. "I want *your* name and hers, buddy."

The woman lay on her back, her head turned away from him, her blond hair a tangled fan against the pillow. Blood covered her chest, streaked her shoulder, the side of her neck, and the inside of the arm closest to him. He stared at it, appalled, sickened, his throat closing. He knew he was going to throw up or pass out or both and grabbed for the damp towel. He pressed his face into it and doubled over at the waist, his head throbbing, the cop's voice stabbing at him, demanding answers.

"I'm talking to you, pal." The cop grabbed him by the hair and flung his head back. "What's your name? Neither you nor the woman got ID."

My name is . . . my . . . Panic bubbled in his throat. He

swallowed hard. He began to shake. "I . . . I don't know. I told you, I don't know."

"Uh-huh." The cop leaned close to him; his breath reeked of coffee and cigarette smoke. "And you've never seen the woman before, right?"

His tongue felt so thick it was an effort to speak. "I don't remember."

"Yeah." The cop stood up straight again. "Okay, we'll play your way for a while, scumbag. I'm going to tell you your name. On the register, you're listed as Peter Ketter. Got that?"

Ketter. Peter Ketter. "What register?"

"What register," the cop repeated with a roll of his eyes, and laughed. "The motel register."

Ketter: it didn't seem right. But if that wasn't his name, then what was it? Who was he? How did he get here? Who was the woman? Why was she dead in his room? What—

The door opened and light assaulted the room. It sliced through his eyes and into the back of his head, where the pain kept pounding, pounding. Another cop stepped in. "Lieutenant Grunwald, forensics just pulled up. You ready to vacate in here?"

"In a minute. You finished running down the license plates in the lot?"

"Not quite. We're checking them against the register as they come through."

"Bring a car around to the side," Grunwald ordered, and turned back to him. "All right, Ketter. You're under arrest for the murder of Jane Doe. You have the right to remain silent . . ."

He sat there clutching the damp towel as Grunwald spoke. That word, "murder," rose and fell around him, an echo, a hideous mockery of what he couldn't remember. His eyes flicked to the woman. *Did I kill you? Jesus, did I?*

He squeezed his eyes shut and reached deeper and deeper for his name. The word "Mac" came to mind; it didn't seem quite right, but neither did Ketter. *Then what's my name?*

The cop threw his clothes at him. "Get dressed, and then hold out your hands."

"I'd like to use the bathroom first."

"Sure you would, buddy. And I'd like the lady's name. You give me her name, then you can take a piss."

"I don't know her name."

"Sure. Put on your clothes, scumbag."

He dressed. The clothes were wrinkled; they smelled faintly of smoke and cologne. As Grunwald handcuffed him, the gold band on his left hand caught the light. *I'm married? Am I married to her, to the dead woman?* He didn't want to look at her, but as he came around the foot of the bed, her open eyes followed him, beckoned to him. *Who are you? Did I kill you? Did I?*

He wished someone had closed her eyes.

Grunwald led him outside into the hot, cruel light. He heard the din of traffic. He smelled the sea. Gulls shrieked and pinwheeled through a clear blue sky. *Where am I?* At the mouth of the parking lot, he saw a hotel sign: DAYS INN. It meant nothing. He knew the name of the county because it had been on Grunwald's uniform, but what city was this? What state?

Florida: the word curled like a wisp of smoke through his head.

What did he know about Florida?

Tourists and sun and Coppertone.

You got the state, now go looking for the city.

Daytona? No. Tampa? Miami? Yes, Miami felt right.

Was Miami in Broward County? What was he doing in Miami?

He was from . . . *where*? Someplace cold.

How old was he?

Where did he live?

Who was his wife?

Who was the dead woman?

What was he doing here?

How'd he get here?

Who the hell am I?

They threaded their way through a crowd of gawkers—young women in bikinis, old men in baggy shorts, kids in jeans and sneakers who peered at them through the fence that surrounded the pool. He dropped his gaze to the ground as they stopped next to one of the three police cars in the parking lot.

Did I kill her?

"All right, Ketter. Inside," Grunwald said, opening the back door of one of the cars.

He got in. Grunwald shut the door behind him. He fixed his eyes on the metal grating that separated the back seat from the front and waited for answers. But there was only a white, empty desert inside him through which a hot wind blew. It was as if he didn't exist at all.

He covered his face with his manacled hands, inhaling the residue of sweat, of blood. He felt like a pocket that had been turned inside out, emptied of change, lint, emptied of everything.

One

THE BLACK FRONT windows of the house signaled that the place was as empty as a new refrigerator. But at midnight on a Sunday, Quin thought, it shouldn't have been. Where was McCleary?

She stepped out of the taxi and waited while the cabbie hauled her bags from the trunk. The warm, wet wind gasped at her legs. Branches rustled and dripped water. Leaves fluttered through the air and scratched at the asphalt near her feet. She wished now that she'd called ahead to let McCleary know she was flying home from Canada a day early. But she had wanted to surprise him.

The cabbie started to carry her bags to the porch, but she stopped him. "I'll get them, thanks." She tipped him a dollar and waited until he'd pulled out of the driveway before she made her way up the walk. You couldn't be too careful in this city. The cabbie might be a raving maniac who picked up solitary women at the airport, swept up behind them like Count Dracula as they were unlocking their doors, and did unspeakable things to them.

Well, hey, welcome back to Miami.

The night swelled thickly with impending rain. More rain. Buckets of rain. The puddles in the driveway and the sweet, lush smell of the yard told her it had been pouring for the two weeks she'd been gone.

The moment she was inside the house, the cats were all over her, meowing and fussing like they hadn't seen a human being in weeks. Quin switched on the light and crouched to pet each one—Merlin, the black cat, came first because he was the oldest and age deserved some consideration. Then she stroked Hepburn, the white Persian, and finally, Tracy, the calico, who by then had gotten bored with the homecoming and was scooting toward the kitchen.

"Mac?"

His name echoed as she turned on lights and followed Tracy into the kitchen. She already knew he wasn't here. The house felt too empty and the fridge confirmed it. It was almost as bad as Mother Hubbard's cupboard: a quart of milk, which one whiff said had gone sour, three bottles of Lite beer, an apple, a couple of open cans of cat food. The freezer wasn't quite as bad. But already her mind had seized on the possibilities: McCleary had been spending most of his time with another woman at *her* house and she was a fabulous cook so why buy groceries; he was on a case he hadn't mentioned when she'd spoken to him the night she'd arrived in Canada; he'd gotten tired of marriage and had vanished; something had happened to him.

But if something had happened to him—*What kind of something? So-so bad? Medium bad? Or the pits?*—then who'd been feeding the cats?

She checked his den, the guest bedroom at the end of the hall, and poked her head into the utility room. Laundry was neatly folded on top of the dryer. The litter boxes in the adjoining half-bathroom were clean. "Lady" his silver RX7, was parked next to her tired old Toyota in the garage.

"Mac?" Quin climbed the stairs to the second floor, turning on lights as she went, suddenly afraid she would find a trail of blood on the carpet, his mutilated body on the bed. . . . She cut off the thought. If you lived in Miami long enough, this was what happened, this insidious corruption of the spirit.

In the bedroom, their king-size bed was neatly made, and the sight of it, corners just so, pillows fluffed up, comforted her. Tidy McCleary. If she'd spent two weeks alone, the fridge would be full but the house would look like the headquarters for a marauding army.

The shades were drawn. She didn't know if that was a good sign or a bad one. But the air was as hollow as the widening pit in her stomach, and that was definitely not a good sign. She sank onto the edge of the bed, reached for the phone to call Tim Benson, then drew her hand back. McCleary wasn't expecting her until tomorrow. He and Joe Bean had probably gone out to dinner, to Maracas, that new Cuban restaurant they'd found before she'd left. Black beans and rice, fried plantains, *arroz con pollo*. Sure.

She shucked her clothes and left them where they fell, a puddle of fabric that smelled like lunch at 35,000 feet. She turned on water for a bath. All day she'd thought about stretching out in a tub filled with water as hot as she could stand it. She'd thought of soap that smelled of fresh pears, of bubbles that hissed and foamed against her skin, of her own tub, her own bed, her cats, her husband. Home.

Any second now, Bean's car would pull in the driveway. Since it was late, he'd just let McCleary out and then be on his way with a pop on the horn and a "Later, m'man." She would hear the front door open and shut, softly. McCleary would see her suitcases in the hallway. She would hear his footfalls on the stairs, in the bedroom, then he would stroll through the door and crouch by the tub and kiss her hello. He would be a proper McCleary, asking how Canada was, how her flight was, measuring her against some image in his head, testing to see if she'd changed in two weeks, and if so, how. He would still be crouched by the tub, listening as she talked, nodding, laughing, but still testing, measuring. She would stop suddenly and crook her finger at him or he would grin in that certain way he had and lean a little closer to her and she would pull him into the tub with her.

Water would sluice over the sides, they . . . The phone rang.

That would be her sister, calling to make sure she'd gotten home okay, that she'd made the connection in New York.

Quin got out of the tub, grabbed her towel, and hurried into the bedroom. But it wasn't her sister on the phone; it was Benson.

"Quin." He sounded breathless, urgent. "I've been trying to get in touch with you for the last four days, but I didn't have a phone number for the place you and your sister were staying."

"I just got in."

"Mac's been arrested, Quin."

"*Arrested?*" The word rolled down her tongue like a giant marble, and she started to laugh. McCleary being arrested was the equivalent of the Pope exposing himself. But when Benson didn't laugh, didn't so much as chuckle, she sat down heavily on the edge of the bed, hugging the towel against her. "For what?" She could barely get the words out.

"I'll be right over."

The line went dead. She sat there just like people did in the movies, the receiver in her hand, her eyes glued to it as if she expected it to speak to her, to explain. Then she replaced it gently in the cradle and got up to put on some clothes, her brain on hold.

The weather in Canada had been crisp and clear. Quin and her sister had bundled up in sweaters during the day, shopping until they dropped, pigging out on French-Canadian food, drinking in the sights like the shameless tourists they were. When they left Montreal to hole up in a mountain lodge as far from civilization as they could get, they'd hiked and canoed during the day, and huddled around the fireplace in their room at night, regressing. It was the first time in years they'd been anywhere together without their husbands or parents or Marcy's kids, and they'd thoroughly enjoyed each other's company. Fourteen days, that was all. But the look on Benson's face said it had been two weeks too long.

At five-ten in her bare feet and a hundred and eight pounds, Quin was thinner than Benson and taller, even when she was sitting. But at the moment, the opposite seemed true. She felt like a fat kid peering up at an adult, waiting for some terrible verdict.

"Just say it, Tim."

He nudged his wire-rim glasses farther up on the bridge of his nose. His eyes were the color of the coffee in front of him. The lemon-colored guayabera shirt he wore gave his face a jaundiced cast. His chestnut hair was cut very short, so he looked vulnerable, like a frightened Marine on his first tour of duty in a war zone. She wanted to put her arms around him.

"It's not simple, Quin, so you'll have to bear with me. Several days after you left, Mac and I had lunch. He asked me to run a check on a nightclub in Lauderdale called Bernardo's—who owned it, whether it had ever been investigated, whatever. He said it was connected to a new case he was working on for a guy named Lans Hitchcock, who was rolled one night outside the club by a woman he'd picked up. He'd lost a Rolex and all his money and whatever jewelry he was wearing. Anyway, I told Mac I'd look into the club and get back to him. I heard from him again, a day or two later. He said he was going to be a reporter and laughed. I didn't hear from him again until the twelfth.'' He paused and Quin didn't like the look on his face. ''I want you to just listen to what I'm going to say, all right? And understand I don't believe Mac is guilty of anything.''

Benson's preface told her it was going to be bad; she didn't understand how it could be worse than it already was. She drew her umber hair back behind her head with her hand and kept her ghost blue eyes on Benson's face. She wouldn't jump to conclusions, even though it happened to be something she did quite well.

Around 7:30 on the morning of June 12, Benson said, a maid at the Days Inn on Lauderdale Beach went into room 110 to clean and found McCleary sacked out on one bed and a dead woman on the other. The maid ran out of the room, the police were called, and when they arrived, they had a hard time bringing McCleary around. They questioned him; he claimed he didn't know his name or who the woman was.

''The arresting officer, Roger Grunwald, is a horse's ass, Quin, and he thought McCleary was lying. He told him he was registered under the name Peter Ketter.''

''It's a name we've used on undercover work,'' she said, and Benson nodded because of course he knew that. Benson had worked with McCleary off and on for ten years in homicide and had been involved with them in numerous cases in the more than five years they'd had their private detective agency. Of course, of course. *I'm already losing it.*

''They finally tracked down who he was through Lady's license plate. She was parked in the lot. Then Grunwald realized he was dealing with an ex-homicide cop and a private eye. He called Metro-Dade and eventually it filtered down to me. I called Doc Smithers and the two of us drove up to Lauderdale. The doc ran some tests on Mac and found traces of a powerful hypnotic in his blood. A heavy-duty tranquilizer called Panzine. He'd apparently been hit over the head, because there was a knot at the back of his skull. The doc said he had a concussion. He's at Broward General in Lauderdale, under guard, where he's been for four days.''

He paused again, a maddening pause to take a sip of coffee. She leaned forward. ''And? How'd he seem when you saw him? Did he talk about what happened? What'd he say, Tim?''

Benson rubbed his jaw. ''He doesn't remember any of it. He didn't even know me, Quin. Or Doc.''

She knew what he was saying. Some part of her seemed to have known it since Benson had said "concussion," said it incompletely, as if there were another word that rode tandem with it, a word that smacked of soap operas.

"Amnesia." She uttered it in a normal tone of voice, like an ordinary word, but it still possessed power. "Is that what we're talking about?"

"Yes. From the concussion."

The next question, the necessary question, was one she didn't really want to ask. "How much doesn't he remember?"

"For the first couple of days, he didn't remember much of anything. His mind was a blank, except for what the doc and I filled in. Now some of his earlier memories are coming back. His skills aren't impaired, so he's not a vegetable or anything."

She heard *the big but* sliding around in what he hadn't said. "He's missing about twenty years, Quin."

He didn't look at her as he said it. He stared into his coffee mug, moving a thumb around the rim of it, as if he were trying to rub away something. *Half his life.* The enormity of it was suddenly everywhere at once—in the air she breathed, in the emptiness of the house, in the sound of the wind outside as it hurled rain against the kitchen windows. She wanted to race upstairs to the bedroom and throw open the closet door and press her face into McCleary's clothes. But she couldn't move. Her body refused to work. She felt weighted, dwarfed, and her mind had fixed on a single thought—that the man she'd been married to for five years and nine months could not remember her.

Benson was talking again. She saw his mouth moving, heard the sounds he made, but she didn't understand him. He was speaking a foreign language. Or maybe he wasn't making any sounds at all. She felt herself standing, her movements slow, languid, as controlled as a dancer's but lacking grace. She poured herself more coffee and her hand trembled. She opened the fridge to get some cream, but there wasn't any. There wasn't anything inside worth eating, and the emptiness mocked her. Enraged her.

I know what it is, Quin. You starved in a previous life and that's why you feel compelled to fill refrigerators and eat all the time. She heard McCleary saying this in his "I've-got-you-all-figured-out" voice. She heard him laughing. She wanted to cry, scream, pound her fists against something. But more than any of these things, she wanted facts, needed them the way she usually needed food. She would break them down like nutrients, analyze them, pick them apart. She turned and faced Benson.

"Who's his lawyer?"

"The firm attorney."

Good. Their attorney was good. Alice had handled dozens of cases over the years for their firm. Quin trusted her; she just didn't trust the system. "Has he been arraigned?"

"Yes."

"When?"

"Yesterday. The trial's been set for September. Alice managed to get the bail lowered from three hundred grand to a hundred and a quarter, Quin, because of Mac's background as a cop and so on. Right now, it's a murder one rap and he's lucky there's any bail set at all. The bondsman is willing to take the house or business as collateral or ten percent cash."

The house, the business, the cars, her life—what was the difference? She would've put up her soul as collateral if she'd thought the devil would have it. She sat down again. Her stomach twisted with hunger, but she barely noticed. Her thoughts raced forward, flipping through what she knew of amnesia.

Damn little.

"Who was the woman, Tim?"

"Her name was Nadia Forsythe. She was a flight attendant for an outfit in Lauderdale called Atlantic Express. It runs shuttles between South Florida and the Bahamas, Atlanta, New York, and a half-dozen other spots in between. Thirty-five, no family, single, no record. According to her personnel record, she was born and raised in Chicago. That's about all we know."

"Since when do motel maids clean rooms at seven-thirty in the morning?"

"She claims it was a mistake; she was supposed to clean room one-twelve next door."

"I want to talk to her."

"We're looking for her, Quin. Two days ago, she didn't come into work, and she hasn't shown up since. No home address. I have a feeling she's an illegal alien and just moves around, working in the hotels along the east coast of Florida."

Great. "Was Mac carrying a weapon?"

"Yes. It had been fired, too. The slug in the Forsythe woman's chest was a .38."

A finger of ice flicked at the back of her neck and worked its way down her spine. She tried to ignore it. As long as she kept asking questions and culling facts, she could maintain the illusion that she was doing something, working toward something, a goal, a purpose. "Anything else in the room or on Mac?"

Benson nodded. "On Mac. A matchbook from Bernardo's with the Forsythe woman's phone number jotted on it and this." He reached into his pocket and brought out an index card that looked like it had been through the wash. Benson's thin fingers smoothed it against the counter. "It was squashed down inside his wallet."

A brief personal ad was taped to the card: *If you have a pleasant telephone voice and would like to make $350 a week for part-time work, call Date-A-Mate at 555-6718.* "Is this one of those sex-by-phone deals?"

"Nope. It's a legit dating service. The idea is that you call the number and the operator asks you questions and then hooks you up to someone of the opposite sex who seems compatible. You get to know each other over the phone first, and if both parties are interested, phone numbers are exchanged. The company's fee is two-fifty; they accept all major credit cards."

Like credit cards sanctioned them. "Does it have anything to do with the dead woman?"

"She worked there part-time."

"What about this guy who hired Mac, Tim? What's he have to say?"

"I got his address from Mac's file and went by his place. Right now, he's out of the country. He's an investor who lives in a ritzy condo on Key Biscayne. Mostly, he seems to play the stock market and commodities. Or so his housekeeper says. She claimed she didn't have any number for him in Europe."

"When can I see Mac?"

"Tomorrow. I'll arrange it."

"Is the amnesia permanent?" *Tell me no.*

"We don't know."

It was better than a definite *yes*, she thought, but not by much. "When *will* anyone know?"

Benson shrugged. "He's got a court-appointed shrink, Quin, who has already seen him a couple of times. She says total amnesia is rare and feels certain that more of his earlier memories will start coming back over the next few weeks. But she can't guarantee anything. It might be a good idea if you spoke to her before seeing Mac."

Quin frowned. "Why court-appointed?"

"The prosecutor wants to be sure he isn't faking."

"Oh, Christ, c'mon. That's ridiculous."

"You and I know that. But to the prosecuting attorney, he's just an ex-cop who shot a woman and is claiming he doesn't remember any of it. Amnesia's evidently an easy thing to fake. Once she's sure he isn't faking, it will work to Mac's advantage. An amnesiac can't assist in his own defense. Alice has already requested a later trial date based on that."

Her brain was overloading. She could feel it, hear it: a lapse in the firing of certain synapses, a faint, sour smell emanating from her skin, a burning way in the back of her eyes. She pressed her fingers to her temple and rubbed absently, in small, tight circles.

"Listen, how about if you stay at our place tonight, with Jackie and me. We've got an extra bedroom, or if you want more privacy, there's the apartment over the garage—if you can put up with Hank's stereo equipment and posters." Hank was Benson's sixteen-year-old son.

"Thanks, but I'll be okay here."

Liar.

"I've got to unpack."

Another lie.

Her clothes could mildew in the suitcase for all she cared. She was going to be hysterical. She sensed it, this hysteria, rallying in her blood, rising in her throat as she nodded, as she smiled thinly, as hot tears gathered behind her eyes and created a hard, pulsing pressure. Now Benson was standing and she was standing and the hysteria was a bratty, spoiled child crouched in a corner of her mouth.

"I'll call you in the morning. Oh, before I forget." Benson reached into his pocket and pulled out a notepad. He tore several sheets from it. "I've included everything I could think of—Mac's shrink, the bondsman, and so on. And Mac's keys." He dug them out of another pocket, handed them to her. They felt cold and heavy in her palm. "Lady's in the garage. I've been feeding the cats. Your neighbor has your mail."

Ordinary life: she seized the details, clutched them as if their banality would protect her. "Thanks, Tim. For everything."

She walked with him to the front door, and the moment the rainy dark sucked his taillights away she pressed the back of her hand to her mouth. Her vision blurred. She stood there on the porch, rain pounding through the yard, splashing against the railing, and waited for answers, guidance, direction, elucidation. But nothing happened. Time had stopped. The world had shrunk to the size of a pea, and a cosmic goblin was tossing it up and down, chanting, *Ha-ha, Quin. Gotcha this time, Quin. Here's your biggie.*

In her mind's eye, she watched the pea swooping up, plummeting down. If the goblin squeezed it too hard, it would pop like a pimple and then there would be only the sound of the rain and the little shit's cackle.

Her stomach growled, and the world clicked forward again. She hurried inside, shut the door, gazed down the hall at the gallery of McCleary's art work. Oils and acrylics, watercolors and charcoal drawings, abstracts, country scenes, portraits, cityscapes. If his skills weren't impaired, then he would still be able to paint. If he could paint, it might trigger a memory. . . .

Big maybe.

She swept into the kitchen for her purse. The goblins hammered their tight, hard fists against the backs of her teeth. *Knock, knock, Quin. Let us out, Quin.*

Food: she needed food in the house.

She would drive over to the all-night Piggly Wiggly for groceries. How could she even think straight with no food in the house? How could she organize a plan with the vacuum of an empty fridge at her back?

But when she was inside McCleary's silver RX7, the familiar scent of leather, of his skin, made her breath hitch in her throat. *He doesn't remember me.* She hit the button for the garage door and it trundled open. *Doesn't remember we're married*. She backed out, pressed the button again, and started to cry.

She cried as she drove too fast to the market, along streets as slippery as satin, the windshield wipers whipping back and forth across the glass. She sniffled and bit at her lower lip as she wheeled her cart down the aisle, grabbing at whatever was closest. Frozen foods. Canned foods. Things she never bought. She nearly burst into tears when the tally on the register came to $132.67 and she realized she didn't have her checkbook with her. She dug into her wallet and found a blank check, then had to go to the office to get it approved.

She wondered if it would bounce.

Count on it, Quin, laughed one of the wicked goblins. *Welcome to the land of Murphy's Law*.

The moment she was inside the car again, she popped the lid on a jar of freeze-dried peanuts, propped it between her legs, and proceeded to consume them by the handfuls. It was irreverent that she could even contemplate food at a time like this, that her hunger churned and burrowed like a mindless mole. She stuffed her face as she drove, the little piggy in the child's jingle, crying all the way home.

Two

"BAHAMAS AIR FLIGHT 412 is cleared to land. Please extinguish all smoking materials and fasten seat belts. We've enjoyed . . ."

The flight attendant's voice pierced her dream, awakening her, and then flowed over her, a dark rushing tide that cooled her burning cheeks. The air vent was aimed at Magali Pintera's face and dried the pimples of sweat across her upper lip. She shivered. *The dream, something about the dream*, she thought, still groggy as she brought her chair to an upright position. She'd had the dream before, she knew she had. But always, the only thing she remembered afterward was that she was running through a dark alley, an alley blacker than pitch. She could hear footfalls. She could hear the breathing of someone behind her. But when her head jerked around, she saw only eyes. They glowed like neon, pulsed like tiny hearts. And they were close, very close, and she knew that if the eyes touched her, she would die.

She shook the dream away and peered through the tiny window to her left. Lights glinted below; they were earthbound stars, chips of moonlight in a black sea. Miami. Now she saw the interstate, an artery of lights slicing through flatness, straighter than a matchstick for miles, then giving way to slow curves, sudden twists, a spill of saffron from the crime lights.

She hadn't been here in five years and found comfort in the fact that at night the city appeared unchanged, static, its topography as familiar as the back of her hand. There: the islands in Biscayne Bay, Miami Beach, the sprawl of Little Havana. And now, as the 767 sped toward its final approach, she saw Liberty City, Little Haiti, and then, beyond it, the deeper darkness of the Everglades, stretching across the width of the state. This tiny peninsula was like another continent, with people from dozens of countries on every block.

Five years.

Lifetimes.

The woman who was returning here was not the same one who had left. In five years, she's moved around like a nomad—Europe, the Far East, South America, and the Caribbean. Her services were in demand in certain circles, and her reputation was such that she dealt only with people who could afford her exorbitant fees. Two years ago, she'd sunk some of that money into an Alpine lodge in Colonia Tovar, a German settlement in the Andean foothills outside of Caracas. It was now the place she considered home, her base of operations, her perfect cover. She was the largest employer in a region dependent almost solely on tourism and paid higher wages than any of the competition. She'd helped elevate the local tourist industry from a second-rate destination to a place so coveted by South Americans and Europeans that nearly every hotel in town was booked solid for the next year. That alone had made her so popular among the locals that no one questioned her about her past. To those people, the present was what mattered.

The town suited her. Its German roots were identical to those in southern Chile, where she'd been born thirty-eight years ago. It allowed her to remain fluent in German, one of four languages she spoke, and she felt secure enough there to be known by her real name—Magali Schmidt. She was a Venezuelan citizen, but rarely traveled on a Venezuelan passport. For this job, in fact, she was traveling on an American passport procured for her by a fed she knew. She was a Cuban-American whose personal history fit South Florida.

If she had to trace her present life to a particular event in her past, it would be to the death of her husband during the overthrow of the Allende government, when she was barely twenty. He'd been struck in the throat by a bullet intended for a line of students in a demonstration in downtown Santiago. He'd died in her arms, his blood oozing over her own skin, his pale blue eyes fluttering open against unbearable pain. Moments later she was accosted by soldiers, beaten senseless, raped, left for dead. It had murdered her compassion. In its place had grown a profound hatred for scum.

She rarely thought of her husband anymore. He was an

American Marine she'd met in a bar in Valparaíso, an ordinary man, really, from Cincinnati. But she had loved him fiercely, passionately, with all the naive hopefulness of youth. Although she no longer mourned him and could barely remember what he looked like, she understood that his death was the heart of everything. She accepted it. She understood the possible consequences of her actions; it didn't frighten her. Her capacity for fear, like her capacity for compassion, had atrophied that night in Santiago.

The plane banked into its final approach. The opaqueness of the Everglades slipped away. Now, in the glass, her own reflection gazed back at her. The natural color of her hair was a rich bronze, but for this job it was black and fell almost to her shoulders in electric curls. Her eyes were wide, deeply set, the dark of bitter chocolate. Her mouth was full, quick to smile, and her nose was slender and straight. Her body—lean, strong, agile—had been honed through a strict regimen of diet and exercise. She was, by her own dispassionate assessment, a striking woman. But through the magic of clothes and makeup, by altering her speech and gestures, she could also appear quite ordinary. She'd long ago learned that the art of disguise was much more than just changing the color of your hair.

The one thing about her that hadn't changed for this job or any other was her fondness for jewelry. She wore several thick gold chains around her neck, half-a-dozen slender gold bracelets danced on her right arm, and a lovely Swiss watch adorned her left wrist. Her rings were a small, deep green emerald in a simple gold setting and a slightly larger ruby crowned by a crescent of diamond chips. Her jewelry always reflected what she needed most on a particular day—gold for a lift, silver or platinum for heightened intuition, sapphires for introspection, rubies for energy. She had a talent for metal, for gems—where they could be bought, bargained for, mined, how they were cut, set, sold. It was not a talent she'd consciously nurtured. It interested her, so it came easily, just as remembering did. Or finding people. Or killing.

Magali followed the departing passengers into the terminal. So many billboards, such a maze of corridors and escalators, all leading to a people-mover which sped them along toward the main building, to immigration and customs. Her flight from Nassau had been blissfully short, but it had been only one leg in her journey from Luxembourg. It was late, and she was tired. She hoped there wouldn't be any delay in customs. The agents were puppets, their faces frozen in grimness, their hands patting, digging, seeking, their voices plangent with courtesy. But American customs agents weren't the paragon of efficiency that they thought themselves to be. They weren't as good as the Swiss, who missed nothing, or as thorough as the Colombians, who, thanks to the drug cartel, now checked your bags before you even left the country. But they were a cut above the agents in Luxembourg, she thought, whose checks were cursory at best.

She had gone to Luxembourg to relax after a long and ultimately satisfying job. Eight months earlier, she'd been hired by the French embassy in Switzerland to track down a man who had abducted several children of French diplomats in various spots in Europe. It had taken her nearly four months to connect him to a string of sex crimes against children in six countries, but once she had, finding him was relatively easy. She tracked him through Austria, Yugoslavia, and Greece, then back up and into the Black Forest, where he was living like a king on ransom money. She spent two weeks working for him as a maid, trying to determine if the abducted children were still alive. When she found their corpses buried in the basement, she sank an ice pick through his throat. A good kill. Quick and clean. Flawless.

She presented her American passport in a room where passengers were separated into two groups—citizens and noncitizens. She followed the rest of the citizens down an escalator to the baggage claim area, retrieved her suitcase, and got in line. One of the customs agents moved down the row of passengers, pausing here, there, asking a few questions, scribbling something on a slip of paper, waving every third or fourth person through.

When he stopped beside her, she caught the scrutiny in his seemingly quick glance that evaluated her according to some arcane customs criteria: Did she twitch? Did she seem nervous? Did she avert her eyes? Was she traveling alone? Was she sweating? Did she fit the profile of a drug smuggler?

As the man paged through her passport, he asked what she'd been doing in Nassau, even though he could plainly see from the stamps that her flight had originated in Luxembourg.

She said as much and he nodded and remarked how beautiful the country was and asked if she had any purchases to declare. Only what was on the declaration slip, she replied.

He waved her on through.

She strolled past the customs counters, one bag clutched in her hand, her carry-on snug on her shoulder. If possible, she traveled lightly and bought what she needed en route. But, depending on the country, it was sometimes a delicate balance. She couldn't travel so lightly that she attracted attention. This time, she had struck the right balance. A good omen.

In the room just beyond customs, she stopped at the line of phone booths and fed a quarter into the slot. She dialed a number in Little Havana and a man answered on the second ring.

"*Dígame.*"

"*Jimenez se encuentra?*"

"*Un momento, por favor.*"

The man who picked up the extension had a low, deep voice. Magali had never met him, but his voice conjured an immediate image—older, perhaps in his early fifties, with white hair and a protruding gut. Too much rich food, no exercise, a life of excess. He hadn't hired her; she wasn't sure who had hired her this time. Jimenez was just her contact, one of the numerous sycophants who made a comfortable living negotiating deals and whose life was played out in anonymity, in a kind of darkness.

"*Sín verguenza,*" she said. *Without shame*: her password.

He provided her with all the details she needed. She thanked him and hung up.

Magali hailed a taxi, which took her to the Carlyle Hotel on Miami Beach. She'd stayed there five years ago, the night before she'd left the country. South Beach had been a war zone of druggies and gangs then, a decaying eyesore at the edge of the sea inhabited mostly by people on Social Security who were afraid to go out after dark. Now Ocean Drive was a yuppie paradise. Police cruised the neighborhood. The hotels had been refurbished in pinks and blues and melons; their lobbies had been gutted and redecorated. Cafés were plentiful. People biked along the sidewalks, pedestrians strolled the beach, music drifted from open doorways.

As she got out of the cab, she stood for a moment on the

walk, inhaling the sweet, warm air. The sound of the surf swelled against the dark. She felt a sudden sharp longing for . . . what? A different life? What sort of life? An ordinary life?

She knew the answer; she just didn't want to think about it. Not now. Not until this job was over. But the longing persisted. It moved through her like the vestiges of a dream. She saw herself and a small child walking the wide beach across the street, pausing to gaze out at the sea. Her child. The child she would have when she was finished here.

She hugged her arms against her and waited for the feeling to exhaust itself. It did, but not as quickly as usual, and then she went into the hotel to register.

Her room was small but charming. Pastel walls, wide windows that overlooked the ocean, a comfortable double bed. She shucked her white slacks and silk blouse, removed all her jewelry, and took a quick shower. Afterward, she knelt in front of her suitcase, studying her clothes. She finally settled on black Italian-made slacks that fit her like a second skin, a short-sleeved cotton blouse, a pair of red patent leather heels, and a red leather purse. She slipped the ruby back on—for energy, because the flight had tired her, and because it matched the shoes and bag. Earrings? Yes, okay. The red hoops would look good. But no gold chains. Not in Miami.

She took a cab to the bus depot downtown and in the ladies' room went into the third stall on her right and locked the door. She reached behind the toilet bowl, patting the cool, damp porcelain until she found a key taped in a dip about a hand's width up from the floor. She removed it and left the stall.

Locker 14 was near the exit. The doors were open, and the exhaust fumes from the idling buses and the noise of their engines assaulted her as she inserted the key in the lock and turned it. She removed the black vinyl briefcase from inside, left the key in the lock, and returned to the rest room. In the stall, she lowered herself to the toilet seat and unzipped the briefcase. There was $75,000 inside, with another fifty due upon completion of the job. In the zippered compartment was a photograph of her mark, along with comprehensive biographical information on him and his wife. It included everything from his vital statistics to his hobbies and personality quirks. The one stipulation was that his death had to look accidental.

Magali flipped through the biographical information, then studied his photograph. *Self-contained*, she thought. His eyes were smoke blue, his hair was thick, dark, laced with strands of gray, like his beard. His mouth said he was stubborn, a man accustomed to doing things his way. His body was lean, sinewy, his shoulders broad. She liked his looks.

A runner.

A man who pursued art as a hobby.

A realist with a capacity for aesthetic appreciation.

Interesting.

When she was back at her hotel, in her room, she spread everything out on the bed, reading through the bio data more slowly, missing nothing. Her eidetic memory was startlingly accurate, and by the time she reached the end of the material, she could recall entire pages as they'd been written.

Ten years as a homicide detective with Metro-Dade, presently a private investigator charged with first-degree murder. Clipped to the page was an article from the *Miami Herald* about the homicide. She looked at the photo of the woman who'd been killed, and her blood boiled. A crooked ex-cop who'd apparently been grabbing a little on the side. Whoever had hired her had one thing in mind: revenge. Good. It was a motive she understood.

But it disturbed her that she would be up against a cop. Those who were good usually possessed an acute sixth sense similar to what she'd observed in certain predators. A man she'd stalked in Rome three years ago—an ex-Italian cop turned Mafia henchman—had taught her a great deal about intuition. He'd not only known he was being tracked but had turned the tables on her and had almost proven to be her nemesis. It was a lesson she hadn't forgotten, and a mistake she did not intend to repeat.

Included in the packet was a copy of the police report, copies of the photo taken at the scene of the crime, everything she needed to evaluate for herself whether the man was guilty. He probably was, but before doing anything, she would snoop a little on her own. She nearly always did, unless she was hired by someone she knew, one to one, no intermediaries.

She was not without a sense of fairness; and besides, she would be paid regardless.

Magali rubbed her eyes, picked up the papers, and carried them into the bathroom. She closed the door and turned on the shower. When steam was rolling through the room, she burned the sheets over the toilet bowl and thought about the child.

Her child.

The child—boy or girl, it didn't matter—was still only an abstract, a tight, hard knot at the back of her mind that refused to go away. Years ago, when she was married to the Marine, she had miscarried. Another time, when she was in her late twenties, she'd gotten pregnant by a Swiss businessman. She'd had the pregnancy terminated—not because the man was married, but because his character was flawed and she didn't want him to be the father of her child. Six years ago, a brief affair with a Spanish artist had resulted in a second miscarriage. But this time would be different. This time the biological clock was ticking. This time her body was primed; pregnancy would be a conscious decision. She would choose the man carefully, deliberately, guided by instinct, just as she chose her jobs.

She held a match to the picture of Mike McCleary. The edges blackened and curled. Magali moved her fingers around to avoid the slender tongues of flames. When there was nothing but a pinch of the photo left, she dropped it into the toilet. It hissed. Thin plumes of smoke rose from it. She flushed the toilet and watched the water swirling, swirling, the smoke gone now, everything gone except for a black fleck of the picture floating in the water like a ship marked for death.

"Bye-bye, McCleary," she said softly, and smiled.

Three

THE ABSENCE OF sound outside his room was fitting, somehow, as though the absence of his memory had drawn the silence to him as a metaphor of his condition. Mike McCleary drifted in it for a few minutes, eyes closed, his body motionless, his hope leaping beyond him like a probe, seeking the bright schematic of the life he'd misplaced.

He wasn't picky; anything would do: a name, face, a place, an event. He would even settle for a brief glimpse of one of those things from the last twenty years, a silhouette his imagination could fill in, part of a name he could puzzle through. *Anything*.

But as McCleary waited, the dull, persistent ache at the back of his head that had followed him into sleep last night rallied like a politician. He winced as he slowly sat forward on his bed and dropped his legs over the edge. The pain slid off to one side, pounding hard. It was as if his memories had grown arms and legs during the night and now hammered against the boundaries in his mind that separated him from them. He poured a glass of water from the pitcher sweating on the nightstand, drank it down, poured a second glass, and consumed that as he got up and went into the bathroom.

He relieved himself, washed up, brushed his teeth, and did not look in the mirror. He wasn't ready to see himself yet. For six days he'd avoided the mirror.

On his way back into the room, he glanced into the hall to see whether the cop was still outside. He was. He was seated in the same chair he'd been in since eleven last night. At seven, some other cop would replace him.

McCleary wandered over to the window and gazed out. His room at Broward General Hospital was on the third floor. The view wasn't great—just a string of shops across the street and the endless stream of traffic—but this evidence of ordinary life cheered him. Although he couldn't see the railroad track, he knew one was close by because at night he could hear the trains whizzing past, wheels pummeling the rails, whistles piercing the still air. The sound awakened him and filled him with melancholy. Did trains hold some special significance for him? Was the sound part of something he couldn't remember? Or was it just one of those things like the smell of rain or the song of a particular bird that made you feel a certain way?

The oldest memories will come back first, his shrink had said. And they had, but piecemeal, like food being doled out to a prisoner as some paltry reward for good behavior.

Distantly, he heard the approach of the first train this morning and imagined himself on it, bound for anywhere, gazing through a dusty window into the urban sprawls. He wanted out, that was all. He wanted out of the room, the hospital, his incarceration, out of this absence of memory.

Anything can trigger the memories. . . .

Like a train?

Don't force yourself to remember, Mike. It'll come. . . .

McCleary jammed his hands into the pockets of his robe, his senses following the train as it hurtled past, whistle blowing. A strange sound, deep, the bellow of a giant bound for someplace it didn't want to go.

He felt the familiar flutter of panic in his chest, the beginning of that insidious terror that he was a nonentity, that the shell of himself for the last twenty years would be forever filled with other people's memories of him, other people's facts, that . . .

Whatever you do, Mike, don't panic. . . .

Right. Do not panic. Rule One.

He moved to the chair and picked up the sketchpad Dr. Clarke had given him. Lorian Clarke. Jungian analyst. Thirty-six years old, hair the gold of peaches, a looker who picked brains for a living. *Sketch anything. It might spark a memory. . . .*

The only thing on the pad was a heading, Sketch #1, as if there was going to be a string of them, and a wobbly circle with nothing inside it. He figured it was what the inside of his head looked like. Empty. Vacant. Folded inside the sketchpad at the back were several typed sheets that Doc Smithers, the Dade County coroner, had brought him two nights ago. They contained facts about him that Smithers and Tim Benson and some other people he had known (and couldn't remember) had put together. As he perused the sheets for the umpteenth time, parts seemed utterly foreign to him, as if he were reading about someone he didn't know. This stranger, himself, had been born in Syracuse, New York, forty years ago. His father was an English professor at Syracuse University, and his mother owned an interior decorator's shop. He had four younger sisters. Fine so far; he remembered some of that. But now he reached the mind lock, the chilled blackness where his memories were on ice, frozen like shrimp.

He'd left Syracuse sixteen years ago, after a stint selling insurance and a year in the Syracuse police department. He spent a decade at Metro-Dade in the homicide division, and when he left there almost six years ago, he was chief of the division.

For the last five years, he and his wife—*no face, no memory of her at all*—had owned a private detective agency in North Miami. They had no children. They shared their home on Poinciana Drive with three cats—Merlin, Tracy, and Hepburn. Merlin had a fondness for beer and Bailey's Irish Cream. Tracy and Hepburn had been inherited during a case three years ago, when he and Quin had been investigating a murder for a movie producer named Gill Kranish.

His hobby was painting. He drove a silver Mazda RX7 —which he'd since found out was a Japanese car—had a talent for cooking, was a compulsive list-maker and an idealist. He'd been close friends with Kranish, originator of the Spin Weaver series, who was now deceased. He was a dedicated runner who put in fifteen to twenty miles a week. During a 10K race last year, he averaged six-and-a-half-minute miles.

McCleary had a brief but vivid image of himself racing down a wide, tree-lined road, chest heaving, arms bent at his sides, shoes pounding black asphalt, and a crush of humanity on either side of him. A woman with dark hair—his youngest sister, he recognized her—was waving a T-shirt and shouting, *C'mon, Mac, c'mon*. On the front of the T-shirt was SYRACUSE UNIVERSITY.

He tried to hold the image in his mind, but the colors leaked out; it faded like an old shirt. *A real memory, another goddamn real memory*. His knees went soft and he leaned back against the windowsill, into a bouquet of roses and baby's breath. College: he'd been running in college. He could remember a race when he was nineteen, but not his wife?

The panic flooded him again. He folded his legs into the chair, clutching the sketchpad in his lap, and flipped to an empty page. He wrote: *I remember . . .* What? Just what the hell did he remember?

The events in the motel room were uneven, hazy. It was like peering through a strip of gauze and being able to detect nothing but shadows. His shrink had blamed the Panzine for that. But he remembered the stink of blood, the back of his skull bright with pain, and he remembered the cop, Grunwald, yanking his head back by the hair and calling him scumbag. He remembered the blonde, the way her hair fanned out across the pillow, and later, he recalled the smell of the sea. Before that, he remembered nothing.

A twenty-year blank, he thought, white as a tundra.

He tore the sheet from the pad and ripped it up. He scooped the pieces into the basket. He didn't need to be reminded that he'd been framed for a murder he didn't believe he'd committed, that someone had pumped him full of a drug, slammed him over the head, left him for dead, and stolen his memories and two decades of his life. Anger pumped through him, then rage. He hurled the sketchpad across the room. It smacked the wall and pages fluttered out like escaping doves. He swept the vase of flowers off the sill. The vase shattered. Baby's breath flew. Roses scattered across the gray rug, marring it like bloody footprints. The noise brought the cop hurrying into the room, a frown throwing his youthful features into confusion. "Hey, what d'ya think you're doing, man? It's not even seven in the morning, and there are still people sleep—"

"Get out." McCleary moved toward him. The cop backed away, his hand on the butt of his weapon. "*Get out!*"

The cop's bloodshot eyes skewed with uncertainty as he surveyed the mess. He glanced back at McCleary and continued his two-step out of the room. McCleary slammed the door and leaned into it, his anger gone, bitterness and dread rising up to take its place. He pressed the heels of his hands against his eyes and wept uncontrollably as he slid down the smooth length of wood to the floor. He drew his legs up against him, face sinking into his arms, and tried to draw comfort from the reality of his flesh, his bones, even from his despair.

"Morning, Mr. McCleary."

The bite of scrambled egg in McCleary's mouth turned sour as Lieutenant Roger Grunwald sauntered into the room. Physically, he didn't seem as thick or dense as he had the morning of McCleary's arrest. He also looked younger than McCleary had pegged him, despite the gray in his hair. Early thirties, McCleary guessed, and ambitious. He suspected this case, his arrest, was quite a feather in Grunwald's cap. When he'd thought about the man over the last few days, he'd hoped Grunwald would shuffle, drool, that he would look slightly simian. But he didn't. If anything, there was a bright glint of shrewd intelligence in his eyes which McCleary found disturbing.

"Ever heard of knocking, Lieutenant?"

"In jail?" He laughed. "You're dreaming, McCleary. I understand there was some trouble in here earlier this morning."

"Nothing serious." *Just a few adjustment problems, Grunwald.*

"Uh-huh." He removed his reflective shades, folded them carefully, slipped them in his shirt pocket. He wasn't in uniform this morning. "So how's the memory?"

"No change."

"Uh-huh." His smile said he didn't believe for a moment that McCleary had amnesia. "Called your wife this A.M. and left a message on the machine. Just wanted to tell her she's cleared to visit you. Lieutenant Benson will probably let her know. I'm assuming you'll be out on bail tomorrow, McCleary, so I think you should understand the rules."

He set his fork aside; his appetite was gone. "Benson explained the rules."

"Benson's Dade County. You're charged in *this* county. We got different rules. You finished with breakfast?"

"Yeah."

McCleary pushed the tray aside and Grunwald picked up a piece of toast, slapped jam onto it from the plastic container at the side of the tray, then bit into the toast and talked as he chewed. "First, you're obligated to see Dr. Clarke as often as she needs to see you, even if it's seven days a week. County pays the cost, so it's no money outa your pocket. Since her office is in Miami, that should make it easier for you. Second, you don't step foot outside Dade or Broward County without a call to me. If you violate that little rule, we got the option of snapping one of those newfangled bracelets on you, McCleary. Heard about them?"

"I don't know."

"Oh. Yeah. Your amnesia." Grunwald smirked. "Well, they're these little electronic gizmos that emit a homing signal so we can track you. Kind of like those sci-fi weirdo movies, you know. But they're the best damn things to come along in law enforcement in a long time. They don't like to use them very often—prisoner's rights and all that shit—but in a first-degree murder rap, no problem."

He polished off the toast, picked up McCleary's untouched glass of orange juice, knocked it back. He set the glass on the table, patted his stomach, and belched. "And just remember that if you get suicidal or weird, your shrink can Baker Act you."

"What the hell's that?"

"It means she can commit you. That fast." He snapped his fingers and laughed. "Glad we had this little chat, McCleary." He strolled toward the door, stopped, glanced back. "Oh, yeah. I forgot. When you leave tomorrow morning, your stuff will be returned to you."

"What stuff?"

"Whatever was in your pockets. But not your weapon. That's evidence." He reached into his back pocket. "And here's your wallet. One of the motel employees found it in the bushes near the dumpster out back of the hotel. Credit cards are all there, but the cash is gone. Too bad." He tossed it. The wallet sailed through the air, overshooting the bed and smacking the wall. "Shit. I never was much good at basketball." Another smirk, uglier, wider, so McCleary could see the pale yellow stains on his teeth. "See you in court."

When hell freezes over, asshole. McCleary barely repressed an urge to heave his breakfast tray at Grunwald's back.

Four

1.

DATE-A-MATE'S AD IN the Yellow Pages was simple and direct: *Tired of the singles' bar scene? Call DAME for a lift to your social life. Confidentiality guaranteed. We take all major credit cards.*

DAME, Quin thought, as in *the dame with the red hair; the good-looking dame; the dame who did him in.* Raymond Chandler tough-guy stuff. She sat at the kitchen table in her running clothes, her mug of coffee in front of her, and dialed the number on the 3 × 5 card that had been found on McCleary in the motel room. A chipper female voice answered. "Date-a-Mate, how may I help you?"

"I'm calling about the ad you had in the paper for phone work. Are you still hiring?"

"Let me connect you with the lady in charge. Please hold."

Music filled the void; she suspected she was in for a lengthy wait. She drummed her fingers against the edge of the photo album she'd gotten out after she'd returned from the grocery store. She flipped it open, feeling the same need she had last night to connect with her past, her marriage, with McCleary. She looked at a photograph of her and McCleary taken by a cab driver in Caracas two years ago in front of the Avila Hotel. The dark bruise of the mountain rose behind them, a necklace of clouds at its throat. They were clowning for the camera—McCleary tipping his Indiana Jones hat and Quin twirling a scarf in one hand, her hip thrust out in a parody of a striptease.

That morning, she remembered, they'd climbed part way up the mountain with a picnic lunch, which they'd eaten under a cluster of acacia trees. The valley spread out below them, windows glinting in the sunlight, the din of traffic reaching them like noises in a dream. They'd made love under the trees, the bright crimson blossoms fluttering down around them whenever the wind blew. She could recall the warmth of McCleary's hands, the way he had moved inside her, the smell of his skin. Memories, she thought, which he no longer had.

Gone, all of it.

She stroked McCleary's face in the photo, stroked as though her touch were magical and could awaken his memories. Then she quickly turned the page. The picture that caught her eye was one of McCleary and Gill Kranish, taken three years ago. They were standing in front of Kranish's sleek Mercedes, the one with the license plate on the front that said SPIN, the name of his most lovable screen creation, Spin Weaver. Shortly before she'd snapped the picture, she remembered, she and McCleary had argued about something, probably Kranish. Despite McCleary's grin, she detected the residue of his foul mood in the set of his mouth and in the dark storm of his eyes. Yes, most of all in his eyes. They were incapable of lies.

Five years. Quin bit at her lower lip, struggling against a dread so huge it threatened to engulf her. She slapped the photo album shut and pressed her hand against the front of it, afraid it might open again on its own.

A woman's voice interrupted the music. "Hello, this is Helen Ziegler. Sorry to keep you waiting. So sorry. May I help you with something?"

Quin went through her spiel again about the ad. "Are there any openings left?"

"You bet. We're still expanding. Uh-huh, expanding like crazy."

A Repeater. The only thing worse than a Repeater was a Speller. "What's the work entail?"

"We're a dating service, and basically what you'd be doing is playing matchmaker according to the system DAME has set up. It requires several days of intensive training. Have you ever done phone work?"

Quin lied. "Yes, when I was in college."

"Are you presently employed?"

"As a teacher," she replied quickly. It wasn't a complete untruth, since she'd spent years as a teacher before becoming a private investigator. "I'm off for the summer now."

"Wonderful. We've hired a number of teachers over the years. Uh-huh. Quite a few teachers. Their schedules are ideal for this kind of part-time work. The pay is quite good. Three-fifty a week to start, with bonuses based on sales."

Sales? What an odd term to use for matchmaking. "If you're interviewing, I'd like to come in and talk to you."

"Let's see . . ." Pages rustled, then Ziegler the Repeater said, "Uh-huh. Okay. I'm going to be out of town tomorrow, but how about the day after. Around three?"

"Great."

"Okay, let me have your name."

She couldn't use her own name, since that had been in the paper, and she couldn't use Ketter, either, for the same reason. "Margo Sillers."

"Fine. See you at three Wednesday, Ms. Sillers. That's three the day after tomorrow." She gave Quin the address, then added, "By the way, your voice is just perfect for this type of work."

And what type was that? She wasn't buying Benson's explanation about a phone dating service. Her idea about this thing ran along more sordid lines, a kind of *dial your sexual fantasy* or *let my voice jerk you off*. But on the other hand, life in Miami had possibly jaded her. DAME might be a perfectly legal business that filled a need for people who weren't into the South Florida singles scene—bars, singles' night at the local grocery store, blind dates.

As she crossed *Call DAME* off her list, her stomach fussed with hunger. *So what's it going to be, Quin oh Quin? The calls and then your run and then breakfast? Or breakfast first?* Food usually took precedence over almost everything else in Quin's life. But she felt the need for the comforting matrix of habit, that symbol of ordinary life, so in the end her run won out over the calls and breakfast.

This morning, she ran for affirmation that her life before the two-week trip to Canada would be returned to her like a lost pet. She ran hard and fast along the track that twisted through the park across the street from the house. She didn't dwell on the fact that she usually made this run with McCleary much earlier in the morning. The important thing was the run itself, its fidelity to consistency. It was important, for instance, that she didn't hedge on the three-mile distance, even though she was tempted. She had to keep within the same parameters of time—twenty-two to twenty-three minutes. She also had to observe the after-run rituals: a drink of water from the fountain in the playground, if it was working; a sprint through the sprinklers—if they were on—to cool down; a spin on the merry-go-round before heading back toward the house.

McCleary called her superstitious—*does he remember that?*—but she really wasn't. There were simply certain procedures that had to be observed. If you did A, then you'd better do B to prevent C from happening. Like that.

Quin rounded the last twist in the path and ran into the shaded playground. It was empty of children, and the sprinklers were off. A breeze nudged one of the swings; its squeaks and complaints rang out in the humid quiet, a solitary, plaintive sound. The water fountain was apparently working, because a man was leaning over it, drinking. A sheen of sweat covered his bare back.

She paused in front of the merry-go-round, noting the stipple of sunlight against its shiny, blue metal surface and the way the grass around it had worn away. The dirt was black and still damp from yesterday's rain. With very little effort she could see herself and McCleary perched at the edge of the merry-go-round the morning before she'd left for Canada. *I'm going to miss you*, he'd said. *Yeah?* she'd asked, smiling. *Tell me more, Mac.*

And he, laughing, looked up at her, winked an eye shut, and played along. He would miss watching her consume four thousand calories a day, he said, and would miss having someone to outrun every morning. She smacked him on the shoulder with the back of her hand. *That's not exactly what I had in mind, you know.*

He chuckled and kissed her, his fingers stroking her damp neck lightly, gently, his mouth sliding to her ear, her neck, moving against her throat as he told her what he would like to do to her body. She dropped her head back, planted a kiss on his chin. *Race you back to the house*. They were neck to neck until the very end, when he suddenly sprinted out ahead of her, rounded the side of the house, and tore toward the swimming pool, shucking his running clothes as he went. They made love in the pool and were late for work.

He won't remember that, either.

She glanced left, across the playground, to the pond on the other side. A family of ducks paddled through the still waters, scooping up bits of something a man on shore was tossing to them. Even if Quin hadn't been close enough to see the man well, she would've known it was Harvey because of the grocery cart. It was piled high with green garbage bags that bulged with his belongings. He was thin and tall, with an unkempt beard the same salt-and-pepper color as his ponytail.

As she approached, it seemed like he hadn't changed his clothes since she'd last seen him, several weeks before she'd left for Canada. His jeans and cotton shirt still looked like they'd come from the Salvation Army. She supposed that buying secondhand clothes helped extend Harvey's monthly disability check from the Army. He'd been wounded nearly twenty years ago in Vietnam, and other than that she knew very little about him, except that he migrated south like the robins every winter.

"Morning, Mrs. M," Harvey said.

"Nice to see you."

He reached into one of his myriad bags and dug around inside, no longer looking at her. "How was your trip?"

It startled her momentarily that he knew she'd been gone. Then she realized he must've spoken to McCleary when he'd come out for his run and wondered if he knew what had happened. "The trip was, uh, good, thanks."

He pulled a rolled-up newspaper from the bag and looked at her. "I know," he said. "About Mike."

"Oh." There didn't seem to be much to say beyond that.

"I reckon you haven't seen this."

He handed her the paper. It was a copy of the *Miami Herald*, and McCleary was one of the front-page stories: EX-MIAMI COP ARRESTED IN SLAYING OF FLIGHT ATTENDANT. Her stomach churned. She didn't bother reading the article, and passed the paper back to Harvey.

"No, I hadn't seen it," she said quietly.

"You talked to Mike yet?"

Quin shook her head. "I just got in last night."

Harvey slid the rolled newspaper up one side of his cheek

and scratched at his temple. "You know how me and Mike had these chats here in the park last winter, Mrs. M?"

She nodded.

"Well, couple, three, four days before I saw the story in the paper we got to talking one morning. He asked me if I had a Rolex watch here in all this mess." Harvey chuckled and slapped the paper against the edge of the grocery cart. "Me. A Rolex. Anyway, he said he needed it for a case he was working on. When I saw him a day or two later, I asked if he'd found the Rolex and he said he had. That night he, uh, moved on the case, I guess."

"Where'd he get a Rolex?"

"Friend lent it to him."

A friend: that was easy. The only friend they had who would own a Rolex, much less lend it out, was Derwin Cody, who'd left at least a half-dozen messages on the answering machine she hadn't returned. Almost three years ago, Cody had hired McCleary to track down someone in his construction company who was taking kickbacks. They'd been friends ever since—not close friends, but that didn't matter to Cody. Once he considered you a friend, he was the sort of person you could depend on for almost anything.

"That's all he said?"

"Yup."

"He didn't mention anything about the case?"

"Not to my recollection. But he gave me something." Harvey dug into another one of his bottomless garbage bags and brought out a small maroon notebook. "He asked me to hold on to this for him. He figured the original would be safe with me." Harvey smiled. "He was right about that."

Quin opened the notebook. On the second page, McCleary had printed the names of three clubs—Bernardo's, Richie's, and Shooters. On another page was jotted a phone number she recognized as Lans Hitchcock's, the man who'd hired McCleary. Under it was a number with "Nadia" to the side of it. On a separate page was written: #21-18-62.

The number to a combination? A phone number overseas? What? "He gave you this the morning before his arrest?"

"That's right."

"I owe you breakfast, at the very least."

"Naw, I really couldn't, Mrs. M, I—"

"Omelets, hash browns, cinnamon toast, freshly ground Colombian coffee."

Harvey grinned. "You're on, Mrs. M."

As they walked back toward the house, Harvey pushing his cart along in front of him, she thought of the night several weeks ago when she, McCleary, and Harvey had sat out by the pool, beneath an obsidian sky dusted with stars, polishing off a bottle of Scotch. Harvey had talked about life on the streets—a life he had chosen, he said, not one he had fallen into—and about the family he'd had before the streets. A wife who'd died of cancer, one son who'd sold out to the Bible thumpers and another who lived with his computers in the Rockies. But he hadn't said anything, she remembered, about what he'd done before he'd hit the streets. There had been Vietnam—and then there seemed to be a long stretch of nothing, a vacuum peopled only by his family, but no mention of a job, a career.

She wondered about that now, as they ate breakfast on the shaded side of the patio by the pool, the cats begging shamelessly for handouts. Harvey indulged each of them as he asked about her trip to Canada, what she saw and ate and where she stayed.

The chatter distracted her from her anxiety about seeing McCleary, meeting with his shrink, all of it. The buzz of her questions—would McCleary remember her when he saw her? What was the worst she could expect? What was the prognosis? —receded to a dull ache at the back of her mind. When Harvey left an hour later, pushing his cart back across the street to the park, she was sorry to see him go. It wasn't just the emptiness oozing back into the house again, but that she no longer had an excuse for not acting. There were calls to return, appointments to make, pieces of an immense puzzle to fit together. And somehow, now that she'd eaten, things didn't seem quite as grim as they had last night.

2.

The old house was tucked back on a shady, narrow road in Little Havana. Vines climbed the front of it, angled around the barred windows, inched along the edge of the roof. Magali imagined that someday she would see this place after an absence and find that the vines had claimed everything, had worked their tentacles through the bars, the glass, under the doors, and curled, snakelike, across the floors inside. Insidious jungle creepers, these passionflower vines, and yet astonishingly lovely. The purple-and-white blooms supposedly told the story of Christ's crucifixion—the nails through His palms, the crown of thorns, His ascension from the dead.

As a child, she'd eagerly peered into the folded petals, seeking the story, but had seen nothing except the flower's anatomy—the pistil, the curves of the petals, the soft meld of purple and white within, the geometry of exquisite beauty. She wondered if her inability to grasp the essential mystery had portended some vital lack in her psyche.

Magali parked her rented BMW at the curb, behind Paco Valenzuela's six-year-old Chevy, and got out. The blast of heat from the sidewalk struck her in the face. She hurried into the shade at the side of the house and knocked on the kitchen door.

An orange tabby, one of the old man's numerous cats, rubbed against her legs, purring. Magali reached down to stroke the animal's head, then picked it up. The cat licked the back of her hand, its tongue, rough as sandpaper, sliding over the skin. Her child would grow up understanding that animals never lied; you knew whether they liked you. Knew it instantly.

She heard the shuffle of feet, the click of the lock being disengaged, and then the old man stood on the other side of the screen, staring out at her. He looked different; he always did when she hadn't seen him for several months. Although he was now close to ninety, he was not as old as the man in her mind's eye, not as hunched, not as wrinkled. His hawk nose wasn't as obtrusive, his mouth wasn't as small, as cockled. It was as if his appearance were shifting constantly, hour by hour, the geography of his face tightening or loosening, following the flow of his moods. But his eyes—dear God, his eyes remained the same—deep blue, liquid, nearly blind; and yet these were eyes that saw too much.

"*Hola, viejo,*" she said.

And now those eyes crinkled at the corners as he pushed the door open with his foot and held out his arms.

"*Mí amor.*" As he reached for her, the cat leaped to the ground and scampered inside. Paco's arms folded around her, arms like wings, arms that took her into themselves. She wanted to purr. She wanted to cry. She loved this man like a father, and yet he was also a friend, a mentor, but more than any of these things, more in ways she didn't yet understand. He held her away from him, his relentless, milky eyes squinting, searching her face, his gnarled hands touching her jaw and smoothing strands of hair from her cheeks, her temples.

"I do not like you with black hair," he said in heavily accented English. She laughed and hugged him again and they went inside, Paco's cane tapping along in front of him. "You are going to bring in your suitcases?" he asked in Spanish.

"They're in the car. I'll get them later."

"Good. Your room is always ready."

The house was small and crowded with *things*—statutes, stones, books and beads, masks and stacks of comic books. Before he'd started going blind, comics were one of his great American passions, as he put it. She guessed he had a small fortune in Superman comic books alone. Decades ago in Cuba he'd been an anthropology professor and had once remarked that comic books were a way of excavating American culture.

She'd known him fifteen years, since she worked for one of his clients—a retired Ecuadorian general who consulted Paco on business decisions. Now the old man was a healer known as El Mago—the Magician. And yet he was more than that. He had discovered certain secrets, she thought, and applied them to his own life, in a practical way.

"Come, we will sit in the courtyard."

The spacious courtyard was shady. There were three ceiba trees and two banyans, their trunks thick and braided, their crowns curved like umbrellas. Spanish moss hung from the branches. A small pool as round as a pancake dominated the center of the courtyard; from it spewed a fountain of water. Along the edge of the fountain were five pieces of coconut. Paco picked up an end piece, snapped it in two, dipped both pieces into the fountain's pool, and handed one to her.

"Eat it."

She nibbled at it as he balanced his cane against the edge of the fountain and sat beside her. Always, when she saw Paco, there were rituals to be performed, gods to be appeased, before they would talk. This particular ritual, if she recalled correctly, was in honor of Elegguá, the god in *santería* who protected, who opened the doors to opportunity. And yet, Paco wasn't a *santero*. He was simply himself, a man with a great deal of knowledge who'd borrowed from here, from there, a man who saw the divine in everything.

He bit into his own piece of coconut and gathered up the remaining scraps. With his thumbnail, he scratched rind from each piece, flicked them into his palm, and touched a dampened finger to them. He then pressed the remnants of rind against the side of the fountain, where a face had been created from chips of tile and stone.

He murmured an incantation, made the sign of the cross, and looked over at her. "Elegguá welcomes you. Let us see what message he has for you, Magali."

His gnarled hands scooped up the remaining rinds and threw them toward Elegguá's image. They smacked the side of the fountain and tumbled into the pool. All four landed with their white sides up.

This pattern, Paco explained, was known as *alafia*. "Elegguá gives you his blessing, but that's all. Do you have a specific question?"

She didn't, so she made one up. How would this job proceed? She nodded, indicating she had the question in mind. Paco let the water rush over the rinds, then tossed them. This time only one of the white sides came up.

"*Ocana sode.*" He frowned. "It sometimes means that something bad is in store."

She didn't believe in the hocus-pocus, but just the same, goosebumps erupted on her arms. "Throw them again, okay?"

This time he asked if there was something wrong, perhaps a danger to Magali. The rinds landed white sides up—*alafia*, but one of the rinds had fallen on top of another. Paco seemed relieved. "*Alafia* with *iré*, with luck. No danger. But you must proceed with caution. You are vulnerable right now." He looked at her, his bushy brows lifting slightly. "Yes?"

She shrugged. *Maybe*, she thought.

The old man gazed at her in that odd, disturbing way he had, as though he weren't really seeing her, and after a moment said, "What's your question, Magali? Your real question."

She tore her eyes from his, hating her transparency. "It concerns a child."

Another throw of the rinds and this one came up two dark,

two white. *Ellife*, he explained, the strongest of the answers. It meant yes, be patient, and all would come to pass.

Magali felt relieved, even though she didn't believe, not really, and got up. She walked over to a bench near the fountain; only then did she breathe more easily. She patted the space on the bench beside her and he joined her, his eyes laughing at her unease.

"Why are you here? In Miami?" he asked.

"Work." He knew the kind of work she did. Although he'd never said anything about it one way or another, she guessed he had an opinion and she didn't particularly want to hear it now. She dropped her head back and peered up through the trees. Sunlight glinted between the branches. A breeze stirred the leaves. "And to see you." She glanced at him, smiling, then dug inside her purse and withdrew an envelope stuffed with bills. She handed it to him; clipped to it was a round-trip ticket from Miami to Caracas, with the date open. "Now you have no excuse not to visit."

Paco set the envelope aside. She knew he would stick it back in her purse when he had the chance and that *she*, when *he* wasn't looking, would tuck it under a book or a statue. "*Mí amor*, I do not want your money. I do not need it. I have plenty of money. But thank you."

"Keep the ticket, then."

"We will talk about it." He knuckled an eye. "I last heard from you when you were in . . . where was it?"

"Zurich."

"Ah. Of course." He grinned sheepishly. "At my age, I am entitled to forget a few things, no?"

His memory, she knew, was not nearly as faulty as he liked to make people believe. But she played along. "Absolutely."

"Let me think now. In Zurich, you were looking for the abductor of children, right?"

"Zurich was one of the places, yes."

"Did you find him?"

"Yes."

"What did you do to him?"

She told him and heard the edge of defensiveness in her voice.

"And this time?"

"Paco, I—"

He whispered, "No more, Magali. I mean it. No more. Stop while you can."

"You don't understand."

She pulled her hand free of his, but it didn't matter. He stood and touched her shoulders. Those deep blue eyes, those nearly blind eyes, commanded hers, held them, seized them. Dappled sunlight played across his wrinkled cheeks. A chill bloomed at the base of her spine. She wanted to jerk her arms up, throwing his hands off, but she couldn't. She wanted to push him away, but she couldn't do that, either. She was helpless and small; she was a bug impaled by the hard glint of his ancient eyes.

"I *do* understand, and that is why you come here. I understand that you kill slime for money. I understand that you also look for missing people as a way of compensating for the killing. Life is never so easily balanced. I neither agree nor disagree with what you do because *what* you do is not *who* you are. Not yet."

The words slapped the walls of her skull and echoed. She laughed, but it was false, and they both knew it. She told him he was a foolish old man, and he stared at her for a long and terrible moment, his thumbs digging painfully between the bones in her shoulders. He could break her with the power of his gaze alone. If he willed it, something inside her would snap like a toothpick and she would cease to be whoever she was. Her memories would rush out of her, a dark, bitter tide.

I love you, viejo, she thought, and his face twitched as if he'd heard the thought. His hold on her loosened, but it was a trick to get her to drop her guard a little, because then he began to speak in the Spanish of southern Chile. It was a sweet, musical sound that touched her all over inside, that softened the parts of her which were hard and ugly. She started to cry, but he was unmoved. He said things she didn't understand in a language that had never been written. His eyes clouded. He'd stepped out of his bones, his muscles and tissue, and drifted into a place where she couldn't follow because she didn't know the way. She felt like she was drugged, like she was drowning in mucus.

Listen to me, she screamed, but he wouldn't. He was gone. He'd been transported, even though his mouth still moved, even though his hands were still against her shoulders. She sobbed. She collapsed against the bench, boneless, a balloon of flesh swept along in the rush of the old man's madness.

Later, when she went outside again to get her bags, the heat revived her. She felt violated, but her mind was lucid. She wasn't sure what had happened, but with him she was never sure. Sometimes she believed that the old man, the house, their past together existed outside of time, that she would return to this spot one day in the future and find nothing here. Or worse, she would find that someone else occupied the house and Paco had never lived at all, that he was someone she'd conjured from the depths of her own madness.

She shuddered in spite of the heat. She opened the back door to pull out her bags but instead slid inside and drew her legs up against her. She squeezed her eyes shut, pressed her forehead to her knees, and tried to shut out the echoes of his voice.

The voice that said, *No more, Magali. No more. Stop while you can.*

Five

LORIAN CLARKE'S OFFICE in Coconut Grove looked like an artist's lair, not a place where a shrink picked brains. The waiting room was done in pastels—pinks, pale silver, blues. Unusual graphics decorated the walls—circles within circles that swirled like melted chocolate did when you stirred it; bursts of color shaped like flower petals; intricate designs that drew your eyes to their pulsing centers. Quin's favorite was of a man and a woman immersed in a circle of pale blue, faces almost touching, arms locked together, their nakedness both elegant and simple. When she looked closely, the light shifted across the shimmering paper and the figures seemed to merge.

Quin's grasp of the various schools of psychological thought wasn't anything to brag about, but she recognized the posters as mandalas, Carl Jung's symbols of the psyche's wholeness. Given the choice between Jung and Freud, she felt more comfortable with the former. Unlike Freud and his repressed sexuality hangups, Jung had sought integration of the personality through an exploration of dreams and the unconscious. That Clarke was evidently of the Jungian school dispelled some of Quin's suspicion of psychiatrists. "Morning," said the cute brunette at the receptionist's desk.

"Hi. I've got an appointment with Dr. Clarke at nine-thirty."

The brunette, whose nameplate identified her as BRIGID NETTLE, ran a rose-painted nail down the slots in the appointment book. "St. James, right?"

"Yes."

"The doctor will be with you in a minute." She plucked a clipboard from the wire mesh basket at the corner of her desk and held it out. "You'll need to complete this while you wait."

"I'm not a patient."

"Oh." Her pretty smile covered her embarrassment and

showed off her white, perfect teeth, the sort of teeth movie stars had. "Sorry. If you'll just have a seat. . . ."

The only other person in the waiting room was an expensively dressed woman who wore enough perfume to gag a whore. She kept consulting her elegant gold watch and finally got up and walked over to the desk. She asked Brigid how much longer her daughter would be.

"Let me buzz Dr. Clarke and find out. . . . Oh, here she comes now."

A teenage girl in tight jeans, a halter top, and high-topped tennis shoes sauntered out, a khaki bag thrown over her shoulder, a cigarette in her right hand. "Thanks again, Doc. See ya next week," she called.

A woman who Quin presumed was Dr. Clarke strolled out behind the girl and greeted the mother. She had thick, honey-blond hair, and wore dove-gray slacks with a matching jacket and a pink silk blouse with a strand of pearls. Her complexion was smooth and creamy, her eyes dark and large, her face heart-shaped. She was one of those women who might've been thirty or fifty, Quin thought, virtually ageless. Her manner was as easy and relaxed as her beauty, as though she'd long since ceased to think about either of them. She didn't fit Quin's idea of what a shrink should look like.

The mother and daughter turned to leave, and Clarke came over to Quin. Her smile was almost musical. "Ms. St. James?"

Quin nodded as she stood and Lorian Clarke introduced herself. Her grip was firm, her palm cool. "Let's go back to my office. Brigid, hold my calls, will you?"

"Sure thing, Dr. Clarke."

Her office was large but not plush. The furniture was mostly wicker with pastel cushions that matched the walls. There were more of the unusual mandala graphics Quin had seen in the waiting room, but these were dream images, surreal, and resembled some of the paintings McCleary had done over the years.

To her relief, Clarke didn't settle behind the imposing teakwood desk. She gestured toward the wicker couch and chairs, which made things less formal, and asked Quin if she would like coffee or anything cold to drink. She said no, thanks, she was fine. What she really wanted was something to nibble on. But it hardly seemed appropriate to ask for food, and she couldn't just dig into her purse for a snack and sit here pigging out. Hello, hypoglycemia.

She sat in one of the wicker chairs and smoothed her hands over her white slacks, hoping for an opening when Clarke stopped chattering about the heat. When it became apparent she wasn't going to shut up any time in the next five minutes, Quin finally blurted, "How's my husband?"

Clarke turned, as if she'd been waiting for Quin to approach the topic first, and smiled as she came back across the room with her cup of coffee. "Better than I expected, considering his situation. I saw him for a while last night. Some of his earlier memories are beginning to return, which is an encouraging sign."

"So you believe he actually has amnesia?"

She settled on the couch to Quin's left, set her mug of coffee on the table in front of her, and picked up a file. "What I think isn't enough for the prosecutor without some tests to back it up. He's one of these guys who likes everything spelled out in black and white. Figures and statistics, test results. So that's what I'm going to give him."

It didn't answer her question, but she overlooked that for the moment. "How can you test someone for amnesia?"

"It's not easy when it has a nonorganic cause. But amnesia happens to be one of my interests, and over the years I've developed a few tests to measure the extent of memory loss. What do you know about amnesia?"

"Not much."

That lovely smile flashed again, putting Quin at ease. "Then you and the medical profession are about even. A blow to the head is the best-known cause of amnesia, but the condition can also develop when the brain is deprived of oxygen—through a blood clot, for example, and through improperly administered anesthesia. Your husband's blood was loaded with a potent hypnotic—Panzine. It's a tranquilizer similar to benzodiazepine, which is one of the most commonly prescribed sleeping pills in the country, but it's about four times as powerful. Administered in improper doses, it's potentially fatal. We know the drug can cause short-term amnesia and impaired motor skills while still in the bloodstream, which is why Mike's memories of what happened when he was arrested are so hazy. But usually it leaves intact any memories stored before the drug was ingested, which wasn't the case with your husband. That left only one explanation for the severity of his amnesia—his concussion."

McCleary's condition, she said, was something called functional amnesia—no damage to the brain itself, no visible change in the organ, only in the way it worked. That was part of what made the mechanics of this type of amnesia so difficult to pinpoint. Amnesia usually manifested in one of two ways. Anterograde amnesia was that in which memory *after* the accident or injury badly malfunctioned. In a case like that, the person was no longer capable of learning and remembering new things because he forgot the day's events as they happened. That was the worst kind. "Mike has *retrograde* amnesia, an inability to recall events prior to the trauma. In severe cases, like his, it can go back years. But it almost always clears up, with the older memories returning first."

Quin didn't like the qualifying "almost," but this was still the most encouraging thing she'd heard since she sat down. "Why the older memories?"

She reached for her coffee, sipping at it. "Well, this is a rather crude comparison, but think of memories as recordings which we mull over, analyze, replay, and consolidate over the years. This consolidation process deepens the groove of the memories. That's not how it actually works, but it's close enough."

"How long will it take?"

"Days, weeks, maybe years. It depends."

Years? It might take years? Distantly, she heard the cosmic goblins laughing. "Depends on what?"

"A couple of things. Your husband has some distinct advantages. He's in excellent health. His hobby is painting, a right-brain pursuit, which might be a way of breaking down the block. And from all indications, you two have had a strong marriage and he has some very good friends who care about him. In other words, he has a support system.

"On the negative side, he's under tremendous stress. The stress of the amnesia itself, and also the stress of being arrested and charged with murder. That could hinder the remembering or speed it up, which will depend, to a large degree, on how Mike has handled stress in the past. I imagine that since he was a homicide investigator for a number of years, he reacts well to stress."

"Yes." Except when Sylvia Callahan was killed, she thought. But that was none of this woman's business.

"His skills remain intact. Anything he was able to do before the injury, he'll still be able to do. Paint, drive, and so on. How long has he been running?"

"Since he was eighteen or nineteen."

"Then it would be to his benefit to resume running as soon as he gets the okay from his doctor concerning the concussion. Anything familiar like that could facilitate the remembering." She paused and leaned forward. "I won't pretend this is going to be easy for you. You're both going to feel like you're living with strangers. His emotions will seesaw. So will yours. Just take things a step at a time. Try to build on the present, and don't worry about the past. It's important that he doesn't feel panicked about his situation, although he probably will from time to time."

Not to mention the sort of panic she was going to feel. Already felt.

"How specific is the amnesia?" Quin asked.

"What do you mean?"

"You said he's missing chunks of the last twenty years. A lot of things exist now which didn't exist twenty years ago."

She opened the file on her lap. "I was just about to go into that. A few days ago, I gave Mike a simple question-and-answer test that covers current events, people, basic facts of life in the eighties. There're some questions thrown in that cover periods of time before 1980. I think this will give you some indication of what you're facing."

The twenty-five questions covered things like, *What is AIDS? How many astronauts were on the Challenger? What is a VCR? What cop show is filmed in Miami? Who is Crocodile Dundee? Who is Spock? Who is President?* The test, said Clarke, didn't eliminate the possibility of faked amnesia. But the individual would have to be quick to figure out which questions he should know to cover the period of time he supposedly didn't recall. "The test is timed—fifteen seconds per question—and the answers are given orally. When Mike took this test, Nixon was the last President he could remember."

A sixties time traveler: swell.

"Anyway, the results of the test helped support his contention that his memories end twenty years ago."

His contention: as if Clarke didn't believe.

". . . and on a bleaker note," she was saying, "it also gives us some idea of what he *doesn't* remember."

VCRs, microwaves, home computers. Mr. Coffee machines, CD players, answering machines . . .

Quin handed the list of questions back to her. Something of what she was feeling must've shown on her face, because Clarke touched her arm. "Look, it's not the worst case of amnesia I've ever treated. Believe me. A couple of years ago I had a woman who, as a result of surgery, had anterograde amnesia—she's unable to recall anything that happened to her afterward. Her case is so severe, she keeps detailed lists of her daily activities so she can remember what she's done. When she travels, she sends three or four postcards a day to herself so she can remember the vacation."

"But twenty years . . ."

"I can't promise that he'll recall everything, Quin. May I call you Quin?"

The way Clarke asked, as if it really mattered, created a huge swell of emotion in her chest.

". . . I can't even guarantee that he'll remember the last ten years or the last five or even that he'll remember your marriage. But I think we've got a real good shot at it."

The tears threatened, but didn't come. Quin dug into her purse for a snack. The hell with impropriety. Anything would do—nuts, dried fruit, a crust of old bread. But she'd neglected to replenish her munchie supply last night. There wasn't so much as a stick of gum in her bag.

"What can I do to help?" she asked.

"I need some answers, Quin. The kind only a wife can give me."

Her questions mostly concerned McCleary's character, Quin's perception of him as a human being, as a husband, a friend. How long had they worked together? A little over five years. Was their working relationship good? The best, Quin replied. Was he a workaholic? It depended on the case. Did he feel comfortable talking about his emotions? Sometimes: it depended on the situation. What kind of cop had he been? What kind of investigator was he? Instinctive. Was he able to recall his dreams? Clearly, Quin said. Did he have a strong sense of right and wrong? Very. Did he observe any particular religion? No. How was their sexual relationship? Great. Was

Quin happy in the marriage? Very. Had McCleary, to Quin's knowledge, ever been unfaithful?

Tricky, thought Quin, how Clarke had led up to that. But now that she had, she understood the reason for the question. McCleary, after all, had been found in a motel room with a dead woman.

"I take it that's a yes?"

"It's a yes, *but.*"

"It's important, Quin."

She ran a hand over her white slacks again, wanting to say this just right so Clarke wouldn't misunderstand. Two years ago when they were working on a homicide, one of their sources was a woman named Sylvia Callahan who McCleary had been involved with a long time before he'd met Quin. His relationship with Callahan had never really ended; it had just gotten lost in the disparity of their backgrounds. When they saw each other again, the old feelings surfaced. "So they resolved it. Or tried to, anyway. She was killed during the investigation."

"You knew about the affair?"

"I knew he was unclear about his feelings toward her, and I told him he'd better find out what he felt so we could get on with our lives. I guess what I'm saying is that Callahan was the exception."

"You met her?"

"Yes."

"What'd you think of her?"

"I liked her. I didn't want to like her, but I did. I could see why Mac had fallen for her." She shrugged. "I realize I'm making this sound like it was easy, but it wasn't." Her voice fell. "None of it was."

"And you? What about you, Quin? Have there been any other men since you got married?"

"No."

Clarke shut her notebook. "Do you know what the river Lethe is?"

Quin thought a moment. "Something in Greek mythology."

"Yes. In the underworld, a person drank of the waters of the river Lethe before he was reborn, so he would forget his previous existence. That's how I think of amnesiacs. As Letheans."

Quin didn't say anything. She felt suddenly vulnerable,

helpless, orphaned. What she wanted most of all at the moment was to lock herself in a room with a mountain of food. It wouldn't even matter what kind of food it was, as long as there was enough to engorge herself. And then she would sleep heavily, dreamlessly, ballooning in this deep sleep until she weighed three hundred pounds. Losing weight would keep her mind sufficiently occupied, wouldn't it?

"I think I've got enough to work with for a while," Clarke said. "Once Mike is home, I'd like to see him regularly. Twice weekly, I think. And I hope you'll feel free to call me or stop by if any problems come up."

"Thanks, I will."

Clarke walked with her toward the waiting room. "Some amnesiacs are apprehensive about seeing and talking with people who know them but who they can't remember. I don't know if Mike will be affected that way, so I've advised him to return to work only when he feels comfortable with the idea. It's unlikely that he would be able to remember what to do at work, Quin, which would only frustrate him."

"I understand."

But she didn't, not really, because she couldn't fathom a life with two decades of memories excised. She tried to imagine what sort of person she would be without the memories of certain experiences that had shaped her. But nothing came to mind. The bottom line was that she had absolutely no idea what to expect from the man she'd been married to for five years.

Denny's Restaurant wasn't exactly gracious dining, but what the hell. Food was the point. She'd managed to postpone starvation long enough to go by the library and check out everything she could find on amnesia. Now it was time to surrender.

She pored over the menu. Limited. Breakfast was definitely the best choice; even McDonald's would have a tough time making breakfast unpalatable. She ordered steak and eggs, hash browns and grits and sausage, biscuits with jam, juice, coffee, and a glass of milk. She consumed it all, then sat there sipping endless cups of coffee, paging through the books on amnesia.

There was the case of Sherwood Anderson, the writer, who

on a routine day in 1926 was dictating a letter to his secretary when he suddenly stopped, got up, and left the house. He was found four days later in a drugstore and was taken to the hospital. Doctors concluded that mental strain had caused amnesia. The longest case of amnesia lasted thirty-seven years. It involved a man known as John Cross who, as a result of a stroke in 1973, remembered that his name was actually John Crosswhite, a fact he'd forgotten when he was in a car accident in 1936. Nice thing to wake up to after a stroke, Quin mused.

One of the more celebrated cases of amnesia was that of Agatha Christie. In 1926, after finding out that her husband was spending the weekend with his mistress, she left her home in Berkshire. Her car was found abandoned on a road the next morning, triggering a massive manhunt that involved track dogs and fifteen thousand volunteers. Ten days after she'd disappeared, she was identified as a guest at a health spa, where she had registered under another name. Speculation ranged from whether the amnesia was real to whether Christie had set it up to spite her husband. Quin vaguely recalled that Vanessa Redgrave had played Christie in a movie called *Agatha* which was based on the disappearance.

So far, the news wasn't too encouraging.

She flipped to a copy of a newspaper clipping from the *Herald*. It was about a 35-year-old woman from Kendall, one of the suburbs, who came to on the bathroom floor of a fast-food restaurant in North Miami and didn't know who she was. Police tracked her identity through the license plate on her car in the parking lot and took her to the hospital. When her family arrived, she didn't know them—not her parents, her husband, kids, nothing. Her marriage broke up, she lost her job, her life fell apart. Although her first twenty-five years came back to her in a matter of days, it had taken her five years to recover the rest of her memories. The only reason her story was in the paper at all was because she'd established an amnesiac support group.

From what she read, the prognosis for McCleary's type of amnesia—no brain damage—was good; that was encouraging. But progress was slow; that was not so encouraging. There were worse types of amnesia—the anterograde kind

Clarke had mentioned, as well as auditory, visual, and tactile amnesia. In the first, the person couldn't interpret spoken language; in the second, written language was forgotten; and in the third, you couldn't identify once familiar objects by the sense of touch. In other words, she thought, making love in the dark would be a forgettable experience.

The fact that there were worse kinds of amnesia didn't console her at all. It was like being told you had cancer, but hey, be thankful it wasn't AIDS. It didn't mitigate the truth—that she was scared shitless.

Six

BAYSIDE ON BISCAYNE Boulevard had been intended as the ultimate in shopping. It was an unenclosed complex of stores, restaurants, and "street stalls" smack on the bay. Its charm was indisputable, Magali thought, what with the cobbled walks, the pastels, the upscale shops. But whoever had designed the place hadn't considered the brutal Florida summers, how the heat would seep through the air from June through October, discouraging even the most intrepid shoppers. The place was nearly deserted this morning.

She was sitting on the low wall outside Sharper Image, paging through today's edition of *USA Today*, waiting for Bartlett. She'd last seen him a month ago in Luxembourg, and before that, in Greece, while she'd been tracking the child killer. She didn't particularly want to meet with him now; he would get the wrong idea. Bartlett was much too possessive, but that was her fault for ever having mixed business with pleasure. All the clichés were true.

It was best that he knew she was in town, though, on a job that had nothing to do with governments and, most of all, nothing to do with rival federal agencies. Feds like Bartlett tended to be extremely competitive among themselves, playing out their one-upmanship games by rules no one else understood. Bartlett called it an occupational hazard. But she thought it was part of that peculiar American drive to excel in competition, regardless of what form it took.

Magali checked the time, got up, and tossed the newspaper into a nearby trash can. When she turned, she saw Bartlett trotting down the steps from the second floor, a package under his arm. Bartlett, the friendly giant—a lean six four, with brawny shoulders, thick arms, hair the color of copper, freckles like a beach boy. He wore navy-blue slacks, a short-sleeved checked shirt, no tie, and Hush Puppies. She could usually gauge what Bartlett was up to by the shoes he wore. Like her jewelry, they reflected his moods. The Hush Puppies meant he was working on a job he had every confidence of settling to the agency's advantage.

"Hi, love," he said casually, as if they'd seen each other only a few days earlier. His large mouth slid into a smile, and he tilted his sunglasses back onto the top of his head. His eyes slipped from her face to her toes and back up again with undisguised scrutiny. From any other man, it would've offended or angered her; from Bartlett, it made her flush with pleasure. He saw it and chuckled. "Have I met this brunette before?"

"A few times," she laughed.

"Well, you look terrific. How've you been?"

"Can't complain. You?"

"Not bad. I think I like you with black hair, Magali."

He rocked toward her then and brushed her cheek with his cool mouth. She thought, suddenly, of this mouth loving her body one winter night in Vienna, and again on a summer afternoon in a field strewn with hyacinths outside of Edinburgh. There were dozens, perhaps hundreds of memories like these scattered through the years she had known Bartlett. They were good together as lovers; the chemistry was right. It was everything else that caused them problems. "How about something cold to drink? This heat is getting to me. There's a café right down here."

"Sounds good."

They walked between two rows of shops, not saying much. She knew he was wondering the same thing she was, if there would be something more after the café. She hadn't intended it when she'd called him, but now that he was here, she didn't discount the possibility. It had been a long time since Luxembourg.

"I heard you were in town," he remarked in his usual calm tone, but it was intended to surprise her.

"Oh, from who?"

"I forget, love. It's just one of those things you hear around, you know? Someone says, 'Hey, Bartlett, I hear Magali Schmidt's in Miami.' 'Yeah?' I reply. 'And what's Magali love doing in this neck of the woods?' And someone shrugs and says, 'Beats the crap outa me.' " He paused, pale eyes questioning.

"I didn't realize my name was on one of your computers, Bartlett."

"It's not. But someone's been tracking your progress since Luxembourg. Word gets around. What're you doing here, anyway? I thought you were going to stay in Europe for a while."

"It's a free-lance job."

"Ah." His head bobbed. "That's good, love. For a minute there, I was thinking that maybe you sold out to the enemy."

They both laughed; it was an old joke between them, bedroom jesting. But it underscored their basic differences. He believed that if you killed in the line of duty for the U.S. government, it was okay. To do it for any other government, for any other reason, was not okay.

"Just making a living," she replied.

"Going to be around long?"

"I don't know."

He held the door to the café open for her, and as she started past him, his fingers brushed lightly against the small of her back, an invitation. She glanced at him over her shoulder; he grinned and his brows arched. *Yes?* asked his eyes. *Was that a yes, love?*

They took a table at the last table near the window. Bartlett sat with his back to the wall, so he was facing the door. Spy rules.

"What information do you need, anyway?" he asked once they'd ordered expressos.

"Who said I needed information?"

He leaned toward her, eyes laughing. "Cut the bullshit, Magali."

"Bartlett, didn't it occur to you that maybe I just wanted to see you? That I didn't necessarily want something from you?"

"It's a real nice thought, love, but I'm a realist, remember? So what do you need?"

"Nothing. I just wanted to check in."

He laughed out loud; it made the freckles slip and slide across the bridge of his nose. He touched her knuckles with his index finger, tapped them, paused, tapped them again, a private code that whispered, *Be straight with me.* Sunlight struck the reddish-blond hairs above his wrist. "Let's get business over with, okay? So we can get on with everything else? I hate like hell when we get off on the wrong foot, love."

She smiled. His bluntness was not without charm. "Information on a man named Mike McCleary," she said, and told him a little of what she knew about him.

"I'll see what I can find out. But the local intrigue usually isn't my area, unless the Colombian boys are involved. Give me the name of the woman he supposedly killed and I'll see what I can find on her, too."

Nothing was written down; it rarely was. But she could almost hear the whir of Bartlett's brain, recording it, filing it away. Twelve years in the spy game had taught him a few things.

Their expressos arrived. He sat back, his huge hands dwarfing the tiny cup, and gave her his usual rundown on the bickering among the various federal agencies. She suspected he was working up to something, that he was constructing a loose framework of the favor he would expect from her in return for digging up information on McCleary. She wasn't surprised when he said, "You never know about these interagency squabbles, love. Sometimes they take weird turns, and if you have to put a certain asshole in his place, you do it, that's all."

"Who does it, Bartlett?"

He didn't reply, but his generous mouth swung into a quick smile, and she thought, *We'll see, Bartlett. We'll see.*

"You free for the afternoon?" she asked.

"It depends," he said, tossing back the answer she'd given him. "What'd you have in mind?"

They ended up at a cottage Bartlett rented or owned on the beach at the southern end of Broward County. She guessed that he kept it "for business" and she was today's business. It made no difference to her one way or the other; she wanted pleasure from him, not love. And business or not, Bartlett was usually a smooth, considerate lover, and when he wasn't, it was because she wanted something different.

They spent the afternoon together—making love in a Jacuzzi in the yard, the sound of the surf around them; up against the railing of the deck, a quick and heated joining; and again in his bedroom. Here it was slow and strange, with Bartlett whispering things to her, ordinary, romantic things, as if they were normal people. He touched her as she liked to be touched, drew her to the edge with his hands, his mouth, and held her there until she begged.

He enjoyed it when he had this sort of power over her, and he knew how to use it. He knew how to suspend her flesh in an exquisite tension by drawing his tongue from her throat to a breast and then nibbling his way down her belly while his hand was busy elsewhere. He knew.

He spread his hand between her breasts like a pianist reaching across an octave and flicked at both nipples simultaneously. "So tell me again how you see American men, love," he said, as if they were chatting over coffee, as if there was nothing else going on between them.

She giggled and he laughed. "Serious question, Magali, really."

"Okay, let's see." She thought about it, but was distracted by his wandering hands, his mouth. "American men make great husbands, but Latins are the best lovers." She grinned as he lifted his head from her breast and looked at her.

"Except me, right? I defy the stereotype. Good lover, but I'd make a bad husband."

She wound her arms around his neck and pulled him down to her, kissing him, laughing, kissing him again.

A long time later, as his mouth paused here at her belly button, there at her hip, and then lower, until she was melting, until she was coming apart and aching like she sometimes did after a kill, she thought that he said he loved her. He slipped into her seconds before she came, his fingers sliding through her hair, his mouth fluttering against hers. She opened her eyes and saw his smile. It chilled her, it seemed to be saying, *It's my game, love, and if you don't believe me, just watch how I play you.* She snapped her eyes shut and drifted away on a dark tide of sentience, wanting to forget what she thought she'd seen, which contradicted what she thought she'd heard.

Seven

1.

McCLEARY STOOD AT the bathroom sink, a towel wrapped around his waist, steam from the shower escaping through the open door. In order to shave, he needed to look in the mirror. But he was afraid of seeing the blank emptiness of his eyes. He knew the texture of that emptiness, because one of the memories that had returned had happened when he was eighteen, touring Rome State Hospital in upstate New York with his psychology class. They'd entered a ward for the severely retarded, and their guide, a nurse, had led them to a middle-aged man sitting by himself at a table.

"This man," she said, "is an idiot savant. You can give him any date since the beginning of the twentieth century and he'll tell you what historical event happened on that date. But if you ask him his name or what he did ten minutes ago, he won't be able to tell you. Anyone have a question?"

The woman standing next to McCleary had tossed out a date: December 17, 1903.

The nurse turned back to the man at the table. "Good morning, Jim. We have a young lady here who has a question for you."

The man had raised his eyes; the light inside had been out for years. It was like peering into a starless sky, a sky blacker than pitch, a sky that preceded some natural disaster. Then the man's mouth had opened and a flame lit up the blackness as he said, "December 17, 1903: Orville and Wilbur Wright flew the first powered heavier-than-air aircraft at Kitty Hawk, North Carolina, over distances of one hundred and twenty to eight hundred and fifty-two feet." His mouth closed and the light blinked out.

Memory was like that light.

If you're going to meet your wife, the least you can do is meet yourself first.

He rubbed his palm in small, tight circles through the steam on the glass. His mouth appeared, the upper lip crossed by a cocoa-colored mustache streaked with gray. The mouth wasn't too bad. He wondered, though, why he suddenly thought of mouths as communicating a complex language of their own. Were mouths of particular importance to him because of his interest in art? Did they have some connection to the dead blonde?

His jaw appeared next. *Stubbly and stubborn.* He had a flash of this jaw sporting a beard. True memory or implanted? It seemed vital to make the distinction between memories he stumbled upon on his own and those other people had fed him. He decided this was a true memory.

Now his nose. It wasn't too bad. Long, slender, just a nose. Then came his eyes: smoky blue, thick, dark lashes. *They aren't blank or empty.* In fact, when he leaned very close to the mirror and peered into the black pupils, he could almost see the light inside. *Hello in there, you can come out now. I need you,* he silently called to the memories.

Nothing happened. There was no abrupt rush of faces or images, no ostensible truths that poured through to greet him. The only thing he experienced was a tightening of the skin between his brows, as if the spot there had been badly sunburned and in another day or two would start to peel. A hunch. At least he remembered the sensation. But a hunch about what?

Nice to meet you, Mike.

Likewise, I'm sure.

You don't look the way I thought you would.

You're remembering me as a twenty-year-old.

"Shit." He would forgo a shave in favor of growing a beard, he decided, and returned to his room to dress.

As he was zipping up his jeans, he heard the cop on the other side of the door say, "Yeah, he's in there," and then the door opened and an orderly he hadn't seen before strolled in, shutting the door behind him with his foot.

The man was short and muscular, with light brown hair that had receded halfway back on his crown, wire-rim glasses that made his deep blue eyes look small and remote, like balls of gossamer silk that floated in his cheeks. His mouth was generous but fussy.

"Time for your enema, Mr. McCleary," he said loudly.

"My *what*?"

He held a finger to his lips, set a tray down on the bedside table, and whispered, "I don't have much time, Mac. That dickhead outside the door is probably smarter than he looks. They aren't allowing you to get calls, and since I didn't know what your status was in terms of anything, I had to get in to see you and . . ." He frowned. "You don't know me." He paused, shook his head. "Jesus. So it's true. The papers weren't just bullshittin'. You really *have* lost your fucking memory. Christ, I can't believe this."

"Who're you?"

"Derwin Cody. We've been buddies for a couple, three years. Point is, a few days before all this shit came down, you borrowed a Rolex watch from me. You remember that?"

"No."

"You said you were working on something and needed the Rolex to look the part."

"The part of what?"

"A reporter."

"I wasn't wearing a watch when I was arrested."

"I know. You returned it to me the night before this mess happened. We were down at this railyard I own. I'm going to turn it into an amusement park. That's why I was showing it to you. Remember any of that?"

"No."

"You said you'd just come from Bernardo's."

"I can't remember."

An awkward moment passed, then Cody said, "What's the story with your bond?"

McCleary repeated what Benson had said yesterday: the house or business as collateral.

"Jesus." Cody ran a hand over his head. "You and Quin got ten percent of that to put up? You got that much cash available?"

"I don't know."

"Hell, the fuckers would take your mother if it were legal. Well, forget it. I'll bring the money by the house tonight. When're you going to see Quin?"

"Sometime today, but—"

"No fucking buts, man. I'm doing it and that's that." Cody squeezed his shoulder. "Sweet Christ, Mac." He shook his head, his words an echo of impending doom. "I kept calling Quin and getting the machine, then when she called me back, I wasn't in. Tell her Cody says not to worry." He jerked a thumb toward the bathroom. "You just had an enema; go flush the toilet or something as I leave, so dickhead won't poke his face in here. Talk to you tomorrow."

And just like that, he was gone.

McCleary flushed the toilet in the bathroom, ran the water, and wondered what his and Quin's financial situation was. Could they afford bail? How much was their agency worth? Their house? His ignorance appalled him. He looked into the mirror; his eyes were as dark and vapid as the idiot savant's.

"Gotta check through your purse, ma'am. Sorry, regulations," said the cop outside the room.

"You're lucky I just cleaned it out this morning," the woman replied. "Am I allowed privacy with my husband, Sergeant?"

McCleary's head jerked up. He was seated by the window, the sketchpad in his lap—*the goddamn blank pad*—and he quickly set it aside and leaped up. Once he was standing, though, he wasn't quite sure what to do. He sat down, stood again, sat again, stood once more, and pressed the heels of his hands to his eyes, wanting this moment to be over, wanting nothing more than to be the hell *out* of here, and on a plane bound for anywhere. Aw, Christ. Now the door was opening. Now he was glancing around. The woman who'd stepped into the room was thin and tall, a couple of inches shy of six feet. In her white slacks, she seemed to be all legs, an awkward colt. She wore a loose, short-sleeve silk blouse the same ghostly blue as her eyes. Her thick, umber hair fell to her shoulders in waves. Her smile was hesitant, a little shy. She clutched a bright red apple in her hand. The fruit of knowledge, he mused, symbol of exile; it was another one of those disturbing metaphors, like the absence of sound earlier this morning.

Wife.

If he hadn't overheard her speaking to the guard, he wouldn't have known she was his wife. He'd desperately hoped that when this moment arrived, he would experience a twitch of recognition, a gut reaction, anything. But the only thing he felt was panic. What was he supposed to do? To say? What did she expect of him? He didn't know what to say, so he just stood there stupidly, looking at her. She spoke first.

"I'm, uh, Quin."

He nodded. "I overheard you talking to the guard."

She motioned toward the sketchpad on the windowsill. "You're drawing?"

McCleary picked it up and showed it to her. "A new art form; your imagination is supposed to fill in the blanks. Would you like a glass of water? That's all there is."

"Sure. Thanks."

Grateful to have something to do, he hurried over to the table, where the sweating pitcher was. He felt her eyes follow him. He heard her move farther into the room, and when he turned to give her the water, he still hadn't thought of anything to say to her.

"This is awkward," she said, holding the glass with both hands, like a child. She'd set the apple on the windowsill, next to the vases of roses and baby's breath.

"I'm sorry, I—"

"I'm not blaming you," she said quickly.

McCleary pulled two chairs closer to the window and they sat down—stiffly, formally, like the strangers he felt they were. She sipped tentatively from her glass; he leaned toward her. "There're a lot of things I need to know, that only you can answer."

Those strange blue eyes latched onto his. "Where should I start?"

He sat back, dizzy from her perfume. It had touched something in him, intoxicating him, and he felt the vague stirring of an erection. Maybe it wasn't just the perfume; maybe his body was remembering what he could not.

"Doc Smithers and Benson put together a bio sheet of sorts, so I don't need facts about myself or anything. At least not those kinds of facts."

"How much do you remember?"

"Nothing beyond the first twenty years."

She flinched. He knew she'd been warned by Benson and probably by Dr. Clarke as well. But the soft shape of pain coiling in her eyes hurt him. A wave of guilt inundated him. *I didn't choose this*, he wanted to say. *I didn't choose to forget you or the marriage or . . .*

"I'm sorry," he stammered.

She waved his apology away. "You don't have to apologize for anything. I didn't believe Tim or the shrink. I had this stupid notion . . ." Her voice trailed off, and she shrugged. "Anyway. Tell me where to start. Ask me questions."

Her eyes followed him as he stood up. As he paced. "Considering where I was found, and that there was a blonde dead in the next bed, I guess what I need to know first is if I was ever unfaithful to you."

He knew from her hesitation what the answer was, and her expression told him the rest of it. He listened to The Story of Callahan, and thought, *Chapter One*.

"You don't remember any of it, Mac?"

"No."

She looked down at her hands, which were curled in her lap. "Benson said there wasn't any evidence that the Forsythe woman had had sex. Or if she had, the man had been wearing a condom."

He noticed how she said, "the man," keeping the things distant, impersonal. "Then what the hell was I doing with her in a motel room?"

"Working on a case for someone named Lans Hitchcock."

"So Benson said."

A sharp, uneasy silence ensued, which Quin finally broke. "I think you were framed. You got too close to the truth about something and you were framed."

"The truth about what?"

"That's what we're going to find out. We've got a few leads. This dating service, the airline where Nadia worked, a set of numbers that could be a combination to something." She reached into her purse and brought out a maroon notebook, which she handed him. McCleary paged through it as she told him about Harvey, but nothing in the notebook or in what she said struck a familiar note in him. "Who's Derwin Cody?"

"You remember that name?" The hope in her voice was unmistakable.

"No. He snuck in here a little while ago."

"Typical." Quin laughed, a quick, free sound, musical. He liked it, and felt less nervous with her now. "You did a job for him several years ago, and you two became friends."

They discussed the Rolex watch. The notebook. Cody's offer to put up the bond. In the exchange flowed a simplicity, an ease that felt right, but he couldn't have said why. When he asked where they stood financially, she seemed taken aback by the question, as if she hadn't realized what the amnesia meant in practical terms.

"We make a decent living, but most of our profits have gone back into the business. We've got an IRA we can cash in to pay for part of the attorney fees, and there's some money in savings and a few stocks we can sell. We can also take out a second mortgage on the house."

"You don't think we should accept Cody's offer?"

"I'd rather not borrow from friends."

He nodded. A moment or two passed. Air seeped through a vent over the door and struck the side of his face, cooling it. Out in the hall, he heard the PA. "Am I, uh, capable of killing someone, Quin?"

"In self-defense."

He held up her response like a mirror and searched it with his mind's eye: it reflected nothing.

"What kind of marriage do we have?" He felt ridiculous asking it, but her answer was quick and assured.

"Honest. It's had ups and downs, but basically it's good."

"What's been bad about it?" *Besides my infidelity.*

She picked up the apple and bit into it, her expression pensive. After a moment, she shrugged. "Nothing bad, really, but just small differences between us. You're very organized and I'm not. You tend to be critical; I tend to speak before I think. Stuff like that. It seems like we've never argued about the biggies—money or in-laws." She paused. "What do you think of your psychiatrist?"

He was physically attracted to Dr. Clarke, he thought, but that wasn't the sort of thing you said to your wife. "She's been great, very supportive. I'm not crazy about the fact that she's court-appointed, but I like her. What about you?"

"The same."

He walked over to the window and looked out. Cars zipped past below, hoods glinting with sunlight. "Are you, uh, sure you want me to come back to the house when I'm released on bond, Quin? I could probably stay with Benson or with Doc Smithers if you think it'll be . . . I mean . . ." He turned; she tossed the apple core into the basket. She smoothed her hands over her slacks, her cinnamon nails bright and shiny against the white. She had nice hands, he thought. *But I don't know her*. How could he live with her? How could he pretend a relationship he had no memory of?

"If it'll be easier for you, I mean," he finished, hating the sliding note of desperation in his voice, the raw plea. It embarrassed him.

"I don't expect anything of you, Mac." Her gaze was level. Her odd blue eyes were tranquil, and yet her voice seemed too soft, like an undercooked egg. "You can sleep in the den, if that'll make it easier for you. All I want is for this mess to be over."

Something in her tone filled him with regret, guilt. He went over to her, crouched in front of her, covered her hands with his own.

"I'm sorry, I didn't mean to—"

"I know. I know you don't." She gave his hand a squeeze and got up. "It's just that this is going to take some getting used to. I think I should go."

She stood so quickly a rolling queasiness seized him. Black dots swelled and popped inside his skull. His head began its hard, persistent throbbing again. She set the sketchpad on the windowsill, next to the vase of flowers.

"I'll see you tomorrow sometime, after the bond's been posted. I'll pick you up here. Or Benson can come by for you, if you want."

He wanted to be cooperative, to do what was easiest, simplest. He wanted this huge, pervasive guilt he felt to go away. "Whatever's convenient for you."

"It's up to you."

She refused to choose for him; he liked that, too. "Then how about if you pick me up?" He thought, but wasn't sure, that he saw relief in her eyes.

2.

The second Quin was outside, a sob squeezed past the tight set of her mouth and slapped the air. She bit at her lip, trying to quell her rising hysteria, and hurried toward her car.

The pavement burned through the soles of her shoes. The sun pressed against her spine, the top of her head. The world had been reduced to a soundless place of heat, of blurred images—cars that melted together, trees that seemed to topple into each other. Against all of it was McCleary's face, McCleary apologizing, McCleary looking at her like he'd never seen her before in his life.

A furnace of heat burst from the Toyota when she opened the door, but she didn't care. She folded herself behind the wheel, rolled down the window, and just sat there, crying until the tears and the heat had robbed every last bit of moisture from her body.

"Very good, Quin," she said aloud. "Now if you're finished, let's get on with business, huh?"

She started the car, slammed it into reverse, and, swinging around, peeled out of the lot.

Nadia Forsythe had lived in a condominium in one of Lauderdale's older neighborhoods, just off Las Olas Boulevard. The building was square-shaped, with a courtyard and pool creating the fourth side. It was upscale but not opulent, and as far as Quin could see, the best thing it had going for it was the profusion of trees around it.

She spotted Benson's Honda wedged into a space at the curb, with a police cruiser doubled-parked alongside it, hazard lights flashing. She guessed it belonged to Grunwald. Too bad. She'd hoped it would be just her and Benson. But considering the way the rest of today had gone, she should've known nothing was going to work the way she hoped.

After leaving the hospital, she'd driven back to Miami and had gone to the bank to arrange a second mortgage on the house. No problem, she was told. She could pick up the money tomorrow, and, hey, guess what, it was only going to boost the mortgage payments by $250 a month. A real bargain.

From the bank, she'd driven home because she couldn't face the prospect of fielding questions about McCleary from the people at work. *How's Mac? Oh, swell, really, he couldn't be better, except that he doesn't remember me, and if he's convicted, he'll be facing the chair. But other than that, he's just great.* She'd spent most of the afternoon making calls—the bondsman, the attorney, Benson, the office, an endless parade of voices and details. This was her last stop before home, a hot bath, and a long night ahead.

As she came into the courtyard, she saw Benson and a man she presumed to be Grunwald sitting at an aluminum table near the pool. They were watching several young lovelies doing laps. She stopped at their table, and Benson introduced her to Grunwald. He looked like a cop. He was one of those men who would probably still look like a cop the day he died—thick, muscular body, dark hair turning prematurely gray, a pair of reflective shades, a mouth that twitched and fussed as he tilted his head back and glanced at her. He didn't get up, didn't offer his hand, didn't do much of anything except nod and mumble, "Nice to meet you," then turned his attention back to the ladies in the pool.

A real charmer, this one.

Benson asked for the key to Nadia's condo. Grunwald slid it across the table and said he'd be along in a few minutes. *Don't do us any favors*, Quin thought. "What a turkey," she remarked when she and Benson were out of hearing range.

"Turkey?" Benson laughed. "You're being too kind, Quin." They climbed the steps to the second story. "He and his boys went through the place real well, so I don't think you're going to find too much here."

"I just wanted to see it. Any more information on her?"

"She died intestate, so the state's getting whatever she had—which was more than I thought she would have. She owns the condo—paid about a hundred grand for it three months ago. Huge mortgage, but that's the only debt we could turn up. Her credit cards are paid off every month. Her car was paid for. She owned a piece of commercial real estate in Palm Beach County that she paid over thirty for in cash about six months ago. She had close to sixty grand in a money-market fund where she banks and another ten or so in savings and checking."

"If flight attendants make that much, Tim, then we're in the wrong business."

"She was pulling in thirty grand a year as a stew and an additional thousand a month as a part-time operator for DAME. That's forty-two grand a year." He unlocked the door to the condo and they walked into the hall, where Benson flicked on the lights. "Not bad, huh."

"Impressive. A lot more impressive than it looks from the outside."

The hall opened into a large room with pale, expensive furniture, abstract paintings on the pearl-white walls, a black-iron spiral staircase that curled to a loft. They checked the rooms downstairs, then climbed to the loft. It had been paneled in wood, and off to one side was a king-size bed with a brass headboard. There was an antique rolltop desk, a wicker couch with matching chairs that stood in front of a TV and a stereo on the other side of the room, three or four more paintings on the walls, a pine bureau with a large mirror. The ceiling was also mirrored.

Quin opened a desk drawer. It was empty. "Grunwald and his boys?"

"Yeah. I went through the stuff when I was at the Broward Sheriff's Department and couldn't find a thing."

"All that means is that someone could've removed the leads, Tim."

He smiled. "I don't like the man either, kiddo. But I can't prove he took anything. Besides, what would his motive be?"

"I don't know." Quin opened the closet door and glanced through Nadia's clothes—designer-label silks, suede and leather, imported handbags, and enough shoes to make Imelda Marcos salivate. She started to say something but heard Grunwald's heavy footfalls downstairs. *Fee, fie, foe, fum,* she thought.

He appeared at the top of the stairs, his sunglasses jammed down on top of his head now, thumbs hooked into the belt on his slacks. "Isn't the bed great?" he remarked.

"Got any ideas how a woman making forty-two grand a year afforded all this?" Quin asked him, not really expecting an answer.

"Nope. Y'all finished?"

For now, Toadface. She walked on past him and down the stairs.

Given the amount of food she put away, Quin had never understood how the art of cooking had eluded her so completely. It wasn't that she didn't know how—anyone could follow a recipe. She simply didn't enjoy it, and the finished product invariably reflected it. *Spices and sauces*, McCleary the gourmet would say. *That's the secret*. Well, she'd added spices to the veal Stroganoff and she'd even made a sauce, and it still tasted boring. She spooned what was in the saucepan into the three kitty bowls on the floor. Hepburn and Tracy scampered over, definitely interested, but Merlin leaped onto the counter and stuck his snout in her glass of beer. He lapped at it, and when the level was too low for him to get at it, he tipped the glass. Quin caught it before it toppled and chased him off the counter. He sat back on his haunches, gazing up at her, licking his chops, and belched.

"Thanks. No telling where your mouth has been, big boy."

She dumped the contents, left the glass in the sink, and helped herself to another beer. Dinner: she still had to solve the problem of dinner. This entire day, in fact, had been a string of problems that begged for resolutions, and it irritated her that the issue of food was no different. *So what's it going to be? Yogurt? A pasta salad? A plate of fruit? Raw veggies?* All of the above, she decided, and went to work.

She'd just finished fixing the pasta when the doorbell rang. She checked through the window first and saw Cody's black Porsche in the driveway—his favorite car in a collection of cars. She unlocked the door. "You're just in time for my yogurt and pasta supreme, Cody."

He wrinkled his nose. "I *knew* it. I just *knew* you were sitting in this big house by yourself, eating shit for supper, Quin. C'mon, I'm taking you out."

"Thanks, but I'd rather stay home."

"Then we'll order and have it delivered." He hugged her hello and swept into the hallway. "How about Italian? I'll call Luigi's and they'll deliver whatever we want."

She laughed. "The yogurt and pasta are fine, Cody. Really."

"Screw it. You sit down. I'll order."

He paced back and forth once he was on the phone, ticking off an order with the same quick, authoritative manner Quin imagined he used on a construction site. She could imagine the people in Luigi's kitchen snapping to attention, jerking things from the fridge, shoving lasagna into the oven, slapping butter on the garlic bread. The restaurant was one of several places where Cody was a regular, and people probably knew they could expect a generous tip if he was pleased with the service. What you had to remember about Cody, she mused, was that his small physical stature had never been an impediment to getting what he wanted.

Except when it came to women, but that was a different story.

Forty minutes after the call, a veritable feast arrived. Ravioli and lasagna, a basket of garlic bread, a huge bowl of antipasto. They ate out by the pool, under the watchful eye of a new moon. Cody chatted away, which Quin knew was intended to distract her. He covered everything from one of the women in his life to a mansion his company was building only a few miles from here to his newest collection—hobbyhorses.

Cody was like a kid when it came to collecting things, and he had the money to indulge his whims. Besides the cars and hobbyhorses, there were antique mirrors, model trains, cameras, houses, tin soldiers, old Coca-Cola bottles, and books. His greatest collection, though, was women.

". . . my therapist thinks it's unnatural, you know."

Cody had been in therapy as long as Quin had known him. "That what's unnatural?"

He speared an anchovy and tossed it to Tracy, who gobbled it up. "That I haven't been able to find a woman to settle down with."

It was a relief to talk about something simple. "I didn't know you *wanted* to settle down."

His blue eyes seemed sad, almost mournful. "I'd like the sort of relationship you and Mike have, Quin."

She squirmed inside. "We've had our problems, Cody."

"Everyone has problems. But you two overcome them." He touched her arm, his fingertips cool, surprisingly smooth. "And you'll get through this, too, Quin."

The tone of his voice and the intensity of his gaze brought the lump in her throat a little higher. She wanted very much to believe he was right, that things would work out. But tonight she was even less sure than she had been last night.

"Oh, I almost forgot," Cody said, reaching into his back pocket. He brought out an envelope, which he dropped on the table. "The bond money."

"I already took care of it, Cody, but thanks very much."

His lower lip thrust out in a pout. The little kid in Cody wasn't getting his way, so now he was going to be a brat. "Took care of it how, by mortgaging your soul?"

"Yeah, more or less."

"Christ, Quin, I wish you'd have let me do this."

She stood to clear the table and planted a quick kiss on the top of his nose. "You've done enough, really."

Besides, this was a dry run for what was ahead, she thought. Tomorrow when McCleary came home, the hard part would begin, and no one could help with that.

No one.

Eight

1.

QUIN MOVED QUICKLY down the busy street. The wind was blowing and whipped her hair in front of her eyes. She brushed the strands away so she could see and spotted McCleary coming toward her, "Mac," she called, waving. "Hey, Mac."

But he didn't stop, didn't look at her. He swept past her with the wind. She ran after him, calling his name, and when she caught up to him, she grabbed hold of his arm. "Mac, hey, hold on."

His smoke-blue eyes were the color of mud in the dream, and looked at her as if she'd lost her mind. His smile was pale, thin, polite. "I'm sorry, you must be mistaken. Excuse me." And he walked away, into the wind.

Quin flew after him, but the harder she ran, the more distant he was from her. Her arms pumped at her sides. Her legs and feet blurred beneath her. The wind pushed against her, holding her in place, gobbling up her cry. McCleary was just a bare speck at the end of a tunnel of people. She could barely see him. She kept shouting his name, shouting, shout—

Her own sounds awakened her, and she sat up and looked wildly around the room, trying to pierce the dark. "Mac?" Her whisper slid through the quiet. At the foot of the bed, one of the cats stirred. She heard the sweet, melancholy lament of a single bird outside; it was almost dawn. She lay back, numbed by a swift tide of memories that seemed to rise from someplace outside her.

The first time she'd met him, she saw McCleary in a town house where the man she'd been living with had been killed. He was asking her questions, watching her carefully, and she'd disliked him intensely.

She saw the two of them crouched in the dark room of a

house they'd broken into, going through someone's files. She couldn't remember the case. But she vividly recalled the way they'd both cracked up with laughter once they were back in the safety of the car, how they'd celebrated their victory—*Over what? Getting the files? Solving the case? What?*—with a bottle of chilled wine which they drank while skinny-dipping in the pool out back. She could taste his skin.

Quin shut her eyes, wondering how she was going to be able to stand this, to live here in the same house with him and know that he considered her a stranger. He would sleep in the den downstairs. He hadn't said so, but she knew he would. She knew it as surely as she'd known two years ago that he would make love to Callahan. He would sleep in the den, and she would sleep here. Beyond this, she knew nothing, was certain of nothing.

Quin turned her face into the pillow, inhaling the scent of the sheets, seeking McCleary. But the sheets were clean and smelled of detergent. *I shouldn't have left. I knew it and I went anyway.* She should've heeded the portents—that her flight to Canada was delayed an hour and a half that morning, that she and McCleary bickered en route to the airport over something she could no longer recall, the way she clung to him when they said good-bye, as though she were afraid she would never see him again.

As she rode out to the gate on the people-mover that day, she fretted that her plane would crash, that McCleary would have an accident on his way back to the office. She thought about both things happening at once. She imagined herself and McCleary meeting after death, if such a state existed. Since they wouldn't have bodies, how would they communicate? Telepathically? Would they have phantom bodies that could touch, that could merge, that could love? By the time she was inside the plane, strapping herself into her seat, she was nearly frantic with worry, with hunger. She pressed her face to the glass of the tiny window and gazed across the tarmac to the terminal windows, hoping to see . . . she didn't know what, perhaps his silhouette. She probably would've gotten up, slung her purse and carry-on bag over her shoulder, and scampered off the plane if the doors hadn't shut just then, sealing her in. Sealing her into her fate and McCleary into his.

I shouldn't have left.

* * *

The offices of St. James and McCleary were located in a comfortable old house in North Miami. In the five years since McCleary's name had been on the door, hibiscus hedges had grown up at either side of it, the pines in the yard had leaped for the sky, and they'd expanded the building until it was large enough to accommodate their staff of sixteen.

Quin parked in the rear lot, next to Joe Bean's black Datsun. She entered through the back door in the hopes that she wouldn't run into anyone until she'd had at least one cup of coffee. But seconds after she'd gotten settled in her office, Bean bebopped in, snapping his fingers and shuffling his feet to whatever inner rhythm he always moved. He was, like his name, as thin as a string bean, with skin darker than tar, and a smile so bright it could light up Pluto. She hugged him hello and he sat in one of the chairs across from her desk and hooked his hands behind his head. "Have you seen Mac?"

"I'm picking him up from the hospital today." She sat forward. "Tell me honestly, Bean. What do you think?"

His long, spidery fingers came together and touched the end of his chin in an attitude of prayer. "He isn't faking the amnesia, contrary to what that shithead lieutenant who arrested him thinks. And I don't like his shrink."

"Why not? She seemed pretty nice to me."

"I guess I just have problems with folks who think they've got all the answers. And it bothers me, Quin, that she's got so much power over Mac's life. Whether or not he gets the delay on the trial is going to depend entirely on her professional opinion about whether he's faking."

"She's already indicated she doesn't think he is. She just has to prove it to the prosecutor's satisfaction."

But even as she said it, Quin knew it wasn't quite true. Clarke had never come out and stated her position.

"The prosecutor is a son of a bitch," Bean was saying. "But all that aside, I've uncovered a couple of things. First, Grunwald is up for a big promotion, and I figure he's got a lot to gain by seeing Mac go to trial as soon as possible. On top of it, I've got the name of a woman who was supposedly real close friends with the Forsythe woman. Another stew. What d'you say we pay her a visit today or tomorrow? The day after, she's leaving on a three-day jaunt."

"How about this evening?"

"Great. I'll come by the house." He patted his hands against his thighs and hummed under his breath as he stood. Then he reached over and squeezed Quin's hand. "We'll lick this thing, lady. Don't worry."

Such undaunted optimism, Quin thought, watching as Bean bebopped out into the hall. She wished a little of his lighthearted attitude would rub off on her.

2.

The McClearys' home on Poinciana Drive was not quite what Magali had expected.

It was larger than she'd thought it would be and wasn't a typical South Florida home. Built of redwood and pine, the style was southern California. The banyan trees at either side of the house shaded it from the worst of the sunlight, and the yard was nicely landscaped: sparges of zinnias and Mexican heather, sprays of ferns, a trellis covered with ivy, six-foot-high hibiscus hedges that provided ample privacy from neighbors.

She had left the BMW parked at a convenience store a couple of blocks away, and had been observing the house from the park across the street. Although she was dressed in jogging clothes, she'd attracted the attention of a bum in the park who was seated on a bench, paging through a newspaper. That bothered her a little. But there was nothing she could do about it now.

She'd seen Quin McCleary leave nearly an hour ago in a silver RX7—McCleary's car, if the biographical data was correct. The woman had been dressed for work, which meant she wouldn't be back for a while. The driveways of the houses on either side were also empty, so Magali decided it was safe to look around.

It was something she did quite frequently on a job, any kind of job, not just a kill. You could tell a great deal about people from the rooms they lived in, if you knew how to read them. Sometimes it only confirmed what she already knew, but occasionally she gleaned information that resulted in a shift in plans because the rooms would tell her what the bios did not.

It didn't take long to snuff out a life—five seconds, fifteen, perhaps a minute. Anyone could do it. But few people could do it as well as she, as successfully, as invisibly, and according to certain specifications. It required not only skill but creativity, a particular way of perceiving the mark. You had to understand your victim in much the same way you would a character in a movie or a book, with the same degree of intimacy—and the same distance. A delicate balance, and one she'd always maintained.

Magali rang the doorbell, just to make sure no one was home, and turned the knob. The door was locked. No surprise. She walked around to the side of the house, under the folds of a banyan. A mockingbird warbled high in the branches, its sweet, melancholy song piercing the hot air. Birdsongs in Miami always seemed mournful to her—a lament, perhaps, for the rapidly vanishing greenery.

At the garage window, she stopped and cupped her hands at the sides of her face as she peered inside. Quin's Toyota. Beyond it was a door that led into the house, probably into a kitchen or utility room. She ran her fingertips under one of the jalousie panes. It would give easily enough, but then she would have to remove several of the jalousies and cut the screen and she would still have to deal with the door inside. She preferred something easier.

The screen door on the back porch was unlocked, but a dead bolt secured the one that led into the house. Magali reached into her purse and brought out a tool that had been custom-made for her in Zurich. It emitted a thin, high-powered laser. It was similar to what was being used experimentally on patients with clogged heart arteries. Instead of risking open-heart surgery or angioplasty, an angiogram was performed in which a catheter was inserted through the artery in the groin that fed to the heart. Laser beams were then shot through the catheter and burned away the fatty deposits in the heart's main arteries. What worked for the heart, she thought, would work for a dead bolt just as well.

She plugged it into the power pack in her bag, aimed the beam of light at the wood around the dead bolt, and fifteen seconds later, a two-inch piece fell away. The hole was as neat and precise as anything made by a surgeon's scalpel, and exposed the end of the dead bolt. With a screwdriver, she worked it back, and the door swung open.

A black cat with luminous green eyes was sprawled across

the newspaper on the butcher-block table. It regarded her with indifference. In the windowsill over the sink, wedged between two flowerpots with begonias in them, was a white Persian cat that watched her suspiciously as she put away the tool and snapped on a pair of latex gloves. She wiped the outside knob, closed the door behind her, and stood for a few moments in the silence, breathing in the air. Part of her detached and floated out into the rooms, learning them, getting a feel for the people who lived in them.

It has to look like an accident. What kind of accident? In a car? Death by fire? Perhaps an accident in the water, while swimming?

She wandered through the rooms, touching things, lingering, absorbing the minutiae of the McClearys' lives. She had dealt with enough scum over the years to know that the accoutrements of their lives were often deceptive. After all, the scum she tracked weren't street people. They often moved in powerful, influential, and wealthy circles. They were polished, sophisticated. They were rarely motivated strictly by greed. Passion spurred them. So did revenge. Quite frequently they simply wanted to beat the system, to get away with something. She sensed that wasn't the case here.

Revenge was involved, yes. But it was also larger than that.

In the master bedroom upstairs, she poked through the bureaus and closets, touching the McClearys' clothes, examining photographs of the two of them together, noting the titles of books stacked in the nightstands on either side of the bed. From the looks of it, the wife read anything. McCleary's tastes were more discriminating: thrillers, suspense novels, nonfiction.

She studied his paintings. His talent was raw, sometimes undisciplined, but masterful at creating a particular mood. *Introspective*, she decided. Through art, he expressed what he couldn't verbalize. Despite McCleary's penchant for order, he was predominantly right-brain.

She moved through each of the remaining rooms, puzzling over the evidence of their lives like an archaeologist seeking to reconstruct the ancient past. When she left more than an hour later, she had more questions than answers.

Outside the convenience store where she'd left her car, she

called Jimenez. He answered the phone this time. "*Sín verguenza,*" she said.

He sucked in his breath. "*Sí, señora, con que puedo ayudarte?*" He addressed her in the familiar "*tu*" form, and it irritated her. She told him to meet her at the Café Domingo on Calle Ocho in an hour. He hemmed, he hawed, he was very busy.

"Be there or you're dead."

"*Sí,*" he said quickly. "*Claro. Una hora.*"

Forty minutes later she was seated in the café sipping an expresso, watching the door. A song by Julio Iglesias pumped from the jukebox. The air smelled thickly of coffee, fried plantains, steamed rice. A clutch of elderly Cuban men played dominoes at a corner table; they were loud, emotional, slapping the dominoes down, cheering, laughing, singing. She loved their outbursts. It was an emotionalism she understood, something Americans needed more of. They were an exuberant people at times, these Americans, but they tended to take themselves too seriously. Even the Chileans, living under the black cloud of Pinochet, managed to poke fun at themselves, to let loose, to give in to their passions.

A corpulent, gray-haired man wandered through the door, patting at his damp moon face with a white handkerchief. His dark eyes flicked uneasily around the room. Jimenez. She knew it.

She lifted her hand in greeting. Jimenez moved toward the table but looked like he wanted to run. He was sweating profusely. He offered Magali his hand, murmuring that it was indeed a pleasure to meet the señora. Anything he could do for her, anything at all, she had only to say the word. She disliked him intensely and immediately for his insincerity. "What I'd like to know, Jimenez, is who hired me," she said curtly in Spanish.

He patted at his forehead with the hanky. "I do not know, señora. It was a referral. The person had my phone number and knew who to ask for."

"Male or female?"

"Female."

"A go-between?"

"That is what she said, but . . ." He shrugged as if to say the vagaries of the criminal mind were vast, imponderable. "*Quíen sabe.*" *Who knows.*

"Do you have a contact number?"

"No, señora. Nothing."

Liar. "Then how were you supposed to let her know I would take the job?"

Jimenez slipped the hanky over his jaw. Half-moons of sweat stained his guayabera shirt. "We agreed that I would leave word with a man at Bernardo's. You know it?"

She shook her head.

"It is a nightclub in Fort Lauderdale."

"What's the man's name?"

"Parchel. Nick Parchel. He tends bar. He works for me from time to time."

"And who passed on the information to him?"

"A man with one eye larger than the other. A glass eye, I think that is what Parchel said. That is all I know, señora."

"The money. How was that worked out?"

"Over the phone. I explained your requirements and told her where the money should be left."

"How did she hear of me, Jimenez? Who was the referral?"

He thrust out his hands, palms up like Shiva, the Indian god. "I do not know. I have many contacts on the streets. It could have been anyone."

That much was probably true. The network on Miami's streets was like that of any large city, complex and efficient. But there were levels within that network, circles within circles, and Jimenez wasn't the bumbling fool he appeared to be. Some of his contacts were powerful. Magali knew he'd gotten her name, for instance, from a Cuban woman for whom she'd done a job several years ago—the abduction of the woman's daughter from her father, who'd whisked the child off to Panama eight months earlier.

A request had been released into the street like a prayer. Jimenez had answered it. Here she was.

She paid for the expresso. They walked outside. He continued to dab at his damp face. He smelled of sweat. Of fear. "Let's take a ride, Jimenez."

Desperation crawled across his face. "I—"

"We need to talk."

When they were inside his Cadillac, she directed him south and then west. While he drove, still sweating, she drew a .38 from her purse. Such an anonymous weapon, really. So common. She rarely used guns in her work, but it was the only weapon a man like Jimenez would understand. She poked it at his ribs.

"I hope you won't try anything foolish, Jimenez."

He stammered that he would not. Orbs of sweat rolled down the sides of his face. "I swear to you, I know nothing more than what I have told you."

"I believe you. But I still think we need to talk."

They drove twenty miles west of the Florida turnpike, into a deserted rock quarry. The sun beat down against the white sand. She slipped on sunglasses; Jimenez skewed his eyes against the glare. He took small, urgent steps away from her when they got out of the car. She leaned against the Cadillac, watching him. Plumes of white dust rose from the ground where his shoes struck.

"I have told you the truth, señora."

"But not all of the truth."

"What?" He said it as if he were trying to hear her above the din in a crowded room. "What is it you want to know?"

"The whole truth."

His tongue slipped across his lower lip. The handkerchief moved over his cheeks, neck, and throat in quick, desperate motions. His plump face squashed up, and he looked like he was going to cry. "I . . . I have told you what I know, I . . ."

She stepped toward him. She cocked the gun; the sound echoed loudly in the still, quarry air. Jimenez fell to his knees, whimpering. "They . . . they will kill me if I tell you."

"And I'll kill you if you don't."

He flattened his palms against his thighs and rubbed them back and forth, back and forth, against the fabric of his slacks. "There is a group of women," he began, his voice a whisper that seemed to lift with the dust that flew when he squirmed. "The Sirenas. They are the ones who want him dead."

"Who? Who do they want dead?" *Say his name.*

"McCleary. The bartender, Parchel, doesn't know anything. He is paid to know nothing, to do nothing except take and give messages."

"Who are these women?"

"Sirenas. That is what they call themselves. That is all I know, señora. I swear."

"You've never met one of them?"

"No."

"Was the woman who called one of them?"

"I don't know. Maybe. Yes, maybe she was."

"Why do they want McCleary dead?"

His hands moved frantically over his thighs now. They were dusted with the white quarry powder and looked like albino rodents burrowing here, there, trying to escape. They left trails of dust on his slacks and against his cheeks when he raised his hands to his face, swiping at his eyes. "The woman, because of the woman."

"Which woman?" Magali snapped. She was losing patience with him.

"Nadia. Nadia Forsythe."

"Did McCleary kill her? Is that why they want him dead?"

"I . . . I don't know. She was one of them. That is all I know."

"You keep telling me that, Jimenez." Magali stepped closer to him. His head was lowered. She could see the bald spot at the center of his crown, a singular pale eye. His shoulders heaved. Those white hands kept flicking, darting. She stifled the urge to shoot them. "Look at me, Jimenez."

He lifted his head slowly, grimacing against the bright sunlight. White dust surrounded his dark eyes; he looked like a nearsighted raccoon. "Please." He whispered it. His fat lips pursed, as if puckering for a kiss. "P-please do not kill me."

Heat quavered in the air, baked the top of her head, embraced her, licked at her cheeks, her arms. She swung the .38 away from him and slowly released the hammer. She told him to get up.

If she allowed him to live, she knew she would regret the decision. But it wasn't fair to shoot him, because he wasn't armed. If she told him to run, he would do so. But the image of Jimenez sobbing and stumbling through the white sand and the heat was abhorrent. She emptied all but three cartridges from the gun. "This is what we will do, Jimenez," and told him.

Rapture swept over his face. His hand jerked up and caught the .38 as she tossed it to him. He scrambled to his feet, moved back. She remained where she was, hand sliding into her purse, fingers closing over the mahogany handle of the ice pick that was her trademark.

"Shoot, Jimenez. I won't move."

She held her arms at her sides, the pick clutched in her right hand, parallel to her body. He raised the gun. His grin widened. The hot sun ground its fist into her face. She would welcome death. It would be a respite, an end to the madness her life had become.

No more, Magali. No more. Stop it while you can. The old man's words whispered through her.

"Go on, Jimenez. Shoot."

His finger twitched against the trigger. Her throat tightened briefly, a spasm of quick pain, then a cool relief flowed into her. It was as if her entire life had been building to this moment. Her own death. *No child, no future . . .*

He squeezed the trigger.

The empty click pierced the quiet. The sound hovered in the heat and the white dust, an invisible hummingbird. Then a dark, twisted grief slammed into her, nearly knocking her to the ground. Jimenez—panting, eyes bulging in his cheeks—squeezed the trigger again. The chamber wasn't empty this time. But his arms jerked up as he fired; the shot flew wide.

Magali's arm snapped up just as Jimenez was about to fire again. The ice pick whistled through the air. It sank into his throat and he stumbled back, his scream eclipsed, finger pulling back on the trigger as he fell.

The shot missed her by inches.

One bullet left, just one.

Jimenez struck the ground.

Dust floated up around him. For an instant, his hands fluttered, his body twitched, then he lay still. Magali walked over to him, gazed down at his plump, moist face, the vapid eyes. "*Cabrón*," she spat, and sank to her knees beside him. She worked the .38 from his hand. She dropped her head back, peering into the unforgiving sky. A vulture circled high overhead, wings dark against the bright blue. She closed her mouth around the end of the gun.

One bullet.

She watched the vulture as her finger pulled back on the trigger.

It clicked.

The vulture descended in tight, even spirals from the blue, a fallen angel.

Please.

Her finger squeezed; the sound of the empty chamber pinged in the stillness.

Magali eased the barrel from her mouth. She squeezed her eyes shut, pressed the heel of her hand against her mouth, then reached over and pulled the ice pick from Jimenez's throat. She twisted it into the sand to clean it, dropped it into her purse with the gun, and walked back toward his Cadillac.

Behind her, the dead man's eyes stared up to where the vulture circled again, waiting.

Nine

1.

"Hi, Doc."

The man hunched over the IBM Selectric, carefully applying white-out to the sheet rolled into the machine, looked up. He broke into a grin and stood quickly. "Quin, honey, it's good to see you."

Doc Smithers hugged her hello, his thick body solid and strong, a father's body. When he stepped away from her, the wisps of gray hair behind his ears—the only hair he had on his head—stood on end. He smoothed them back with the flat of his hand. "Have you seen Mac?"

"Briefly. I'm picking him up in a while. You're my first stop in a bunch of stops. How do you think he is?"

Smithers was the Dade County coroner. Like Benson, he'd known McCleary since his days at Metro-Dade. She guessed he was in his early sixties, but he seemed both older and younger to her—younger in his approach to life and older in his wisdom. Considering his line of work, his cheerful disposition had never ceased to astonish her. Even now, perched at the edge of his desk as he carefully thought about her question, a sparkle of optimism lit up his eyes.

"I think he's doing damn well. He's taking things a step at a time." He rubbed his large hands against his thighs, as if to work out a kink in the muscles. "He's already said he intends to find the bastard who framed him. He's angry. That's good. As long as he's angry, he can't feel sorry for himself."

She asked if he knew Dr. Clarke; he did. Unlike Bean, he thought she was tops. "How about you? How're you doing?"

She shrugged; her thin smile communicated everything. "Would it be possible to get a copy of the autopsy report on Nadia?"

"I'm a step ahead of you, Quin. I made a copy for you this morning. Her body's downstairs, if you want to have a look."

"What's she doing here? She died in Broward County."

"The coroner in Broward is a friend of mine. Once I found out about Mac, I asked if we could do the autopsy here. He was delighted to have help. We found something that may be significant. Let's hit the deep freeze and I'll show you."

As they descended the stairs, Smithers's presence, the familiar smell of his after-shave, stirred a throng of memories. It was like being a miniature person inside one of those glass paperweights, and the snowdrops that fluttered around her were her recollections: here, she, McCleary, and the Doc sitting on the deck of a houseboat they'd rented with several other people last winter, putting up the Kissimmee River; there, she and McCleary in the Doc's kitchen, poring over court documents on a case seven months ago; and there, the three of them sipping tepid Corona beers at a café in Coconut Grove shortly before she'd left for Canada. Her memories of him were triggered by smells, the taste of food, certain tunes, his laugh, the sound of his voice. How could McCleary not remember Smithers, who'd been a part of his life three times as long as Quin? She couldn't fathom what it would be like to look at him and not connect with some part of herself.

The morgue was a cold cavern with walls of metal drawers. In an adjoining room was the autopsy table, washed in the glare of fluorescent lights. The stink of antiseptic hung in the air. The click of their shoes against the tile echoed in the quiet. An empty gurney stood against one wall, waiting. There were no windows. With the lights off, she thought, the claustrophobic gloom of the place would be like amnesia. A black hole. When the lights were off, did the spirits of the dead commune in here? Did they dance? Did they celebrate or mourn?

Smithers went over to the far wall and slid open a drawer in the middle. He pulled the sheet away from the body's face. Nadia Forsythe was pretty; Quin had expected she would be. But she hadn't expected her to have hair the color of light, and such soft, delicate features.

"A gunshot wound to the chest, fired from a distance of less than five feet, with a .38. She was killed almost instantly. The bloodspatter expert who was called in says she was facing the door when she got it and fell alongside the window. She was then lifted onto the bed."

"How come no one heard anything?"

Smithers shrugged. "Windows closed, TVs on, people asleep. Gunshots in South Florida are about as common now as firecrackers on the Fourth of July. Unless you're the person being shot at, who pays attention? But this is what I wanted to show you. This mark."

He folded the sheet back farther, exposing the sutures from the autopsy that ran like a zipper from just under Nadia's throat to her pubic bone. She was slender, with full breasts, a flat stomach, and hips with just the right amount of flare. The mark Smithers had mentioned was on the upper part of her right thigh, a scar shaped like an X.

Quin traced it with her fingertips; the skin was cold, clammy. She quickly drew her hand away. "Very neat."

"Yeah, it is." He touched Nadia's appendectomy scar. "This is old, probably from childhood. But you can still see the tiny markings where the stitches were." His fingers moved to the thigh scar. "This is a lot more recent, within the last, oh, nine months to a year. It was fairly deep, but there weren't any sutures."

"Meaning what?"

"That it isn't the result of surgery. The curious part is that when I saw the scar, I knew I'd seen something like it on another woman who passed through here."

As though the morgue were nothing more than a pause between two points, instead of the final stop, Quin thought.

"I went through my records and found the woman's name. Karen Rappaport. She was a secretary for a local law firm, and her body was found out in west Dade, in a vacant lot, head blown away. No apparent motive, no suspects. The case is still open. One of Tim's men is assigned to it. The only bit of information he's turned up with a link to this case is that the secretary worked for Date-a-Mate for six months or so, a part-time job. They claim she'd been fired about a month before she was killed."

"Tim didn't mention any of this."

"I just spoke to him about it late last night."

"What about the drug you found in Mac? Was there any trace of it in Nadia?"

"No." He drew the sheet over her. "But traces were found

in one of the glasses in the motel room. My guess is that Mac drank out of it.''

"I know Panzine's a powerful hypnotic, but what else should I know about it?'' she asked.

Smithers ran his hand over the back of his neck. "Mostly it's prescribed for insomnia and anxiety. It's nonaddictive, which makes it safer than Valium in that way. But it's so potent, it's usually prescribed only in small doses, around five milligrams.''

"How much was in Mac's blood?''

"Minute traces. But keep in mind that I didn't see him until seven or eight hours after his arrest. It'd probably been twelve to fifteen hours since he'd ingested the drug. I figured he must've taken twenty milligrams or so of the stuff. Panzine can be lethal if mixed with alcohol, Quin. If Mac had been drinking, it's likely he would've been dead when they got to him.''

The inside of her mouth turned dry and sour. "Was any of it found in Nadia's belongings?''

"What belongings? They didn't find anything of hers, except for the airline pass card, which was in the pocket of her skirt. That's how she was finally identified.''

She asked how difficult it would be to track down the names of people in Dade County who'd been prescribed Panzine. Smithers shook his head. Insomnia was the most common sleep disorder in the country, he said. In Dade alone, there were probably ten thousand people or more using Panzine. It wasn't the kind of thing she needed to hear.

"If you were me, Doc, where would you start?''

"With the dating service.'' He tilted his head toward the drawer that held Nadia. "And with her.''

2.

McCleary imagined his lost memories hovering close to the surface of a pool like young, eager fish. To recover them, he had only to slide his hand into the water and grab. But when he did, his fingers closed over nothing but water and air.

He turned away from the window where he'd been standing for the last fifteen or twenty minutes, anxiously scanning the parking lot below for some sign of Quin. He picked up the empty sketchpad and set it in the bag with his pajamas and robe on the top of the bed. Then he returned to the window, to the huge slice of sky visible in the glass.

I want out of here. C'mon, Quin, hurry up.

Yet, as badly as he wanted out, a part of him dreaded it. He dreaded having to deal with people who knew him but whom he couldn't recall. Their faces would inhabit the black room in his head, pleading for illumination. Their mouths would whisper to him as he slept. Their eyes would gnaw at him, turn away from him, seek him out like radar. Then there was Quin—his apprehension at being around her, living in the same house with her, not knowing what she expected of him. But all this aside, there was the larger problem, the fact that the society he remembered had leaped ahead two decades, into a future he had once only imagined.

He'd had ample time to read and had consumed every newspaper and news magazine he could get his hands on. Okay, so he knew Nixon was no longer President, that the Vietnam War was over, that an ex-actor had spent eight years in the White House. He knew about Watergate and test-tube babies, AIDS and the Concorde, the explosion of the *Challenger* and the Middle East fiasco. But there were hundreds of other details, like home computers and VCRs, CD players and microwave ovens and electronic technology that made him feel like the protagonist in Heinlein's *Stranger in a Strange Land*.

"Afternoon, McCleary."

Roger Grunwald strolled in. He wore his ugly brown uniform today; the buttons at the belly strained against the fabric. His reflective shades rested on top of his gray-flecked hair. His eyes wandered around the room, probably looking for a lunch tray to pillage, McCleary thought. "Just got the word that your wife posted bond. As of right now, you're a free man." He grinned. A bit of tobacco stained one of his front teeth like a cavity. "Free until court."

"You came all the way over here to tell me that?"

"Nope." He poured himself a glass of water from the sweating plastic pitcher on the nightstand, knocked it back, poured another. Beads of perspiration stood out on his forehead. "Just wanted you to know I'll be keeping an eye on you, McCleary."

"I'd be disappointed in you if you didn't."

Grunwald wasn't amused. "Yeah, I bet." He gulped down the second glass, wiped the back of his hand across his mouth. "You might say I've taken a real interest in this case."

"Sounds like you're up for a promotion."

It wasn't a guess; Bean had called earlier and told him as much. Grunwald didn't deny it. He moved his shoulders in a way that reminded McCleary of a rooster puffing out its chest after a conquest. "Frankly, McCleary, you're a real catch. The former chief of homicide for Metro-Dade. Not too bad for a thirty-two-year-old cop, huh," and he laughed. "See you around."

Fat chance.

As Grunwald turned, he nearly collided with Lorian Clarke, who stood in the doorway, her expression bemused. "You badgering my patient again, Lieutenant?"

She flicked her honey hair off her collar. McCleary thought there was something defiant in the gesture, as if she were challenging Grunwald to an old-fashioned duel—pistols, ten paces, and all that. "Nope, just defining the rules, Doc. Mind if I have a word with you? In private?"

Clarke glanced at McCleary and smiled. *Her* mouth, he thought, was infinitely more interesting than Grunwald's. "Be with you in a second, Mike."

She and Grunwald walked out into the hall. The lieutenant partially closed the door behind them and the drone of their voices sounded like a horde of bees. McCleary capitulated to the quick burn between his eyes that urged him toward the door.

The PA system was blaring, but through the crack in the door he heard Grunwald say, " . . . I've got Saturday off. How's your schedule look?"

"I think I've got a patient coming in Saturday morning, but I'll check."

"We could fly over to Sanibel for Saturday night."

"I'll let you know. I'd better get back inside, Roger."

Roger: my, aren't we chummy. An overnight trip sounded like they were more than friends, but Jesus, *Grunwald*?

He ducked into the bathroom, shut the door, ran water in the sink for a couple of beats, then returned to the room. Dr. Clarke was studying the chart hooked to his door, her back to him. Wisps of hair strayed over the curves of her shoulder. Her perfume sweetened the air.

"Does it look critical?" he asked.

She turned with a laugh. "Hardly. You probably have the lowest blood pressure and pulse on the entire floor."

Your taste in men sucks, Doc. "So when do you want to schedule our first appointment? The lieutenant says I'm supposed to be at your beck and call."

"The lieutenant," she said, "gets carried away. Let's start out twice a week, Mike, and play it by ear from there, okay?"

"Suits me."

She slipped her hands into the pockets of her blue silk skirt. "If you ever have anything you want to talk about in between sessions, feel free to call or stop by the office."

"You're supposed to be the enemy." He smiled as he said it to show Clarke he was just kidding. *Sort of.* "Hired by the prosecutor to prove I'm faking amnesia."

Her frown threw her beauty out of balance. "I was hired by the county, not the prosecutor, Mike."

She hadn't mentioned where she stood on the amnesia issue—whether she thought his was for real. He wondered if she'd discussed it with Grunwald. Over dinner? Drinks? In bed? "The lieutenant's aiming for a speedy trial in September, not a delay," he said.

If she caught the implication of the remark, she ignored it. "And I'm aiming for what's best for you, as my patient." She smiled, and they set a date and time for their first session.

The last car McCleary recalled owning was a black '65 VW bug christened Snoopy by the woman he'd been seeing at the time. It had cost him $800 used, had carted him all over New York State, to Washington, D.C. for a peace march, to Connecticut for a Jefferson Airplanes concert, to Woodstock, Vermont, and Colorado. He'd slept in the car, made love in it, gotten stoned in it. He couldn't remember what had happened to it; perhaps a part of him had been expecting to see the VW parked in the hospital lot. Instead, a sleek silver vehicle baked in the hot June sun. The Mazda RX7. And she was beautiful.

Her name, Quin explained, unlocking the door and tossing him the keys, was Lady. She was the third RX7 he'd owned, and was about six months old. The first had been riddled by a spray of bullets in southwest Miami not long after he and Quin had met. The second, she said, he'd traded in.

Compared to Snoopy, Lady was a Rolls. Leather seats, a dashboard that looked as complex as the instrument panel on a plane, electric seat belts, an electric sunroof, an "autoputer" that computed everything from gas mileage to engine temperature.

"How much did she cost?" he asked once they were inside.

"More than seventeen, less than eighteen. I forget the exact amount."

"Seventeen thousand?" He nearly choked.

She snapped on her seat belt. "A loaf of bread costs more than a buck, coffee runs between two fifty and five a pound, depending on where you buy it, milk is nearly two bucks a half gallon. Here in South Florida, you probably can't buy an outhouse for less than eighty grand."

Welcome to the future. "How much are record albums?"

"Between ten and twelve dollars."

"Books?"

"Hardbacks as high as twenty-two, paperbacks from four to five."

"Gas?"

"It's been up and down, but right now it's more than a dollar a gallon for unleaded."

"What's unleaded?"

Her eerie blue eyes looked pained or startled, he couldn't tell which. "Gas with the lead removed."

"And it costs more than a dollar a gallon?"

She nodded.

"Jesus." He remembered gas costing about thirty cents a gallon. "Movies?"

"Four to six at the theater, a lot less to rent a video." She paused. "There are these things called VCRs that—"

"I read about them," he said quickly.

Mike McCleary, idiot savant.

He started the car, backed slowly out of the parking spot, drove to the exit. "You mind if we swing by that nightclub? Bernardo's?"

"No problem. Turn right and head east at the light."

Lady hummed. She purred. She glided across the roads through the sticky heat, responding to his lightest touch.

He tested her gadgets. The radio. The wipers. *More than seventeen grand*. For that money, the car should've been under lock and key, sealed up, protected.

He flexed his fingers against the steering wheel. "Who shot up the first car?" he asked, realizing he was eager for details about the life he couldn't recall. She seemed relieved to talk.

"A couple of drug boys." She told him the story, including details on how the two of them had met. Some of this he'd heard from Benson, but not in quite this way. Quin had been living with a man named Grant Bell, who'd been murdered; McCleary had been the investigating officer. At the time, McCleary's partner—and lover—had been a woman named Robin Peters, who eventually proved to be the connection between McCleary's life and Quin's.

Benson had told him about Robin. Their affair, that she was crazy, that he'd wanted to marry her, that she was dead. But he hadn't told the story the way Quin did, and he'd also been stingy with details. McCleary sensed Robin's importance in his past, but didn't know how to tactfully question Quin about her.

"How'd she die?" The question seemed safe enough until she answered it.

"You killed her in self-defense."

The words hung there.

"Take a quick right over the bridge," she said, then told him about how Robin had died. The hurricane. The knife. The wind. Her madness. The .357.

And somewhere still, he thought, somewhere inside him, Robin Peters was dying, and he and Quin were meeting for the first time, and he was playing cop and detective, and someone was framing him for murder. He just couldn't remember any of it.

He might not ever remember it.

3.

Bernardo's was one of a half-dozen bars and clubs between the intracoastal canal and the Atlantic, just off Oakland Park Boulevard in Lauderdale. It was the largest building on the block, painted a flamingo pink, with the name written in huge neon letters across the side. Nouveau Tacky, Quin thought.

In the lot that said VALET PARKING ONLY there were fewer than a dozen cars. "There're some public meters nearby," she said. "Let's park there."

He went around the block and swung into a parking spot. A quarter would buy you an hour. It was, McCleary pointed out, five hundred percent higher than it had been twenty years ago. She couldn't remember what she had looked like twenty years ago, much less what things had cost. But to him, 1969 was last week.

"What date did Neil Armstrong walk on the moon, Mac?"

"July 20, 1969."

"When was Woodstock?"

"August sixteenth through nineteenth, same year." He glanced at her over the roof of the car, as he was locking the door. "My memories stop about a week into 1970."

"Then they're still coming back?"

"Apparently."

If this new McCleary was anything like the old one, his clipped tone meant he didn't feel comfortable talking about memory just now. She changed the subject. She briefed him on her visit with Doc Smithers, about DAME, Harvey the vagabond, Grunwald's promotion. He countered with Grunwald and Clarke and the possibility of a personal relationship between them. She didn't know what that might imply beyond a conflict of interest, but filed the fact away and focused instead on the exchange of information. This was one of those *grooves* of memory, she thought, one of the habits they'd developed during the years they'd worked together. In the past, they'd exchanged information in the most unlikely places—jai alai, workout rooms, the dog track, supermarkets, Jacuzzis. By concentrating on what their strengths had been, perhaps she could activate one of those grooves and nudge it from hibernation.

The inside of Bernardo's was dark, cold, and smelled of stale smoke. There were two bars downstairs, a raised area with tables to the right, a small, shiny black dance floor to their left. Synthetic disco music pounded from the sound system.

McCleary winced and leaned toward her so she could hear him. "Whatever happened to acid rock?"

"John Travolta happened."

"Who?"

"We'll rent the video."

"Of what happened to acid rock?"

Quin laughed. "Yeah, one of the things."

They claimed stools at the smaller of the two bars. "Oh, before I forget." From her wallet, she brought out a wad of bills and an electronic bank card. "I figured you might be short on cash."

He thanked her, pocketed the money, and examined the card. "What kind of credit card is this?"

"It's not." Stick it in the slot at the bank's outside window, she explained, punch your secret code, how much money you want, and fast cash appears. At the supermarket you could use it to charge groceries to your account. He nodded, kept turning the thing over in his fingers, and she knew he was thinking *Orwell*. If *this* was strange to him, what was going to happen when he got to the house and tried to make sense of the microwave? The VCR? The computerized security system?

Which I forgot to turn on before I left the house this morning. What else had she forgotten?

"What'll it be, folks?" Except for the earring in his right ear and his longish hair, the bartender looked like a model in a Coppertone ad—young, virile, handsome, and very tan. Quin wondered if he was Nick Parchel, the bartender who'd been here the night McCleary met Nadia.

"Polar for me," Quin said.

McCleary asked for the same. They'd consumed their share of the Venezuelan beer on their trip two years ago, but it was obvious he didn't have any idea what it was.

"Right." The bartender knocked his knuckles against the bar, started to turn away, then stopped. "Ketter, right? Peter Ketter, alias McCleary. Or so the paper says." He paused. "You were in here the other night. With Nadia. I served you a Perrier with a twist of lime. The lady had a screwdriver." He leaned toward them; Quin caught a whiff of after-shave and suntan lotion. "Cops have been bugging me ever since, man. Dates, they wanted dates. I told 'em you were in here June tenth. I remember, because it was the night before Nadia was killed. You talked to her for oh, maybe forty minutes, an hour, something like that. You left. She left. Then the night crowd rolled in and rocked until four in the A.M. The cops were trying to get me to say I'd seen the two of you splitting together. I told 'em to take a hike. You left first, she followed five, ten minutes later. She said you were a reporter. Anyway, once people are out the door, I got no idea what happens, you dig?"

"You knew her?" McCleary asked.

He reached under the bar and brought out two bottles of Polar beer. He snapped off the tops and set the bottles on napkins in front of her and McCleary, "She came in three, four, sometimes five times a week. Looker like her is hard to miss even if she'd only come in once in a blue moon. I knew her as well as a bartender knows anyone. I know who's going to drink too much, who I'm going to have to turn off. I know who tips well. Nadia tipped well." The dance song ended, and he lowered his voice. "Sometimes Nadia came alone, sometimes she didn't. But she hardly ever left alone. Well, maybe I should qualify that, huh. Be fair to the dead and all that. Recently, she left alone a lot more often than she used to."

"Did she date anyone in particular?" McCleary asked.

"Hey, man. She was a good-looking woman. She had guys falling all over her. But once in a while, if she'd had a lot to drink, she'd talk about this dude she was seeing. A guy with bucks. He wanted to get married; she didn't."

Benson hadn't mentioned this, Quin thought. "Who was he, do you know?"

Parchel shrugged. "Naw, she never said. Women like Nadia . . . hell, they whine and gripe about the men in their lives, but they never give names and never do too much about their complaints, either. You folks want anything else?"

"Just the bill," McCleary said.

"Coming up."

Parchel busied himself with the bill. Quin saw him scribbling on a napkin and wondered if that was where he did his math figuring.

When they walked outside a while later, McCleary reached into his shirt pocket and pulled out a paper napkin from the bar. He unfolded it. "Take a look at this. Parchel clipped it to the receipt."

McCleary: Watch your ass. Dude named Raúl Jimenez left message here that Araña would take the job for a hit on you. Five days ago, I passed that on to a guy with a glass eye. Call me at 555-1682 after midnight or before 2 p.m.

Dread sat in her throat like a weight. "What's 'Araña' mean?"

"Spider." He let out a sharp, wonderful laugh, an *old* McCleary laugh that momentarily lightened the gloom. "Where did I learn Spanish?"

"On the streets. When you were with Metro-Dade."

"*Araña*." He repeated the word to himself, testing it, apparently trying to connect it to something else, to something familiar. In Spanish, it sounded dark and sinister, even if you didn't know what it meant. For Quin, it conjured images that were quite specific: thick, milky-colored cocoons, webs that were lovely and deadly, primal creatures that stung their prey into paralysis and then consumed them alive.

4.

Magali watched them from the parking lot of a restaurant across the street. As they passed beyond the point where her car was parked, she got out, crossed the road, and followed them on foot. If they happened to glance back, they would see a flashy brunette in short, tight shorts, a skimpy blouse tied at the waist, high-topped pink sneakers. She kept a safe distance behind, but was close enough to observe that they didn't touch.

She walked as far as the end of the block, where they turned left, toward the public parking. Magali slipped her sunglasses back into her hair, and smiled absently to herself. *Soon, McCleary.*

Ten

1.

THE ROOM WAS filled with ice. It rose from the floor in jagged hills, hung from the ceiling in stalactites, crusted his desk, the window, the furniture. It covered everything in a pale, pulsing blue. Clouds of vapor thickened the air, freezing his cheeks, stinging his eyes, his hands, the inside of his nose. The cold made everything sparkle. The room crackled and snapped like popping corn. Behind that sound, McCleary heard harsh, grating whispers. *Touch me, McCleary. Remember me, McCleary. Over here, McCleary.* His head jerked right, left. But the vapor was so thick he couldn't see the source of the whispers.

He grabbed hold of a stalactite and his hands slipped away from it, covered in blood. He screamed. He lunged toward where the windows should've been, but there was only a wall of ice as shiny as a mirror. Mouths swirled inside of it, mouths without faces, mouths that opened in hideous screams, that pursed, mouths smacking and rasping, *Remember us, McCleary. Remember.* He pounded the walls with his fists. The ice cracked. Mouths slipped through the fissures and stuck to the backs of his hands, the tops of his feet, to his fingertips.

A tongue lapped at his ankles.

A lip inched up his arm.

A huge white tooth worked its way into his shin. He screamed again and ran, his lungs burning, the vapor blinding him. The ice was so slick he couldn't keep his balance. He stumbled and slid through the closet, crashing into a wall of ice. It exploded around him. The tiny shards glittered brilliantly, *ting*ing as they fell.

The room was gone.

He lolled in a field of ice. White, vaporous ribbons of ice struck through with sunlight hung from the barren branches of the surrounding trees. They quivered with life. *Over here, McCleary,* whispered a ribbon that was now growing a head, limbs, a face, breasts. *Remember me?* she cackled, and leaped down from the branches, shaking the ice from her hair. *We are your memories,* she said softly, moving toward him, arms outstretched.

Now, beyond her, he could detect the events of his forgotten life impaled on the ends of the branches like Christmas tree bulbs. *Here,* they shouted. *Here we are. Claim us, McCleary. We're yours, McCleary.* They rushed toward him, these memories and events, these people, and clamored around him, grabbing at him, tearing his clothes, clawing his arms, suffocating him. He fled across the field of ice, weeping, stumbling. He fell and skidded out of the dream. He came to in the dark, heart drumming, fists clenched against his chest, something warm, wet, and rough sliding over his cheek.

He flew forward, grappling for the light, clawing at his face. *The tongue. Jesus!* The tongue had followed him out of the dream. The tongue and the lips and the huge white tooth embedded in his shin were here in the den with him. Any second now the door would burst inward and all those people and events from the ice field were going to rush in, overwhelming, crushing him.

But when he finally got the light on, there was only Merlin, sitting back on his haunches on the floor, looking at McCleary as if he were a traitor, the enemy. *You hurt me,* accused those eyes. *You're not my friend anymore.* McCleary slumped to the edge of the couch, rubbing the heels of his hands against his forehead. *Memories on ice:* who needed a shrink to figure that one out?

The cat jumped onto the couch, insinuating himself under McCleary's arms, and settled in his lap. "Decided to give me a second chance, huh, boy?" Merlin purred as McCleary stroked him. Gradually, his heartbeat slipped back to normal. The sweat on his face dried. The silence in the house sprang up around him, mocking his solitude, and he glanced at the clock on his desk to see how long he'd slept. *Forty minutes? That's all?*

He'd stretched out shortly after Quin and Joe Bean had left to talk to a stew who had worked with Nadia. He'd spent most of the afternoon alone. He'd called Benson to tell him about the note from Parchel, then he'd wandered from room to room, studying his own paintings, the contents of his den, photo albums, seeking his past. He hadn't found it. But he'd discovered a few of the wonders of the last two decades. He'd mastered the microwave and the VCR, but the computer and jet laser printer in his den still seemed as foreign to him as the evidence of the life he couldn't recall.

The most fascinating invention of the last twenty years was the CD player. It redefined music. He had gone through the collection of disks and listened to all the music he remembered —Hendrix and Janis Joplin, the Stones, the Doors, the Grateful Dead. He'd listened and made endless lists of things to do, people to talk to, of possible tactics in solving the lubricious riddle of who had killed the Forsythe woman.

Now and then, when he'd jotted down a particular detail or observation, the burning sensation had sprung across the skin between his eyes. At least his hunches weren't on ice, he thought. During the first twenty years of his life they'd been sporadic, fickle, and had concerned small things—which horses to play at the track, how to approach a particular woman, who was on the other end of the ringing phone. He suspected his years as a cop had strengthened the ability, so he'd checked the items on his lists that had brought on the burn.

Merlin lifted his head from McCleary's lap, ears twitching, tail swishing, and leaped to the floor seconds before the doorbell rang. The sharp, intrusive peal startled him. Panic, his old hospital foe, marched across the floor of his gut. *No one's home. Go away.*

It rang again.

It would be someone he couldn't remember.

On the third ring, he reluctantly got to his feet, stomach churning, and padded into the living room. He peered out the window. A black Porsche was parked in the driveway and Derwin Cody stood on the porch, a brown paper bag cradled in the curve of his arm. McCleary's anxiety subsided.

I've met him. He knows about the amnesia. I won't have to explain or apologize. Okay. No problem. He could deal with Cody.

He unlocked the door. The warm night air surged into the room, a tide sweetened with the scent of gardenias, jasmine, June.

"Mike. I didn't think anyone was home."

"I didn't hear the doorbell. C'mon in, Cody."

In the kitchen, Cody pulled a bottle of Grand Marnier from the paper bag. A bright yellow ribbon was tied around it. "Welcome home, Mike."

McCleary grinned. "Open this sucker and I'll get some glasses."

"Great." Cody laughed and rubbed his palms together. "I'm in the mood for a drink. Just had a session with my therapist, and I always feel like getting shitfaced afterward. Where's Quin, anyway?"

"She and Bean are talking to a friend of Nadia's."

"Yeah? Another stew?"

McCleary didn't want to talk about it, so he lied and said he didn't know. He set out two glasses and thought instead about the ritual he was enacting. How many times had he and Cody stood in kitchens or bars, doing exactly this? Just how well had they known each other? He asked, and Cody's blue gossamer eyes flicked from the glasses he was filling to McCleary's face. McCleary thought for a second that the question had offended him, and was relieved to see Cody smile.

"Well, let's see." He handed McCleary a glass of Grand Marnier, moved around to the other side of the table, and sat down. McCleary pulled out a chair across from him. "Once every couple of months, we make it a foursome for barbecue or dinner before a concert or something in the Grove. Sometimes when you're in Lauderdale on business or I'm on a job in Miami, the two of us have lunch. During football season, we'll occasionally get a bunch of guys together, and go to a Dolphins game." He'd been fingering the Swiss Army knife he'd used to break the seal on the Grand Marnier. Now he ran his thumb over the tiny red caboose attached on a ring at the end of the knife, stroking it like a good-luck charm. "We may not see each other that often, but as far as I'm concerned, we're good friends. And as you get older, it seems that good friends are tougher to find, you know?"

No, he didn't know. But he nodded and sipped at the liqueur. Its sapid taste burned a path through him. "What was involved in that case you hired us for, Cody?"

He sat back with a sigh and moved a hand over the top of his head. "Three of my men ripped me off to the tune of three hundred grand or so. At the time, all I knew was that something didn't feel right. Anyway, you went undercover as manager for one of the construction crews, and within three months you had the answer."

"What happened to the three men?"

Cody's desolate smile said it all. "The men got heavy-duty time, but they'd already spent the money." He shrugged. "It put a bad dent in the company for a while, I can tell you that."

Hepburn rubbed up against McCleary's leg just then, crying to go out. He scooted back from the table and opened the door for her. She scampered into the dark, and he frowned and ran his fingers over the burned wood in the jamb. His knuckles fit into the neat, precise hole that used to cover the dead bolt when it was engaged.

"Take a look at this, Cody."

He walked over. "Goddamn. You sure couldn't make this kind of hole with any blowtorch. You just noticed it now?"

"Yeah. This is the first time I've opened the door since I got home."

He stepped out onto the porch, his eyes slipping slowly through the yard. The moon hadn't risen yet, and the water in the swimming pool rippled with starlight. Pockets of darkness crouched under and between the trees. He was suddenly conscious of how the smallest sounds seemed amplified in the stillness—the cry of crickets, the rustle of leaves in the mild breeze, the distant blare of a horn. A chill touched the back of his neck, and he barely resisted the urge to throw on the floodlights. He stepped back quickly into the house and shut the door ever so softly. It was a second or two before his hand came away from the knob, another second before he turned and moved toward the phone to call Benson.

2.

Liz Evans looked like a stew. She was thin enough to be anorexic, her makeup was perfect, her shiny dark hair had a perm. She talked fast and bounced as she moved over to the coffee table to set down a platter of cheese and crackers surrounded by raw veggies and dip. Quin nibbled from the platter, noticing that Evans ate nothing at all.

". . . don't know what I can tell you about Nadia, except that she was weird, that's all. Just one weird chick." She tucked her feet under her like a bird as she sat down across from Bean and Quin. "I flew with her for three years, and just when I would get to the point where I thought I'd figured her out, she'd do or say something outrageous and I would realize I didn't know her at all."

"Was she involved with anyone?" Quin asked.

Evans laughed. "Nadia was always involved with someone. I'd see her on flights, coming on to a passenger, then later she and the guy would be having drinks or dinner and she'd go back to his room for the night. Then that was it."

Bean asked if there was anyone special in Nadia's life.

"They were all special. That's how Nadia would rationalize her affairs. But there was one man she didn't talk about much. Never even told me his name. I got the impression he was married. Maybe he wasn't and she was just being secretive, I don't know." She shrugged her thin shoulders. "I know he had money, though. One time she came to work wearing this rock of an emerald, I mean an absolute beauty. *He* gave it to her. Who hired you two, anyway?"

"Someone who knew her." Bean's reply was quick. Too quick, thought Quin, but Evans didn't seem to notice.

"But they already arrested the guy who killed her," Evans said, as though McCleary had been tried and convicted and was already on death row.

"There's some question about whether he's guilty," Quin told her. "That's why we were hired." She chewed anxiously at a radish. If she kept her mouth busy with food, she would be less likely to blurt the wrong thing. "Is there anyone you know of who would want to see Nadia dead?"

"No." She twirled a strand of hair around her finger. "But how would I know? I don't even know if this McCleary fellow was someone she met on a flight or what."

"Ms. Evans, there was a mark on Nadia's thigh," Bean said. "An X-shaped scar. You have any idea what it was from?"

"Oh, yeah, that. She said she'd gone to a guy to have a tattoo done and then changed her mind. That's what I mean about Nadia and outrageous things. A tattoo, right?" She laughed. "It's just the kinda weird thing she'd do. First time I saw it, Nadia and I were on a beach and it was still kind of pink, like it was recent."

"When was this?" Quin asked.

"A while ago, like summer or fall, I'm not sure. Before the tourists started arriving."

"Did she go to bars a lot?"

"Sure. As much as any of us do. I like, uh, knew her but didn't know her, see. We crewed together on a lot of flights, so whenever we were traveling we like bunked together and shopped and went sightseeing. But I didn't see that much of her when we were off duty. I don't even know who her friends were. I told all this to the cops."

Quin glanced quickly at Bean, who was frowning, who was sitting at the edge of the cushion as if he believed Evans intended to bolt for the door and he would have to catch her before she made it into the street. "Which cops?" she asked.

"This lieutenant. Grunwald. Yeah, that was his name. Lieutenant call-me-Roger Grunwald." She rolled her eyes. "Now *he's* the kinda guy you *don't* want to meet on a flight, believe me. He's the type who sits at the back of the plane because he's heard it's safer to be there if you crash, and he's sucking down double Scotches, getting loaded on the puddle jumper to Nassau. He wants you to sit down and chat so he doesn't have to think about the plane crashing, so if we hit turbulence, he can grab on to your arm and make you explain what's happening."

"How long did Nadia fly for Atlantic Express?" Bean asked.

Evans's eyes skipped to Bean. " 'Bout as long as me. Three years. Our stews don't exactly have a reputation for longevity. The pay's not so hot, and you get sick and tired of walking across the Atlantic Ocean. So three years means you've pretty much got your pick of flights. Nadia used to squash her flights all together in a two-week period, which left her time for her other job."

"With DAME?"

"Yeah. Right. She'd been working there since . . ." She thought a moment. "Last summer or fall, I think. A year, nine months, something like that."

That would make it somewhere between June and October, about the same time Evans had first noticed the pink scar on

Nadia's thigh. Was there a connection? "Did you tell the lieutenant about it?"

"He didn't ask. I didn't think it was important. I know she made real good money with them, working as an operator. I even called in one night and charged my two-fifty just to see what it was about. You're single in this town, you eventually get tired of trying to meet men in bars. So I called in and spent two hours on the phone with this dipshit in Ocala." She shifted around on the couch, unfolded her legs, and stretched them out until her heels rested on the hassock in front of her. Then she crossed her legs at the ankles and folded her hands at her waist, her movements as torpid as a cat's. "Well, he wasn't really a dipshit. We talked about stuff you just *don't* talk about with a guy you've only met. I wouldn't have minded meeting him, but suppose he was really great? There would've been a logistics problem—me in Miami, him in Ocala. I'd still be spending Saturday nights alone."

Evans, hungry for company, for an audience, wandered off on a tangent. When she resisted Quin's gentle nudges to get her back on track, she realized the woman had told them all she knew. She and Bean left a few minutes later. They drove through the warm June night, analyzing what they'd learned from Evans, picking apart the information, doing what she and McCleary had always done so well together.

Not once did Bean ask how things were between her and McCleary. Perhaps he thought it was none of his business or that it was just too soon to tell. Whatever his reason, she was grateful he didn't prod. She didn't want to voice her opinion out loud for fear that it would give it more validity, cast it in stone. In her heart, though, the prognosis already looked terminal.

3.

The music was fast, heated, impersonal. Her body absorbed the rhythm, translated it. Magali didn't have to think about it. She didn't have to puzzle over how she should move, what her feet should do, where her arms should be. She simply danced. She didn't know who her partner was and didn't care. He'd been seated several stools away from her at the bar, tapping his feet and drumming his fingers in time to the music, and she'd suggested they dance. So here they were, spinning and twisting in the flash of lights, in the smell of sweat and booze and smoke. Her steps and motions were fluid and Latin and natural. His were contrived, and slurred like his voice by the drinks, but it didn't matter to her.

When the music ended, she hurried away from her partner before he could speak to her, before he could offer to buy her a drink. Her shirt was damp and clung to her skin as she threaded her way through the crowd. She retrieved her purse from behind the bar and saw Parchel tallying up his register. He glanced at her, tapped his watch, and held up three fingers. She nodded and smiled and gestured that she would meet him outside.

She had spent the last two hours here at Bernardo's, dancing with strangers and playing coy with Parchel as he tended bar. He'd asked her out for a drink or a bite to eat when he got off at midnight, and of course she'd accepted. He had information she wanted about Jimenez.

Outside, a breeze stirred the warm, humid air. She smelled salt, the sea, scintillas of perfume from two women who swept past her, laughing. She thought she caught a whiff of blood on her hands, Jimenez's blood. She was imagining it, she knew she was; she had showered twice since returning from the quarry and had even perfumed her hands. A woman she'd met in Rio several years ago who'd spent two decades in this business claimed she'd retired from it after she started awakening at night with the odor of blood as thick as fog in her room, its viscous feel on her hands and between her fingers. Had *she* played Russian roulette? Magali wondered. Was it part of a burnout syndrome?

The double doors behind her whispered open and Parchel said, "Ready for that drink?"

She glanced around at his naive, handsome face. "You bet. What'd you have in mind?"

He smiled, and it was obvious what he had in mind: a ride to his place for that drink, that bite to eat, and then into the bedroom. In that case, she would need her car, and a great deal of time would be wasted. Before he could suggest it, she said, "How about that little bar just down the street?"

His disappointment was obvious, but he quickly masked it. "Uh, yeah, all right. Then we could head over to my place for omelets. My omelets are the best in South Florida."

"Sounds good."

He grinned and took her hand. His presumptuousness annoyed her, but she didn't draw her hand away. They started across the street toward Shamrock's, a small neighborhood bar set back in an alley. He commented on her dancing; she asked about his job. Her right hand, her free hand, was sliding into her purse. Her fingers closed over the .38.

The alley was deserted. Light from a nearby street lamp offered enough illumination to see but not so much that they would be noticed. Magali paused, reached down to adjust her sandal, and when she straightened, she pointed the gun at him.

"What . . ." Parchel murmured, stepping back, hands patting the air in front of him. "Hey, be careful with that thing."

"I'm very good with this gun, Nick. And if you want to remain alive, all you have to do is answer a few questions for me. Do we understand each other?"

"Uh, yeah. Sure." He folded his arms, unfolded them and let them hang at his sides, then folded them again. "But I—"

"A man named Raúl Jimenez gave you some information. Who did you pass it on to?"

He twisted the gold post in his right ear. "To a, uh, dude with a glass eye. Never saw him before. But he's so ugly I can tell you his mother's probably still shittin' bricks." He laughed nervously, and when she didn't even crack a smile he fell silent.

"Jimenez says you work for a group of women who call themselves Sirens, Nick." Jimenez hadn't said any such thing, but she needed to have some idea how much Parchel knew. "Tell me about them. You've got exactly five seconds."

"Who?"

"You're down to three seconds." She cocked the gun.

"I don't know. I swear. I've never heard of any group called the Sirens. This . . . this dude with the glass eye . . . he just came in and asked if I was Parchel. I said yeah, and he wanted to know if I had a message from Jimenez. I told him Araña would take the job."

"How much did Jimenez pay you to pass on the message?"

"Five hundred."

"How many jobs have you done for him?"

"Four or five. He pays well. Whenever I needed the money, I pass a message. No big deal."

"And you've never heard of the Sirens?"

"No, I swear."

"What kind of job is Araña going to do?"

"A hit."

"On who?"

Silence.

"Three seconds and counting." She spoke softly.

"McCleary." He gasped the name. She smelled his fear now, saw it in his face, his eyes. "Guy named Mike McCleary. I think that's who."

"Why McCleary?"

"I don't know. I swear. Maybe it has something to do with his murder rap. You . . . you know about that."

"I'm asking the questions," she snapped. "Did McCleary kill the woman? Nadia?"

He twisted the gold post in his ear again, then shoved his hands into his pockets. "How should I know?"

"Tell me exactly what Jimenez told you."

"He . . . he said, 'A guy with a weird right eye who's uglier'n sin will be coming into the bar. Tell him Araña will take the job for the hit on McCleary.' But I . . . I had problems with that. I'd never passed on a message about any hit. That wasn't the same as passing the word about a drug deal going down. So I asked him what McCleary had done. He . . . he told me it was none of my goddamn business, that if I didn't want to pass the word, he'd find someone who would.

"I got pissed, you know? I figured I needed to cover my ass. I told him he'd have a tough time finding someone as dependable as me, especially at Bernardo's, and that if I was gonna pass a message about a hit, I needed to know some details. I knew about McCleary by then because it'd been in the papers, and hell, I waited on him and Nadia that night. Only he was using a different name. He said McCleary had pissed off some people. I left it at that and told Jimenez I'd pass the message. He paid me, and I haven't seen him since."

"Who hired this Araña?"

"I don't know. The . . . the only other thing Jimenez told me was that Nadia was the star at this dating service where she worked. The way he said it made me think that maybe someone there had contracted the hit. But I might be wrong. I was gonna look into it, you know, but then I decided I'd better stay out of it.''

''What was the name of the dating service?''

He thought a moment and told her.

''Have we had this conversation, Nick?''

He shook his head vigorously. ''No. No way. I can keep my mouth shut.''

''Turn around.''

''I . . .''

''Turn. Around.''

He did.

''Kneel and lock your hands at the back of your head.''

''Jesus,'' he whispered. ''Please don't—''

She slammed the butt of the weapon against the back of his head, silencing him, and he slumped to the ground.

''Sweet dreams, Parchel.'' She hurried out of the alley to her car.

Eleven

1.

THE HANDS OF the clock didn't seem to have moved at all since McCleary last looked. It was still 3:16 A.M. But he was sure he had closed his eyes, dozed, and awakened again since he'd last consulted the time. Suppose this was one of the side effects of his amnesia? Suppose time for him remained stuck at 3:16 A.M. until he recovered his memories? Was such a thing possible? Was this an aberration science hadn't discovered yet? If so, what would the ramifications be? Would it prevent him from perceiving daylight? How could he possibly be prompt for work? For appointments? For anything?

He toyed with his speculations about what his life would be like with his perception of time stalled at 3:16 A.M., but the abstract stumped him because he couldn't imagine variations on a life he didn't even remember. His mental gymnastics only returned him to the circle of the present: to the hole in the doorjamb, the fingerprints forensics hadn't turned up, the call that Parchel hadn't returned, to what Quin and Bean had learned from Nadia's friend. The murder rap, the very thing he should've been most concerned with, was easier to push out of his mind than his situation with Quin. At the moment, that seemed more immediate, more pressing, an impediment to be overcome before he could deal with the rest of it.

Earlier, when the house had emptied of everyone and it had just been the two of them, they'd been awkward and uneasy with each other. They'd talked and exchanged information and she'd shown him how the computerized security system worked and where the linens were for the hide-a-bed, but beneath it it had lurked their strangeness with each other. His absence of memory had surrounded them, pinioned them.

She loved him and he couldn't reciprocate; that was the bottom line.

As he was making up the hide-a-bed, she'd paused in the doorway to say good-night and he'd turned suddenly and said he thought it would be better if he stayed elsewhere. Better for who? she'd asked. Better for both of us, he'd replied. She told him no one was pressuring him to do anything. It sounded good, but they both knew it wasn't entirely true. He felt the pressure of her needs and expectations just as surely as she did.

"Maybe what I'm trying to say is that it would be better for you if I moved out."

"Let me worry about what's best for me." Her voice had been too soft, her eyes too blue, too intense, and he'd left it at that.

Now, in the dark, he thought about the thickness of her hair, the blue of her eyes, the soft outline of her breasts against the T-shirt she'd changed into when she'd gotten home. He thought about how her mouth was incapable of lying, flinching when he said something that inadvertently hurt her, tightening when she was annoyed, sliding into an easy smile when something pleased her. Earlier, he had wanted to touch her mouth with his thumb, trace its shape, feel its texture. He'd imagined kissing her, stroking her, making love to her. But when, in his head, her face kept changing, he realized it wasn't Quin that he wanted; anyone could have satisfied the need for physical intimacy.

When the phone rang, it seemed he hadn't really been asleep, that he had just been dozing. He grabbed for the receiver before it rang again, and Parchel said, "Sorry about calling this early, Mr. McCleary."

The hands of the clock stood at five. "I spoke to your roommate earlier, and he said you weren't in."

"Uh, yeah. I had a run-in with someone who seemed to know quite a bit about what's going on. A woman. I woke up in an alley with a goddamn knot on the back of my head."

McCleary listened as Parchel told him what had happened, and jotted down a couple of items. He underlined Sirens twice. "What'd she look like?"

"A dynamite brunette, five eight or so, nice body."

Hormones talking, McCleary thought. "Can you be a little more specific?"

"Specific?"

Like he didn't know what the word meant. "Yeah, you know, eye color, what she was wearing . . . details, Parchel."

"Shit, man, I don't know. Lemme think. Electric hair, shoulder length. Tight clothes—skirt with a metallic top. And jewelry, yeah, she wore a lotta jewelry. And spiked heels. She looked like she was Spanish. The heavy makeup and tight clothes, you know, but she didn't have an accent."

"Spanish. You mean Cuban?"

"Hell, man, I dunno. Cuban, Nicaraguan, Colombian. They all look the same to me."

"Where's this Jimenez fellow live?"

"Look, I got no idea what-all Jimenez is into. I don't fuck with people like him."

"Your name won't be mentioned."

"Look, I don't even think he's in town. I called him when I got home and no one answered."

"I need a lead, Parchel."

"Christ," he breathed. "The only reason I passed you that note to begin with is because I hate seeing anyone get fucked and I wasn't feeling none too good about this hit. But I'm not going to play jeopardy, man. You're on your own."

"I'll keep you out of it. You've got my word."

Parchel sighed. "Your word. Great. Shit. Okay, you got a pen?" He reeled off a phone number. "That's all I know. You're on your own.

"Right. Thanks for your help."

"Good luck, man."

Like luck had anything to do with it.

McCleary opened the huge dictionary on a corner of his desk and looked up "siren." *A seductively beautiful or charming woman, esp. one who beguiles and deceives men.*

Was it just an arbitrary name for a group of people or did it mean the group was actually composed of women who beguiled and deceived men? If so, how? And what had Jimenez meant when he'd told Parchel that Nadia Forsythe was the star of the dating service? Was DAME somehow connected to the group? With an acronym like that, it certainly seemed possible.

He got up and went into the kitchen. He made himself a

mug of hot tea and sat at the butcher-block table. The only light came from the panel over the stove. It tossed off tight, buttery circles that ended at the outer rims of the front burners. The night pressed up against the windows at his back, at his right side. Although the vertical blinds were closed, he felt uneasy and shifted around so his back was to the refrigerator.

His fingers closed around the spoon inside the sugar bowl. He removed it, set it on the table, reached for the salt shaker. The pepper shaker. The Honey Bear container. The straw place mat everything had been on was now empty, and he slid that over in front of him too and put his mug in the middle of it all.

Now his fingers arranged and rearranged the items. He named them. TV, double beds, doors, walls, Nadia, McCleary. The image in his mind's eye crystallized until he no longer saw the objects as they were but as what he had made them. He was inside the room at the Days Inn. He was . . .

What? What the hell happened that night?

He and Nadia had met at Bernardo's. They'd talked awhile. Nadia had been drinking a screwdriver, and he'd been working at a Perrier and lime. He'd been wearing a Rolex Cody had lent him. He'd left before Nadia by a few minutes. Presumably, she followed him to the Days Inn or they'd met there, where he was registered as Peter Ketter. But if Parchel was right about dates, then he'd met Nadia at Bernardo's on the tenth of June. Then he'd met Cody at his railyard, where he'd returned the Rolex. He'd been found in the motel room on the twelfth, so he'd met with Nadia in the motel on the night of the eleventh.

What happened in the room? Had she given him something? Told him something? Why would he pose as a reporter? What had he told her? And what did the numbers in that maroon notebook he'd given to Harvey mean? 21–18–62. Was it the combination to something? He didn't belong to any clubs where he might have a locker. The safe-deposit box at the bank was opened with a key. The floor safe here at the house had a combination lock, but that was nine digits, not six. *If* the numbers belonged to a combination for a locker or safe or something else, then did that mean he'd hidden something in it? Something Nadia had given him?

The idiot savant inside him laughed. He reached deeper for the memories. But the deeper he groped, the less attainable the memories became. They were planets spinning out of orbit, plunging through the dark, cold vacuum of space. The wall loomed in his head, huge and impenetrable, and he suddenly swept his arm across the table, knocking everything to the floor.

The salt and pepper shakers rolled noisily across the tile. His mug broke. Tea splattered and splashed across the lower part of the wall. The sugar bowl shattered; granules spewed across the floor. Tracy, the calico, poked his head into the kitchen, hesitating to make sure the clamor was over, then scampered for the sugar, lapping it up.

McCleary pushed away from the table, threw open the back door, and walked outside. He stood at the edge of the pool, where moonlight varnished the surface of the water; nearby trees cast navy-blue shadows against it. He dropped his head back and peered into the belly of the obsidian sky. Its vastness, the incomparable loveliness of the stars, eclipsed his anger. He sank to his knees, feeling small and diminished, twisted with a terrible hopelessness. He was trapped by the same system that had fathered him. He wasn't so sure that anyone's efforts—Quin's, his attorney's, a shrink's, Benson's, Bean's—was going to change that, because they were part of the system. He needed to escape, to get away from everyone in order to find himself, and maybe in the process he'd answer the questions that plagued him.

But how would he escape?

By dying.

Okay, yeah, maybe there was something to it. What kind of death? Fire? Explosion? A drowning? It would have to be convincing enough so Grunwald wouldn't suspect a setup, and since there wouldn't be a body, the best he could shoot for was a *Presumed Dead.* It meant the reactions of the people closest to him would have to be authentic, because Grunwald would be questioning them, watching them closely. They already knew about Araña: could he use it to his advantage?

What sort of death would be the least suspicious?

2.

He didn't know the route they had run nearly every morning for the last five years. He didn't know it, and Quin wished someone were here to witness the fact. Someone like the prosecutor. Or Dr. Clarke. She explained the track as they limbered up in the front yard, in the sweet morning air, then they set off across the street to the park.

For the first mile and a half they were neck to neck, their shadows sliding across the sidewalk, the damp grass. When they reached the trees, Quin's lack of sleep began to catch up with her; her energy fizzled. She fell back a couple of paces, watching McCleary from behind, wondering how he'd filled his sleeplessness last night.

Around two, she'd tiptoed down the stairs to fix a snack and had seen a light under the door to the den. She'd been tempted to knock, but as she'd neared the door, it had seemed so imposing, so formidable, she'd beaten a hasty retreat. From then on, she'd been up and down all night, flopping this way and that on the bed, fluffing the pillows, kicking off the covers, yanking them back up, hating the emptiness of the place where McCleary had lain for five years.

When the phone had rung at five, she'd given up and had gone downstairs to fix coffee. McCleary had come out a few minutes later and told her about his conversation with Parchel. They had watched the sun rise.

McCleary slowed, and she caught up with him. Now he paced himself with her and she glanced furtively at him, seeking an indication in his expression that this ritual of running had triggered a recollection. But what she saw was an intense concentration. His awareness of her, she knew, had receded to a remote dot at the edge of his thoughts. This was that reticent McCleary she had met more than five years ago, churning singularly through the waters of his own being.

They loped down a shallow hill to the playground. The sprinklers were on, snapping like hungry gators as they whirled. He suddenly broke into a sprint. It left a rush of warm wind in his wake, and Quin slowed to a walk, pressing her hand to the stitch in her side. Just beyond the south border of the pond she spotted Harvey and his grocery cart, moving toward McCleary, who was leaning over the water fountain.

Harvey stopped. McCleary glanced up. Quin imagined Harvey introducing himself, explaining how he'd known McCleary *before*. They talked. McCleary nodded. Harvey nodded. Birds sang from the trees. The sprinklers whirled. Several other runners pounded into the park. She could almost believe it was business as usual, a day out of any week in her life before the trip to Canada. Almost, but not quite.

As she neared the two men, she noticed Harvey was still wearing the same faded jeans, and a different shirt, which was badly wrinkled. He scratched at his beard as he greeted her and smiled. "I was just asking Mike if that maroon notebook helped at all."

McCleary had pulled off his T-shirt and wiped his damp face with it. He didn't add anything to Harvey's comment and neither did she. "You two got company staying with you?"

"No," Quin replied. "Why?"

"Yesterday morning, I noticed this woman jogging through here, and then later I saw her over at your place. I thought she was staying with you because she went around back and I didn't see her again for . . .well, it musta been forty minutes or an hour. She left the house and walked down to the end of the block. I got to thinkin' about it and walked over to the house to see if one of you were home."

Quin and McCleary looked at each other; he asked Harvey to describe her. "Dark, curly hair," he began, and Quin hugged her arms against her, riding out the deep, ugly chill that chewed hungrily at her bones. The description matched the one Parchel had given McCleary of the woman who'd knocked him out.

The DAME offices in Coconut Grove were located in a small, Spanish-style building with pink stucco walls and black iron bars on the windows. Its heart was a splendid courtyard with a skylight where plants and trees burgeoned with greedy abandon: bromeliads and ivy, dracaenas and ferns, pinwheel jasmine. When she reached the second floor, she realized the entire south side of the building—both floors—belonged to DAME. Legitimate or not, she thought, it was definitely a lucrative little biz.

The waiting room could've belonged to a dentist or a gynecologist. Piped-in music was tuned to an FM New Age station. It was strictly snooze stuff—breaking waves, a harp, a little jazz.

She gave her name to a cute receptionist and said she had a nine A.M. appointment with Helen Ziegler. The woman passed her a clipboard and asked Quin to complete the attached questionnaire. There was also a flyer included. It had been printed on fancy, pale-blue paper with navy-blue lettering, and explained that DAME was a "sensible alternative to today's haphazard ways of meeting other singles." There were thirty DAME franchises in twenty-five states and three foreign countries, with another twenty due to open in the next two years.

The company, said the flyer, was highly selective in choosing its "front-line employees"—an embellished name for operators. Each applicant was carefully screened in terms of personality and professional goals, and if you were interested, would you please take a few minutes to complete the questionnaire?

Quin filled in her bogus name—Margo Sillers; address—a Coconut Grove apartment that belonged to a friend; Social Security number. By the time anyone realized the number was as phony as her name, she'd be long gone from DAME.

The questions were as transparent as the elaborate terms for the different kinds of available positions, and the choice of answers ranged from *Strongly agree* to *Strongly disagree*. Mark one, please. Quin could barely suppress a laugh. *Romance is very important for a marriage*. Well, hey, it helped a whole lot. *I rarely lose my temper. I enjoy touching more than talking. Pornography is one of our greatest evils. A fulfilling sex life is the basis of a good relationship. Welfare benefits should be raised annually*. And so on. The gamut was wide enough to cover sex to politics. At the bottom of the page were questions on annual income—check the appropriate range, please—and marital status, single, divorced, or widowed.

Quin was finished with the questionnaire by 9:15. At 9:30, the cute receptionist informed her it would be just another few minutes. At 9:40, another woman entered the office. Her gaze connected momentarily with Quin's and seemed to flicker with recognition. Quin was sure she'd never seen the woman before, but there was something vaguely familiar about her—that thick black, electric hair, a complexion as flawless as a baby's, high cheekbones, dusky eyes. It wasn't until the woman paused at the desk that Quin realized who she looked like—Robin Peters, McCleary's old love.

"Hi," she said to the receptionist. "I'd like to apply for an operator job."

"Do you have an appointment?"

"No."

"Well, we usually require appointments. But if you don't mind going in with someone else . . . ?"

"That'd be fine."

The woman had to spell her name for the receptionist, then enunciated each syllable clearly: it was obviously something she'd done a lot over the years. Ma-ga-lee. Magali Pinto. Then she took the seat one over from Quin, the personality profile in hand.

She wore a pale shirtwaist with low-heeled shoes—a conservative *interview* outfit—with just a touch of makeup. She wore a lot of jewelry—several rings, four or five gold chains, bracelets. There was something disturbingly regal about her, Quin thought. She was the sort of woman who probably looked great before she'd even brushed her teeth or combed her hair in the morning.

"Are these for real?" she said suddenly, glancing at Quin.

"Take a look at number fifty," Quin said. *I enjoyed taking the personality profile*. They both laughed.

"What the hell, I need this job," Magali said.

"Same here. You can't beat three-fifty a week for part-time work."

She leaned across the chair that separated them; her hair brushed her cheeks. "You think this is erotic phone talk?"

"I don't know."

"Well, it won't make any difference. As long as the horny callers don't come looking for you." She fished in her bag, brought out a pen, set her purse on the chair between them, and went to work on the questionnaire. Her purse was still unzipped and Quin thought—but wasn't sure, couldn't be sure—that she saw what looked like the handle of a knife protruding from a leather case.

Robin had carried a knife.

Crazy Robin who . . .

"Oh, I should've introduced myself," the woman said. They exchanged names and pleasantries and Quin noticed how Magali reached for her purse and zipped it shut. She did it in a way that led Quin to believe that what she'd seen *was* a knife. Well, so what? In Miami, lots of women armed themselves.

"Y'all can go on in now," said the cute receptionist "Helen's free. Through the double doors." She pointed a long, red fingernail. "Fourth office on your left."

The hall was as quiet as a tomb. No ringing phones, no typewriters, not even the tap of computer keys. All the doors were closed. Magali whispered, "How do you suppose someone named Helen will look?"

"So-so."

"So-so slender?"

"So-so attractive, plump, and blond, I think. Mid-thirties."

"Hmm. I was thinking a slender brunette, nice-looking."

They laughed.

"You a gambler?" Magali asked.

"Depends. Why?"

"Loser buys coffee."

"You're on."

Helen Ziegler was so-so attractive, plump, and very blond. But Quin was about ten years off on her age; she appeared to be in her mid-forties. Still, three out of four wasn't bad. She was dressed casually but well in dark slacks that trimmed her figure. As they settled into the matching leather chairs in front of her desk, Helen paced and smoked, giving them a rundown on the company. That word, *selective*, spilled from her mouth at least half a dozen times.

When she was finished with her spiel, she stopped pacing and leaned back against her desk, plump ankles crossed, a metal ashtray in one hand, her cigarette in the other. She knew Quin was a teacher, she said, but what sort of work was Magali presently doing? Free-lance translating for local corporations. Uh-huh, perfect, Ziegler breathed, nodding, stabbing out her cigarette. Such flexible schedules, uh-huh, just perfect.

She prodded and poked at their lives as though she were a physician kneading flesh in search of tumors. Now and then she referred to one of the questionnaires or made a notation on a notepad. She said the profiles would be evaluated before they left, but that she was usually a good judge of character, uh-huh, she sure was, and she didn't think there was going to be any problem with either of them. No problem at all.

At $350 a week for part-time work, Quin thought, what woman in her right mind would even dream of making trouble?

"I'd like to show you the phone room and explain what you'll be doing once you come on board."

"Once," not "if": like it had all been decided.

They followed Ziegler into a room broken up by soundproof booths. Each booth had a computer terminal and two phones. "This is our training room. It's quite pleasant, don't you think? Uh-huh, quite pleasant, even if I do say so myself. It's similar to the room where our front-line girls work. You'll be given a list of screening questions to ask each caller. Each and every one. The computers will analyze the answers, and anywhere from six to ten names will then appear on the screen. Those are your matches. You'll connect the two parties. They take it from there. Our success rate is quite high on matches. Uh-huh." Her head bobbed like a bird's stabbing for worms. "You'd be surprised at how much people are willing to tell a stranger over the phone. The right kinds of things. Intimate things. We accept all major credit cards and are tied into the Quick-Check system, which verifies if the credit-card numbers are valid. The fee is two-fifty. For that, the client gets to come back to us for up to a year or six matches. We *like* success, uh-huh, we want our clients to be *satisfied*. So we give them plenty of chances. Each week, we have a bonus for the girl who handles the most calls."

"How many hours a week are we required to work?" Magali asked.

"We like our girls to start with fifteen hours a week. Flexible hours. We're open around the clock." She spun her index finger in the air. "Our busiest times are late afternoons and evenings. But since we service three counties—Dade, Broward, and Palm Beach—there're enough calls coming through in the morning to keep everyone busy. Everyone." Another smile, another cigarette.

"Any obscene callers?" asked Quin.

"Uh-huh, sure." The words tumbled out in a cloud of smoke. "You'll learn how to deal with them in training."

"How long's the training?" Magali asked.

"Three days. But an intense three days. Eight hours. You'll be paid fifteen an hour during your training, uh-huh, we don't shortchange our girls." She hooked a hand to her ample hip and looked from one to the other. "Any questions?"

Both women shook their heads.

Ziegler's eyes slipped over Magali from head to toe, then did the same to Quin; she found it vaguely obscene, "We like our girls to dress well because it comes across in their voices.

You both look fine, just fine, uh-huh. Any problem with evenings and nights? With weekends? Weekends are *very* busy."

No, no problem, they said.

Ziegler brought her hands together. They made a soft, squishing noise. "Good. Now let's go see how you fared on the profiles."

"Well, I lost. How about coffee?" Magali said when they were outside in the still heat. "There's a café right around the corner from here."

Quin couldn't quite move past this woman's resemblance to Robin Peters. It was a little too coincidental for comfort. But on the other hand, she was paranoid enough these days to see something suspicious in almost everything. The woman was probably nothing more than what she appeared to be—a translator in need of a job.

Besides, she was awfully hungry.

Twelve

1.

THE STREETS OF Miami were like a web spun by a spider injected with amphetamines, McCleary thought. Roads twisted erratically, angled into dead ends, melted into other roads where the names or numbers changed for no apparent reason. He ended up on streets that hadn't been included on the map and had to backtrack and stop at gas stations to ask for directions. If he could believe the date on the map, which he'd found tucked in the side pocket of Lady's door, it had been printed this year.

It would've been simpler to take the Palmetto Expressway to the morgue. But he'd wanted to reacquaint himself with the city and had hoped that something he saw would incite a memory, however small. The only thing he'd triggered was a bad mood, stepchild of the frustration that had shadowed him since his arrest.

Dying's looking better all the time. But how to do it?

He turned into what he hoped to Christ was the right block and pulled to a stop in front of a building with the windows boarded up. A large sign on the front door said the county morgue had moved to a new address. He swore under his breath, checked the notepad he'd dug out of his desk at home, and flipped to the list of addresses. There it was, county morgue, this street, this number, right goddamn here. So the list was outdated. When Benson had called and asked him to drive over to the morgue, he'd forgotten that McCleary wouldn't know now where the morgue was and had neglected to give him the address. Rather than call him back and ask, McCleary had consulted the notepad and the map. So much for pride, he thought, and drove to the nearest phone booth.

The receptionist gave him directions, and within twenty

minutes he was hurrying around to the front of the building, site of the most fitting symbol for the twenty years of his life he couldn't recall. He saw Benson trotting up the steps, accompanied by a short, squat man in gray dress slacks and a guayabera shirt the color of cantaloupe. He called Benson's name, and the two men stopped on the steps to wait for him.

"Mike, hi." Benson turned to his companion. "This is Señor Turbera, a friend of the deceased."

What deceased? "Mucho gusto," McCleary said, offering his hand.

Turbera's smile was tight and uneasy; his moon face shone with sweat. He looked like he wanted to be anywhere but here. *"Un placer."*

As they continued up the steps, McCleary caught Benson's eye over the other man's head. *What's going on?* he mouthed.

Just hold on, said Benson's gesture. *I'll explain in a second.*

The cool air inside the building was a benediction. The place had a faintly medicinal odor, like a hospital, but there were no nurses scurrying around like busy ants, no blaring PA, no physicians pronouncing terrible verdicts. Here, the verdicts were in.

They met up with Doc Smithers in the front office, Smithers with his wisps of white hair like Tweedle Dum, Smithers with his avuncular smile, his belly laughter. He gave McCleary's shoulder a pat. "Good to see you, Mac, how's it going?"

"Okay."

Smithers's expression said he knew there was more to it than that, but because of Turbera's presence, he merely nodded. "Whenever you have some free time, you know where I am."

They descended into the chilly morgue. Smithers opened a metal drawer in a wall of drawers. He pulled a sheet back from a man's body and Turbera sucked in his breath. His head bobbed once. "*Sí*. That is him. That is Raúl Jimenez."

Jimenez?

"What was your relationship with Mr. Jimenez?" Benson asked him.

"He was my brother-in-law, señor." He spoke quietly; his face was white. "Former brother-in-law. He used to be married to my sister. We remained friends after they divorced."

"Who would want him dead?"

Turbera turned away from the drawer with a shrug and

tugged at the hem of his guayabera shirt. "I do not know, señor. I did not see him that often."

"What'd he do for a living?"

"He owned a clothing store in Little Havana. But in the past six months, a year, he was away a great deal. He worked as a consultant for people in the Caribbean and Latin America. I do not know what kind of work it was, except that it was not legal."

"Drugs?" McCleary asked.

"I do not know. He never told me."

"How do you know it was illegal?"

"By what he did not say."

"Is there anything you can tell us that might help us find who did this?"

He thought a moment, his bushy brows fanning together. "There is only one thing I can think of. Three nights ago, I think it was, I was at his home. A woman called. I went to get him, but he had already picked up on the extension. Before I hung up, I heard her greet Raúl with *sín verguenza.* It means 'without shame.' I thought it was a strange way to open a conversation, so I listened to part of what they said. She asked him for directions. He told her to go to the Miami bus station, to a locker. I hung up then, and they talked a while longer. Later, I asked Raúl who had called and he said, '*Una araña*.' That means spider."

Goddamn, McCleary thought. "Did he say anything else?"

"I thought he was making a joke with me. But Raúl looked frightened, and I knew it was not a joke. Nothing else was said."

Benson thanked the man for his time and walked him back upstairs, leaving Smithers and McCleary in the morgue. "What killed him?" McCleary tilted his head toward the drawer.

"Something sharp penetrated his esophagus. He suffocated. They found him in a rock quarry west of town. He was definitely killed there. The dust was embedded under his nails and was caked on the soles of his shoes. Some workers found him early this morning. He had ID on him. They tracked his Cadillac to a gas station in Little Havana. Quarry dust was all over the tires and bumpers. Tim said they checked the car for prints but couldn't find any that were clear enough."

"So whoever killed him drove his car back into town."

Smithers nodded.

"The weapon. Any idea what it was?"

He ran his hand over his nearly bald head. "A slender blade. An ice pick or something similar. What's going on anyway, Mike?"

"Looks like I'm someone's mark," he said.

2.

This is the wife of the man I have been hired to kill. The thought drifted through Magali's mind, a dry leaf against the surface of a cool stream. She could see it, this leaf, struck through with sunlight that exposed its tiny veins, chipped edges, its elemental truths.

Is this the kind of woman who marries scum?

She wasn't entirely sure yet. After all, when it came to men, most women suffered from selective vision. She supposed the same thing afflicted men as well, but not in quite the same way. Still, the fact remained that Quin McCleary might be one of those women who'd chosen not to believe that her husband might be capable of murder.

But wasn't it just as possible that she was posing as someone she wasn't because she was *not* one of those myopic women? Because she believed completely in McCleary's innocence? Because their marriage had been, until now, an honest, solid relationship? "Do you always eat like that?" She asked with a laugh, gesturing toward the plate heaped with more food than she consumed in two days.

"Whenever I can."

"How do you stay so thin?"

"I fret a lot." She stabbed a strawberry garnish at the side of the plate. "I figure that fifteen minutes of fretting burns up about five hundreds calories."

"You jog, don't you?"

Quin's glance was sharp, immediately suspicious, "How'd you know that?"

From the bio on your husband.

"Lucky guess. I run, too."

"Hmm." She polished off the strawberry. "I figured you probably did. You're not exactly Totie Fields yourself."

Magali laughed. She said she belonged to a health club, and, although she hated running indoors, she felt it was safer, Miami being what it was.

"We run in a park across the street from where we live," Quin—as Margo—said.

"We?" She'd slipped up, but in the next moment she recovered nicely, admirably.

"My boyfriend and I. We just started living together." She wasn't so sure it had been the wisest decision she'd ever made, she added. Her boyfriend wasn't exactly what she'd thought he was when they'd started dating. Since they'd moved in together, she'd discovered he had numerous compulsions. The worst was his hand-washing. "Fifty times a day, over and over again," she said, rolling her eyes.

Her story was convincing enough so that Magali began to wonder if McCleary actually *was* a compulsive hand-washer. "You never know a man until you live with him," she remarked.

And just how would you *know, mí amor?* She could hear the old man's whisper in her head. *When did* you *last live with anyone besides me?*

She shook the thought away, but it was too late. A sudden gloom claimed her. It pushed through her with all the subtlety of a hurricane, stripping away her capacity for idle chatter, scraping at the polish of her disguise. The longer she remained in the booth, the more painful it became. A physical pain, this, an aching in her joints, a discomfort in the center of her spine, a soft, persistent throbbing at her temple.

For long moments there was only the sound of Quin's fork scratching across her plate, muted laughter from somewhere else in the café, and the wild rush of blood through her veins, her capillaries.

When they finally left, her dejection had rooted inside her, fast and hard, a cancer. They parted company in the DAME parking lot, then Magali walked another two blocks to where she'd left the BMW. It was the longest two blocks in her life. Hot, buttery sunlight melted around her, through her, scorching the top of her head, the back of her neck and arms. She was so parched, she could barely swallow. The swell in her chest ached.

The instant she was inside the car, inside the sweltering balloon of heat, the tears came, stinging the corners of her eyes, eroding the skin on her cheeks. She rolled her lower lip against her teeth and pressed the heels of her hands against her eyes.

What's wrong with me? What?

She started the car and screeched out of the lot, headed toward Paco's.

3.

McCleary consulted the map as he worked his way south again, into Coconut Grove to Lorian Clarke's office. He got lost only once, when he made a left instead of a right and ended up in downtown Miami. By the time he parked in the lot adjacent to her office, it had started to rain, and he was twenty minutes late for his appointment.

He was not looking forward to this.

In the waiting room, he gave his name to Clarke's secretary. Her eyes, her hesitant smile, said she recognized his name and would he please not stand too close? Bad luck might be contagious.

He waited on the couch by the window, buried in a magazine. The McCleary he remembered, the twenty-year-old McCleary, would have struck up a conversation with this woman, joked with her, won her over, prodded her with questions about Clarke and her relationship with Grunwald. The old McCleary would've made love to Quin last night.

Rain struck the window behind him, driving furiously against the glass. Its din was like the clamor inside him, like the voices in the ice-room dream. *Remember us, McCleary. Remember.*

He got up quickly, asked the secretary—*Brigid, her name's Brigid. Charm her, Mac. Make her laugh, Mac*—where the rest room was. She directed him down the hall.

In the men's room, McCleary leaned over the sink, splashed cold water on his face, drank water from his cupped hands, pressed wet towels against his eyes. Water soothed, water cooled, water calmed. *How can I arrange my own death and make it look convincing?*

You can't. Forget it. Bad idea.

The towels slipped to his mouth, and he raised up slowly, looking at himself in the mirror.

Blank eyes. Hello, idiot savant.

But light surged in them, surged as if a question had been posed to the idiot. The light grew and he saw a woman.

The light pulsed and the woman moved toward him, her face in shadow, a drink in her hand.

The light brightened and he shivered.

The light was terror.

Deep down, I don't want to remember what happened that night. Is that it?

McCleary flattened the towels over his eyes again, and gasped as his stomach heaved. He got violently ill in the sink. His gut kept twisting even when there was nothing left inside it. He heard the voices in his head, whispering, hissing. *Ha-ha, McCleary. We are here, McCleary. Remember us.* His stomach kept churning; he vomited again.

He ran water in the sink, yanked fresh towels from the dispenser, wet them, held them to the back of his neck. He rinsed out his mouth. He avoided looking at himself in the mirror. He silently talked himself out of whatever space he'd plunged into and backed away from the sink.

When his spine was against the hard, cool wall, he closed his eyes, rooting himself. *Easy does it. You'll be okay now.* The message rushed through him, he felt it, he felt it leaping synapses, commanding nerves, muscles, tendons. When he walked out into the hall a few minutes later, his knees were rubbery, but he was calm. The door to Clarke's office was ajar and he looked in.

She was at her desk, scribbling something, her blond hair pulled back away from her face. "Hi," he said.

Her smile when she glanced up was quick, mercurial, as bright as a shooting star. She turned the legal pad over and stood. "Let's sit over here. It's more comfortable."

They settled in a wicker sitting area, a parody of someone's family room. She offered coffee, but he shook his head and watched as she poured herself a mug from the pot on the bookcase. She chatted—about all the rain they'd been having, the hot weather—trying to put him at ease. McCleary tuned her out and distracted himself by absorbing the details in the room.

His gaze settled on one particular poster on the wall for a symposium in Bollingen, Switzerland, on Jungian psychology. Across the top left-hand corner was written: LE CRI DE MERLIN. Below was a forest with a beam of light slicing through it that drew the eye to a white unicorn bounding from the green thicket. A man in a black robe, his face hidden by a black hood, straddled the creature's back.

"What's the significance of the poster?" he asked.

"The cry of Merlin. Do you remember the legend of Arthur and Merlin?"

"Vaguely. The grail, Lancelot, Camelot, Guinevere."

She sat in one of the wicker chairs. "The poster refers to Merlin's life in the forest, after he disappeared from the world. The legend said that men still heard his cries, but they couldn't understand or interpret them. Jung thought of Merlin as an attempt by the medieval unconscious to create a parallel figure to Parsifal, who was a Christian hero. Merlin, son of the devil and a virgin, was Parsifal's 'dark brother,' as Jung called him. In the twelfth century, when the legend came into being, there was no premise by which the meaning could be understood. So Merlin ended up in exile, and *Le Cri de Merlin* resounded in the forest. Because no one understood it, Merlin lives on in unredeemed form." The unicorn, she said, was her own addition. "A magical creature as enigmatic as Merlin. I see them as two sides of the same coin."

"The good and the bad?"

She smiled. "Or the light and the dark, two aspects of the alchemical force that leads to transformation. More specifically, *Le Cri de Merlin* is the amnesiac's cry."

Her calculated pause had the desired effect. He drew his eyes from the poster to her face, and suddenly, in that moment, he hated her. He hated her for knowing which buttons to push, how to burrow into his softest, most vulnerable self, how to trigger all the live, raw wires that had fired simultaneously only moments ago in the rest room.

"I don't think I'm ready for this," he said, and stood.

"Sit down, Mike."

He disliked her for that, too, for the sharp authority in her voice that reminded him just how much power she had over him, over his life. "I'll call you in a few days," he said, and walked out of the office. Clarke followed him, her footsteps quick, as sharp as her voice had been seconds ago.

"Mike, just a minute."

He turned. Thrust his hands into his pockets. Stared at the

smooth perfection of her skin, the curve of her jaw, the strand of pearls at her throat, and waited for her to speak again.

"I realize you're under a lot of stress." Her voice had shifted into neutral, a cool, professional voice, devoid of emotion. "But I still have a job to do, and I need your cooperation to do it."

"Not now. I'll call you and reschedule." He hurried down the hall, out into the waiting room, and into the rain.

Cody Construction was located in south Lauderdale and was one of the most unusual structures McCleary had ever seen. It consisted of eight rusty red boxcars arranged in a square, with a plexiglass dome over them. A six-foot-high hibiscus hedged surrounded it. The soft pink blooms on it were half the size of McCleary's hands.

McCleary entered the complex through the north boxcar and gave his name to the receptionist. She made him a badge and directed him through the sliding glass doors across from her. Mr. Cody's office, she said, was at the top of the escalator on the third floor.

When he stepped out into the dome, he felt like he'd arrived in another country. Rubber trees shot up eight and ten feet and looked like giant green umbrellas. A small wooden bridge arched over a creek fed by a fountain. Wildflowers burst from all the green, blanketing the shallow banks of the stream. Wooden benches and tables peeked out here and there, some of them occupied by people having coffee or early lunches. It was as if he were standing in South Florida's future, in a time when developers had razed all the greenery and the only remaining bastions of wilderness would be places like this, preserved through private or government funding. Even the absence of birds in here might fit into that version of the future, he thought.

He rode the escalator to the third floor, through the tap dance of rain against the dome, and spotted Cody at the railing, talking to a man in jeans and a hard hat. ". . . tell that goddamn turkey we can't have the house finished three weeks early," he was saying. "No, never mind. I'll call him and tell him myself."

The hard hat's eyes flicked to McCleary, and Cody glanced around, his anger breaking up into a smile. "Mike. What a great surprise." He dismissed the hard hat with: "Tell him I'll be calling him."

"Right, Mr. Cody."

"Problems in paradise?"

"Paradise, shit," Cody snorted. "You agree to build a house by a certain date and then the owner wants to leave for Europe and you're supposed to finish nearly a month early. This is that place we're building not too far from you." His cheeks puffed out with agitation, and he poked at his glasses with his index finger, pushing them farther up onto the bridge of his nose. "In this business, we meet a lot of assholes. C'mon, let's go into my office."

It was a capacious, wonderful room, mostly glass, with the gray, pendulous sky filling the dome, rain running over it. Beyond them, the New River twisted through the wetness, a rippled strip of aluminum foil.

On a table in the corner was a model train. It's track curved through a miniature New England town replete with clapboard homes, a white steepled church, a school, a railyard and station, a market, lawns and trees. Cody flicked a switch and the train chugged forward, whistle blowing. Lights came on in the homes. The bell in the church tolled.

"As a kid, I always had this fascination with railroads and trains. The town took me about six months to build," Cody explained. "I used scraps from our construction sites."

McCleary crouched until he was eye level with the church. "Real stained glass in those windows?"

"You bet. Everything but the greenery is real. Even the church bell in the tower there. My next project is for the *National Enquirer*."

"What's that?"

"You don't know what . . . ? Oh. Yeah, I forgot." He laughed nervously, embarrassed now. "It's a supermarket tabloid with headquarters just up the coast, in Lantana. Every December they ship in a Christmas tree that must be fifty feet tall and decorate it. They build these incredible life-size displays on the grounds. This year I'm building one that's going to have a train, railroad station, the works. Like this, except it'll be much larger. I told you about the railyard I bought south of here. It's eventually going to be an amusement park. And there'll be a model-train museum. For kids. Big kids and small," he added with a chuckle. "But I already told you about that. Even showed you the place." Cody turned off the switch. The train stopped, the lights went off, the town shut down.

"That night, Cody. Did I say anything to you about the case I was working on?"

"No. Just that it was heavy duty."

McCleary nodded and glanced around the office. "How many times have I been up here?"

Cody shrugged and poured them each a finger of cognac. "Dozens of times, I guess. One Sunday you and I sat up here watching the Super Bowl and getting loaded. You passed out on the couch and Quin nearly had my head." He laughed. "Another time, you and Quin and one of my ladies and I came back here after dinner and played poker until four in the morning. It was raining that night, and we played downstairs, in the dome, where you could hear the rain. It was nice." He handed McCleary a glass. "Cheers, Mike. Nothing better than a sip of this stuff on a rainy afternoon."

McCleary sampled the cognac. He wondered if drinking in the middle of the day was something he usually did. He rather doubted it. "So who won the poker game that night?"

"I did. But I lost the girl." His mirth vanished. "I have this terrific knack, see, for meeting the greatest women and for four, five months, things are perfect. Then something goes haywire and it all gets fucked. I still haven't figured out exactly what screws things up. But at least I've learned if I have enough ladies to play the field with, then I can slow down the process and stretch the four or five months into eight or ten." Melancholy weighted his voice; he stared sullenly out into the rain. "But what the hell. My therapist hasn't figured it out yet either. Even the experts don't know squat, Mike."

He changed the subject—asking what had happened with the doorjamb, if forensics had found anything. As McCleary explained, the cognac loosened his tongue and he suddenly blurted, "How would a man go about disappearing, Cody?"

The words hung there like the smell of old food. Rain drummed the glass dome overhead. Cody's blue gossamer eyes finally looked up from his snifter. "I guess that would depend on his reasons for disappearing. Does he want to disappear as who he is and then become someone else? Does he just want to drop off the face of the Earth? Does he want to die so his wife can collect the insurance money and then the two of them meet up later in Madagascar?" He smiled a little. "Or does he want to die to get the assholes off his tail, Mike?"

The assholes, the spider lady, all of them. "He just wants to know what his options are."

"His options." Cody nodded. "Well, if it were me, Mike, I guess I'd set up some type of fire so it'd be real difficult to tell who died. I would make sure something of mine was found near the scene. I'd already have a safe place where I could lay low. If this place was outside the country, I'd make sure I had my phony documents first. It's always best to negotiate things like this when you still have the upper hand." He paused, rubbed the side of his face, and lowered his voice. "And I'd keep it to myself, so that when the cops came snooping around, the grief of the people who knew me would be real."

McCleary swallowed some more cognac. He felt that Cody was waiting for him to say something. When he didn't, the other man touched his arm. "What the hell's going on, Mike?"

"I can't do this."

He vomited nearly everything that had happened since his release from the hospital. Cody listened. He advised McCleary to think things through. He was rational about it. Reasonable. Had he discussed this with Benson? No way, McCleary replied, shaking his head. Benson was a friend, yes, but he was still a cop. Had he mentioned it to Quin? No, he hadn't said anything to anyone.

"Look, man, if you still feel the same in a week or so, then we'll look at the options. And in the meantime, how about if I get a date for the Grove Arts Festival and we make it a foursome? It's a week from Saturday. In fact, why don't you think things over till then?"

Ten days.

He didn't know if the spider lady would wait that long. He didn't know if *he* could wait that long.

4.

"This is Bartlett."

"Without shame," she replied.

"Give me your number. I'll call you right back."

On an unsecured line, she thought, and read off the number in the booth where she stood. Less than a minute later, it rang. "Any news, Bartlett?"

"A couple of things, love. The evidence against this McCleary fellow looks solid. But when you consider his background, it's almost *too* solid. I get real nervous when I see cases as airtight as this one."

"You mean his background as a cop?"

"Yeah, that's part of it. Now don't get me wrong, love. There're a lotta dirty cops in Miami and a lot of dirty ex-cops. But usually they're dirty because there are drug bucks involved. Big bucks. The only thing I found on him prior to this was an internal investigation when he shot his ex-partner nearly six years ago. The department eventually ruled it as self-defense and that was the end of it. Turned out his partner was a nasty little lady with oh, maybe six homicides to her credit."

"Anything else?"

"That's not enough?"

"What about the Forsythe woman?"

He recited facts that she already knew. But she listened, the rain drumming against the phone booth, traffic streaming through the road in front of her. She thought of Bartlett's hands, of the light hair that covered his arms like fur. She thought of his eyes, of what she'd seen in them. When he asked if she had any free time this afternoon, it was this memory of his eyes that prompted her to say no, she was much too busy, but she would call him in a few days.

"Wait, love."

"What?"

"If you have something on your mind, just say it, okay? We've always been pretty straightforward with each other."

She didn't agree with him, but let it pass. "I've just got a lot to do, Bartlett. I'll call you soon."

"Where can I get in touch with you?"

That's not how we play this, she wanted to shout it at him. But it was only partially true. In Europe, he had almost always known how to contact her. But America was a continent of different rules. "It'll be simpler if I call you," she said, and hung up before he could reply.

She opened her umbrella as she stepped out of the booth. A part of her believed that any second now the phone inside would ring and if she picked it up, she would hear Bartlett's voice whisper, *You can't get away from me* that *easily, love.*

And he would say it as though she were the enemy.

Thirteen

1.

THE HEAT DURING the last week of June and the beginning of July broke and set records for that time of year. The temperature hovered in the high nineties, with little or no reprieve at night, even when it rained. Which it did.

Every day, rain swept across the peninsula in fierce, buffeting gusts, causing power outages and more than the usual number of traffic accidents on the interstate. It blew leaves from the trees in the McClearys' front yard, blanketing the lawn. Pine needles created vivid green swirls against the sidewalk and driveway. Clutches of white and lavender periwinkles, clover and ivy sprang up where none had existed before, and the air always smelled sweet and clean.

But the profusion of growth, the green richness of everything, seemed like a mockery to Quin of the sparse landscape her life had become. She felt like Dorothy in Oz, caught in a place she didn't want to be, longing for home, hoping the wizard would set things right when she found him.

The problem with the analogy about Oz, she thought, was that she inhabited a world where wizards were as extinct as yellow brick roads. In her world, you got out of a place you didn't like. You quit your job, divorced your husband, traded in your car, redid your life. If you didn't know how to do any of those things, then you bought a book that told you how or consulted an expert who did it for you.

But what book did you read, what expert did you consult, if all you wanted was your old life back? What magic could restore what had been?

Opportunity, she thought. That was a kind of magic. Tonight was the first time in two weeks that Ziegler's office was empty. She didn't know if a search of it would bring back her old life, but it was worth a try.

Quin rubbed her eyes, logged off on her computer, and flicked the switch on her phone that would automatically emit a busy signal on her line when someone called. It was just past midnight. The twelve-to-eight shift was settling in. Ziegler's assistant, who'd been monitoring the progress of the "new girls" on the four-to-midnight shift the last two weeks had left half an hour ago. Now or never, Quin thought, and pushed away from the booth.

In two weeks at DAME and sixty hours of work she'd uncovered nothing even remotely suspicious. The only odd thing was something that had *not* happened—Magali, Robin's look-alike, hadn't taken the job. Helen "Ziggy" Ziegler said she'd demurred at the last minute. Quin suspected Ziggy had found something objectionable in Magali's personality profile. But that hardly qualified as *suspicious*.

The background check Benson had run on the board of directors had yielded no dark and desperate secrets. As far as they could determine from public records, there was only one owner and he was living in Europe. If he had a silent partner, he wasn't on the books. DAME seemed to be exactly what it claimed to be—a dating service.

Quin headed toward the staff kitchen and greeted several of the operators who were on their way in. The ones she'd gotten to know seemed to be what they appeared to be as well—women in need of well-paying part-time work. They all remembered Nadia Forsythe, but none of them had known her well. *She wasn't real friendly,* one operator had said. *She was distant,* remarked another. *Nadia was a snob,* sniffed a third. Another operator observed that Nadia was one of Ziggy's favorites, which was probably the most revealing assessment on Nadia that Quin had heard.

How did you get to be one of Ziegler's favorites? Quin had asked.

The answers to that ranged from the sublime to the obscene, and told her virtually nothing.

Quin retrieved her bag of munchies from the fridge in the staff kitchen. To bide her time until the graveyard-shift operators got settled, she polished off what remained of the freeze-dried peanuts in the bag, then returned to the hall.

No one was around.

The crew had gone to work, and so would she.

Quin took a quick look over her shoulders and ducked into

the hall to her left. It led into Ziggy's secretary's office. She picked the lock on the desk with a bobby pin, opened the middle drawer, and patted around inside until she found the master keys. Then she let herself into Ziggy's inner sanctum.

The room smelled faintly of smoke and the woman's cheap cologne. She went through the desk first, found Ziggy's stash of Hostess Twinkies, her "secret" vice, but nothing of interest. She booted up Ziggy's computer, located *Personnel* on the menu, but when she tried to get into the document, the machine beeped. *Password required* flashed on the screen.

Sirens, she typed.

Invalid password.

Dame.

Invalid password.

Ziggy.

Invalid password.

Twinkie.

Invalid password.

Fuck you.

Invalid password.

"Yeah, yeah." She tried to get into the document through another program, and when that didn't work, she returned to the menu. The only files she could get into were those that had nothing to do with DAME. She finally gave up on the computer and started in on the filing cabinets. None of the drawers was labeled and all were locked. She picked the locks one by one, and in the third drawer found the personnel files. Ziggy was apparently one of those people who didn't entirely trust computers and had kept backups she could touch, feel, hold.

The files were divided into categories—administrative, front-line, clerical, and so on. She started with the front-line, in F's, for Nadia Forsythe. She didn't find anything, but noticed that some of the folders had gold stars on them, the kind you received on neat homework in grade school. She pulled one of the starred files and looked through it. The top sheet was a brief summary with the woman's name, position (front-liner), shift (day, which explained why Quin didn't know who she was), earnings ($25 an hour), and the date she'd started with the company (six months ago). Under it were her profile tests, résumé, background information, training scores, a record of her matches. Nothing unusual—except for the gold star on the front.

Quin reached S and pulled her own file—*Sillers, Margo.* A silver star was pasted on the front of her folder. She flipped through it, looking for something that would explain what the star meant. Clipped to one of her profile tests was a typed note that said, *Possible candidate. Observe.*

Candidate for what?

She put it back and moved on to the rest of the drawers. She stopped at one labeled TERMINATED. Ugly word, that. No wonder the damn drawer was locked. She picked it with her bobby pin, slid it open. There were only five files—Nadia Forsythe's among them—and each was marked with either a silver or gold star or both. She considered taking Nadia's file with her, then decided it would be safer to copy it. The copier had an automatic feeder, and a couple of minutes later she'd duplicated the file. She slipped it into her bag, returned the original to the drawer, and started jotting down the other four names with starred folders. The last one was *Rappaport, Karen.* "Rappaport," she whispered. "Rappaport." She knew she'd heard it before, but where?

Then she remembered. Rappaport was the woman Doc Smithers had mentioned, the one with the X-shaped scar on her thigh like Nadia, who'd come through the Miami morgue about a year ago.

Terminated: both Rappaport and Nadia Forsythe were in this drawer, and they were both dead.

Were the other three women also dead?

She decided to copy Rappaport's file as well.

A few minutes later, she stole out of Ziegler's office, her secrets zipped into her purse.

It was the scar she thought about as she drove home. Two women who worked for DAME and had identical scars on their thighs had been chosen for something and murdered. If the star marked you for death, it would be easy enough to find out by running a check on the other three names in the TERMINATED file. But suppose the scars marked you as a possible candidate in an elite club known as the Sirens? After all, members of street gangs often had identifying marks like tattoos or wore certain kinds of clothes or carried a particular weapon that marked them as a member of the gang. But was it a fair comparison? She decided it was. When you were brainstorming, anything was fair.

All right, then. She would assume, for the moment, that

the Sirens was a gang of women who preyed on men in a certain financial bracket. Lans Hitchcock, who'd hired McCleary, had supposedly lost his Rolex when he was rolled. McCleary had borrowed a Rolex from Cody the night he went to Bernardo's. So the Rolex, symbol of the good life, might be a way of quickly identifying a mark. But who would believe that a reporter made enough money to own a Rolex?

She set this aside in her mental discrepancy column, and concentrated instead on the Panzine. Had Nadia intended to drug McCleary or had the killer done it? Who had knocked McCleary out? Someone who'd been at the motel with Nadia when he arrived? Maybe Nadia and the killer had been working together. That theory had possibilities. Quin imagined that Nadia and this other man, the killer, had marked McCleary because of the Rolex and had intended to rob him that night in the motel. Or perhaps they were setting him up for something else because they believed his story that he was a reporter and were afraid he was going to blow their operation. Instead, Nadia and the man had argued. The man had shot her. Perhaps he'd intended to kill McCleary as well, but had panicked or something and just left him there to take the rap. If that were true, then McCleary had never seen the killer, and the man was afraid of what McCleary might remember, so he'd hired the spider lady for a hit.

She sensed that some of her theory was correct, but knew there were pieces missing or elements she knew nothing about. The riddle of DAME, of the Sirens, bore some disturbing similarities to her marriage. In neither instance would she wager on the odds for resolution or success.

2.

Le Cri de Merlin: the magician's namesake was stretched out along the left side of McCleary's desk. He purred. His ears twitched. He was dreaming. He was in the dark forest of his exile, seeking light.

To die but not die would also be a kind of exile.

McCleary got up and went into the kitchen. He fixed himself a mug of hot tea and added a shot of rum and a slice of orange. He opened the back door. It now had a metal jamb, a practically impenetrable jamb into which fit the most secure dead bolt on the market, the locksmith had assured him. He drew in deep breaths of the humid night air, and stepped outside.

Would death by drowning be the right choice?

Crickets cried out in the stillness, a piercing, melancholy sound. There was no light in the bottom of the pool because he'd turned it off. Why warn an intruder that there was a pool in the middle of the yard? Let the bastard fall in. But even an intruder would see the pool, he thought, because its dark waters had seized the quarter moon and fractured it.

He could disappear in the Everglades. He would rent a canoe from one of the outfitters down there and simply not come back when he was supposed to. A search party would be sent out. They would find the canoe with no one in it. Would the police assume he had drowned or that he'd split? Would it get Araña off his back?

He walked out to the pool, sipping at the drink. His bare feet whispered against the damp, spongy grass. He curled and uncurled his toes against it. The humidity licked at his arms, his face.

He couldn't disappear in the Everglades; too much would be left open to doubt. He had to do better than that. His death would have to be convincing.

A scythe of clouds wrapped itself around the lower tip of the moon. The crickets stopped chirping, and the stillness chilled him. Too much like death, he thought. Or like exile. The whole idea of dying yet not dying was madness; he was better off not doing anything rash. He would keep digging for answers.

And how long's that decision going to last, old buddy? Until tomorrow morning? The day after?

For two weeks now, he had vacillated. He'd drawn up plans, discarded them, created new ones, buried them. At night, he didn't sleep. He sat up plotting his options like a sociologist charting some new fad. When it started to get light, he fell into bed in the den, into a sleep like death until the dreams started. The ice-room dream, dreams about Quin, Dr. Clarke, erotic dreams where he made love to women he didn't know—or did he? dreams in which he never came. But invariably, he awakened from these dreams with an erection, his heart racing.

When Quin got up, they went running, then he fixed

breakfast. Once she'd left, he puttered around the house, executing tasks he'd set for himself—laundry, cleaning, vacuuming, straightening out closets, fixing things. Sometimes he repeated a particular chore three or four times during a day so he wouldn't have time to think. To speculate. To make himself paranoid. One day he'd gone grocery shopping three times. Another day he'd spent an hour in an Eckerd's Drug Store, investigating all the items that hadn't existed twenty years ago.

He'd spent an inordinate amount of time, it seemed, in the birth-control aisle, marveling at the dozens of products—spermicides and sponges, foams and condoms, diaphragms and vaginal suppositories. Good ole reliable rubbers were now sold in boxes with soft-focus photos on them and came in umpteen varieties—thick and thin, lubricated and nonlubricated, with ridges and without. There were even condoms marketed with women in mind.

Sometimes Quin came home for lunch before she drove to DAME, and when she did, a gourmet meal was waiting for her. Other days, he ate lunch alone, then spent the afternoon reading and watching videos he'd rented, trying to catch up on twenty years. Occasionally, he slept in the afternoons, but rarely for more than an hour, because then the dreams would come again. Twice, he'd gone over to the park to shoot the breeze with Harvey and they'd ended up in a bar. He'd gotten loaded. He'd slept well, but the hangover wasn't worth it.

It was the nights he dreaded. The nights when Quin was home, the nights when he went through the rituals of their pretend marriage, when he fed the cats, took out of the garbage, made dinner, the nights when they both tried too hard to make things work. The best times, the only times with her that made sense, it seemed, were when they were puzzling through clues, facts, trying to bridge the two. But even those times were punctuated by the awkwardness, the unease of separate rooms on different floors. His room and hers.

He walked back inside and saw Quin's black silk jacket draped over the back of the chair. Her shoes had been abandoned near the kitty bowls. Her purse was on the kitchen counter. A thick folder lay in the center of the butcher-block table, next to a vase of wilted periwinkles. He heard the showers upstairs. The tea kettle was on.

His gaze swung back to the clothes, the purse, the shoes,

the discarded objects of her night life. Her secret life at DAME. Every goddamn night it was the same. And in the morning he would find things right where she'd left them, unless he took them upstairs. When he came in here in the morning, in fact, he was never quite sure what he would find—books and magazines, a pair of stockings, sandals, a comb, lipstick. He had refrained from saying anything. He was too grateful for her help to make waves.

But tonight he was short on patience.

Tonight he wanted to die but not die and didn't know if it was madness or wisdom.

Tonight he yanked the jacket from the back of the chair. Tonight he plucked up the shoes, the purse, and marched into the front room with them. He set everything on one of the lower steps of the staircase. She would see it when she came downstairs for her inevitable snack.

Snack, hell. She would put away a four-course meal in nothing flat. If the figures in the checkbook were accurate—and it was hard to tell because Quin never subtracted or added anything—their grocery bill ran almost $700 a month. His wife, a woman he didn't remember, didn't love, but to whom he was forever grateful, ate like a goddamn horse.

Where did the food go?

He rubbed the heel of his hand against his temple and returned to the kitchen. He knocked back half of his drink. He paced. He heard the shower go off. He sat down at the butcher-block table and opened the file on the table. Papers spewed out. He stacked them, went through them slowly, and saw two familiar names—Nadia and Karen Rapapport.

Quick on her feet, said a notation in Nadia's papers. *Smooth . . . Sounds convincing . . . Excellent candidate.*

"Hi," said Quin from the doorway.

She wore a pale blue terry-cloth robe. She was rubbing her wet hair with a towel. She smiled. "You're going to find that file real interesting." She padded over to the stove, where the tea kettle began to whistle, and explained what she'd done, what she had found. When he didn't say anything, she glanced back. "What's wrong?"

He didn't look at her. "Nothing. Just tired."

She busied herself with her tea and didn't say anything. She made a lot of noise—slamming the cupboard door, dropping the kettle back on the burner, opening and shutting the fridge.

"Okay, something's eating you. What is it?"

She leaned against the counter, the towel draped over a shoulder now, the mug at her mouth, her blue eyes bloodshot from her shower.

"I'm tired of picking up your stuff in the kitchen every morning."

"No one asked you to pick it up."

"Someone has to pick it up, and since you don't, I do."

She stared at him. She glanced at the window. She looked up at the ceiling. She gave an odd, curt laugh, and her cheeks flushed with color. "I don't believe this. I don't believe we're having this conversation." She moved across the room, slammed her mug against the table. Tea splashed out. "For your information, Mac, I haven't put in sixty fucking hours at DAME because I like it, okay? I don't sit there answering calls from lonely hearts and perverts because it's my idea of a good time."

"I'm talking about the stuff you leave in the kitchen, Quin, not about what you're doing. I appreciate what you're doing. I'm grateful for it. But that has nothing to do with leaving your things all over the house, all right? So cut the shit with the guilt trip, with—"

"Fuck. Off." She spit the words, her voice soft, deadly. "Just fuck off, McCleary."

He watched her march out of the room, heard her footsteps on the stairs. The bedroom door slammed. He sat there, hands clenched against his thighs, the rum still warm against his tongue. He had said his piece, he had gotten it off his chest. So how come he felt like shit?

He remained where he was for a long time. The ticking of the clock filled the silence. One of the cats munched on Friskies. He didn't know which cat because he didn't look. He didn't care. Outside, the crickets cried.

He finished his drink.

He wondered if he should die in a fire. But what kind of fire?

He made another drink, and now the silence in the house settled around him like a fine mist. The backs of his eyes burned. He felt the rum in his blood, rushing to his head. He wanted to go upstairs, but what would he say? What was there to say? That he didn't love her because he didn't remember her? That he'd already spoken to Benson about moving into the apartment over his garage? That Benson had said the place would be ready by tomorrow?

She would hate him. He wouldn't blame her, but he couldn't stand the thought of Quin hating him. He would go upstairs and apologize for what he'd said. He was right about her clothes, her *things,* but it didn't matter. What mattered was that she had supported him, believed in him, that she had been a friend to him when what she'd wanted most of all was to be his wife again.

He had to lose himself, and he had to make it look good. But how?

He tossed the remainder of his drink into the sink and turned off the lights as he walked from the kitchen to the living room. Merlin tagged his heels.

Upstairs, the bedroom door was still closed. No light seeped from under the door. He didn't want to wake her if she was asleep, so he didn't knock. He turned the knob. The door didn't squeak as it swung open. He stepped into the room where he had slept for five years, the room he hadn't been in except to get clothes, since he'd left the hospital.

The fragrance of perfume and soap lingered in the air. Dim, pale light from the street fell in ribbons across the rug and stopped just short of the bed. He could make out the shape of her body under the covers. "Quin?" Although he whispered her name, it seemed to echo as if he'd shouted it. She didn't reply, and he moved closer to the bed into the distinctly female scents, and undressed. He draped his clothes over the back of the chair near the window and slipped into bed beside her, trying not to rock the bed. He barely breathed. He barely moved. His head sank into the pillow. The cool sheet and the weight of the blanket felt good against his skin.

McCleary closed his eyes and listened to her breathing. He couldn't tell if she was really asleep or not and rolled onto his side. Her back was to him, the covers drawn up so high around her shoulders he could hardly see the shape of her head.

He touched her back under the covers, touched it lightly, as if to test its solidity, its reality. The heat of her skin under the T-shirt she wore warmed his fingertips.

"I'm not asleep," she said.

"I'm sorry," he said.

"It doesn't matter."

"It does matter."

She rolled onto her side, facing him in the twilight. "What matters? What are we talking about anyway?"

He reached for her, and she moved into his arms, burrowing her face in the curve of his neck, sliding a leg between his. He stroked her damp hair, the back of her neck, and felt her trembling. He realized she was crying, and it filled him with remorse, with guilt, and he murmured over and over again that he was sorry, he hadn't meant to hurt her. She pressed up against him, her mouth seeking his, and he kissed her. It felt good to hold her, to hold anyone, and her mouth tasted sweet and warm, and he couldn't help himself, he wanted her.

The beat of her heart quickened against his chest. His hands moved under her T-shirt, against her soft skin, over the articular flare of her hips, and hers fluttered down his spine and against his thighs, hands as urgent as her mouth, as demanding as her mouth, hands that caressed him with an intimacy borne of familiarity.

They made love quickly, wordlessly. Their very different needs to connect and affirm, to communicate, erupted into a hot tide of passion that submerged him. He stayed inside her afterward, his fingers lost in her hair, his mouth touching hers now and then. The pale light from the street lamp outside illumined the dampness on her cheeks, the long, fine lines of her neck. He dozed off, his cheek against her chest, her hand against the small of his back. When he came to, he could tell from the soft, even rhythm of her breathing that she was asleep. He was still inside her, and he was hard again. He drew his tongue over her lower lip, tasting her cool sleep. He slipped away from her, a hand brushing over her breast, and she stirred awake and reached for him. "Don't go," she whispered.

They made love again, more slowly this time, savoring each other. His body seemed to respond with its own deep memories of how and where to touch her, of what she liked, of what made her sigh or shudder with pleasure. When it was over, though, he sensed an incompleteness—not in the act, but in what had been left unsaid. She voiced it first by asking where this left them. He said he didn't know. She was quiet for a few moments, her hand resting lightly in his, unobtrusively, then her fingers tightened over his and she said, "You're moving out, aren't you."

It wasn't a question. It was as if she'd sensed the shape of his omission, its silhouette, and had filled it in. When he didn't reply, she lifted up on an elbow and looked down at him and said that the only thing she was asking for was honesty.

"I need time, Quin."

"Time," she repeated.

"It isn't you."

"Yes it is." She tried to draw her hand away, but he wouldn't let it go. He trapped it like a small bird in his own hand, his thumb sliding over the knuckles.

"No, you're wrong. It's me. This Araña person knows where I live. I don't want to endanger you any more than I already have. I need some time, that's all, to throw her off, to sort things out."

He tried to explain what he felt, but it didn't come out right. She asked him to clarify. He couldn't. She asked where he was going to move and when. In with Benson, he said, tomorrow or the next day.

She lay back when he said it, the pillow sighing as her head sank into it. "Oh," she said. Then, "Is that what you really want to do?"

"I think so. Yes, I think it's better for now."

Suppose something broke with DAME? she asked. What then? Should she get in touch with him at Benson's or what? They worked out the details. It became a little easier after that; they were veering away from the personal, away from the marriage, into safer waters.

They talked until there didn't seem to be anything left to say and the hands of the clock stood at 4:30 A.M. The last thing McCleary heard was the solitary chirp of a bird, launched out into the dark like a probe searching for morning.

3.

Quin poured her baggie of munchies onto a paper plate on her desk at work—carrots and radishes, slices of apple, a small brick of cheese, whole-wheat crackers, and a dozen of the plumpest strawberries she'd seen in a year. She cut a slice of cheese from the brick, pressed it to a cracker, bit into it, and went to work.

She propped three small corkboards against the window. She labeled the first NADIA FORSYTHE and on it she pinned copies of the photos taken in the room at the Days Inn. On strips of masking tape, she printed:

> killed with Mac's .38; worked for DAME; silver & gold stars on file; mysterious lover; met Mac (as Peter Ketter) at Bernardo's; spent less than half an hour with him at club; they left separately, w/Nadia following several minutes after Mac; went to Days Inn.

As she munched on two more crackers and a strawberry, she arranged the strips vertically and made a second column of strips with observations and questions. She then labeled the second corkboard MCCLEARY, cut up more strips of masking tape, and jotted:

> hired by Lans Hitchcock, who's supposedly no longer in the country; client told Mac he was robbed of $ and jewelry—including Rolex—outside Bernardo's; checked into Days Inn as Ketter the night after meeting Nadia at Bernardo's; Panzine found in Mac's blood; concussion & amnesia; arresting officer (Grunwald) and court-appointed shrink (Clarke) possibly having affair; borrowed Cody's Rolex; numbers found in maroon notebook 21–18–62; La Araña hired for job (hit?) involving McCleary; Araña possibly hired by dead man named Jimenez; bartender at Bernardo's passed on Jimenez's message that Araña would "take the job" to a man with a glass eye; any connection between Araña and what happened at Days Inn?

She nibbled at a slice of apple as she arranged the strips vertically, and left room at the bottom in case she thought of something else. A second column on the corkboard consisted of her observations and questions. She suspected McCleary had borrowed the Rolex from Cody because Hitchcock's Rolex had been stolen from him outside Bernardo's. Stolen by a woman. Maybe by Nadia? So why had Hitchcock left the country so soon after hiring McCleary? Why was McCleary posing as Ketter, a reporter?

Why is he going to move out?

No, scratch that one.

Nothing personal belonged on the corkboards.

Except that it was all personal.

She looked at the third corkboard, which was still blank. *What's your name? What should I call you?* Miscellaneous? Etcetera? No. She picked up her pen and, bearing down on a strip of masking tape, wrote THE ICE ROOM, after McCleary's dream.

He can tell me his dreams, but he's going to move out.

Today? Would he move out today?

Last night happened, but he's going to move out.

On the third corkboard went everything from information on DAME to Jimenez to facts on amnesia. Here she taped the five names she'd found in the TERMINATED drawer. Nadia and Karen Rappaport were definitely dead, but Benson said the other three women were alive. He had tracked them through the Motor Vehicle Department, talked to each of them, and confirmed they'd been employed by DAME and were subsequently fired. Why were they fired? he'd asked. Because they didn't like the work and didn't perform according to Ziegler's specifications. So TERMINATED had a dual meaning.

THE ICE ROOM corkboard also contained questions and possibilities, speculations and connections. Here she would put the names of suspects, when she had them.

There was a quick rap at her door. "It's open, Bean," she called.

He shambled into the room, humming a disconnected tune. "How'd you know it was me?"

"The way you knock."

His eyes flicked to the corkboards as he sat down, then back to her. "I just got off the phone with Benson. We got us a lead."

"What kind of lead?"

"Dude who claims he picked up a fine chiquita at a bar in the Grove and they went back to his place and she drugged and robbed him. He's got Panzine in his blood and his Rolex is missing. That's just for starters. Got his address right here." He held up an index card. "You ready to see what's what?"

Quin scooped her snack back into the baggie and dropped it in her purse as she slung it over her shoulder. "Let's go."

Fourteen

MAGALI HELD HER breath as the BMW turned onto the old man's street. *The house won't be there.*

She'd been gone only a few hours, running errands, doing the grocery shopping for herself and Paco. But even so, she was afraid she would return here to find a vacant lot or a home that had been occupied by other people for the last decade. Then she would have to admit what she'd suspected for years—that she was *una loca,* a crazy, a functioning crazy, perhaps, but mad as a hatter nonetheless. Then she would have to admit that the old man whom she loved like a father had never existed, or if he had, had not existed here.

But the house was there, as it had always been, bleached white in the hot light, the passionflower vines climbing the walls, twisting around the bars in the windows. A Jeep was parked behind the old man's battered Chevy. She wondered who it belonged to. A client? Despite his failing eyesight, Paco still had a dozen or so clients, people who wanted glimpses of their futures and for whom he threw the *caracoles,* or shells, or sometimes, bits of coconut; people who requested his *curandero* potions, his healing hands; men and women who believed he had powers.

A strange word, that, weakened by its own ambiguity. After all, power was different things to different people. In the unpleasant facet of her work, power was control over life and death. To a politician, it meant the opportunity to influence things on a large scale, and to a cop, an honest cop, righting what was wrong. *And to me? To me, personally, what is power?*

She no longer knew.

She carried two bags of groceries up the walk, her door key in her hand. But it didn't work because the dead bolt was engaged. She rang the bell. It was several moments before the door opened. A handsome man with sharp blue eyes and hair the color of Ivory soap said, "Ah, you must be Magali. Here, let me help you with the bags."

"Who're you?" She refused to surrender the groceries.

"Diego Rincón. A friend of Paco's."

"I don't remember him mentioning you."

He smiled. "Friend, client, apprentice."

The last word convinced her that he was who he said he was. No one but a close friend of the old man's would think of himself in relation to Paco that way. So when he offered again to help her with the groceries, she handed him a bag and followed him into the house.

As she entered the kitchen, she heard the drone of the TV from the courtyard and saw Paco seated under a ceiba tree. He was watching the afternoon soaps on Channel 51, the Spanish station. The soaps had gained in importance once his eyesight had started to fail and it had become more difficult for him to read comic books. But there was nothing at all wrong with his hearing, she thought, so why was the volume turned up so loud?

She began unpacking the groceries and putting them away. Rincón helped her, puttering around with an easy familiarity that annoyed her. "I'll do that," she said. "Why don't you see if Paco wants some lunch?"

He smiled again, that clean, affable smile, and walked outside where the old man was. She saw them talking, but couldn't hear them because of the volume on the TV. He didn't come back in to tell her whether Paco wanted lunch, so she fixed it anyway. She made sandwiches for the three of them, tuna fish and Swiss cheese, Paco's favorite. She sliced up some papaya, tossed it in the blender, added milk, and made papaya shakes.

She carried everything out into the courtyard and set it on the chrome-and-glass table in the shade. The TV was off, Diego Rincón was nowhere around, and Paco was sitting on a straw mat on the ground, under the ceiba tree. He was dressed completely in white. His feet were bare. His fingers busily worked at ribbons of straw, braiding them into what she knew would eventually be a small rug.

A straw rug meant a sacrifice. For what purpose? A celebration of some sort? As payment for help from the gods?

Over the years, she'd seen Paco sacrifice chickens and

pigeons, roosters and goats, whatever a particular ritual called for. He'd always done it quickly, mercifully. If the animal or fowl was used for a cleansing of some sort, the carcass was usually buried or burned. But if its purpose was to strengthen or heal or to imbue one with power, almost every part of the animal was used in some way. The meat was eaten. The bones were pulverized, and the dust was used in other rituals. The blood was drained. She did not pretend to understand what was involved or why he did it. She didn't understand his rituals or his magic; it all made her uneasy.

"Do you want lunch?" she asked.

His liquid eyes looked up. "In a while. Did you finish all your errands?"

By "errands," she knew he meant McCleary. "Groceries, post office, like that." She lowered herself to the ground beside him. "Is it going to be a rug?"

"Hmm. For you, *mí amor*. So tell me about your errands. Your real errands."

"There's nothing to tell."

That much was true. For the last fourteen days she had followed McCleary. Watched him. One night when he was home alone, she had called him just to hear his voice, to see what she could detect from the way he spoke. She'd pretended she was conducting a survey for a consumer company and asked if he would participate. He asked what consumer company. She made up a name. He said okay, a reluctant okay, and he'd answered her five or six questions. She had learned a little more about him from the sound of his voice, and had liked him for taking the time. He'd also said he'd hever heard of three of the products she'd mentioned—well known products including Memorex tapes. He'd laughed about that one, and said it sounded like something he needed. The longer she observed him, the less certain she was. She should've acted by now and hadn't. She said nothing of this to Paco.

His eyes darted over her shoulder, and she glanced around. Rincón had materialized in the doorway like a ghost. He carried a tray with the papaya shakes. "You have met Diego?" Paco asked.

"Yes."

"I added ice to the juice," said Rincón, moving toward them. He, too, was now dressed in white, and his feet were bare. She knew the color was significant, but didn't know why. Rincón brought the juice over to where they sat and joined them.

"Two or three times a week," said the old man, his fingers still working at the ribbons of straw, "Diego is my driver. Other times, he is my apprentice. The sorcerer's apprentice," he added, and laughed. Rincón laughed. She felt excluded and didn't like it.

Magali sipped at her shake and wished Rincón would go away. He was sitting uncomfortably close to her, legs stretched out on the ground, back leaning against one of the chairs.

"Nice rug, no?" said Rincón, gesturing toward the thing Paco was braiding.

Magali nodded. The shake tasted too sweet. Perhaps the papaya had been overly ripe.

"The rug is for magic," Paco said.

"Your rugs are always for magic," she replied.

He laughed, his lips drawing away from his tired yellow teeth. "True, *mí amor*. True. But today's magic will be . . ." He paused, smoothing his gnarled hands over the rug. "Special. Diego, did you know Magali doesn't believe in magic? And yet she listens to the oracles."

"One doesn't have to believe." Rincón's friendly smile showed his white teeth. "That is the magic of magic. It is always hidden."

The rug was finished. Paco passed it to Rincón, who stood and walked over to a patch of sunlight. He dropped the mat in the light, on a bed of leaves. "For you, please, Magali," he said, gesturing toward the rug.

She drank more of the juice and met his gaze. She realized his eyes weren't the sharp blue she'd thought, but a pale almost transparent blue. She felt that if she leaned close to him, she would be able to peer through the thin membrane of blue into his brain. "I'm quite comfortable where I am."

Paco chuckled. "I told you she could be most difficult, Diego." He pushed himself to his feet. She thought she could hear his bones creak and complain as he moved away from the shade of the tree, toward the far gate that led outside, to the chicken house.

Rincón also stood. He went inside the house. Magali finished the juice and realized that everything she looked at had a peculiar, lovely clarity. In the trunk of the ceiba, for instance, she could see the thick strata of bark, like layers of color in an oil painting. In its leaves, she could make out the tiny, fine veins. Even her sense of touch seemed acute. The ground was a sponge against her hand, but softer, silkier. The glass that had held her juice was cool, as slippery as the fruit itself.

She heard footsteps and looked up. Funny, she had forgotten momentarily about Rincón. He had emerged from the house with a white tablecloth draped over an arm and a vase of fresh flowers in his hand. He covered the table with the cloth and fussed with the flowers in the vase. Except for his bare feet, he might've been a waiter in one of those ultra-expensive restaurants where the menu was oral and bottles of wine started at a hundred bucks. She giggled and quickly covered her mouth with her hand when Rincón looked over at her.

Now Paco returned with a squawking chicken. He gripped it at the feet and carried it as far as the shade of the ceiba tree. He stopped at the rim of the shade and asked the tree for permission to cross into its shadow. He waited. His head was cocked as if he were listening for the tree's response. From the pocket of his slacks, he drew out a handful of coins which he tossed onto the ground around the trunk. After a moment, he stepped into its shadow, murmuring something she couldn't hear.

The chicken squawked again. Its wings fluttered. She thought she could see the frantic beat of its heart against its soft, downy chest.

Now Rincón came over to her, his pale blue eyes glazed and distant. He silently passed the mat inches above her head, as if in benediction, then turned and moved to the old man. Rincón paused at the outer rim of the ceiba's shade and he and Paco began to chant.

The ceiba tree, she knew, was considered sacred among many Latins, who believed it possessed great spiritual force. According to legend, it was the only tree not covered by water during the Great Flood; people and animals who had sought refuge under it had survived. Whatever the truth about the tree, it was essential to the old man's magic. He revered it. He paid homage to it. He spoke to it.

As a healer, he used its root and leaves in herbal teas to treat urinary tract difficulties, anemia, and certain types of venereal diseases. The bark was steeped for a special tea for women who wanted to conceive. But on a darker note—and Paco's magic always seemed to have that darker side—the ceiba's shade was believed to attract spirits. Its roots and the ground around it were used for blood offerings. Its trunk and the dirt in which it grew were intrinsic to the black arts.

She listened to the chanting. Lost herself in it. The soft, susurrous sound moved around her like water and through her like pain, like pleasure. She started to close her eyes, but a swift, abrupt movement caught her attention. With a flick of his wrist, Paco tore the chicken's head from its neck. Blood spurted from the wound, splattering his white clothes, splashing against his feet. Her stomach twisted, heaved. Bile surged into her throat. *Leave now,* screamed a voice inside her. *This instant.* But she sat there, paralyzed, watching in fascinated horror as Paco bent his head over the fountain of blood and drank. Rincón, still chanting softly, now moved alongside him, the mat extended. The old man lifted his head. His lips shone bright red, his eyes were feverish when they connected with hers. *"Para tí, Magali." For you for you.* The words echoed. The words rose and fell in the hot and terrible stillness. Then the old man shifted and blood spurted onto the mat, soaking it.

Sweat sprang across her back.

Her skin burst into flame.

Her stomach turned inside out.

She stumbled to her feet, arms clutched at the waist. Her vision blurred. The heat was a tongue that scorched its way through the center of her chest, the middle of her forehead, deeper and deeper.

She was burning up.

She smelled charred flesh.

She smelled death.

She was in the dark alley of her nightmare, running, arms pumping at her sides, the eyes of her pursuer impaled against her spine. She stumbled toward the fountain. She fell to her knees. She thrust her hands into the water, splashing her face, her neck. She heard the chanting behind her. She heard the birds. She dropped her head back, water dripping from her cheeks, her hair, and peered up, up past the trees, into the quavering blue sky. The sun rolled like a beach ball. The sun spun toward her. The sun hurt her eyes, forcing her gaze to the pool. There, floating on the surface of the water, was the face of her American husband, her dead husband. His youth and his innocence were a rebuke of what she had become.

A sob exploded from her chest. She slapped a hand against

her mouth to silence it, but it bit at her hand. It drew blood. She tried to stand. She willed herself to stand. Her body refused to listen.

The juice, she thought wildly. *Rincón put something in the juice when he added ice.* She couldn't lift her head. Her eyes refused to close. The sun whipped the top of her skull. The face of her dead husband broke apart. The water swirled, bits of his ruined face rearranged themselves like a mosaic, like bits of colored stone, like a child's connect-the-dots, and became the image of the soldier who had raped and beaten her in Santiago, and left her for dead.

She screamed.

The face shifted again. Now it was Bartlett, a giant with a giant's smile, a giant's hands, Bartlett whispering that he loved her, whispering it even as his eyes said something different. Now the face belonged to the scum she had killed in the Black Forest, the child murderer. Now it was the Mafia henchman in Rome. On and on through the years, the faces became those of lovers and victims, clients and friends.

An unbearable pressure throbbed in her chest. She could barely breathe. The stink of blood thickened. *The juice, what did he put in my juice? Oh God, my eyes, my head . . .* Now the image in the water changed again. She gasped. It was Paco. But he was ancient. His face was so wrinkled the lines were sucking his features into themselves, consuming them. The face turned hideous with old age. Skin began to sluff off, exposing muscles, bones. She cried out. She pressed her hands to the rim of the fountain, struggling to rise, but couldn't.

Her palms slipped. She struck her chin against the rim, splitting the skin like a grape. Drops of blood struck the water, turning it pink. The grotesque image of Paco broke apart. A new face formed.

"No more," she whispered, shaking her head, wiping the back of her hand across her chin, pushing herself up. But hands gripped her head, shoving her to her knees again. Whatever had been put in the juice had weakened her enough so she couldn't throw the hands off.

"Watch the water," hissed a voice close to her ear. "Watch and remember. Watch and learn."

His hand held her head in place, and her chin kept bleeding, and she stared at the water, unable to tear her eyes from it. The new face was small and smooth. An infant's face. Its tiny mouth opened like a flower. It wailed. It laughed. It cooed. Her heart trembled. Her heart broke. She reached for the child, her child, she reached and her hands shattered the image as they struck the water.

Bits of the infant floated away, into the dried leaves that dotted the surface. She wept. She called to it. She wanted to follow the child, to float away with it, to piece it back together. But the hands still clutched her head. The old man hissed in her ear again. "Keep watching, Magali. Watch, closely."

Another face appeared and it belonged to McCleary.

"Do you understand?" Paco whispered. His breath was hot and stank of blood. *"Do you understand?"*

She sobbed. She jerked her head up and down. *Yes, yes,* she understood; but it was a lie, and the old man knew it. He wouldn't release her head. He kept hissing at her. His spittle bloodied her feverish cheeks. The terrible pressure of his voice slapped at her, demanding that she say it aloud, that she tell him she understood.

Yes. She bellowed the word. She didn't know if it was truth or lie, but it didn't matter. She screamed, *Yes yes,* and instantly the hands fell away from her head and it dropped to her arms.

She wept.

"What did Rincón put in that juice?" she asked.

It was later. She didn't know how much later. She was now stretched out on a lawn chair in the courtyard. The sun had moved in the sky. She guessed it was early afternoon, but of which day? Which week?

She swung her legs off the chair and glared at Paco. He was sitting under the ceiba tree, watching his portable TV. It was as if he hadn't moved since she'd been in the kitchen, putting away the groceries. Maybe he hadn't. Maybe none of it had happened.

"Did you hear me?" she snapped.

"I am nearly blind, not deaf," he replied, pushing his thick glasses up on his nose. She hadn't seen him in his glasses for a long time. They made him seem very old. She noticed he was no longer wearing his white—*blood-splattered*—

clothes. Had he ever worn them? Had a man named Rincón actually been here? *Did he drug my papaya juice?*

"What was in the juice?"

He turned his head slowly toward her, as though he had a stiff neck and the movement hurt. "Just the truth. You apparently find the truth quite reprehensible, Magali."

"Truth." She spat the word. She rubbed her fingers against her temple, which ached. Her legs felt weak and rubbery when she stood. The courtyard tilted. Her hand flew out and gripped the back of the chair. She steadied herself. She forced herself to say, "Truth is subjective."

"I think not."

She walked over to where he sat and squatted beside him. The sun was hot and bright. The air was too still. Sweat pimpled her upper lip. "I'll have my child, Paco, regardless of what truths you show me."

"They are not my truths or your truths, *mí amor*." He spoke quietly, evenly. "They are simply truths. The visions the ceiba gave you were not just about your child. They were about what you do. About what you are. Two weeks ago, three, whatever it's been, I told you to stop what you are doing while you still can. You are developing a taste for killing that is frightening."

She started to interrupt, to tell him he was wrong, but he held up his hand. "Please. Allow me to finish." He touched the trunk of the tree behind him. "The ceiba does not discriminate between good and evil as long as it is paid for its services and respect is shown for it during rituals. But you are not a ceiba, Magali. You have lost respect for the lives you take."

"I kill vermin, Paco, people who . . ."

His expression silenced her. The sun crouched on her shoulders and spat in her face. "You are merely a human being who has done some good things, some bad, but who believes she is above terms like good and evil. Do you really believe McCleary is guilty of murder?"

"Yes. Yes, I think he is. I think there are other things involved, but yes, I believe he killed that woman."

"And I think you are wrong, *mí amor*, and that you are lying to yourself."

When she smiled, the skin around her mouth felt tight and strange. "How can you have any opinion at all? You don't even know anything about the man or what happened. Except what I've told you."

"I'm telling you that if you cross the line you're treading by killing him, there will be no child. Nothing can be simpler than that."

"You're talking nonsense."

"Believe what you want."

She was suddenly so tired it was an effort to keep her eyes open, to move. "I'm going to lie down."

"Pleasant dreams." He laughed and turned back to his TV, and she knew her dreams wouldn't be pleasant at all.

Fifteen

1.

THE DEARTH OF trees in South Florida always became more apparent to Quin when she was driving through a neighborhood where they were plentiful. The banyans along the wide road in Coral Gables loomed huge and lush, with branches that had braided together overhead, creating a canopy of shade, a tunnel of green. It was as if these sentient giants were watchful guardians who, if threatened with demise by developers, would rise up and wage battle.

She followed Bean's black Datsun into another neighborhood where acacia trees proliferated. They were in full bloom, their saffron buds so abundant the leaves were barely visible on the branches. Flowers littered the thick shade beneath them, birds pecked at the seeds that had spilled from the trees' pods, cats stalked prey through yards. She saw no bikes, no toys on front porches, no evidence of families. She spotted BMWs, a Mercedes or two, Volvos, sports coupes—and guessed the area was geared toward singles and couples, all on their way *upupup*.

Bean slowed, then pulled to a stop in front of the brick home. A Porsche like Cody's was in the driveway, except this one was bright red. "Not a bad little palace," Bean remarked as they got out of the car. "Benson said the guy's a defense attorney."

"Does he know about us?"

"Only that we're investigating a case involving another person who had traces of Panzine in his blood."

The man who answered the door was straight out of a beer commercial: mid-thirties, about her height, sandy hair, a tan that hinted at heavy windsurfing, sailing, fishing on weekends. He wore khaki shorts, a T-shirt that said AUSSIES DO IT DOWN UNDER, and sandals.

"Are you Ian Granger?" Bean asked.

"Yes. Yes, I am." He smoothed a hand over his hair, a self-conscious gesture, almost shy. He sounded like an Aussie. "You must be the folks Lieutenant Benson told me about."

Bean introduced himself and Quin. "We'd like to ask you a few questions, Mr. Granger. Unless this is a bad time."

"Hopefully my bad times," he said with a laugh, "are over for a while. They say this stuff comes in cycles. Come on in."

They settled in a nicely furnished, sunken living room. It was orderly and neat, everything in its place. No clutter, no dust, a room in a magazine, in a model home. Bean got right to the point and asked Granger to tell them what had happened to him. He seemed eager to talk about it, the kind of eagerness that indicated this was the most dramatic, horrifying, and exciting thing that had ever happened to him.

"Two days ago, I, uh, left work late, around nine, I guess it was. I went by Richie's, this bar in the Grove, for a couple of drinks. I met this woman. A schoolteacher. We started talking and what not and came back here. I put on some music, made us drinks, and just when things were going along pretty well . . . *Bam!*" He slapped his hands together once. "I'm gone."

"Gone?" Quin repeated.

"Out. I wake up around fourteen hours later to find the woman nowhere around. My Rolex was gone, my camera equipment gone, my VCR, compact discs, my portable TV, even my phones gone, all of it. The inside of my mouth tasted like kangaroos had crapped all over my tongue, if you'll pardon the expression, ma'am, and I could barely walk. I got my ass over to the ER at Mt. Sinai. Turns out my blood's loaded with this Panzine stuff. For insomnia, the doc tells me. 'You got insomnia?' he asks me. 'Christ, no,' I tell him. 'I sleep like a baby.' I figure he thinks I'm maybe an attempted suicide who changed his mind. Then I remember the drink, right? I race home, haul the glass to this cop I know at Metro-Dade. He sends it to the lab. The drug was in my drink."

"You'd never seen the woman before?" Bean asked.

"No."

"Describe her," said Quin.

"That's easy," he replied. She was a typical schoolteacher

type. Cute. Dark hair. Dark eyes. Softly spoken. Slender. Cultured. Thirty or a little older. The description, unfortunately, probably fit several thousand women in South Florida. "What school did she teach at?" Quin asked.

"That whole thing about teaching was a lie, ma'am. She said she taught at the high school here in the Gables. Eleventh-grade science. I called. There was no teacher there named Sheila Wells. At first, when I woke up and realized what had happened, I wasn't going to do anything. I mean, how embarrassing, right? You pick up a lady at a bar and not only does she rob you blind, she drugs you too. But then I took a little inventory of the stuff she hauled off and I got mad. I knew I wasn't going to be able to make an insurance claim unless I reported it to the cops. On top of it, I felt lousy and I started getting paranoid about what she'd given me. That's why I hit the hospital."

"Were you wearing your Rolex?" Bean asked.

"Yup. Sure was."

That made three Rolexes—the man who hired McCleary, McCleary, and now Granger. The Panzine link was the second thing both incidents had in common. Robbery fit two of the men. It looked like the beginning of an MO. She visualized her corkboards and took a long shot. "Mr. Granger, have you had any contact whatsoever with a dating service called DAME—Date-a-Mate?"

The expression on his face was all the confirmation she needed. "Uh, yeah. Yeah, I have. A month or so ago, I guess, I heard about it through another lawyer in the firm. Why?"

"It might be significant. Can you tell us what your involvement was?"

He called the number one night, he said, when he was feeling low, thinking about his ex-wife and all. The woman who answered had explained how the service worked, asked if he was interested, and when he said yes, she requested a credit card number. He used his American Express for the $250 fee. The operator then asked him about two dozen questions which covered everything from his profession to his personal interests. She also requested general ranges for his income and age, then asked what traits he was seeking in a woman. He was put on hold for several minutes as the information was processed and matched with the names of women he would most likely find compatible. When the operator came back on the line, she said she'd already spoken with a woman on a list of eight possibilities and would give her, if he didn't object, his number. She would call this evening.

Up to this point, his story adhered to the standard procedure Quin had followed during her weeks at DAME. "So what happened?"

"The woman called me. We musta talked for, oh, maybe an hour. Very weird thing, I'll tell you, talking like that to someone you've never met. We agreed to meet the next night at Richie's. Around nine. I was there. She wasn't."

"When was this?" Bean asked.

"Maybe three weeks ago."

"Did you call the service again?"

"No." He combed his fingers through his hair and shifted in his chair. Quin sensed he was feeling uncomfortable with the story now. "I mean, it's really humiliating to get it from someone you've never even met. I knew I could've called back and gone through the whole rigmarole again, with the second name, but I just wasn't up to it.

"Anyway, the day before yesterday, the chick calls me again. She's real apologetic, says a relative died suddenly and she had to leave town. Yeah, yeah, I'm thinking. Sure. It's the kind of story I hear all the time from clients. But then I figure maybe I've gotten cynical over the years and when she suggests trying again, I said okay. I told her I *might* be at Richie's that night. *Might.*"

"Then isn't it possible your schoolteacher was the woman?" Bean asked.

"No. Her voice was different. The woman on the phone—the DAME woman, Marilyn—said she was a blond, short, around five foot three. This woman, Sheila, was a brunette, taller, around five six. I don't think there's any connection. I think it's just a coincidence."

Voices, thought Quin, could be disguised, and the rest of it could be written off as a lie. What puzzled her was Granger's obtuseness. But then again, Granger obviously had been short on self-confidence since his divorce, and wasn't interested in seeing the truth.

"What about your attorney friend, Mr. Granger?" asked Bean. "What kind of experience did he have with the service?"

"Great. His second name panned out. They've been seeing each other every day for weeks."

"You know anyone else who's tried the service?"

"Yeah, a judge. No problem. He's dated a couple of women. He thinks the service is terrific, worth every penny of the fee."

What's the pattern of selection? Income was probably a factor, but there had to be more than that. "On the DAME questions, Mr. Granger, the incomes are given in ranges, with the highest as over sixty thousand a year. Is that where you fall?" Quin asked.

He nodded.

"And your attorney friend?"

"He probably makes twice what I do."

"Is his lifestyle different from yours?"

Granger laughed. He crossed one leg over the other as he shifted again in his chair. Sunlight streaming through the window struck the side of his head, bleaching the color from his hair. He looked just then like a small boy, lost but eager to cooperate, to be accepted. "Guy—that's his name—is a real unconventional character. He lives in a trailer and socks all his money into Swiss bank accounts. If you saw him on the street, you'd think he was anything but an attorney."

Lifestyle. Yuppies living the good, conventional life are targets.

"When you and this woman—Marilyn—agreed to meet, how did you describe yourself?" Quin asked.

He shifted again, thought a moment, frowning slightly. "I don't think I did. I think what happened was that she said, 'Let me guess what you look like.' Yeah, that was it. Then she went through what she thought I looked like."

"Did she mention your Rolex?"

His frown deepened. "I don't remember. She might've said something like, 'I bet you wear a Rolex.' Or, 'I bet you drive such and such a car.' Like that."

Income, lifestyle, the Rolex as an identifying mark. They would mess with a yuppie attorney, but not with one living in a trailer and not with a judge. *They? Who're they?* A gang of women who worked the yuppie clubs and bars, preying on affluent men who'd been screened through DAME's dating service. But who at DAME was in charge? Ziggy? Did she maintain a list of lonely hearts who were actually members of the Sirens? Was that how it worked? If so, then there had to be operators who were working with her. *The stars. The silver and gold stars on the file folders. Those operators were tapped.* The *silvers* were candidates, the *golds* were chosen.

Nadia had been a *gold* operator at DAME.

Then what had she been doing with McCleary as Ketter the reporter in a motel room? Where had she gotten the Panzine to drug him? Did the operators also work the clubs?

"What d'you think?" she asked Bean when they were seated in a coffee shop on Miracle Mile a while later.

"That we're hot and you better cover your ass at this dating service, Quin."

She sipped at her iced tea and poked at the chef's salad she'd ordered. "*If* it's a ring, Joe, then presumably there've been a lot of other men who've gotten ripped off in the same way. How come none of them have gone to the cops?"

Bean tore a piece of bread from the loaf in the basket. "Hey, lady, if it were me, I'd keep my mouth shut. I'd be too embarrassed to go to the cops."

She laughed. "C'mon, Bean, from Granger I expect to hear something like that. But not from you."

"Okay, okay. I'd go to the cops because of the business I'm in. But I understand where these guys are coming from. You pick a woman up in a bar. Go back to your place. Instead of spending the night with her, you wake up the next morning minus everything that can be carried out. You've been taken. It'd be humiliating. Male pride and all that, Quin. I know it sounds like a crock to you, but believe me, it's pride. Even the guy who hired Mac went to a private detective, not a cop."

She conceded he had a point. But to her, a man going home with the wrong woman amounted to nothing more than an error in judgment. So what? Women misjudged men all the time—the good-looking guy who stopped on the interstate to help you change your flat but robbed and raped you instead; the competent handyman who cleaned you out when you weren't looking; the amiable husband of a neighbor who turned out to be a wife beater. No one was ever surprised when these things happened to women. But for a man to be drugged and rolled in this own home . . . All right, she could see how that might be interpreted by another man—like a cop—as indicative of some fundamental weakness in the person. She could understand how the man himself might consider it humiliating. Yes, she understood. But she didn't agree.

"I heard from Mike earlier this morning," Bean said, changing the subject. "He told me he'd be moving in with Benson."

She didn't look at him. "I figured he would tell you."

"If there's anything I can do, Quin, or—"

"Just make sure Mac knows you're his friend, Joe."

Bean nodded, his discomfort emanating from him like an odor. She sensed he felt as if his loyalties were being divided and he didn't quite know how to deal with it. He'd wanted to tell her that he knew McCleary was moving out and yet seemed uneasy now that he'd done so. Was this what happened when a couple separated? Did your friends choose sides? Were the years reduced to *his* and *hers*, like towels? Bed sheets? TVs?

Are we separating? Is that what's happened? Is this the prelude to divorce?

When they'd discussed it last night, she'd thought of it as temporary. Until McCleary regained his memory. Until he was exonerated of the murder charge. Until he'd had sufficient time to make sense of what had happened to him. Until. But now, suddenly, the separation assumed a new dimension. She felt the emptiness that would echo in the house. She saw herself running alone in the morning. She saw breakfasts for one, dinners for one, one car in the garage, one towel in the bathroom. One.

Long after Bean had left, she remained at the table, sipping tepid coffee that she didn't taste. She watched shoppers, undaunted by the heat, strolling the Mile. Cars whizzed by. Everyone was in a hurry. Everyone had someplace to go.

She decided she would sit right here until the restaurant closed. She would order something to eat whenever she got hungry. She would watch the Mile empty of people, of cars. She would watch the sun set. She would wait for the stars to come out, for the moon to rise. Maybe she wouldn't move until she had answers, even if it took weeks.

A sit-in, a protest, like the old days. She would make the local six o'clock news. People would gawk at her through the picture window, thinking it was a publicity stunt, and some of

Chapter 15

"Sadie! Sadie!" cried Jennifer as she rushed into the clinic's recovery bay and saw her dog awake in a padded cage.

Her tail wagging, Sadie lurched to one side, banged against the padded wall and finally heaved herself to a half-sitting position. She was so happy to see her that Jennifer's eyes blurred with tears.

"Hey, there, girl. You're feeling better, huh?" She unlatched the cage and reached inside. "You had me so worried."

Sadie opened her jaws and a slack tongue slapped at her hand, the dog's feeble attempt at a loving lick.

"You're still a little groggy, right?"

The dog's eyes were a little glazed, Jennifer thought, but she was alive. Yesterday, all she could do was pray Sadie would survive. Not only was her dog alive, but she was recovering.

"Sadie's doing remarkably well," said the technician as

Jennifer slipped her arm around her dog, careful not to touch the bandage on her neck.

"When can she come home?"

"Dr. Bustos says it'll be a few days."

Running her hand over Sadie's smooth coat, Jennifer said, "I'll come get you the minute you're well enough to leave, okay?"

In response, the dog leaned against Jennifer. Sadie valiantly attempted to give Jennifer another sloppy kiss, but her tongue missed the target. Jennifer's heart did a slow backflip. She leaned down and nuzzled Sadie, brushing her nose against the dog's silky ears.

"I'll be back," she promised as she pulled away. "I have to get to class. I'm late. Kyle will have started already."

At Kyle's name the dog cocked her head to one side and began wagging her tail so hard it thumped against the padded wall. Jennifer closed the cage, promising, "I'll be back later. Understand?"

The bloodhound whimpered, a low, soul-piercing sound as Jennifer closed the cage. It took all Jennifer could do to walk out of the clinic. She knew this was best for the dog, but it was so hard to leave her alone in a cage.

As she hurried to her car, Jennifer tried not to think about last night. What would have happened if Thelma Mae hadn't called to her to ask about Sadie.

Was she falling into Kyle's trap again? she wondered. Was she being pulled back in time to when she'd been a lovesick teenager?

No . . . she . . . was . . . not!

Remember what happened. You were an emotional wreck. You don't want to go through that ordeal again.

She chalked up her foolish behavior last night to the craziest day of her life. She'd been grateful to Kyle for all he'd done . . . and vulnerable.

* * *

Kyle pretended he didn't see Jennifer come into class late. He'd known she'd reported to the firing range before dawn. He assumed she'd gone to the clinic the minute it had opened to visit Sadie. He'd been stalling by discussing tactics of various types of terrorists groups until Jennifer arrived.

"This morning's paper had an article about one of the emerging types of terrorist groups. Did anyone catch it?" he asked.

"Yeah, I read it," responded one of the men. "Environmentalists claimed they set fire to the Forest Industries headquarters somewhere in Oregon."

"That's right. The Earth Liberation Front said the fire was 'in retribution for all the wild forests and animals lost to feed the wallets of the greedy corporations represented by the Forest Service Industries.' "

"Isn't that the same group who set the fire in Vail that burned some buildings and destroyed several ski lifts?" Jennifer said.

Kyle tried to keep the smile off his face. All the men had puzzled looks, none of them seeming to recall the earlier fire by the same underground group. She was quick and smart. And sexy as hell.

Last night proved to him that there was more than just the past between them. She might not be ready to admit it, but she was *not* in love with Chad Roberts. Still, he'd have to go easy with her. After Thelma Mae had interrupted them, he'd knocked on Jennifer's door and got nothing more than a curt "good night" from her.

"Yes," Kyle replied, putting his private thoughts aside and concentrating on the subject. "The ELF is the same environmentalist group who took responsibility for the fire at Vail. Like Timothy McVeigh and some paramilitary groups, these environmentalists are part of the terrorist threat that's home grown. Let's talk about how you all might handle such groups. Any ideas?"

"Most of us on the Miami-Dade County Antiterrorism Task Force are assigned specific duties," said one of the men. "Bomb squad, sharp shooting, K-9. One person is responsible for staying in contact with FBI and local undercover agents. They're supposed to alert us if there's a threat."

"True, but we can help ourselves," Jennifer piped up. "Using the Internet and reading papers, we can anticipate problems. The Everglades is an environmental hot button right now. The ELF group struck in Colorado, then in Oregon. They're all over the map. South Florida, our territory, could be next."

The men murmured their agreement. Apparently, none of them had considered the ELF a threat in their area. Typical, Kyle thought, most Americans tended to think of terrorists as a group of crazed Middle Easterners.

"We have no choice but go into action after they've struck," commented one of the men.

"This is a game of contacts," Kyle told the group. "One person shouldn't have to shoulder the entire responsibility for gathering info on potential terrorists. All of you need to cultivate people who can help.

"Get to know the fire arms dealers and the people who sell timing mechanisms and components that may be used in bombs. Incendiary devices start fires and accelerants to keep the fire going, giving the terrorists time to get away.

"Someone, somewhere sells this stuff to the terrorists. You, as a group, can anticipate and head off problems if you have good contacts. Heathrow Airport security in London has stopped more terrorists from getting on planes. How? They have luggage checks and dogs and sophisticated equipment, but what has proven the most reliable? Gut instinct."

"That's right," one of the men said. "I remember the woman who boarded a plane for Israel. Her boyfriend had hidden a bomb in her cosmetics case. The man at the passport station sensed something was wrong and discovered the bomb."

"Correct," Kyle told him. "People selling firearms or components that might possibly be used in bombs have gut instincts, too. Something doesn't seem right about a person. It's your job to stay in contact with as many of these people as possible. Ask them if they sold something to a suspicious character."

"Isn't paying large amounts of cash instead of using a credit card or a check another red flag?" asked Jennifer.

Kyle had planned on mentioning it next. He nodded, giving Jennifer a smile, but she stared back at him, her face blank—all business.

"Right. Large sums of cash is always a warning." Kyle stood up and stretched his bad leg. "Let's take a break while I set up the new piece of equipment we'll be using."

He wanted to go over to Jennifer and ask about Sadie, but the other men were clustered around her. Everyone wanted to know all about the rescue operation yesterday. Kyle set up the DNA field unit he was demonstrating.

"Time's up," he said a few minutes later. "Let's talk about the benefits of DNA testing in the field."

"How fast do you get results?" several of the men wanted to know.

"In a matter of minutes," Kyle answered. "One day, every police station in America will be able to check DNA instead of having to wait months for test results."

"Around Miami, there are billboards saying something about home test kits if you want to know the father of your child," said Jennifer. "They're for sale on the Internet, too. Are these kits for real?"

"I don't know. I'm careful not to hang around with women who wonder about their child's paternity."

Kyle's comment drew a laugh from the guys, but Jennifer stared at him as if he was a wad of gum stuck on the bottom of her shoe.

"I haven't seen these kits, but I understand they're reliable," Kyle said when the chuckles subsided. "As I said, it's a technology that will be widely available very shortly. What we have here"—he held up the small black device—"is a field unit designed for special forces."

"Why would they need a DNA test kit?" Jennifer asked.

"Good question," he responded. "If you come across physical evidence, you will want to quickly analyze it so you'll have a better idea who you're looking for. Example: You're called in when a suspicious package might be a mail bomb. We've had lots of those in the last few years."

"Too many," someone commented.

"If it is a bomb, there may be some physical evidence on it. A hair. A speck of blood. You'd be surprised how often people scratch themselves and leave a trace of blood."

The group nodded, obviously excited about the possibilities of DNA field test kits such as this one.

"Instead of making anyone bleed," Kyle said with a grin, "I'm going to test this kit first on Jennifer. Place a short strand of hair on this." He held up a disk that looked like a photographer's slide.

"What am I supposed to do?" she asked.

"Use these tweezers to pull off the sterile cover strip." He picked up a pair of tweezers from his desk. "Then put your hair on the tacky surface in the center."

She walked up to his desk with a mischievous grin. While she worked on it, Kyle explained the finer points to the rest of the men.

"It's important to keep your fingers on the cardboard rim. That way you don't deposit any of your own DNA material on the slide and get a false reading."

"I'm finished," Jennifer said. "Now what?"

"Drop it into the slot at the top of the machine." He waited until she'd inserted the slide, then added, "Now press the On button at the left. Take your seat and we'll wait five minutes for the machine to give us a readout."

Jennifer returned to her chair while one of the men asked, "What kind of readout will it give us?"

"There's a small screen like you see on pagers. It will print the message there."

"You've got the machine plugged in," Jennifer commented. "In the field, it must run on batteries."

"That's right." He nodded, then asked, "What information will the DNA test tell us first?"

"Racial background," guessed several of them at once.

"Good guess. That's the second bit of info the machine will give us. The first is sex—male or female."

They discussed other types of information the field DNA machine would provide them until the machine made a low-pitched *ping.*

"It's ready," Kyle said with a smile at Jennifer. "Let's see if it tells us the DNA sample belongs to a female Caucasian."

Jennifer smiled back and winked. At last he was getting somewhere. He picked up the machine and tilted it slightly to read the small screen.

"Female," he said, reading the first bit of info to the class. He looked at Jennifer again after the kit had determined her sex. She was grinning like a TV evangelist raking in the bucks. "It got that part right. Let's check the rest."

He read the next line to himself. Aw hell! He'd been taken.

"Canine." He looked at Jennifer who now appeared as innocent as she possibly could. "You put one of Sadie's hairs in the machine."

"You said to place a hair on the slide. You assumed it was my own hair, but I felt compelled to test the accuracy of your device."

The men chuckled and cast admiring glances at Jennifer. Even Kyle had to admit she'd been clever. Jennifer would prove to be the most valuable member of this team.

Jennifer finished class late that afternoon and called Paws N Claws. Sadie was better, improving with each hour. The news put a bounce in her step, despite her sore ankle, as she went over to the firing range to practice for the second time that day.

She'd learned her lesson. She refused to put anyone in jeopardy because she wasn't a crack shot. She was becoming more accurate each time she practiced, but there was still a long way to go.

It was nearly dark when she arrived at Paws N Claws to see Sadie. The reception area was closed, so she walked into the recovery room. Sadie wasn't in her cage.

"Oh, my God. Did something happen?" she said, then noticed the technician wasn't in the area either.

She found the woman in the adjacent area, inserting an IV in a cat's paw.

"Where's Sadie? Is she all right?"

"She's out back in the grassy area with Kyle. We like to get the dogs up and walking as soon as possible. Just like people in hospitals, animals need to get moving again."

Jennifer thanked her, then hurried out back. What was Kyle doing here? She should be the one helping Sadie.

Behind the clinic was a grass yard surrounded by a wooden fence painted Key West blue, a bright tropical shade. Most of the fence was concealed by bougainvillea and tree ferns. A single floodlight lit the area.

At the far side of the yard, Sadie was hopping along beside Kyle on three legs. The dog's tail swished back and forth, the way it did when she was happy. No question about it. Sadie adored Kyle.

And Kyle had saved Sadie's life. Jennifer had no right to be upset about him being here with her dog.

Jennifer shrugged out of her day pack and dropped it on the ground. "Sadie, girl, how are you doing?"

The dog looked over at her, tail now wagging furiously. She would have attempted to bound across the grass, but Kyle held her back.

"She's doing great now," Kyle informed her as she approached them.

"Now?"

"When I first took her out of the cage, Sadie had a hard time making it on three legs." He pointed down to the white cast covering her paw. "I held her up with one arm, and she got the hang of it."

Jennifer petted Sadie, wondering how to handle the situation. She did not want Kyle inserting himself into her life. She needed to distance herself from him as much as possible.

"I'll take over," she said with surprising calm.

"Sadie's just about had it. I've walked her three times around the yard. She's gone to the bathroom. The technician said to take it easy the first time. Tomorrow morning, Sadie will be raring to go. Right, girl?" He fondled Sadie's long ears and the dog gazed up at Kyle as if he'd hung the moon.

"Let me take her in then." She took the leash from Kyle and walked away. With any luck, he'd get the hint and disappear.

She hadn't been born under a lucky star. Kyle was waiting for her when she came out of the recovery room.

"There's a party for Logan McCord over at Sunset Key. You're invited."

Logan McCord. The name rang a bell but she couldn't quite place him.

"Who's Logan McCord?"

"The ace on Cobra Force," he said, and she recognized

the elite antiterrorism unit of the Marines. "He knows more about terrorism than anyone around. You may remember reading about him a while ago. The high tech computer at FBI's Nation Crime Information Center was brand new then and combining fingerprint information from a number of databases. It discovered Logan McCord had been kidnapped as a child."

"I remember now. *Exposé,* the news magazine, scooped everyone with a special report on him. Logan didn't realize he was Senator Stanfield's son who had been kidnapped when he was very young until the computer matched the fingerprints, right?" she said, and Logan nodded. "Imagine finding out you were someone else at thirty-something. You were really filthy-rich Haywood Stanfield's son."

"It's an amazing story," Kyle agreed. "Do you want to meet Logan McCord?"

She thought a moment, recalling more about the unusual story. "Didn't he marry Kelly Taylor, the reporter who scooped everyone?"*

"Yeah, that's right."

"Well, she's the person I really want to meet."

*See *Tempting Fate* by Meryl Sawyer

Chapter 16

Jennifer stood beside Kyle at Sunset Pier, waiting on the dock for the water shuttle to the exclusive island Sunset Key. She'd been so excited at the prospect of meeting Logan McCord and Kelly Taylor that Jennifer hadn't thought about what she was wearing. Since class this morning, Kyle had changed into white linen shorts and a pale blue polo shirt.

Even if his nose was a bit too long and his jaw slightly angular, Kyle looked tanned and devastatingly handsome. There wasn't a woman they passed who didn't check him out—twice.

Jennifer's own clothes were wrinkled and . . . tacky. She had on beige cargo shorts with deep pockets and a red T-shirt with a funky message:

So Many Men
So Few Bullets

Her hair was a mess. What else was new? And she didn't have on a stitch of makeup. This morning when she'd rushed out of Thunder Island, it hadn't mattered. Well, she thought, mentally kicking herself, there was nothing to be done about it now.

"Who is giving this party?" she asked as they boarded the launch for Sunset Key.

The private island was just across the channel from Key West, a stone's throw away, but it was so exclusive most people never went there. She'd noticed how carefully the attendant had checked his list for Kyle's name before allowing them to board the sleek cruiser for the short trip to Sunset Key.

"Trevor Adams is throwing the party. He owns Half Moon Bay—"

"Half Moon Bay? I saw that estate featured in *Architectural Digest.* His home is really impressive."

"The house is nice, but it's no better than any of the other homes on Sunset Key. It's the beach that makes it special. Locals call it Half Moon Bay because of its shape, so Trevor gave his home the same name."

Jennifer asked, "How did you meet Trevor?"

"I was house-sitting next door. Trevor's very friendly. He invited me over." The boat rocked unexpectedly, and he put his arm around the back of her seat. "It's not usually this rough. Must be that tropical storm south of here."

The shuttle pulled up to Sunset Key's private dock where Kyle's name was again checked against a list before they were permitted to disembark. They left the boat and walked down a brick path lined with colorful flowers and lit by subtle downlights.

"No cars are allowed on Sunset Key," Kyle told her. "They use golf carts to bring in groceries and heavy stuff."

"How did they build these houses?" she asked, looking at the magnificent homes, modern versions of the classic Key West homes.

"They bring everything in on barges."

They walked to a home at the far end of the exclusive

key. The double-wide door was open and the festive noise of a party greeted them even though no one was in sight. Without hesitating, Kyle led her into a large foyer filled with sculptures.

"This is new," commented Kyle as he paused near a bloodred sculpture contorted into a weird shape. "What do you think?"

"It looks like the work of some ax murderer to me."

Kyle chuckled, a low, sexy rumble that came from deep in his throat.

"Kyle! Kyle!" called a stunning blonde as they walked out of the house onto the terrace where the group was having cocktails. The beauty threw her arms around Kyle and kissed him.

Granted, it was a short, friendly kiss, but something about the greeting made Jennifer's blood simmer. Get a grip, she told herself as she plastered a smile on her face.

"Jennifer, this is Amy Conroy," Kyle said, his arm still around the beautiful woman. "I mean Amy Jensen. She married Matthew Jensen."

Matthew Jensen? The publisher of *Exposé* magazine. Logan McCord, Kelly Taylor, and now Matthew Jensen. Kyle was on a first name basis with some of the most important, fascinating people in the country.

Amy Jensen rolled her eyes. "Matt and I had twins a few months ago. The little devils, Kyle and Logan are asleep—finally."

Kyle. The Jensens had named a baby after Kyle. Apparently, they were much closer than she ever could have imagined.

Amy looked directly at Jennifer. The other woman, dressed in a black slip dress, smiled at Jennifer with genuine warmth. Amy Jensen was the type of person you couldn't help liking—even if she had just kissed Kyle.

"Come on, Jennifer. Let me introduce you to everyone."

"Lord Almighty! It's, like, Kyle." A redhead rushed up

to Kyle and threw her arms around him, pressing her body flush against his as she gave him a kiss straight from a porn flick.

"That's Bubbles McGee," Amy told her as the kiss continued. "They're old friends."

"Right," Bubbles said, breathlessly breaking the kiss. "I used to, like, sell Alien Abduction Insurance on the sidewalk in front of Jimmy Buffet's Margaritaville, but Kyle got me into mud."

The last word came out muh-ud. Mud? Surely the woman's southern molasseslike drawl had distorted the word. Bubbles handed Jennifer a card: Club Mudd. Oh, well. This was Key West. Anything goes.

"People come to my spa for, like, a mud dip. Then they dry in the sun. Hunks"—she looked suggestively at Kyle—"scrape off the dried mud. What better way to exfoliate your skin and get rid of, like, the worst toxins on the planet?"

Jennifer found herself nodding even though this was the most hair-brained thing she'd heard in ages. But it was probably expensive and all the rage.

"There's Matthew with Logan McCord," Kyle told her.

He steered her away from Bubbles and Amy toward two handsome men standing on the grass with yet another striking blonde. Once again, Jennifer kicked herself for not at least putting on mascara. Then a bell sounded in her brain and she stopped dead in her tracks.

She asked Kyle, "I read about Amy, didn't I?"

"Probably. Her story was in all the papers. Two women were in an auto accident. Amy was mistakenly identified as the dead woman. No one realized the error including Matthew Jensen, who had known the woman quite well."

"Didn't Amy go along with the error because a killer was after her?"*

*See *Half Moon Bay* by Meryl Sawyer

"Yes. I'll tell you all the details later, if you like." He took her arm and guided her forward.

"Hey, Kyle. How's it going?" asked one of the men, but his eyes were on Jennifer, and he extended his hand. "I'm Matthew Jensen." He dipped his head toward the blonde. "This is Kelly McCord, and the infamous Logan McCord."

"I'm Jennifer Whitmore," she said with as much self-confidence as she could muster.

Logan greeted her with a nod, then slapped Kyle on the back. "How does it feel to be a civilian?"

"I don't know. How does it feel?"

Everyone laughed except Jennifer. The men didn't notice her silence, but Kelly did.

"Kyle and Logan were both in antiterrorist units in the military. Logan was with the Marine's Cobra Force and Kyle was with the SEALs. They're both civilians now."

"I see."

"Come on," Kelly said. "Let's get you a drink." When they were a few feet away from the men, Kelly whispered, "Male bonding time. We're outta here."

As they walked toward a bar set up under a tall palm where the grass met the sandy beach, Jennifer took a close look at the small cove. With its crystal white sand gleaming in the moonlight and the regal ranks of palm trees, it was a postcard vision of paradise.

From behind a dwarf palm, bolted the oddest looking dog Jennifer had ever seen. It was the color of tarnished gunmetal and had part of one ear missing. Chasing the dog was a huge marmalade cat. The pair ran off into the house.

"That's Bingo hounding Jiggs again," Kelly told her.

"Jiggs, the half-eared dog," she said, suddenly recalling a bit more of Amy's story. "Didn't he and Amy hide in the trunks of cars to get across the country without some crazy man finding them?"

"Yes. That was just before the horrible accident when Amy had to have all the reconstructive surgery."

Jennifer looked back at the crowd on the terrace and easily spotted Amy. If she'd required extensive surgery, it had been done by a master.

"I've been wanting to meet you," Jennifer told Kelly after the bartender had handed them each a glass of Chardonnay. "You were the reporter who broke Logan's story. I wanted to ask how you learned he'd been kidnapped as a young child and had grown up thinking he was someone else."

Kelly leveled her green eyes at Jennifer. "Do you believe in fate?"

"No . . . not really."

"I didn't either, but now I know better. My husband had been killed, and I thought I would never love again. Then I met Logan." Kelly smiled wistfully and sipped her wine. "Fate brought us together just as fate brought Amy and Matt together. What about you? Has fate cast its spell on you and Kyle?"

"Kyle? No. We're . . ." What were they exactly? "Old friends."

"Is that right? I must have been mistaken about the look on your face when Amy greeted him, and when Bubbles the Airhead was kissing him."

There might have been a challenging glint in Kelly's eyes, but Jennifer ignored it. "I'm engaged to another man."

A long beat of silence, then, "Congratulations."

Kyle caught up on his old buddies with Logan. The two were from different branches of the service, but they'd gone through SEAL training together. While Kyle was talking with Logan, he kept his eye on Jennifer.

She had chatted for a while with Kelly, then she'd joined

Clive and Trevor, their hosts. The twosome were sure to entertain her, and they were no threat to Kyle. They were gay as were many of the other males at the party. There wasn't much competition in sight until Brody Hawke walked out onto the terrace and beelined toward Jennifer.

"Who in hell invited him?" Kyle asked out loud.

"I had Trevor invite Brody," Logan said. "I started a private security firm. You know, high tech corporate accounts. Brody worked on a project for me while he was on leave. I encouraged him to become a SEAL."

"Hawke's the most talented of the group I just put through my antiterrorism course."

"Well, if Hawke was hustling my woman, I wouldn't stand here chewing the fat with an old friend." Logan made a circle with his thumb and index finger, the Special Forces signal for "got your back." *I'm covering you.*

With a chuckle, Kyle walked toward Jennifer. Too late. Brody was leading her onto the small wooden dance floor set up for the party. The reggae group who usually worked at the Hard Rock Cafe had been hired for the evening and were playing a slow song with a Caribbean beat.

Kyle stalked across the lawn to the bar and ordered his usual, a long neck Corona with two twists of lime. He stood there watching the whitecapped waves slapping the beach, his back to the dance floor. The storm, though miles away, was churning up the seas. He expected the breeze to have kicked up, but it was dead still.

Just as the song was finishing, he put down the beer and went over to the edge of the dance floor and saw Jennifer peering up at Brody as if he were God's gift to women instead of just another SEAL with a death wish.

"My dance," Kyle told Brody with what he thought was a smile.

"Yes, sir!" Brody responded with a mock salute.

He pulled Jennifer into his arms, holding her closer than necessary. She didn't look too thrilled about it, but she didn't shove him away. The band played another slow tune with an exotic sound. Jennifer moved lightly with the music, swaying provocatively with the beat.

The gleaming moonlight wove silver threads through her tousled ash-blond hair. He slipped his fingers through the hair at the back of her neck and gently rubbed her bare skin with the rough pad of his thumb.

"Don't," she warned, but her voice was a little too breathless to be convincing.

He dropped his hand and let it coast down her back while encouraging her soft body to press against his solid frame. Her breasts nudged his chest, the nipples hard, a reminder of their late night swim. An upward surge of heat shot through his groin. Aw, hell. What she could do without even trying.

"Why didn't you tell me you knew all these people?" she whispered.

"Why didn't you ask?"

The small dance floor was shoulder to shoulder with dancers. Kyle deftly maneuvered Jennifer to the center of the area, letting his knee flex between her legs to the erotic beat of the music. He placed her hand against his chest and used his free hand to draw her even closer. The supple softness of her body sent another surge of desire through his, but this time passion mingled with an aching tenderness he couldn't remember experiencing until now.

It was the urge to protect, and something more that his body didn't want to give him too much time to examine. Yet there was no doubt about one thing. He communicated better with her physically than verbally.

He didn't give a damn about the group around them, didn't even think of them when he lowered his head to meet her warm lips.

"Don't you dare kiss me."

Jennifer was staring over his shoulder at Kelly and Logan

who were dancing nearby. Kelly winked at Jennifer. Women. Go figure.

His hand at the back of her neck, he held her still as she parted her lips with a breathy little sigh. They were only swaying slightly now, not even pretending to dance.

Her lips opened even more, seeming to invite him to kiss her. He couldn't disappoint her. He bent down and touched his lips to hers while his hand slowly inched down her back until he touched the soft flare of her hips.

He pressed firmly, pushing her into the hard heat of his sex. A soft purr rose from deep in her throat. The erotic sound was as powerful as any narcotic. This wasn't just a kiss. It was the promise of things to come.

The song ended on a long roll of steel drums in a Caribbean finale. The group around them broke up, some moving away, others waiting for the next song to begin. But Kyle and Jennifer didn't move. They kept kissing until someone bumped into them.

He pulled back, gazing down at the dark gold fringe of her lashes casting wispy shadows on her high cheekbones. She looked up at him, and he noticed minute shards of silver in the depths of her blue eyes. She looked away, obviously trying to hide her emotions. He cupped her chin and gently turned her toward him again.

"You always were a good dancer," he said, referring to their youth.

Something sparked in her eyes, anger no doubt, but he refused to give her the opportunity to argue. His hand fisted, clutching the silky hair at the back of her neck as he brought his lips down on hers, smothering her response. For a moment, her body went rigid, but he kept kissing her.

In some distant part of his brain, he realized the music had begun again, this time with a more rapid beat. People jostled them, but he kept kissing her, and letting his other hand rove up and down her back, lightly stroking her, encouraging her to relax while they swayed slightly, barely pretending to dance.

A few moments later, her body softly gave in, allowing him to pull her against him as her tongue eagerly mated with his. Heat surged upward in his groin, hard and bittersweet.

So many women had paraded through his life, but never had any kiss been as emotionally arousing as this one. Or as carnal. He wanted her, all of her, not just one lousy kiss.

The song ended and the band announced a break. *Come on, Parker. Think fast.*

"Let's call Paws N Claws and check on Sadie," he said.

"Why?"

He didn't bother to answer. This was nothing more than an excuse to get Jennifer alone. He quickly led her into the house and took a fast turn into the nearest bedroom. He closed the door behind them and didn't even bother to flick on the light.

"What are you doing?" she asked.

He backed her up against the door. "You know what I'm doing."

"Kyle, don't," she said, but made no attempt to move away.

He pinned her against the door with his body and angled his mouth over her parted lips, but he stopped short of kissing her. He took her face in both his hands and tilted it upward. Enough moonlight gleamed through the open windows in the dark room to see her moist lips, wide blue eyes, and the wild strands of honey-blond hair framing her face. Jennifer wasn't the most beautiful woman he'd ever seen, but she was the sexiest—bar none.

"You don't want me to stop. Do you, Jennifer?"

He waited a fraction of a second for her response, the iron heat of his sex demanding action. Then he lowered his lips the scant inch to hers as his arms circled her buttocks and brought her up on her toes flush against his rock-hard erection.

"A-a-ah," she moaned beneath his lips.

His skilled hands found the cargo shorts' zipper, and he had them undone while his tongue explored the sweet channel of her mouth in a primitive, sexual parody of the act to come. He shoved her shorts off her hips and would have smiled, if he hadn't been kissing her.

Son of a bitch. She was wearing silky bikinis no bigger than an eye patch. His blood thickened, pulsing through his entire body and hammering in his groin.

"Sexy," he heard his raspy voice say. "You're so damn sexy."

Her arms were around his neck, and she pulled his head down, silently making him kiss her again. As he did, he caressed the soft roundness of her hips and the baby-fine skin between her thighs, carefully avoiding the bikinis. She arched against him, again begging without words.

Sensing her desire, his pulse kicked up another notch, and his cock strained for release. It took all his willpower, but he forced himself to take his time.

He whipped his head back to gulp in a fresh breath of air. The leather band holding his hair back broke, and his thick hair swung free. He tipped his head forward, his hair brushing her cheeks as he kissed her.

Finally, he inched one finger under the silky bikinis and rubbed it against her warm mound, determined that she needed to be as fully aroused as he was. Hot and achingly hard, he gently probed, finding her wet and slick.

She pulled away from his lips just enough to whisper, "Oh my goodness."

He intimately stroked the tender flesh, steeling himself so that he was gentle even though he longed to bury his entire length to the hilt. He fondled her, concentrating on the small, tight nub between the slick folds of skin.

"Parker! Parker, where are you?"

Aw, hell. What did Hawke want? He froze, his penis inside her panties, intimately pressed against her. It took several gulps of air before he could muster a response.

"What the hell do you want?"

"Dowd called. There's a Code 11 at the base."

Just his luck. Interrupted two nights in a row.

Chapter 17

Kyle let out a string of four letter curses under his breath as he forced himself to stand up straight. The movement was an act of self-castration that left beads of sweat across his upper lip. He swiped at his mouth with the back of his hand.

"It's an emergency at the base. Trevor will see that you get back to Thunder Island safely," he told Jennifer, his hand on the doorknob. "Later, babe."

Hardly able to walk, he staggered into the hallway where he found Brody Hawke waiting for him. Brody had such a shit-eating grin that Kyle almost believed the guy had the balls to make up the Code 11 just because Kyle had gone off alone with Jennifer.

"What in hell's going on?"

"Dowd beeped me." Brody pointed to the beeper attached to his belt. "He's enacted a Code 11. Let's get out of here."

Code 11. A "priority" situation. Commander Dowd

never would have called one unless something important was happening.

Fuming, still cursing under his breath, he hobbled after Brody down to Half Moon Bay's private dock instead of going to the community pier the way he'd come with Jennifer.

He walked out on the Half Moon Bay's private gangway and recalled the night Amy Conroy had nearly died on this very spot. He'd had a small part in saving her life, and a surge of pride welled up inside him as he stood there, gazing across the narrow channel at the lights of Key West.

The wind had kicked up, he noticed. Chains of seaweed was being beaten against the shore by angry, white-capped waves.

"Trevor sent his house boy to take us back to Key West as quickly as possible," explained Brody.

"Good thinking." Kyle jumped into the launch, knowing that if they'd had to wait for the Sunset Key shuttle to take them across, they'd be stuck here for nearly an hour.

A prickle of alarm waltzed down Kyle's spine. Jennifer and the others were isolated here on Sunset Key. Their only link to the mainland, Key West, was the shuttle and the private boats like this one. In rough seas, lightweight boats like these weren't worth a damn.

In a few minutes, Trevor's boat reached the Sunset Pier, and Kyle stepped onto the dock. The wooden pier rocked beneath him as he waited for Brody to get off. The water was much more turbulent than when he'd crossed with Jennifer.

"I've got my Harley chained to a palm tree," Brody told him.

It figured, Kyle decided. Brody Hawke had a Harley-Davidson motorcycle. There was something a bit wild, a bit defiant, about both the man and the machine.

Without talking, they walked the short distance to the palm where the Harley was chained. Raucous sounds roiled out of the open air bars lining nearby Duval Street. With the noise came the moist, tropical scent of Key West perfumed by night blooming jasmine and fragrant plumeria.

Brody unlocked the motorcycle and gunned the engine. Kyle straddled the leather seat behind him. The Harley shot forward like a rocket. Feeling uneasy because he wasn't driving, Kyle set his jaw and tried to forget kissing Jennifer during the ride from hell.

Finally, they slowed down at the Navy Base, where they parked the Harley and crossed the pitch-black grounds to the commander's headquarters. At the main desk, they announced themselves, then an ensign led them to Commander Dowd's office.

"What's going on?" Kyle casually asked the commander.

"Tropical storm Frances has been upgraded to a hurricane," Mike Dowd said. "I've ordered our men to secure the military equipment in the underground bunkers."

"Is the storm headed this way?" Kyle asked.

"Not at present, but remember Honduras. Hurricane Mitch unexpectedly veered inland, destroying everything in its path."

Kyle asked, "Shouldn't civilians be notified?"

"I'm under orders to protect Navy property," Dowd answered. "It's up to the Civil Defense authorities to notify the civilians. I spoke with the brass at their headquarters. They claim alerting the population prematurely would panic people unnecessarily."

"People? They aren't worried about locals. All they give a damn about are tourists."

Mike shrugged, but he was too honest a guy to deny it.

"What about the danger?" asked Kyle, thinking about Jennifer and his friends isolated on Sunset Key. They could be killed or stranded for days without food or water.

Mike Dowd lifted his hands, palms upward. "This is just a precautionary measure. We need to be ready in case it's a rogue hurricane and changes course."

Dowd assigned a team to help Kyle move his valuable antiterrorist gear to underground bunkers. When they finished, it was the middle of the night. The moon was obliterated by bands of dark, sulky clouds. The wind was blowing harder now, bending the palms sideways.

"What does the satellite say about the storm?" Kyle asked one of the Navy intelligence officers.

"Hurricane Frances is still headed due north straight up the Gulf of Mexico. It's projected to make landfall on the Alabama coast."

Kyle wondered if Jennifer and the others had gotten home, or had they stayed on Sunset Key because the water in the channel was too rough to cross? He tried to telephone, but the lines were down, which wasn't surprising. In a strong wind, Sunset Key's phone lines went down much sooner than the lines on Key West. The cell phones were out as well.

A few minutes after Kyle left so unexpectedly, Jennifer went out to the terrace and watched the others at the party. She didn't feel like celebrating. Her emotional compass was way off kilter. Once again, she'd let Kyle Parker get to her.

And what had he done?

He'd left her, the way he had before, when he'd broken her heart. Would she ever learn her lesson, she wondered. The man was poison—pure and simple—yet she melted in his arms without blinking.

"What's wrong with you?"

She walked along the beach where the turbulent surf pounded the shore, sending frothy spume high into the night air. Wind-whipped clouds sailed across the moon like streamers, and a hot, seething restlessness filled the tropical air. Harbingers of a summer storm, she decided, then her thoughts drifted.

She should go back to the terrace and talk with some of the interesting people, but she didn't feel like it. She was too depressed about shooting Sadie and too disturbed about the way she'd behaved with Kyle. What was wrong with her?

Trying to concentrate on Chad and their future together, she walked across the beach to Half Moon Bay's private pier. Trevor and Clive were putting several people in a boat.

"If you have to be somewhere early in the morning, I suggest you leave now," Trevor told her. "The sea's so rough because of the storm, we may not get everyone back to the mainland tonight."

"There's plenty of room here, if you want to spend the night," Clive added. "It's up to you."

"I'd better go. I have to be at the base at dawn tomorrow," she said. "Thanks for a wonderful party."

"We'll get together again," Trevor said as he helped her into the boat.

She waved good-bye as the launch pulled away from the dock. They were such fascinating people, she thought. She wasn't surprised to find Kyle knew Logan McCord. They'd both done antiterrorist work. But the others didn't seem to have anything in common with Kyle, yet they all knew him and seemed to genuinely like him.

Kyle was so much different than she'd expected. Granted, her assumptions were based on old, old memories. Years had passed. They were both different people now.

As much as she wanted to hate Kyle for what had happened back then, it wasn't entirely his fault. The mess her mother had made of her life and the tragedy that followed was as much Jennifer's fault. She'd fallen for Kyle, knowing he intended to join the Navy and follow in his father's footsteps.

Was it any wonder that he never tried to find her?

It was an old wound, one that should have healed long

ago, but it always lurked in the corner of her mind. When she least expected it, she would experience an aching sadness too deep for tears.

Why was she subjecting herself to more heartache? By allowing Kyle to kiss her and . . . everything, she was ruining her relationship with Chad. What would he say if he knew?

It had taken her years to find the right man. True, it then had happened with astonishing speed, but she knew Chad was the man she wanted to marry.

How could she possibly be susceptible to Kyle after what had happened? Years had passed, yet her body seemed to operate independently of her more rational mind.

She mulled over her feelings and still didn't have an excuse for her behavior when the boat pulled up to Key West. It was well after midnight, but, as usual, the town was just getting going. Music blared from the bars and groups of people who roved the streets laughing and talking. It would be safe to say many of them had "wasted away" in Margaritaville.

She headed toward Thunder Island, then changed her mind. What point was there in going home? She would never be able to sleep. Her time would be better spent on the firing range.

After finding her car, she drove out to the base. The guard at the gate checked her security pass and told her the base was being prepared for a hurricane.

"Is Frances heading toward us now?"

"It's just a precaution."

Good, she thought. She would have the firing range all to herself. Her car was the only one in the lot when she parked at the range. It was lucky she hadn't had the time to turn in her smart gun after the search.

The person who usually checked out weapons wasn't at his post, and no one seemed to be around. She made her way into the depths of the dark building. It was the first time she'd set up her own targets, and it took a little longer

than she anticipated. She stood behind the firing line, thinking of the alligator and seeing Sadie.

"I'm going to be a crack shot or die trying," she said to trigger the voice activation mechanism.

"Oh, my stars! Not another hurricane."

Thelma Mae stood on the widow's walk outside the secret room, listening to the wind lashing the palm trees. Behind her the radio was giving the latest weather forecast. Hurricane Frances was still heading north and was expected to hit near Mobile. Even though the storm was miles and miles away, it wasn't unusual for it to cause rough surf and strong winds.

As a precaution, she'd had the beach chairs moved into the storage shed on top of the pool chaises. The shutters on the windows of the lower floors served as storm shutters and were closed just in case. If the wind was worse in the morning, she would be forced to tape the windows on the upper floors.

She hated taking such precautions because it upset the guests. No doubt some of them would panic and leave even though the storm wasn't expected to come anywhere near Key West. It couldn't be helped. She had no choice except to protect her home. Last year hurricane Georges had unleashed its fury on them. Thunder Island had narrowly missed being destroyed.

She couldn't chance having that happen. The guest house and the inhabitants' private affairs were her whole life. She couldn't imagine what she'd do without them. Thunder Island was more than just a place to call home.

She'd sold her soul when she gave up her baby and married a wealthy man older than her father. Fate had been cruel. She'd been unable to have another child.

Her husband had indulged her by purchasing the dilapidated old mansion. She'd lovingly restored Thunder

Island, so named by the original owner because the cannon at Fort Zachary Taylor sounded like thunder to his young son. The house became more than just a project to Thelma Mae. It gave her direction and purpose especially after her husband's death.

Finally, fate had smiled on her again: the baby boy she'd given up walked back into her life again. Of course her son didn't understand the importance of Thunder Island, but it didn't matter.

Having him back was all that counted.

Chapter 18

Kyle helped the other men secure laptops and sensitive files in another underground bunker near where he'd put his equipment. They were stashing gear so quickly that Kyle hoped someone was keeping a log or they would play hell finding everything again.

Commander Dowd stormed in, yelling, "Hurry up! Hurry up!"

"What's the rush?" Kyle asked.

"Frances is a goddamned rough hurricane. She just changed course and is gaining strength as well as speed. She's dead-heading for Key West."

"Aw, shit!" Kyle hustled to put things away, but his mind was on Jennifer and the others on remote Sunset Key. Trevor's home had a basement, and he knew Trevor had lived in the area long enough to be prepared for a disaster like this. Still, he couldn't help being uneasy.

They completed the project and Dowd ordered his men to remain in the bunker until the hurricane passed over. Dowd could order his men to remain on the base, but Kyle was free to leave. If he went to the dock, he could get some kind of boat to Sunset Key.

Even if he couldn't rent or borrow a boat, he could swim the narrow channel. Hell, he had been a SEAL and had swum longer distances in rougher water. He had to make sure Jennifer was safe.

Leaving the bunker, Kyle spotted Brody. "Hawke, may I borrow your Harley? I'll stow it in a safe place."

"Ah, yeah. Sure, man." Brody handed Kyle the keys, but he didn't look too thrilled about it.

Kyle raced out of the building and streaked across the parking lot, ignoring the hitch in his knee. The wind howled through the palms with a snapping sound like whips. The heavy air was rain scented and crackled with electricity. Any second the heavens would open and rain would pummel the earth. He'd been through three hurricanes and knew what to expect. It would be the leading edge of the storm. Worse would follow.

He jumped on the Harley and gunned the engine, intending to drive to the docks, stow the Harley in one of the warehouse basements. Hell-bent for leather, as his father used to say, he sped down the dark black top road leading off the base. He leaned hard into the turn near the firing range.

He blinked twice, not quite believing he'd spotted Jennifer's car. What in hell was she doing here? He swung the Harley to the side and drove into the lot and parked next to Jennifer's car.

Inside, his footsteps echoed through the empty corridor as he rushed to the firing range. He figured Jennifer must still be blaming herself for shooting Sadie, but practicing during a hurricane was damn stupid.

He found her standing there without earphones, firing away. The back of the range was littered with discarded paper targets. From the looks of them, Jennifer was improving.

"What in hell are you doing?" he yelled.

She spun around, pointing the gun at him. Instinctively, he ducked and lunged for her. His hand locked around her wrist. The gun dropped to the floor with a clank.

Eyes smoldering, she glared at him and yanked her hand away. "I'm practicing. Is there a law against it?"

He quickly picked up her gun, saying, "Didn't you hear? Hurricane Frances is coming right at Key West."

"No. The guard at the gate said it was heading toward the Alabama coast."

"She changed course."

"Oh, my God. What about Sadie?"

He put his hand on her arm. "The vet has a basement. I've seen it. They'll take the animals down there."

"We have to evacuate to Key Largo. I—"

"There isn't time. But we may be able to help batten down Thunder Island. Let's go."

Jennifer grabbed her gun and shoved it into her backpack. They raced to the parking lot, but when Kyle opened the door a blast of wind driven rain hit them full-force. He slammed it shut.

"I've got Hawke's motorcycle. We'll take it instead of your car."

"So we can get soaked? Sounds like a great plan."

There were times he was so damn tempted to put his hands around her cute neck and squeeze. "The way the wind's blowing, trees are bound to fall. I can lift the Harley but not the car. I—"

"Right. Let's get going."

Jennifer hunkered down, her head against Kyle's back in a futile attempt to keep the blinding rain out of her eyes. She had no idea how Kyle could possibly see where he was going. Arms around his powerful chest, she hung on as the motorcycle barreled down the road, littered with palm fronds ripped from the trees by the relentless wind. He swerved unexpectedly to avoid trash cans and plastic beach chairs that had blown into the street.

Thunder boomed, shaking the ground, and chain lightning arced across the dark sky, searing the tops of the palms. Kyle skidded to a halt, and the Harley tipped sideways. Her backpack lurched to one side and the shifting weight nearly toppled her into the rain-filled gutter. The ruthless wind had destroyed a stately royal palm. Its majestic crown of huge fronds blocked the street.

"Get off and walk around it," Kyle yelled above the howl of the wind and the pelting rain ricocheting off the pavement like a hail of machine gun fire.

She did as she was told and climbed over the palm's massive trunk, barely clearing it without scraping her leg. Standing on the other side, shivering because the wind was blowing through her wet blouse, she watched Kyle. He hoisted the Harley up sideways until it straddled the palm. Then he hopped over the trunk and pulled the motorcycle to the other side.

He wasn't even breathing hard when he said, "Hop on. Let's go."

Waves blasted out of the sea, shooting high into the air and swamping the road in places. Twice the Harley stalled out. When it stalled for the third time a few blocks later, Kyle stopped and got off.

"The Harley's flooded. We're not going to make it back to Thunder Island before the hurricane hits full force. Let's try for the house Trevor's renovating on Angela Street."

She had no idea what he was talking about but assumed Trevor, who owned Half Moon Bay, was renovating one of Key West's historic homes in the Old Town section. Kyle hauled the Harley off the street up onto the narrow sidewalk. Head bent to keep the rain out of her eyes, she followed.

They must have walked several blocks with Kyle pushing

the motorcycle before he shoved aside a gate hanging by a single rusted hinge and guided the bike onto a flagstone path. Jennifer stayed two steps behind him, and took a quick glance at what once must have been one of Key West's finest historical mansions.

Kyle led her around to the back where he leaned the Harley against the side of the house while he opened a rickety storm door into the cellar.

"Got a flashlight in that backpack?" he hollered over bellowing wind.

She dropped the pack to the weed-choked grass and unzipped it. Shielding its contents with her body as best she could, she pulled out the small, high-intensity light and handed it to Kyle. He propped it up on a beam inside the building. He rolled the Harley into the cellar, and she followed.

Kyle pulled the storm door shut. The cellar was dank, the air heavy from mildew and the moist earth. The support beams were festooned with cobwebs. In the deep shadows beyond the circle of light, something scuttled away. Piled near the door were empty burlap bags stamped: Aker's Extra Fine Steel Wool.

"What are they doing with so much steel wool?" she asked, water dripping into her eyes from her hair.

During the ride, the leather thong holding Kyle's hair back had fallen off. His chin-length, wet hair fell around his face in wet hanks. He finger-combed it off his face and squeezed the water out of it. In one deft motion, he secured it at the nape of his neck by tying two strands of hair together.

He stripped off his soaked shirt and hung it from one of the Harley's handlebars. She ignored her body's unwilling reaction to him. If Kyle had been just handsome, Jennifer was positive she would be more detached. It was the size and power of his body that she found so intriguing. He took his strength for granted, moving with a natural, athletic grace.

Hoping he hadn't noticed her staring, she dragged her gaze down to her hands. She busied herself by attempting to wring the water out of her cargo shorts. Then she yanked her T-shirt out of the shorts and tried to get the water out of it.

"They use extra-fine steel wool to lightly sand the wood in the house," he said, answering her question. "Knowing Trevor, he's probably saving the bags to recycle them."

"I see," she managed to respond as she wiped her soaked hair off her face. He was unzipping his wet shorts. "What are you doing?"

He stepped out of them and draped the dripping shorts over the Harley's seat. His Joe Boxers were soaked, too, and clung to his body. If she hadn't noticed how impressively built he was before, there was no mistaking it now.

He turned, caught her staring, and flashed her a cocky grin. "See something you like?"

She ignored him, repeating her question. "Why are you taking off your clothes?"

He scattered some of the burlap bags on the stone floor. "No sense in sitting around in wet clothes. We're here until the hurricane is finished with us."

They would be alone together for hours. He glanced at her, and she looked away. She had seen that expression more than once. Even in the dark, she recognized that look and felt it touch her body like a lover's caress. She cursed herself and promised she would get through this . . . somehow.

He smiled again, only this time his grin was all male arrogance. "Turn around or you'll get a real show."

Oh, my God. He's going to strip bare. She whirled around, telling herself that one of Key West's voodoo queens had put a hex on her. Luck had most definitely taken a powder the moment Kyle Parker walked back into her life.

A rustling noise was followed by a wet slapping sound. Out of the corner of her eye, Jennifer saw his undershorts hurl through the air and hit the Harley's front fender. For a moment, the underwear clung to the metal, then slowly slid to the stone floor in a wet slosh.

The cellar seemed eerily silent now except for the *plink-plink-plink* of the rain dripping from a broken board overhead. The thick walls protected them from the storm's fury, but through the plank door, she heard the frightening sound of tree branches being ripped away and hurled like javelins at the house.

She tried valiantly to concentrate on the almighty Frances and her power to destroy Key West. It was difficult for Jennifer to stay focused. Her mind kept straying to what Kyle might be doing behind her.

Kyle Parker buck naked.

Despite her wet blouse plastered to her chilled skin, prickles of heat rose from her body in shimmering waves. She reluctantly recalled another time—long ago—when she'd seen him without a stitch of clothing.

Their parents had been living together in a small house near the Navy base. They all shared one small bathroom. Believing she was alone in the house, Jennifer barged into the bathroom and saw Kyle as he stepped out of the shower and reached for a towel.

It had been a defining moment for both of them. He'd stood there, nude. She'd stood there, awestruck.

The air between them had crackled with sexual tension, then he tossed her a towel, saying, "Dry my back."

She'd been a year younger and totally in love, yet she'd managed to hide her feelings. Despite her shock and embarrassment, she brazened it out, refusing to run like the stupid little kid he believed her to be. She grabbed the towel and rubbed his back for all she was worth.

Before she'd finished, he snatched the towel away, then hooked it around his waist. The whole time she never looked down. Still, she remembered what she'd seen when he stepped out of the shower.

"You ain't seen anything yet," he had informed her.

Jennifer had bolted from the room, but not this time. She was older now, experienced, in control of her emotions. She turned to face Kyle.

She inhaled a gulp of air, then burst out laughing. Kyle was reclining against the pile of burlap bags, a single bag negligently draped across his midsection.

"Do you know how ridiculous you look with 'extra fine' blazoned across your . . . your—"

"Cock?"

"Private areas."

"As opposed to public areas?" he replied with another grin some women would have found hard to resist. "You didn't used to be such a prude. I seem to recall that you were one hot number."

She refused to allow him to bait her. Still, a long buried memory surfaced, startlingly vivid despite all the years that had passed. She had been a virgin the first time they'd made love, and he'd held her in his arms all night. What had happened to that sweet, tender young man?

"Don't tell me you're going to spend all night in those wet clothes," he said with another adorable smile.

"They're not bothering me," she fibbed.

He rolled his eyes heavenward and settled back against the stack of burlap bags. "Suit yourself."

She pulled a few bags of a stack and arranged them on the floor as far away from Kyle as she could get and still be able to lean against the bags to support her back. Sitting down, she tugged at her wet shorts.

"You're gonna get crotch rot."

"Very funny. There's no such thing."

"Yeah? Tell that to guys working in the rain forest. It's worse than athlete's foot."

For a second she wondered if he could possibly be telling the truth, then decided some men would say anything to get a woman to take off her panties. She was itchy and clammy, but nothing could make her take off her clothes when Kyle was so close. She leaned back, closed her eyes, and tried to go to sleep.

The somnolent drip-drip, drip-drip of the rain leaking into the cellar irritated her rather than made her sleepy. She realized less noise was coming through the cellar door. Ready to ask Kyle if he thought the storm was over, she opened her eyes.

"Oh, my God!" She sat bolt upright.

Without making a single sound, Kyle had moved right next to her. He lay on his side, the burlap bag draped over his hips. One elbow was bent to support his head as he stared at her with that intense gaze of his.

"What are you doing?"

"Looking at you," he answered, his voice a shade shy of a whisper.

"Well, stop. I don't like it."

"Not unless you tell me why you're so damn mad with me, yet want me in spite of yourself."

"In spite of myself. What's that supposed to mean?"

"You still have the hots for me even though you're engaged to another man."

Her first reaction was to deny it, but decided to deal with it instead. "I understand why you may have deluded yourself—"

"Deluded?" He slapped his bare thigh. The sound echoed through the dark cellar. "Yeah, right. That's why you turn into a porn star every time I—"

"Porn star?" She whacked at him with her left hand and succeeded only in hurting her wrist when her hand hit his powerful shoulder.

To herself, she admitted she had given him good reason to think she was crazy about him. She wished she had an explanation, but she didn't. All she could think was that her mind had never quite let go of the past.

Chapter 19

Jennifer tried to decide what to say without stripping her heart bare. This was more difficult than she could possibly have imagined. During the long, lonely years since she'd last been with Kyle, she'd lived with the consequences of what had happened. And suffered for her mistakes.

Finally, Hiram Whitmore, her stepfather, had brought her out of her funk by telling her she would end up like her mother. It was then that he began showing her how to train bloodhounds. She'd enjoyed the work, but the hurt remained, buried deep inside her head.

She had imagined this conversation a thousand times, but had never actually thought it would take place. She'd never dreamed she'd be in a deserted cellar, with a hurricane threatening their lives, explaining her feelings to a nearly naked man. A man who had no intention of asking forgiveness.

"Kyle, I understand why you were confused—"

"Confused? Babycakes, I'm not one damn bit confused. I know exactly what you want."

He ran the tip of one finger along her cheek, then brushed a wet strand of hair away from her face. The mere touch of his hand sent a warming shiver through her.

"I . . . want . . . to . . . marry . . . Chad Roberts." She paused to put special emphasis on each word to make certain he understood she loved Chad.

"Why?" He arched one eyebrow.

"Why?" She sat up straighter. "I—we want to start a business."

"A buddy of mine wants me to go into business with him, but we never discussed marriage. Maybe we should."

"Very funny." In the sheen of the flashlight, his smile challenged her. "You know what I mean."

"No, I don't. Explain it to me."

"Chad and I have similar goals and a vision for our future."

His smile vanished. "What kind of business?"

"Specialized security, like what corporations use. I will do sweeps."

"Sweeps?"

"You know, taking dogs like Sadie to facilities to sniff for drugs." She tried to sound positive, but it was difficult. They had discussed this, yet Chad hadn't made any definite plans to leave the DEA and start a business. "Sweeps are the bread and butter of security firms. Insurance companies insist on drug-free workplaces, so I'll handle the sweeps while Chad develops high tech corporate accounts."

"High tech. Chad? He's an expert on South American drug smuggling."

"Yes, and those experts are in tremendous demand."

His eyes narrowed until the green was barely visible between his dark lashes. "In demand for what? Sex?"

There was no point in talking about Chad. For whatever reason, Kyle was determined to bait her rather than have a serious discussion.

"You started to tell me why you're so pissed off."

"That sounds crude."

"A pitcher of margaritas in the face. Now *that's* crude."

Silently conceding she'd behaved extremely childishly, she decided to tell him part of the truth. An instinct for self-preservation told her not to completely open up the old wound. It had taken her years to come to terms with what had happened. Why depress herself?

"I shouldn't have thrown the pitcher of margaritas. It was a really stupid thing to do. It was a gut reaction." She choked out the last words. "I'm sorry."

He smiled, a cute grin that struck her as incredibly funny. She giggled a moment, then broke into a laugh.

"What's so damn funny?"

"I was just thinking you have weird outfits. You sometimes wear margaritas. Now you're wearing nothing but a smile and a burlap bag."

"I could always take off the bag. Women tell me I look best wearing nothing but a smile."

"Don't you dare!"

He put his hand on the edge of the burlap sack carelessly draped over his hips. "Talk or this comes off."

She was fairly sure it was an idle threat, but with Kyle you never knew. "I threw the margaritas because I was angry with your father."

"My father? What in hell does he have to do with it? Your mother *left* him."

"She left because he refused to marry her."

"Look, he had a bad experience with my mother. He didn't want to get married again. He said so right from the beginning."

She couldn't deny it. Her mother had been warned when their relationship started. Still, her mother had secretly hoped she could change Vincent Parker's mind by living with him.

"If he'd come after Mom, it might have helped. She would have known he cared."

"Dad cared," Kyle said, his voice suddenly husky. "Believe me, he cared."

But not enough to come after her. Vince hadn't made the effort and neither had Kyle. She longed to ask him about it even though she'd known the truth for years. To Kyle, their relationship hadn't been about love. It had merely been sex, a moment in time easily forgotten.

It had been radically different for her. The experience had drastically changed her life, leaving a hidden scar.

"Within eight hours of your mother's leaving, Dad's unit was called to Greneda."

How long had that "conflict" lasted? She tried to recall, but couldn't. "Greneda? I'm sorry I don't remember much about—"

Kyle barked a laugh. "That's the hell of it. Ask the average American and they can't remember why we were in Greneda, yet the government sent the military in like it was some big deal. World War II all over again, or worse."

Granted, Vincent Parker had been sent to Greneda, but Kyle hadn't. Why couldn't he have called her? There wasn't any excuse she could imagine.

"SEALs hadn't seen action since—"

"Vietnam," Kyle finished, his smile as stiff as his emerging beard.

"Your father always talked about going into combat."

Kyle responded with another of those looks she couldn't quite decipher. She waited a moment, knowing Kyle had idolized his father. He had followed in his father's footsteps and become a SEAL, too.

"How is your father?" She hated to ask because she didn't want to tell him about her mother and what had happened after her death.

Kyle stared off into the darkness beyond the dim circle of light. The rain must have stopped; the leak was no longer dripping onto the stone floor. A cryptlike silence filled the dank cellar. Suddenly, she . . . knew.

"Your father died."

Kyle slowly turned to face her, sorrow etching the masculine planes of his face. "He was the first SEAL killed trying to take the airport in Greneda."

"Oh, God, my mother never knew," she blurted out before she could stop herself. She should have told him first that she understood how traumatic it was to lose your only parent at such a young age. "I'm so sorry."

"Didn't your mother read the papers or watch television? There weren't many casualties."

She shook her head, and the still-damp curls slapped her cheek. "No. We didn't have much money. We stayed in a flea bag without a TV for a month. There was a pay phone down the hall. Every time it rang, Mom rushed to answer it hoping your father was calling."

"My father died thirty-six hours after your mother skipped out on him."

She couldn't blame him for the bitterness so evident in his voice. There were two sides to every story. Kyle had his own take on the situation. What did it matter now? They were both dead, but their memories lingered, haunted.

"I'm sorry about your father. Truly I am. He was a good man. During the time we lived with him, your father was wonderful to me."

"Yeah," Kyle replied, a fond note in his voice. "He would have blistered both our hides if he knew what was happening."

"True. So true."

She gazed at him . . . remembering. She recalled more than she wanted about those hot, sultry summer nights when they'd lied to their parents, pretending to be going out with friends only to meet in their secret spot in the woods. She had been crazy about him in that uninhibited, totally devoted way young girls love for the very first time.

Then you grew up—and paid the price.

"What happened to you, Jennifer? Where did you go?"

It was the very question she wanted to ask him. Of course, she knew the answer. She hadn't been as important to him as he had been to her.

"An old friend of my mother's had a farm in rural Georgia near Macon. We went to live with him. They got married."

"I guess she wasn't that crazy about my father."

How could she explain? she wondered. She'd never really understood why her mother had married. "Hiram Whitmore had been in love with my mother since high school. He caught her on the rebound."

"Whitmore adopted you."

"Yes. He expected it to make my mother love him, but it didn't." She sucked in a calming breath of air. "Mom never stopped loving your father. He meant more to her than life itself. Without him, she didn't care about living. That's what she said in her suicide note."

"Sonofabitch!" He stared at her a moment, slack-jawed, then put his arm around her and drew her close.

She was acutely conscious of where his warm flesh touched her. A strange inner excitement filled her making it hard to concentrate.

"She left you alone in the world."

She opened her mouth to defend her mother, but her eyes met his and she acknowledged . . . the truth. A thousand times she'd asked herself the same question. Didn't her mother love her enough to want to live to help Jennifer when she had most needed a mother? In a way Jennifer blamed herself. She should have been able to do *something* to save her mother.

"She loved me, but she was obsessed with your father." She hesitated, torn by conflicting emotions. "If she'd known he had died, it might have made a difference. Especially if she believed he loved her."

His large hand cradled her chin, the touch almost unbearable in its tenderness. "Dad loved your mother. He planned to marry her. He told me so the morning he left."

"If only he'd phoned her."

"I gave him the number you left with me. He kept calling and calling, but the line was busy."

She let out a long sigh and allowed herself to lean against him for support. "I wish—"

He silenced her with a cool finger to her lips. "Hush. Even if they'd spoken, Dad still would have died. Your mother probably would have killed herself anyway." The smoldering anger she detected in his voice startled her. "I often blamed your mother for my father's death."

"What?" She pulled out of his arms. "That's ridiculous."

"The last thing a SEAL in combat needs is to let a woman distract you." He paused, now seeming more pensive than upset or angry. "Dad went into combat worried about your mother."

"Are you saying she was responsible for his death?" she gasped, unable to imagine it. Of all the scenarios she'd envisioned, and there had been hundreds of them, she had never considered her mother might have caused Vince Parker's death.

"She didn't fire the machine gun that pumped the bullet into his body. But when he left, Dad was so upset about your mother skipping out on him that I don't think he was focused on combat the way he should have been."

A pulsing knot formed in her stomach as she realized how selfishly she'd looked at the situation. She'd never stopped to consider Kyle's point of view.

"I'm sorry about your father's death. I truly am. My mother would have shot herself even sooner if she suspected she played any part in his death."

He shrugged. "Who knows? He might have died anyway."

"The whole thing was a tragedy." Of course, what she'd

told him was only part of the story, the part she could force herself to tell.

They sat in silence, the sounds of the storm filling the dark cellar. Finally, Kyle spoke.

"That was then and this is now. What about us?"

"Us?" she retorted more sharply than she intended.

The time for "us" had been years ago. The raw ache that had never quite gone away reminded her of the love she'd once felt for Kyle. He had been her first love. She could tell herself Kyle was *nothing* to her, but she wasn't being honest.

"We're friends." She couldn't keep the teary undertone out of her voice. "We'll always be friends."

"Friends? Friends?" He swept her into his arms. "We're more than friends."

His last words were nearly smothered against her lips. His kiss was surprisingly gentle, almost thoughtful, as if he were giving her time to think about their relationship. She intended to push him away, she honestly did, but somehow she found herself returning his kiss—in spite of herself. She told herself to remember what had happened the last time they'd made love. Don't allow yourself to be hurt again.

"Friends, huh? Gimme a break."

Before she could even attempt a clever comeback, he was kissing her again. In some distant part of her brain, she realized he was unbuttoning her blouse. He pulled back and gazed down at her.

"You know, Jennifer, all things considered, I think we should upgrade our relationship to best friends."

Chapter 20

To hammer home his point, Kyle repeated, "Best friends."

He ran the tip of his finger up her arm as he stared into her eyes. He wondered just what she was thinking. He knew she wanted him, yet something held her back, and he had the distinct feeling more than Chad Roberts was bothering her.

"Don't get any ideas," she said without looking at him.

"Ideas? Ideas?" he said. "Hey, you catch on quickly. Don't you?"

He slipped his arm around her and drew her close. The rain had soaked her hair, turning it a burnished gold in the warm glow of the flashlight. The heat of her body caused the scent of some intoxicating fragrance to rise from her soft skin. A fluid warmth seeped through him, pooling in his groin.

A sense of urgency, both physical and mental, spurred him on. As weird as it seemed, this was the time—and stranger yet—the place—to make love to Jennifer. They'd come close earlier in the evening. If he allowed her to talk him out of it, he might never have another chance with her.

He lowered his head to capture her lips in a fierce, hot kiss. His tongue invaded her mouth commanding her to respond. Flattening the mound of her breasts, his chest pressed against hers.

She didn't protest when his hand stole under her T-shirt. Beneath the damp fabric, her skin was moist, but smooth. He inched his way upward, taking his sweet time.

A flare of desire smoldering in her eyes told him that she wanted this as much as he did. She gasped as his hand covered the lacy cup of her bra. With the pad of his thumb, he caressed the taut nipple.

"Like this?" he asked, the need to hear her voice suddenly hitting him.

A beat of silence. "Oh, yes."

The hard heat building in his groin kicked up a notch. His cock pushed against the scratchy burlap bag covering him. He tossed it aside, then angled his body across hers.

His lips explored the gentle curve of her neck while his hand stroked the warm fullness of her breasts. He sucked her skin against his teeth, tasting, feeling the fine texture. Then he nuzzled her neck hard with the stiff bristles of whiskers emerging along his jaw as he flicked his tongue across her earlobe.

"You're so damn sexy," he whispered into her ear.

In response, she arched up a little and turned her head toward him. Her lips were parted and moist and begging for another soul kiss. Her eager response matched his, startling him. His mouth covered hers with a hunger that bordered on desperation.

Take it easy, he told himself. Don't rush her.

He plowed his fingers through her damp hair and arched her head back as he pressed his open lips against hers. His tongue delved deep into her mouth. His free hand slid behind the cup of her bra and found her taut nipple.

Her wet clothing got in the way, and he pulled her upright, then peeled her T-shirt over her head. He flung it in the direction of the Harley. A peach-colored demi-bra supported breasts that weren't centerfold material, but they were the sexiest set he'd ever seen.

Above the rain pummeling the cellar and the howl of the wind, their ragged breath filled the dark room. He gently lowered her onto her back again. Through the moist lace, he suckled first one tight nipple, then the other, flicking it roughly with the tip of his tongue.

She moved beneath him, obviously responding to his erection pressing against her damp shorts. His bare leg nudged her thighs apart, and he settled himself between her legs. She sucked in a gulp of air, then raked her nails across his shoulders.

"Oh, Kyle!"

The raspy sound of her voice kicked his pulse into high gear. His blood seemed thick and heavy as it pounded in his temples. Hot, demanding need raced through his body and throbbed in his groin.

He unhooked her bra, then pulled it off and tossed it over his shoulder. Nuzzling her breasts, he cupped them with his hands and inhaled deeply. The warm, moist scent of woman mingled with a trace of perfume, overloading his senses. He'd never slowed down to enjoy a woman this way before now. The thought had never occurred to him, but Jennifer was different. He wanted to enjoy her fully, completely.

She arched her hips upward, shoving herself against his pelvis. He rocked back and forth, then up and down. His fingers scaled downward, playing across her baby-fine skin and stopping just above her warm mound.

His hand inched downward, possessively covering the downy rise. With a single finger, he parted the delicate folds and found the tight nub at the heart of her sex. The air left her lungs in an audible rush.

"Let's get you out of these damn shorts," he said to her.

She lifted her hips and helped him unbutton and shove her wet clothes down over her hips. He threw them in the same general direction of her bra. The poor excuse for panties—nothing more than a triangle of fabric—went next.

Taking her hand, he guided it to his turgid erection. "See what you do to me?"

Her throaty sigh echoed through the dark cellar. She pulled back her hand and he rose to his knees.

Jennifer gazed up at Kyle who was wearing nothing but a captivating smile. Everything about him seemed strong, hard. Irresistibly masculine. A whisk of dark hair unfurled into a coarse dense thicket below his navel. Aimed right at her, his shaft surged out from between powerful thighs.

"Jenny," he said, his tone as seductive as his eyes, which were exploring her body a scant inch at a time.

Her name on his lips, an echo from years past, sent a stab of raw pain to the depths of her soul.

She stared up at the shadowy ceiling, its beams casting dark bars of light above her. What was she doing? she asked herself. In an instant, the answer came.

She had wanted this man. No matter what the consequences. She intended to lose herself in him, in this moment—to forget the past.

And what troubles tomorrow might bring.

Kyle bent down and brushed her tummy with his lips. Trailing moist kisses, he roved lower and lower until his mouth found the forbidden heat between her thighs. The rasp of his beard against her sensitive skin was unbelievably arousing. Her heart beating in erratic, uneven lurches, she couldn't resist arching her buttocks asking for more.

Suddenly, she sensed herself fracturing in a thousand tiny, explosive pieces, then Kyle pulled back.

"Keep going!"

He smiled, a cocksure grin that said he had her number. Balanced on his knees, he guided the velvet-smooth tip of his penis between her thighs. Slipping slowly up, then down, he stroked her ultra-sensitive skin with expert precision. Each caress threatened to trigger a core meltdown.

She gasped, "Oh, my. I—I—"

"Sweetheart, now's not the time for an intellectual discussion," he said in a raspy undertone. "Trust me on this."

She tried to giggle, but a choked sound came out instead. He kept fondling her with the tip of his penis and smiling down at her.

"A-aren't you going to . . . you know."

"No, what?"

"Don't joke. Get on with it."

He eased the bulbous head of his shaft into her body. She stiffened, already realizing how large he was and bracing herself.

"Is this what you want . . . Jenny? Tell me."

Her pulse, already tripping over itself, skyrocketed. "Yes, oh, yes."

"Say it."

"I . . . I want . . . you."

"Who do you want? Tell me."

"I—I want you . . . Kyle." The words came out in a breathless rush.

"And I want you, Jenny. I always have. I always will."

He repositioned himself, his upper body settling heavily against hers, the mat of hair on his chest flattening her flushed nipples. His hips cocked and the iron heat of his sex penetrated her, stretching her thighs apart with a forceful thrust.

He delved deeper, hunkering down and burrowing further into her body until he could go no more. The mindless, shuddering satisfaction of having him inside her knocked her breath from her lungs. True, she didn't have much experience making love, but she thought she knew what pleasure sex could give.

Wrong.

This was altogether different and totally unexpected. Her throat constricted as he began to move inside her with a moan so tortured it sounded as if he was in physical pain. His groan came from deep in his chest, but it reverberated through her entire body in a way that was uniquely erotic.

With both hands, he lifted her hips to deepen the angle of his thrusts. Her heart thrummed noisily, painfully. She shuddered as he cradled her face in his hands, and sighed as his lips smothered hers in a mind-searing kiss.

Jennifer forced her eyes to open and found she was gazing directly into his. The white-hot green of his irises bored into her with mind-startling intensity. There had always been something so compelling about Kyle.

He pumped up and down, entering her body, then withdrawing in seconds only to reenter again. She gasped, attempting to draw vital air into her lungs as the tempo of her body matched his. The sweet feel of imminent release spiraled through her in a heady rush.

Heaven help her! This was it!

A rainbow of stars blinded her for a moment, then she floated, serene on an imaginary carpet of sweet-smelling rose petals. She closed her eyes and tried to catch her breath.

Kyle had to admit this was the best sex he'd ever had, and yet it had been so much . . . more. Jennifer touched a part of him, a place he would have sworn had been snuffed out long ago on an airstrip in Greneda. His father's friends had described in detail his father's heroic death. Losing his only parent, a father he loved, had taken something out of Kyle.

In the two years that followed, living in foster homes too brutal to think about, he'd developed an emotional shield. Only once since his father's death had he allowed his guard to slip and to care about what happened to another person. That chink in his emotional armor had damn nearly gotten him killed.

What in hell was he doing with Jennifer?

Jennifer hadn't made him feel sorry for her—the way the woman in Libya had. No, Jennifer had reached him on another emotional plane entirely. She'd brought back the past, the wonder and passion of their brief time together.

Making love to Jennifer had been an unexpectedly moving experience. But as he looked at her now, he knew something was troubling her. No doubt she was giving herself hell for having sex with him while engaged to another man.

Chad Roberts was history. No way could Jennifer make love to him and still want to marry Chad. She wasn't the kind of woman to be disloyal.

Her lips were still moist from his kisses. The lower one appeared fuller than usual, making him tempted to kiss her again—and start all over. As if reading his mind, she looked away, drawing her knees up to her chest and wrapping her arms around them.

She's withdrawing, he thought, but he didn't know what to do or say. Putting his feeling in words wasn't something he'd ever been comfortable doing.

"Jen?" He put his hand on her smooth shoulder.

She turned her head to face him. His instinctive response to her was so powerful that it stunned him. How had it happened so quickly?

A searing bolt of lightning so intense its light speared

through the gaps in the cellar's door lit up the room. Almost immediately a bolt of thunder rocked the earth, the jolt so ferocious the stone floor beneath them rumbled.

"Jeez-us!" Kyle pulled Jennifer into his arm.

Cree-aaak! The strange sound was followed by a reverberating crash, then a series of splintering sounds.

"Oh, my God! What is it?" Jennifer cried.

"I think lightning struck the big gumbo limbo tree in the garden. Sounds like it fell against the house."

"That's too bad. I couldn't see much, but it looked like a grand old mansion like Thunder Island."

"This is one of the oldest historic homes in Key West," Kyle said, his arm still around Jennifer. "I'd better check the radio and see what's going on out there."

Jennifer almost looked away when Kyle stood up and walked across the cellar without bothering to cover himself. Wait. She'd just made love to this man. Why was she feeling so self-conscious?

She watched him, not quite believing she'd actually made love to him again. How many years had she waited to feel his arms around her again, to feel his powerful body filling hers with a surge of raw energy too awesome to describe?

He was even more exciting than she'd remembered. He'd been a boy the first time they'd made love, a little too eager, a little too hurried. Now he was a man, an experienced, inventive lover.

He had an edge to him now that hadn't been there years ago. It suddenly struck her that Kyle was so much like his father. Kyle was the image of Vincent Parker, something she hadn't noticed as much when he'd been younger. He had the same way of holding back his emotions that had prevented his father from committing to her mother until it was too late.

She told herself it didn't matter. She'd been down this

road before, and she knew where it led. Straight to heartbreak.

How could she have been so utterly stupid?

Why on earth had she allowed herself to make love to Kyle while she was engaged to another man? It went against everything she believed. Love and loyalty were synonymous.

She owed it to Chad to discuss . . . Discuss what? She pondered what to tell him while she gathered up her clothes and put them on. Didn't she love Chad? She would have sworn she did, but tonight made her question her feelings.

Was it unfinished business with Kyle, or was it something more?

Kyle shoved the radio back into its case, saying, "The storm's changed course again. It's veered north toward Key Largo. The brunt of it missed us. The worst is over."

He stepped into his shorts without bothering to put on his underwear. Fascinated, she watched him shrug into his shirt.

He said, "Let's get out of here and see how bad the damage is. We may be able to help."

"Right. They'll need S&R units."

"He's coming home. Thank You, God. Thank You." Thelma Mae said the words out loud as she hauled another deck chair onto the beach behind Thunder Island.

The hurricane had spared Key West, this time. Electricity was out as well as the telephones, and a water main was broken, according to the radio, but this was nothing compared with Georges' devastation.

How lucky could she get? Her prayers had been answered. Thunder Island and been spared.

And he was coming home.

"Let me do that."

Chuck came up on Thelma Mae, taking her by surprise. Beside him walked Raven and Lisa. Thelma Mae allowed them to line up the beach chairs and Italian café style umbrellas in the sand.

"We have the beach to ourselves," Plotzy proclaimed as he sauntered toward Thelma Mae, wearing his usual outfit of Speedos and leopard-print suspenders. "The tourists hightailed it the minute the sun came up."

"I'm not worried. People have short memories. By the weekend, Hurricane Frances will be ancient history, and tourists will pour back into Key West."

"Right-o," Plotzy responded in his absentminded way, his gaze tracking the trio on the beach. "Golly, looks like Chuck has the hots for Raven and Lisa doesn't like it one bit. She's sticking to her brother like white on rice."

"Maybe she's afraid Raven will hurt Chuck. You can't blame Lisa for being protective of her brother. After all, when she had leukemia and needed a bone marrow transplant, Chuck came through for her."

"Lisa had leukemia? You don't say. You could never tell by looking at her."

Thelma Mae silently sighed to herself. They'd broken the mold when they'd created Plotzy. They'd discussed Lisa's leukemia and bone marrow transplant several other times. Plotzy retained only what was important to him.

"If you ask me," he said in a conspiratorial whisper, "Chuck and Lisa are a whole lot closer than twins should be."

Thelma Mae shrugged off the comment even though she agreed. There was something unusual about the twins. "A life threatening illness and the bone transplant brought them closer."

"Right-o. Inheriting billions from their parents' pharmaceutical company probably helped, too."

What Plotzy chose to remember was amazing. She'd mentioned their inheritance only once. She'd marveled at

Lisa's remarkable recovery many times, but Plotzy hadn't retained that part of the story.

"Like you, Plotzy, Chuck and Lisa made their money the old fashioned way. They inherited it."

"Right-o," Plotzy agreed with his goofy smile. It never occurred to him to be apologetic for never having worked a day in his life. "Like me, Chuck's a hunk. A rich hunk."

Thelma Mae stifled a laugh. Plotzy was gay, but he was a misfit even here in Key West where just about anything could pass for normal.

Lisa left her brother with Raven and bounced across the sand to them. "Kyle didn't make it home last night. Have you heard from him?"

"No. I assume he stayed out at the base." Thelma Mae considered Lisa's interest in Kyle healthy. She didn't need to spend every waking moment being her brother's keeper.

Plotzy released a noisy sigh as Lisa rushed back to where her brother was helping Raven set up an oversize umbrella. "Kyle Parker. Now there is a hunk to end all hunks."

Kyle was the essence of masculinity, she thought, but another hunk who was even more gorgeous would be arriving soon. She wandered off to tend her orchids, wondering what he would add to the sexual highjinks going on at Thunder Island.

Chapter 21

Kyle sat on the rail while Chuck poured cocktails for the group gathered on Thunder Island's back porch. Three days had passed since Hurricane Frances decided to spare Key West. During that time Jennifer had done everything she could to avoid him. He'd given her space.

What choice did he have?

Every day after class, she rushed off to the clinic to visit Sadie. Then Jennifer spent hours on the firing range. It had been well after one each night when she tiptoed up the hall and quietly let herself into her room.

Why was she avoiding him?

"Nothing to drink for me," Raven told Chuck, breaking into Kyle's thoughts. "The club reopened. I'm dancing tonight."

"That's too bad."

Kyle silently agreed with Chuck. Even though the hurricane had done little damage to the key, the tourists had fled. Most of the bars and restaurants on Duval Street had been closed. It was a rare moment in paradise—locals only time.

"Oh, my," Lisa said. She'd been sitting in the long shadows cast by the setting sun, not saying anything. "Who's the stud with Thelma Mae?"

Kyle looked toward the side of the house where Thelma Mae was showing the beach to a tall man with black hair and dark, striking eyes.

Chuck gazed at Raven, presumably to gauge her reaction to the handsome stranger, but Raven hadn't bothered to turn around. "Fun's over," declared Chuck. "The tourists are back."

"You mean the fun's just beginning," his sister said with a wink.

Kyle could have been annoyed at how quickly Lisa went for another man after she'd spent the last few days coming on to him, but he wasn't. His mind was on Jennifer. The next time he saw her they were going to have a serious talk.

Thelma Mae promenaded across the lush lawn on the stranger's arm. The man was young enough to be her son, but any fool could see how taken she was with him. She giggled at something the guy said and lowered her lashes flirtatiously.

This was a side of the cool Thelma Mae that Kyle hadn't seen. She was an insular woman with a dark undertow to her personality. Kyle wasn't positive he would like her if he really knew her.

"This is Tyler Langley," Thelma Mae announced with unmistakable pride.

As she proceeded to introduce Langley to everyone, Kyle studied the man. It was hard to dislike the guy. Tyler Langley had an easy smile and an unaffected manner despite his good looks.

"Right-o," Plotzy called as he bounded up to the porch from the beach. As usual he had once again avoided "the curse'' by being in the ocean when the sun set, but he'd spotted the handsome stranger anyway.

Kyle gave Langley credit for acting as if everyone wore faded Speedos with leopard-print suspenders when they went swimming. Tyler said, ''Hi, there,'' as he shook Plotzy's extended hand.

Raven might not have bothered to look at Tyler when they had first seen him, but now she couldn't keep her eyes off the guy. Chuck was not a happy camper, Kyle decided as he watched the way Chuck was frowning.

Out of the blue, Plotzy told Tyler, ''Jennifer threatened to turn me into a toad.''

Now, that would be an improvement.

Tyler chuckled. ''I haven't met Jennifer, but I like her already.''

Look, buddy, don't even *think* about Jennifer.

''Where is Jennifer these days?'' asked Chuck. ''We haven't seen much of her lately.''

''She'll be here soon,'' Plotzy told Tyler, even though the stranger didn't know Jennifer and hadn't asked the question. ''She's bringing Sadie home this evening.''

Unfuckingbelievable! The looneytune Plotzy knew more about Jennifer than he did.

Jennifer lifted Sadie out of her car and gently put her on the footpath leading to Thunder Island. The dog hobbled along, doing amazingly well on three legs.

''Atta girl, Sadie. You're almost home.''

The sun had set but the sky was fired with its afterglow, backlighting the trees lining the path with a hazy wash of gold. Ahead near Thunder Island's gate, she saw a man leaning against the white picket fence. Sadie spotted him and immediately her tail surged upward, wagging joyfully.

Kyle strode toward them, but it was too shadowy to see the expression on his face. She'd successfully avoided him for the last few days. She didn't want to see him now. No matter how she'd suffered in the past, no matter what her rational brain told her, something inside her traitorous body responded to Kyle.

In spite of what had happened.

"Hey, Sadie," Kyle said. "Look at you. We're going to have to call you gimp."

Sadie's tail chopped the air, and she danced a three-legged jig. Kyle bent down and fondly petted Sadie's head. He took one long ear in each hand and jiggled them.

He looked up at Jennifer, saying, "You should have asked me to help you."

"We managed."

Kyle stood up and stared down at her. "What's going on? Why are you avoiding me?"

She gazed into his intense green eyes and saw something she didn't quite recognize. She wasn't sure if he was angry, or something even more ominous.

"I don't know what I was thinking. I love Chad."

Before she could protest, he hauled her into his arms. "You sure as hell have a strange way of showing how crazy you are about Chad Roberts."

She pulled away and silently cursed herself. "It's just because you were the first man I cared about. Puppy love."

"Well, call me a dog."

There was something so cute about the way he said it that she almost smiled. Almost. Experience had taught her to be cautious where Kyle was concerned. She was far, far too vulnerable to his charm.

"Look, Kyle, I've got to think."

"About what?"

"How I feel about . . ." She intended to say "you," but stopped herself, astonished that she wasn't thinking of Chad first.

"About me?" he asked with another adorable grin.

"Hey, Kyle! Jennifer," Chuck called from the porch. "Hurry up. Dinner's being served."

Thelma Mae loved stirring the pot. She loved to cook and throw in unusual ingredients. Even more, she loved to throw odd people together and see what fireworks followed. She glanced around the table, terribly pleased with herself.

Tyler Langley had ratcheted up the testosterone level at Thunder Island. Chuck was glowering at Tyler while Kyle silently ate his dinner. All the women were fascinated by Tyler's deep sea diving stories.

"Now that Mel Fisher is dead, Key West could use another treasure hunter," Jennifer said.

Kyle silently watched Jennifer as she spoke. Thelma Mae smiled to herself. A new box of condoms—French Ticklers—had appeared in Kyle's nightstand two days ago. So far, not one had been used.

Jennifer was too loyal to fool around with Kyle, Thelma Mae assured herself. She had made an exception by letting Jennifer move into Thunder Island ahead of the others on the waiting list. She didn't want to be disappointed in Jennifer's character.

Tyler smiled at Jennifer, then turned to Raven and Lisa seated to his right, saying, "I believe the Atochia is not the only wreck in the area. Mel got lucky when he found it."

"Lucky," scoffed Chuck. "The man searched for years and spent a fortune to find the Atochia."

"Right-o," added Plotzy. "I knew Mel and he was a hard worker."

Thelma Mae nearly gagged on the cold cucumber soup with just a hint of sorrel. Mel Fisher had been one of the friendliest men in town, never failing to smile and wave at the locals. That's how Plotzy knew Mel, but, like the women at the table, Plotzy was enchanted by Tyler and was angling for a way to get his attention.

"I have the greatest respect for Mel, but I have some ideas of my own."

As Tyler said this, he winked at Thelma Mae. She beamed back at him. The world was full of men. Only a few of them were special.

"Whose soup is that?" asked Raven, indicating the empty place across from Thelma Mae.

Thelma Mae had been wondering when someone would notice. She had a very strict rule about showing up for dinner on time. If you didn't arrive when the first course was served, the china was removed and you missed dinner.

She'd never made an exception. Until now.

"I'm expecting a guest. His plane must have been late. He'll be along shortly."

"Really?" Chuck and Lisa said in unison. Sometimes she thought the twins were joined at the hip. Their minds were often on the same track. "You're making an exception to Rule 9?"

"Some rules are meant to be broken," Tyler said with what could only be interpreted as a suggestive smile at Raven.

Chuck's brows drew together so tightly a furrow appeared between his eyes. He looked as if he was preparing to break something, but it wasn't a rule. Thelma Mae smiled inwardly. Boy, oh, boy did she love stirring the pot. And it was only going to get better.

Kyle watched Tyler bullshit everyone, laying it on with the devil's own smile. Kyle didn't know what to make of the man. He was full of himself in a strange way. Tyler Langley didn't seem to be taken by his looks, which had captivated every female at the table, but Langley wanted everyone to be impressed by his abilities as a treasure hunter.

Why? Kyle wondered. Tyler hadn't mentioned any experience to speak of, unless you counted commercial scuba diving with tourists in the Cayman Islands. That Tyler could even think about stepping into Mel Fisher's shoes took balls.

"Tell us about the treasure you've found," Jennifer said. She hadn't spared Kyle more than a quick glance, but she looked at him for an instant as she questioned Tyler.

Tyler hesitated for the briefest of seconds—hardly enough time to blink—but long enough to make Kyle suspicious. "I've uncovered several significant pieces." He leaned forward with a smile, implying he was letting them in on a deep dark secret. "I can't say what because word might get out—"

"And someone else might steal your find," Lisa finished for him.

Kyle's eyes met Jennifer's. He knew they were both thinking the same thing. Tyler Langley was not in Key West to hunt sunken treasure. What was he after?

"Oh, my stars!" cried Thelma Mae. "There you are."

Kyle looked toward the doorway and saw Spike—Chad—Roberts walking into the dining room. Just his luck. When he was finally getting somewhere with Jennifer the cocky jerk shows up.

Kyle had no doubt women flipped over Chad. He had blond sun-streaked hair and pale-blue eyes, the type of looks and attitude Kyle associated with surfers. Sure as hell, you'd never think Roberts was with the DEA just by looking at him.

"Chad! What a surprise. I thought you were going to call." Lisa jumped up and raced over to Chad. She threw her arms around him, pressing every inch of her voluptuous body against his. The deep-throat kiss that followed left the table in astonished silence.

Kyle's gaze cut to Jennifer. She was staring at the couple with something too intense to be mere shock. She bit down on her full lower lip, then her eyes shifted to him.

"Hey, you two," Kyle said to break the tension. "You'd better come up for air."

As he said it, Kyle noticed the tight expression on Thelma Mae's face. Chuck seemed to be pissed off at the spectacle his sister was making of herself. For some strange reason, Plotzy appeared to be as upset as Chuck, which didn't make any sense. How could Plotzy know Chad? What was Chad doing here anyway?

"Thelma Mae, baby," Chad said as he wrenched himself out of Lisa's clutches. He had the gall to smile at everyone as if the scene with Lisa had been totally natural and head for the open place opposite Thelma Mae. "Sorry I'm late."

Kyle noted Chad neglected to say why he'd been late. Thelma Mae didn't ask. Her pinched expression disappeared as Chad dropped into the seat opposite her.

Kyle stole a sideways glance at Jennifer. She was idly playing with her wine glass as if this man meant nothing to her. Chad had yet to look at Jennifer or even glance in her direction.

Why not?

Granted, Roberts might want to keep his so-called engagement from being public knowledge to protect Jennifer from drug lords, but Kyle clearly recalled what Sam Halford had told him. The son of a bitch might have used the engagement bit to lure Jennifer into bed.

Jennifer waited, silently fuming while Chad flirted with Lisa. What was going on here? Lisa acted as if *she* were the one engaged to Chad.

She concentrated on the main course being served, conch chowder. Thelma Mae prepared the traditional dish with a unique flair by adding calamari and bay scallops to the dish. It was usually one of Jennifer's favorite meals, but tonight she had to force herself to eat.

She was all too conscious of Kyle watching her, and she didn't want him to know how upset she was. Upset and confused. On one level she was furious with Chad for ignoring her, yet on another level, she was relieved. She couldn't possibly love Chad the way she'd thought and still have become involved with Kyle.

How do you feel?

Jennifer's silent question to herself was difficult to answer. For so many years, she'd worked hard at *avoiding* heartfelt emotion. Precisely because there was a casualness about Chad, she had felt safe with him, knowing he didn't expect too much from her.

Kyle was completely different. He would accept nothing short of total commitment, something she could not give without opening a door to the past that she was determined should remain shut.

"How did you find out about Thunder Island?" Kyle asked Chad, interrupting her thoughts.

Chad glanced at Lisa, then looked across the table at Thelma Mae. The older woman smiled, a fond almost affectionate smile. Jennifer found Thelma Mae's reaction odd. The woman was usually all business, yet tonight she'd saved a place for Chad and now was smiling at him with the same pleased expression she'd shown with Tyler. If she had a thing for younger men, it didn't include Kyle or Chuck.

"I was down here on a top secret project," Chad responded to the question. "Someone brought me to Thunder Island, and I've been coming ever since."

What? Jennifer silently contradicted Chad. When they'd been in Miami, he had told her in detail of how he'd sought out Thelma Mae Horton. She had been the mother of a DEA buddy who had been killed in Colombia. The two had become friends, and he visited when he could.

Why would Chad deliberately not tell the truth about such a simple matter?

Finally, the group rose and went out onto the terrace to enjoy dessert and coffee. Instead of following everyone, Jennifer went down the hall and into the laundry room to check on Sadie. Although the dog could walk, Sadie wasn't able to get up the stairs to Jennifer's room. Thelma Mae had agreed to let Sadie stay down here until the cast was removed.

She opened the door and flicked on the light. Lurching to one side, Sadie staggered to her feet, tail wagging. Jennifer dropped to her knees and fondled Sadie's ears the way Kyle did, jiggling them.

"You're wondering what you did to get shut in here, aren't you, girl?"

Sadie licked her hand and wagged her tail even harder.

"I could carry her up and down the stairs for you. That way Sadie could stay in your room."

She started, turning slowly, not having heard Kyle come up behind her.

"That would be great. Thanks. I'll need to walk her outside first."

Sadie scrambled toward Kyle, ridiculously happy to see him. They walked the dog out to the side yard near the swimming pool. Jennifer waited, expecting some smart-aleck comment about the way Chad had taken up with Lisa, but Kyle remained silent as they let Sadie do her business.

It wasn't until they were back in the house at the bottom of the stairs that he spoke, "Okay, Sadie, here we go."

He effortlessly lifted the bloodhound into his arms and carried her up the stairs. Jennifer opened the door to her room, instantly regretting she hadn't taken the time to put things away. The T-shirt she slept in was tossed across the unmade bed. The message in hot pink script was still visible:

Anyone Who Says Money Can't Buy Happiness
Doesn't Know Where To Shop.

Kyle put Sadie down on the braided rug next to the bed. He towered over Jennifer, asking, "What in hell is going on with Roberts?"

Jennifer shrugged, acting as if she didn't care, but the way Chad ignored her had been terribly embarrassing. Worse, she'd discovered the man she thought she wanted to marry was a liar. Being involved with him demonstrated what poor judgment she had when it came to men. It would be a long, long time before she allowed herself to become involved with a man.

She turned away from Kyle, but he spun her around to face him. "Roberts is a nut case. If I'm away from you for five minutes, it's all I can do to keep my hands off you. I'd be damned if I could be separated from you for weeks and not kiss you the second I saw you again."

Before she could respond, he bent down and gently kissed her lips. It was a short, fleeting kiss, but one of indescribable sweetness. Without another word, he turned and walked out the door.

Chapter 22

Jennifer made herself wait and see if Chad would come to her and explain his behavior. She sat in her room and watched Sadie make herself comfortable on the rug next to her bed. She thought about Chad, but her mind kept straying to Kyle.

"If I'm away from you for five minutes, it's all I can do to keep my hands off you. I'd be damned if I could be separated from you for weeks and not kiss you the second I saw you again."

Kyle had sounded so sincere, and the look in his eyes echoed his voice. He did care about her. What about Chad?

She walked over to the French doors that opened onto the balcony and swung them open, thinking. Through the half-closed plantation shutters she caught a glimpse of Kyle standing by his desk, his back to her.

He'd taken off his shirt, and his low-riding cut-offs gloved his slim hips. He was built like a V from the breadth of his shoulders where they joined the column of his neck to his lean, powerful legs. Except for the scar on his knee, he was perfect. Physically.

Kyle was nothing like Chad. Nothing. Chad was shallow and a liar, she reluctantly admitted. Who knew what went on inside his head.

She forced herself to look away from Kyle and truly examine what was going on inside her mixed up brain. Had the episode with Chad been some sort of weird interlude? At the time, it had seemed so *right.*

The way Chad behaved tonight confirmed he wasn't as much in love with her as he had seemed. No wonder he hadn't given her a ring. Had he been playing a game with her?

She walked back inside, trying hard not to steal a glance at Kyle, who was still standing near the desk. He'd never seemed so appealing as when he'd carried Sadie up the stairs, knowing she couldn't possibly carry the dog and realizing how much she wanted to keep Sadie with her.

"I made a terrible mistake with Chad," she whispered to the sleeping dog.

Sadie didn't move, but Jennifer recalled the bloodhound barely tolerated Chad, but she was crazy about Kyle. She'd flipped for him right away.

"What is Chad's game?"

Sadie didn't answer, of course. The dog seemed to be dreaming about S&R work. Except for the paw in the cast, her other legs were twitching and her nostrils kept flaring in and out as if she were trying to pick up a scent.

"What are you waiting for?" she said out loud. "Find out what's going on with Chad."

She slipped out of the room, taking care not to awaken Sadie, and went down the stairs to look for Chad. She pivoted around the bend in the stairs, hand on the newel post, and nearly slammed into him.

"Hey, sweetheart, there you are," he said with a smile.

She refused to allow him to con her. "I want to talk to you."

"Ditto," he said, taking her arm and turning her so she headed up the stairs with him. "Let's go to my room."

Before she could protest, he stopped on the landing near a watercolor of a famous Key West landmark, the Donkey Milk House. He pressed a panel of highly polished oak next to the painting. The panel slid back to reveal a secret stairway.

"Sheesh! I've walked by this every day and never knew it was here."

"There's a lot you don't know." He nudged her up the stairs.

She climbed the narrow stairs and found herself in a small but airy room lit by a single lamp. A quick look around told her that she was in the widow's waiting room behind Thunder Island's widow's walk. She had seen it from the outside of the house many times.

"Thelma Mae said this was a false room," she said over her shoulder to Chad. "She claimed there wasn't any way up here."

He slid his hands around her waist. "It's top secret—reserved for very special people."

She shoved his arms away. "Let's talk."

He gestured toward the bed where his duffel had been thrown. The only other place to sit down was the small stool in the corner near the telescope trained on the beach. On the small nightstand next to the bed was a military-style knife.

She stayed where she was. "What's going on?"

He folded his arms across his chest with an angry glint in his eye. "I think it's pretty clear what's happening. You're getting it on with Kyle Parker."

"What?"

How could he pick up on that from the brief interlude at the dinner table when Chad had been so absorbed with Lisa that he'd barely noticed her?

"Any fool can see the two of you have been humping like weasels."

Chad couldn't know anything about what happened with Kyle—unless Kyle had told him. While she doubted it, she couldn't rule out the possibility.

"I'm engaged to you. Why would I—"

Chad barked a sound that didn't come close to a laugh. "I've known Parker for years. He's the original ass man. Did you tell him we were engaged?"

She hesitated, knowing Chad had sworn her to secrecy.

"I told you not to mention it to anyone. The cartel wouldn't hesitate to kill you to get back at me," he reminded her with a disgusted look. "And Parker would consider it a challenge to screw you knowing you were my woman."

"My woman?" She hated that term. This wasn't the man she'd known in Miami. The Chad Roberts standing before her was another man, an arrogant jerk. "I'm not your woman. I'm not anybody's woman."

Chad raked his fingers through his sun-bleached hair. "I didn't mean it the way it sounded. I just meant Kyle Parker would do anything to get you if he knew we were engaged. Did you tell him?"

She shrugged as she nodded. "We're old friends. I knew him when we were kids. It's safe to confide in him."

"Really?" Chad responded, his tone implying he didn't quite believe her. "You never mentioned Parker."

"Why would I? It was years ago. I didn't realize you two knew each other."

"Did Parker tell you about Panama?"

"He said he'd run into you down there."

Chad flopped down onto the bed and lounged against the pillows that were propped up along the rattan headboard. "Did he tell you about a certain *señorita* who decided she liked me better than she did him?"

"No-o-o," she slowly conceded, wondering what else Kyle hadn't told her.

"Don't get me wrong. Parker was an ace when it came to operations, but his weakness is women. It almost got him killed in Libya. Did he tell you about that?"

She shook her head, realizing Kyle had told her virtually nothing about himself. The warning bell inside her head had been correct. She had been wise not to tell Kyle *everything.*

"Funny." Chad smirked. "Kyle will always walk with a bit of a limp because of a piece of tail, yet he hasn't told you about her."

She mustered a half smile as if this bit of information didn't mean a thing to her, but inwardly she was shocked at how hurt she was. She had almost forgiven Kyle for what happened years ago. After all, they had been so young then, hardly in charge of their own destinies.

That was then and this was now.

Kyle had avoided numerous opportunities to discuss the past with her. He could have shared part of himself with her, but he hadn't. Once again it struck her how much he was like his father.

"I think we should put our engagement on hold until you figure out how you feel about Kyle Parker," Chad said.

"You're right," she replied without hesitation. "Since I never had a ring, it wasn't a real engagement anyway, was it?"

Chad gave her a sheepish smile, obviously pleased to be getting off the hook. "Yeah, I guess not."

Jennifer left the secret room without closing the door behind her. She was down the stairs opening the hidden panel before she realized how smoothly Chad Roberts had turned the tables on her. He hadn't given her a chance to ask about his flirting with Lisa. He'd cornered her and made her defend herself, seizing the opportunity to back out of their engagement.

On one level she was relieved. She had nearly made a dreadful mistake. But on another level, she was even more disturbed than before.

"What is wrong with me?" she whispered to herself. How could she ever have thought she was in love with Chad? He was nothing like the man she had fallen in love with.

Nothing.

Her problems went back to the time she *never* thought about, the time after her mother had killed herself.

"Don't go there," she said out loud, opening the door to her room. "Don't even think about it."

She closed the door, marveling that Sadie hadn't awakened. She tiptoed across the room and forced her thoughts away from that depressing time. Had Kyle deliberately seduced her because he had some macho thing going with Chad? It didn't seem that way to her.

But she obviously wasn't much of a judge of men. Going back to her first love, Kyle, then returning to the present time, she had made more than her share of poor choices.

Thelma Mae hid in the shadows outside Chuck's room. The twins were arguing, but Thunder Island's walls were too thick to hear what they were saying.

"Stirring the pot again, huh?"

She flinched at the raspy whisper, even though she recognized Plotzy's voice. How had he managed to sneak up on her? Was she losing her touch?

"Pot. Did you say 'pot'?" she asked, positive she'd misunderstood him.

"Remember back in '82 you told me you loved to stir the pot by mixing explosive personalities."

Slack-jawed, Thelma Mae motioned for Plotzy to follow her down the hall where they could talk. The man barely remembered to put on clothes before leaving his room, yet he recalled something she'd told him years ago.

"You've really done it this time," Plotzy told her. "All the women were drooling over Tyler, then Chad arrived. Now we wait for the fireworks."

That had been exactly what she planned, but she was astounded to learn Plotzy had picked up on it.

"Chuck and Chad and Tyler. What hunks," Plotzy said with a sigh. "Kyle's not bad, either."

"Forget it, Plotzy. They're straight."

"What a waste."

"What are the twins arguing about?" she asked, even though Plotzy couldn't hear any more than she could.

Plotzy rocked back on his heels with a smug smile. "Money."

"That's ridiculous. They're richer than Midas."

"Right-o." Plotzy toddled off down the hall.

Thelma Mae went into her own room where she found Chad waiting. He'd made himself at home and was lounging on the balcony chaise sipping a bottle of Red Dog Ale.

Thelma Mae attempted to hold her breath, but every time she saw Chad, her heart did a silly backflip. Other men were more handsome and smarter, but there was only one man like Chad.

His father.

"Welcome back," she said with a smile.

He swung his feet to the ground and faced her, the bottle of beer dangling from one hand. "No more wandering around third world countries. I've quit the DEA."

She clapped her hands. "Good for you."

"Money talks and bullshit walks. That's what I've learned. This time I'm going for the brass ring."

Based on earlier conversations, she guessed, "You're marrying for money."

"Isn't that what you did?" His pale eyes darkened dangerously. "Marry for money?"

She swallowed hard against the lump rising in her throat and forced herself to look directly into Chad's pale-blue eyes. Finally, it was out in the open. They had never discussed it until now.

"Yes, after your father left me, I had no choice. I was young, barely seventeen, and I didn't have anyone to help me." The pleading tone in her voice had no impact on him. His brows drew into a censuring frown. "Delbert Horton asked to marry me—"

"But he didn't want to get stuck with someone else's brat."

"Del thought we should have our own children."

"So you put me up for adoption just like that." He snapped his fingers so close to her face that she flinched.

"It was a terrible mistake. I—I've regretted it every day since. I—"

"Would you have given a shit if you'd been able to have another kid?"

Thelma Mae stepped back, the words hurting her as much as a physical blow. "It had *nothing* to do with not having children. I regretted giving you up immediately, but Del wouldn't change his mind."

"How hard did you try? You must have been a looker back then. You could have played the sex card—if you'd wanted to."

She felt as if her breath had been cut off. Chad could ooze charm when he wanted. Yet when the chips were down, Chad was his father all over again, a chameleon who could be sweet or as brutal as Attila the Hun.

Still, he was her son—even if the outside world didn't know it.

He stalked into her room and threw open the door of the minibar. While he helped himself to another Red Dog, Thelma Mae looked down on the beach and saw Raven walking alone.

Feeling a hand on her shoulder, Thelma Mae turned

and found Chad smiling at her—all charm again. He was his father, all right, Jeckyl and Hyde.

"It's okay. So, I was adopted by the family from hell. It wasn't your fault."

His white-toothed smile said he'd forgiven her, but she knew better. He'd suffered terribly. He would never forgive her.

And she couldn't forgive herself.

For all his faults, this was her baby boy. He'd spent years and a lot of money to find her. In his own way, he loved her as much as she loved him.

"Who are you marrying? Lisa?"

"No way. I'd have fucking Chuck hanging around all the time. Besides"—he took a long swig of beer—"I'm talking *real* money here."

"Lisa's heir to a pharmaceutical fortune."

"Carina Maria Estevez is practically royalty in Bogotá."

It sounded like drug money to Thelma Mae, but if she didn't ask, she wouldn't have to deal with it.

"What about Jennifer?"

A moment of hostile silence followed. He finally responded, "What about her?"

"You had me give her a room here. She thinks you're going to marry her."

"Did you ever think I was?"

"I had my doubts," she conceded, "mostly because of Jennifer. Like I told you earlier, she's much too interested in Kyle to be in love with you."

"Ask me if I care."

But he did care, Thelma Mae knew. The apple never fell very far from the tree. Chad was his father all over again. He didn't want Jennifer, but he didn't want anyone else to have her, either.

Chapter 23

It took a lot of willpower but Jennifer managed to temper the urge to confront Kyle. There would be plenty of time in the morning, she assured herself as she changed into her bikini for a swim. She needed to think things over once more and examine her own feelings more closely before talking to Kyle.

Restless, she slipped out of the room and left Sadie still snoozing beside the bed. The shadowy corridor was strangely silent, thanks to the tourists who'd fled Key West after the hurricane. A few had returned, but the guest house was less than half full.

Outside, the balmy air carried the fragrant scent of magnolias and night-blooming jasmine. A cat's paw of wind lofted the fronds on the trio of royal palms guarding the back terrace. The yard lights went off each night at eleven, but a lover's moon rode high above a single bannerlike cloud and lit the terraced area leading down to the water.

At the tide line, Jennifer saw someone standing and almost turned back, recalling the time she'd met Kyle on the shore. Then she realized Raven was wading in the ankle deep surf, her back to Jennifer.

What was she doing here? Raven should be fan dancing at the club now. The statuesque brunette's hair cascaded down her back, stopping at her hips where the thin strap of a gold lamé thong caught a ray of moonlight.

"Hi, there," Jennifer called softly, not wanting to startle Raven.

Raven slowly turned and fluttered her eyelashes. The light sparkled off her dark eyes, and Jennifer realized the woman had been crying. Raven swiped at her eyes with the back of her hand.

"Silly, isn't it, crying over a man?" Raven asked Jennifer, a catch in her voice.

Jennifer didn't know how to respond. She wasn't comfortable discussing her own problems. Talking about Raven's troubles made her want to walk away, but there was something so sad in Raven's voice that Jennifer forced herself to stay put.

"I've cried over a man, too," Jennifer admitted after an uncomfortable silence, "and it's never worth it. Later, you'll kick yourself."

Raven giggled, a choked sound. "I'm a two-time loser. You would have thought I would have learned my lesson with Chad."

Chad's name exploded inside Jennifer's head like a grenade. For God's sake, how many women had he been involved with?

"Chad? I thought you and Chuck . . ." Jennifer let the sentence dangle like a baited hook.

"Chad used to come from Miami to see me every weekend," Raven said. "Then he met someone else."

"When was that?" Jennifer asked, hoping she hadn't been the other woman.

Raven dug one toe into the sand. There was something graceful yet provocative about the movement, and Jennifer could well imagine Raven onstage mesmerizing the male audience. "Three years ago."

Jennifer stifled a sigh of relief.

"It took me all this time to get to the point where I could have another relationship."

"We have something in common," Jennifer explained, telling more about herself than she normally would have. "Chad pulled the same thing with me. I even believed he wanted to marry me."

Stunned, Raven gazed at her for a long moment. "Don't blame yourself. He's great at conning women."

Jennifer stared out at the ribbons of moonlight reflected on the incoming waves. "I can't believe I was such a sucker."

Raven laughed, a low, choked sound. "Now Chad's met his match."

"Lisa? His match?"

Raven gazed at her with knowing eyes. "You bet. Chuck and Lisa are much closer than ordinary twins. No one will ever come between them. I learned that the hard way. Now it's Chad's turn."

Jennifer thought for a moment, realizing Raven was correct. The twins did seem to be closer than any siblings she'd ever known. She hadn't really paid much attention, but she had picked up on something strange about them that she'd attributed to Lisa's illness.

"When Lisa had leukemia, Chuck donated his bone marrow for the transplant," she explained to Raven, although she was fairly certain the other woman already knew the story. "A traumatic experience like that brings people closer together."

Raven arched one finely sculpted eyebrow, indicating this did not satisfactorily explain the twin's relationship.

"What makes you think Lisa can hurt Chad?" she asked Raven.

"Because she has something he wants very badly." Raven paused, then added, "Money."

Jennifer thought a moment, not recalling Chad being overly interested in money, but then, she'd missed so much about him. This might not have been an aspect of his personality she'd seen when they'd been dating.

"The twins inherited the Leftram Pharmaceutical fortune, right?" Jennifer asked, vaguely recalling what Plotzy had told her—not that the man was terribly reliable.

"True, but they've run through a chunk of it. Chuck's been day trading stocks on the Internet."

"Uh-oh," Jennifer said. "It's dangerous to speculate how a stock will do based on a single day's performance. It's a good way to lose a fortune overnight."

"That's what I told Chuck," she replied, her tone fond yet sad. "He wouldn't listen. Now, Lisa's giving him hell for it." Two beats of silence followed while Raven gazed out to sea. "And she's giving him hell for being involved with me."

Jennifer reached out and touched Raven's arm with her fingertips. "Don't cry over Chuck. He isn't worth it."

Something sparked in the depths of Raven's eyes. "Yes, he is. He understands me."

"But will he cross his sister?"

"He says he will, but I doubt it. That's why I'm so upset."

"Maybe he will," Jennifer said without conviction. "Stranger things have happened."

It was after eight o'clock when Kyle knocked on Jennifer's door the following morning. No answer. Not that he was surprised. He'd lain awake for hours, staring at the ceiling fan slowly rotating over his bed, thinking about Jennifer. When he'd finally fallen asleep, he'd been so exhausted that he'd overslept for the first time in years.

"Jennifer's gone."

Kyle whipped around and found Chad Roberts standing behind him. Where in hell had he come from? Okay, okay. He must be losing it. Jennifer had so dominated his thoughts that his SEAL training hadn't kicked-in. He hadn't heard Chad come up behind him. A mistake that could prove fatal.

Chad's smile was just a hair too cocky to suit Kyle. "I carried Sadie downstairs for her."

"Great. Thanks." Kyle turned and walked down the hall, set on putting distance between himself and Chad.

"Everyone's going over to the house Trevor Adams is restoring on Angela Street," Chad said as he followed Kyle down the stairs.

Kyle wondered if "everyone" included Jennifer and decided it did. Since it was the weekend, there weren't any classes at the base. She probably would spend time at the range, then go help Trevor.

"I hear you're teaching at the base," Chad said from behind him, his tone just a touch too friendly.

"I'm teaching antiterrorism techniques." Kyle hit the main floor and headed toward the dining room where Thelma Mae put out a continental breakfast each morning.

"I quit the DEA," Chad informed him.

"That so?" Kyle helped himself to a bagel and a cup of coffee. He turned around with the full cup and almost bumped into Chad.

"Yeah, I'm tired of dragging in drug lords and being on the cartel's hit list." Chad grinned with a self-deprecating shrug, and Kyle had to admit he was handsome and charismatic, the type of man women fell for. "It's time to get married and settle down."

"Really?" He choked out the word. He'd heard Jennifer leave her room last night. He'd assumed she'd gone to settle things with Chad.

Had they made up instead?

Aw, hell. From the shit-eating grin on the guy's face, they had.

There were several other guests in the dining room, but Kyle didn't know them. He walked over to an empty table and hoped Chad got the message. Of course he didn't. Chad grabbed one of Thelma Mae's famous cinnamon rolls and a mug of coffee, then came over to sit with Kyle.

"Will you continue to teach at the base, or do you have other plans?" Chad asked as he sat down.

"I'm not sure." Kyle was so pissed he could barely get the words out.

After the way Chad had treated Jennifer last night at dinner, how could he act as if everything was okay? Was this any way to treat a woman? How could Jennifer take it? Didn't she realize she deserved better?

"I'm going to sit back and let my old lady support me," Chad said between bites.

"You're going to let Jennifer do all the work?"

"Jennifer?" Chad looked at him as if he were speaking in tongues. "You *seriously* think I would marry her?"

I would. In a heartbeat.

"Hey, Kyle, women like Jennifer are skanks. Sluts. They put out for every cock that comes along. She—"

"You sonofabitch!" Kyle lunged across the table and grabbed the prick by his throat. Before he could stop himself, Kyle slugged Chad. Like a geyser, blood erupted from Chad's nose, and he toppled backward, knocking his chair to the floor and collapsing beside it.

"Hey there, Kyle," someone called as he walked through the door of the home Trevor was restoring.

The house was a hive of activity, typical of all the rebuilding going on in Key West the last few days. Although the loss from Hurricane Frances hadn't been severe, many of the historic wooden buildings in Old Town had been damaged. The locals, always a tight-knit group and none closer than the gay community, had chipped in to help each other with the repairs.

"Langley, I'm surprised to see you here," Kyle said when he realized who had called his name. He'd been expecting Matt Jensen or Logan McCord, but not Tyler Langley. Recalling the b.s. he'd given everyone at dinner last night about becoming a treasure hunter, diving for sunken booty, it seemed out of place to find him here.

"I'm helping Trevor," Langley told him. "He's up in the attic fixing the rafters the tree split in half."

"Have you seen Jennifer?"

"Don't I wish." Langley moved closer, saying in a low voice, "You're the first straight person I've seen."

What a crock, Kyle thought. Langley's tone pissed him—big time, but his knuckles still smarted from decking Chad. Trevor and his friends were stand up guys, men you could count on to help you. That's why he was here.

"If it bothers you, leave."

Kyle bounded up the stairs without a backward glance. But he couldn't help wondering about Langley. He seemed easygoing and likable—most of the time. Yet he was lying, hiding something.

Kyle spent the rest of the day at the Angela Street house, helping Trevor and his friends repair the roof. It was tough work, since no nails could be used and still meet the Preservation Society's standards. Instead, they hammered in wooden pegs to secure the rafters and boards like the ships' carpenters who had originally built the home in Old Town.

The sun was beginning to set, and Jennifer had yet to appear. This surprised Kyle. Raven had arrived around noon with the twins, and eventually Plotzy had ambled into the house, although no one had actually caught him doing anything except talking. The permanent residents of Thunder Island were present except for Jennifer.

Thelma Mae handed Chad another ice pack to put on his nose. "The swelling's gone down. It's not broken. You should be fine by morning."

"It'll never look the same. Never."

She gazed out the window across the widow's walk at the sky washed with amber light. The sun was beginning to set. No doubt if she looked down at the beach, she would see Plotzy ready to go into the water to ward off the curse for yet another day.

She had been up in Chad's special room the best part of the day, nursing his bruised ego. This was a side of her child she might never have seen if it hadn't been for Kyle Parker. Her son was vain—to a fault. X rays at the Emergency Room showed nothing more than a minor crack, but he'd been terrified his nose had been ruined.

His cell phone rang, and he answered it. "It's no big deal," he told whoever was calling. "My nose didn't even swell. You don't think a wimp like Kyle Parker can get the best of me, do you?"

Kyle a wimp? That was stretching the truth beyond its limits. Thelma Mae would have laughed except Chad was so much like his father. It was positively chilling.

He could lie even more easily than he told the truth. Like father, like son, she thought with an inward sigh. After saying how anxious he was to marry her and give their child his name, he vanished the day after she'd told him she was pregnant.

Still, even without having met him, Chad was remarkably like Lance Peterson. The resemblance wasn't physical. Their personalities were so similar that it frightened her at times.

"A party in Truman Annex?" Chad perked up as he said this, sliding the ice bag off his nose. "Sounds like a winner."

Truman Annex. The exclusive enclave adjacent to the Little White House, used first by Truman and later by Kennedy, was home to some of the wealthiest residents in Key West. She wondered who was giving the party, and secretly hoped Chad would bring her along.

She lived just outside Old Town in an area of restored mansions mingled with others yet to be brought back to their original glory. Truman Annex was brand new, but built in typical Key West style with wooden buildings encircled by wide verandahs and eaves dripping with gingerbread scrollwork. It would be interesting to go inside one and compare it to Thunder Island.

There would be no comparison, of course, but it would be fun to look anyway. She hadn't had much social life since Delbert died nearly twenty years ago. Thunder Island was her life.

Until now.

Now she had a son, someone in her life besides a rambling old mansion that required constant upkeep, and a garden full of rare, exotic orchids. Having Chad back, despite his faults, energized her in a way nothing else had since the day she'd looked into his adorable face.

Then handed him to the nurse, giving him up for adoption.

Chad surged to his feet, his nose momentarily forgotten. "That was Lisa. The gang's meeting at Mallory Dock to watch the sunset. Then we're going to party at Clive Burrough's home."

He shrugged out of his T-shirt, tossed it on the floor and pulled a fresh polo shirt off a hanger in the closet.

"Don't get into any more fights with Kyle."

"Not to worry. I can fix his ass anytime."

She didn't want to ask how, so she kept her mouth shut.

"Jennifer Whitmore is his hot button. All I have to do is get into her pants again." He shoved his shirttail into the back of his khaki shorts. "Shit! That'll be like taking candy from a baby."

He was out the door and halfway down the stairs before she could say, good-bye.

Chapter 24

Jennifer questioned the wisdom of taking Sadie to meet the gang at Mallory Dock. It was the scene to end all scenes in Key West. The fabled sunsets had become a sideshow. Droves of tourists gathered at Mallory Dock each evening at dusk to see the weird acts.

"You never know what act will turn up," she said to Sadie. "My favorite is the Dalmatian who yodels 'Dixie' while balancing on her front paws."

Sadie hobbled along beside her as they trudged through the crowd standing shoulder to shoulder watching the various acts. Ahead, she spotted Raven with Chuck and Lisa. The brunette waved, seeming very happy, and Jennifer wondered if she'd been wrong. Maybe Chuck had chosen Raven over his sister.

"Stranger things have happened," she said out loud.

A man in a Key West Sunset T-shirt and Hawaiian print swim trunks stepped in front of her, blocking her way. "Strange, babe. Wanna see strange?" He grabbed his crotch.

She elbowed him aside. "Get a life!"

Kyle walked up just as she joined the group. "Where have you been all day?" he asked.

"The rest of us were helping Trevor," added Lisa. "It took all of us to repair the damage that tree did to his roof."

Jennifer waved at Tyler, who was shouldering his way through the crowd toward them and kept her eyes on him as she responded. "I was out at the firing range, and a couple of the guys were showing me how to use a sharp shooter's rifle and scope." Out of the corner of her eye, she saw Kyle's expression tighten. "My shoulder's killing me, but I'm getting better."

Tyler was now standing beside her. "Better at what?" he asked with a suggestive wink.

"Jennifer's a crack shot," Raven told him.

"No, I'm not, but I'm trying to improve." She leaned down and stroked one of Sadie's long ears. She waited, reluctant to discuss shooting Sadie, but Tyler didn't ask.

Instead, he wanted to know, "What happened to the guy who swallowed swords? He was right over there last time I came to Key West."

"You know how it is," Chuck said, his arm around Raven. "Acts come and go. I haven't seen the sword eater in months."

The group bought margaritas from a stand and strolled around the dock looking at the various acts. Vendors sold everything from cotton candy to hats woven from sea grass and topped with small, wind-driven fans to keep the wearer cool. Jennifer thought the people watching was even more interesting than the performers. Where did some of the tourists get their clothes?

"Everybody's out to make a buck," Tyler commented as he pointed to a golden retriever, who had just completed an amazing high wire act. The dog had a bucket in his mouth. People threw dollar bills on the ground, and the dog picked them up and dropped them into the tip bucket.

"Sadie, you're not earning your keep," Jennifer joked.

"Everyone collects tips after their act," Lisa told Jennifer. "It's the only way most of these people make a living."

Jennifer noticed that Lisa had attached herself to Tyler and seemed very cool to her brother and Raven. Jennifer caught Raven's eye and the brunette looked at Lisa and rolled her eyes heavenward. Obviously, Lisa was still giving her brother trouble about Raven.

Kyle hadn't said anything. Jennifer could feel him watching her and wondered what he was thinking. She wanted to question him about what Chad had told her, but this wasn't the place to have a private conversation.

"There's Chad!" Lisa cried.

Jennifer looked through the crowd and saw Chad approaching slowly, his progress impeded by the closely packed people watching shows and awaiting sunset.

"What happened to his nose?" Tyler said.

"Don't go there," cautioned Raven with a quick glance at Kyle.

Jennifer noticed Chad's nose appeared a little red and might have been slightly off-kilter, but his appealing smile was right on target. The others returned his wide grin, but she knew the artifice behind the smile too well to respond.

"I hear it's party time," Chad announced almost too brightly.

"Clive is having a barbecue for everyone who helped fix the roof on the Angela Street house Trevor is restoring," Chuck said.

"That lets me out," Jennifer said. "I didn't lift a finger."

"Me either," Chad said, "but I helped restore one of the old homes in Coral Gables. I'll bet I could give them some good advice."

"Really?" Lisa said as if she'd just heard God Himself speak.

"Sure, honey. I had a great time doing it. There's nothing like preserving history to make you feel good."

Chad said all of this in his easygoing, sincere tone. If Jennifer didn't know better, she would have believed him, but Chad had told her that he despised construction work of any kind. Or maybe that was a lie.

She didn't know, and she was proud of herself for no longer caring. Raven caught her eye, then winked. So, Raven doubted Chad's story, too.

"Come with us anyway," Kyle said. "Trevor and Clive won't care."

Raven tugged on Chuck's hand. "We're missing the sunset."

Kyle bent over, picked up Sadie as if she were a toy poodle, and tucked her under one arm. "Don't you think she's walked enough for one day?"

"Probably," Jennifer conceded, "but I didn't want to leave her at home. She hates being alone. Sadie's used to being with me."

Kyle's eyes met hers and, surprisingly, the look wasn't censuring. "Better let me carry her over to Clive's."

She nodded, desperately trying to throttle the dizzying current racing through her. Despite everything that had happened now and in the past, she constantly had to battle her attraction to this man.

Kyle angled his shoulders sideways and plowed his way through the crowd to the edge of the dock where people were crowded against the rail to watch the setting sun. Jennifer followed, and he scooted aside, making a very small space for her.

Her rib cage pressed against the rail, Jennifer felt Kyle's free arm go around her. The evening air was warm, his body warmer yet against her back. She shivered slightly and something caught in her chest.

The three of them together. It seemed so . . . right. She

glanced up at him and the heart rendering tenderness of his gaze startled her.

Flustered, she trained her eyes on the horizon where nothing more than the top rim of the sun was still visible. Through the jewel-clear air, crystal-like shards of light sprayed across the sea, turning the turquoise water to molten gold. High in the sky, brushstroke clouds caught the last embers of the day and were transformed from stark white to russet and crimson and copper.

Dong! Dong! The bell rang, signaling another sunset in paradise. A raucous cheer from the crowd shot up to the heavens, and people began to clap and whistle. Jennifer and Kyle kept watching, not joining in the cheering.

"What are you thinking?" Kyle whispered in her ear.

She gazed into his green eyes and saw pinpricks of gold reflecting the setting sun. "I'm thinking of my mother and your father. They'll never have a chance to see a magnificent sunset like this again. I think you appreciate nature's beauty even more when you realize someone you love will never have the opportunity."

She quickly turned away before the tears came. He kissed the back of her head and hugged her. "You're right. Never forget to take the time to smell the flowers."

The sun had disappeared, and the crowd turned its attention to the amateur acts on the dock. Kyle and Jennifer watched the brilliant light slowly fade until nothing more than a lavender twilight hovered over the channel.

"Jen, what happened with Chad?" he asked quietly.

Chad and the rest of their group had also moved away from the rail and were heading toward a man in a turban who was sitting cross-legged, playing a flutelike instrument to coax a python out of a basket. As embarrassing as it was to admit she'd been a complete fool, she had no choice.

"Chad didn't want to marry me, not really. He accused me of having an affair with you, but that was just an excuse to get rid of me."

"He's a damn fool."

"No, Kyle, I'm the fool. Chad seemed to be so much fun, so easy to be with that I saw what I wanted to see. I didn't see the real man."

His gaze bore into her in silent expectation. "Why, Jen? You're so bright. Why didn't you see the real man?"

Because of you! Because of the past! She knew the answer, but she couldn't bring herself to discuss it with Kyle. She'd built a dam, a barrier in her head, and if it broke, she didn't honestly know if she could handle it.

"I thought we'd be good together," she began, certain she sounded like an idiot. "We were both so interested in our careers."

"What about having a family?"

She hesitated, then told half the truth. "No. Chad was adopted. It was a bad experience. He didn't want children."

Kyle seemed set to press the point, then changed his mind. "Okay, Chad can be pretty convincing."

"Jennifer, Kyle," Raven interrupted them. "We've had all the fun we can have. We're going over to Clive's. Are you coming?"

"In a minute," Kyle answered for her. He waited until Raven had walked away, before saying, "Do you want to go over there?"

"Not really. I'd better take Sadie home. Poor thing's exhausted."

The leg with a cast outstretched and resting on the rail, Sadie was asleep, cradled against his hip and supported by his arm. Jennifer couldn't have held her like that for two minutes, yet Kyle had picked up Sadie at least ten minutes ago.

Kyle slowly turned so Sadie's injured leg didn't suddenly fall off the rail, saying, "Let's catch a rickie to your car."

"I didn't take the car. I saw Brody as I was leaving, and he gave me a ride."

"On his Harley?"

"Sure. I put Sadie between us." She gave the dog a quick stroke. "You loved it, didn't you?"

Sleepy-eyed, the dog gazed at her. Kyle's jaw tightened, but he didn't comment. In silence, they made their way through the crowd still packed around the performers. The acts would continue until there was no one around to tip them.

"Shouldn't you let Clive know you aren't coming?" she asked Kyle.

"I'll call him from the house."

Across from Mallory Dock was Mel Fisher's Maritime Museum where Key West's rickshaws lined up to get rides. The "rickies" were two-wheeled carts pulled by buff locals who sat up front and pedaled the modified bicycle. They made their living driving tourists around the island, darting between automobiles that were often gridlocked for over an hour just to go a few blocks.

Kyle held up his arm and whistled. A rickie shot out of the line and over to them. The driver wore black bicycle shorts and a tank top cropped short to reveal a muscular torso and a tattoo of a dragon.

He skidded to a stop in front of them, saying, "It'll be extra for the dog."

"Okay."

Kyle stepped back, motioning for Jennifer to get in. Then he set Sadie at her feet, and the dog put her head on Jennifer's toes. Kyle climbed in, rocking the vehicle to one side. He settled into the seat, taking up all of the empty space.

"Thunder Island," he said, and the rickie lurched off over the uneven cobblestones. Kyle put his arm around the back of the seat, touching her shoulders without actually putting his arm around her.

The driver worked hard, standing up to pump the pedals as he turned up Green Street. They passed Duval Street, the main drag, and the tourist mecca of bars and T-shirt shops. Even though the sunset celebration was just breaking up, the open-air bars were full and different types of music blared out at them. Not that any of the commotion woke up Sadie.

The hotshot driver sped up the street, dodging between cars and skillfully avoiding pedestrians. They passed a huge poster reading:

RED NECK FESTIVAL

"Redneck Festival," she commented, trying to make conversation. "That's a new one."

"I guess Hemingway Days and the October Fest isn't enough to keep the tourist board happy. They're advertising this big time on the Internet and inviting rednecks from around the country to come for the hub cap toss, the tobacco spitting contest—"

"You're making this up."

Kyle held up both hands. "No. Honest. There's also a chance to dive for pigs' feet the way you would bob for apples. There's more, too, but I can't remember everything I read."

"Just what Key West needs," she said with a laugh.

"If Thelma Mae served dinner, we've missed it," he told her. "What about grabbing conch fritters from Frit Ta Ta?"

"Sure, sounds good."

Frit Ta Ta was a rolling cart that no one had ever seen move from the corner near Planet Hollywood. Papa Joe-Joe, one of Key West's Hemingway look alikes, ran the popular stand. Kyle told the driver where they wanted to go.

"I'll have to double back," the driver responded. "That'll be extra."

Jennifer and Kyle shared a laugh. With rickie drivers

even a handbag was extra. They worked hard and made a good living. No one seemed to mind their "extras."

They pulled up at Frit Ta Ta and Kyle jumped out. "I'm getting one for Sadie, too."

"She eats kibble. People food is bad for her."

Of course Kyle paid no attention. He got into the line at the stand with a cute grin. She couldn't help smiling, especially when Sadie sat up and looked around for Kyle. No question about it; her dog adored Kyle.

Minutes later, Kyle returned with three baskets of conch fritters and two sodas. Sadie completely forgot how tired she was and sat up while Kyle shared fritters with her. Bouncing along, eating the fritters, and looking at the historic homes in Old Town, they made small talk about the house Trevor was restoring.

She put off asking him questions about Chad or about Kyle's past in the hopes that he would turn the conversation in a more personal direction, but he didn't. They pulled up at Thunder Island and Kyle paid the driver, then carried Sadie up the path toward the dark house.

"Looks like no one's here," he said, putting Sadie down on the verandah that wrapped around the building.

"I guess everyone's over at Clive's," she said lightly to hide the uneasiness she felt at being all alone with him. Thelma Mae rarely left the house in the evening. Jennifer had been counting on finding her at home. "I'll go fill Sadie's bowl with kibble and bring it. She's starved, aren't you, girl?"

Sadie looked hungry all right, hungry for Kyle's attention. He sat down on the swing and Sadie hobbled up to him, silently begging to be petted. Jennifer left them on the side porch and went for the dog food.

When she returned with a bowl of kibble and Sadie's water bowl, she found Sadie up on the swing with Kyle, her head in his lap.

"Din-din, Sadie."

Kyle lifted her down, and the dog took her sweet time—when normally she would have bounded over—getting to her meal. Jennifer stood nearby, leaning against the railing and watching Sadie eat. She was waiting for the right moment to ask Kyle about . . . about what? Well, she could start with Chad, then see if Kyle would open up enough to tell her about Libya.

"Come here." Kyle patted the space on the swing next to him.

A familiar shiver of awareness rippled through her along with the note of caution sounding in her brain. She walked over to the swing, skirting Sadie and thinking of the first litter of motherless puppies that her stepfather had put her in charge of. The nonstop work had brought her out of her deep funk.

Looking back, she knew she'd been on the verge of a severe depression like the one that drove her mother to commit suicide. She wanted no part of the black abyss. By taking up with Kyle she was only courting disaster.

She sat on the swing, steeling herself to his virile attraction, and asked, "How did you meet Chad?"

Chapter 25

"How do I know Chad?" Kyle repeated, Jennifer's question taking him by surprise. She nodded quickly, a determined set to her sensual mouth. The last thing in hell he wanted to talk about was that cocky prick, Chad Roberts. What was it with women and Chad?

"I'm waiting," she responded, her voice tight.

"Look. It's a small world out there. DEA, ATF, and the military antiterrorist units all operate in the same parts of the world." He put his arm across the back of the swing, wanting to hold her, but knowing now wasn't the time. Something was on her mind.

"I thought the military couldn't be involved in drug activities without congressional approval or something."

"Right, *but* the military is always involved in antiterrorist operations, and *often* the two overlap."

"Like Cuidad del Este where Brody's going."

She knew more than was good for her, Kyle decided as he nodded. "Cuidad del Este, Bogota, Rio, San Salvador—they're all the same. Drug kingpins and terrorists from as far away as Afghanistan live in each other's pockets. They coexist because they all operate on the dark side of the law."

"I see." Jennifer rocked back slightly and the swing moved, a gentle, lulling motion. "So you and Chad were in the same circles."

"Not exactly. I ran into him in Panama where the DEA has an ongoing operation."

She looked at him expectantly, and he wondered what she wanted from him. After a moment, she said, "And?"

"And that's how we knew each other." He didn't want to sound petty by saying he thought Chad was a cocky hotshot who would tell anyone who would listen how great he was.

She arched one delicate brow, then looked down at Sadie. The dog had finished her dinner and was sprawled out at their feet.

"Was there a woman?" she asked.

"A woman? What are you talking about?"

"Did you and Chad go out with the same woman?" she asked, her voice seeming a bit forced.

"We were on special assignments. It wasn't exactly party time." Then the light dawned. "Is that what Chad said?"

She nodded with an apologetic expression. "Sorry. I should have known better. Chad told me something about you being with a woman, then he came along and she left you for him."

"What else did he say?"

"Well, let's see," she hedged.

"Wait a minute." He slammed the heel of his palm against his forehead, recalling an incident in Panama City. "One night I was in a bar, hanging around, waiting for an informant to show, and this waitress kept flirting with me. She was sitting on my lap when Chad came through the door with a group of guys from the DEA. I told the woman to take a hike, and she went after Chad next. Turning that incident into stealing my girl takes balls."

"I'm sorry. I *should* know better than to believe a word Chad Roberts says." She paused a moment, and at the base of her slender throat a pulse beat swelled, tempting him to lean over and kiss her there. "It's just that you haven't really told me very much about yourself."

He put his arm around her shoulders and pulled her close. "What would you like to know? Ask away."

The tender, yet excited gleam in her eyes touched him in a way that nothing had in years. "I want you to tell me what happened in your life that's important to you."

Aw, hell. That's a woman for you. Couldn't she just say what was on her mind? He didn't want to rake through the muck that was his life, asking himself what had been important and what hadn't.

He tried to joke. "Hey, we don't have all night, and that's how long it would take to tell you about SEAL training, then the special antiterrorist courses."

"Can't you be serious?"

"Can't *you*? Tell me what you want to know."

She glared at him with burning, reproachful eyes, then asked, "What happened to you after Mother and I left?"

"I told you. Dad's unit was called up. He left for Greneda, and I stayed with friends. You remember Bud Felder, don't you?"

"Of course. He was your best friend."

"I was staying with him when Dad was killed." He rushed the story, the memory of his father's death triggering a raw ache deep in his chest. "After the funeral, I was sent to live with my dad's only relative, a distant cousin. The woman had never been married. She hadn't a clue about what to do with a rebellious sixteen year old. Within a month, she gave up, and I was sent to a foster home."

"Oh, Kyle. I'm so sorry. If only Mother had known where you were. You could have lived with us."

"Like I told you, Dad and I tried to call, but the line was always busy. After he left, I had to use a pay phone because I didn't want to run up the Felders' bill. I finally got through, but they said you were gone."

"You tried to reach me?" she asked, utter disbelief coloring every word.

"Damn right. I promised, didn't I?" Before the words passed his lips, he realized what she'd been thinking all these years. "You thought I blew you off, right?"

She nodded, her full lower lip trembling as she met his gaze. "What else could I think?"

"I thought you trusted me enough to know I would contact you unless something bad had happened. If you had called Bud, he would have told you where I was."

She covered her face with trembling hands, and he had to steel himself from pulling her closer, but he was as mad as hell at her. Hadn't he meant anything to her?

It was pitch dark now, and one by one the yard lights came on, thanks to the automatic timer. A small wall lantern on the verandah flicked on at the same time, giving off a dim glow.

Finally, she dropped her hands, but she didn't look at him. Her eyelashes cast forlorn shadows across her cheeks. She slowly turned to him.

"I would have called except Mother kept harping on how terrible your father was and I . . . didn't know what to do, so I did nothing. I never dreamed your father had been killed. I always thought you two could find us if you wished. Then Mother remarried and we moved so far away. I . . ."

He could have let her off the hook, but her distrust was a blow to his pride. All those years ago, he'd fallen in love with Jennifer. Time and life had moved on, but his feelings remained the same. He'd never considered committing himself to anyone else. Never.

"Is there anything else you want to know?" he asked, trying unsuccessfully to keep sarcasm out of his voice.

She measured him with sad, wary eyes. "I'm sorry. I don't know what I was thinking. All I can say was it was a terribly difficult time for me. Losing you, then my mother . . ."

In her gaze he saw something he intuitively recognized because he'd experienced it so often himself. Loneliness. He looked down at Sadie recalling Jennifer saying this dog was her only friend.

It was no way to live life, he decided, remembering something Jen had said earlier. When you look at something beautiful like a sunset and realize someone you love is dead and will never have the chance to see nature's beauty, you appreciate it all the more. He'd missed so much. Nature's beauty and the companionship of a special person.

Being angry about something that happened years ago, when they were hardly more than kids, was infantile. Fate had given him a second chance with Jennifer, and he wasn't going to blow it.

He rocked the swing with his foot as he pulled her closer. The dark sky was spangled with pinpricks of stars and a magnolia moon, he noticed, proud of himself.

"What happened in Libya?" she asked out of the blue.

He sucked in a stabilizing breath and held it a second. "What did Chad tell you?"

"Not much. Just that you fell for some woman when you were supposed to be on a mission, and that's how your leg was injured."

"The sonofabitch! Know what he does? He takes a kernel of the truth and twists it to suit his purposes."

"Yes. I learned the hard way, but I still want to know what happened to you."

It had been a defining moment in his life, and it had ended the career he loved. Many times he'd replayed the incident, changing what he'd done. But now he could admit the truth. He would never have done anything differently.

"Posing as a Russian bomb expert, I went to Libya to crush a terrorist cell. While I was there, I noticed a woman being treated worse than a dog by her husband and his family.

"You have no idea what life is like for women in that part of the world. Over there, you marry into a family and become a slave to your mother-in-law and nothing more than a baby machine for your husband."

"I know how good we have it," she said. "I'm a member of Amnesty International. I always read their reports. Rape isn't even a crime in many countries. It's disgusting."

Kyle nodded, then continued. "My mission was going great. I had them fooled, so I tried to ignore what was happening to Shalah, telling myself there were hundreds of thousands of women in the same predicament and I couldn't save them all. Then one night, I found her outside the village, wandering, her clothes covered with dried blood."

"What had happened to her?"

"Her husband and his family wanted another son, but the woman had delivered a daughter that morning. They stoned the baby to death, then beat Shalah with rakes and hoes. There was nowhere to go, no one to help her. I had to do something."

"I'm so proud of you," Jennifer said softly.

He shrugged off the compliment, silently acknowledging he'd done the right thing. He couldn't say he was proud, but he knew he could never have lived with himself if he'd turned his back on that woman. It would have haunted him for the rest of his life.

"I hid Shalah in a granary and told her I would take her out of Libya when I left. Over the next few days, I brought her food, and she seemed much better."

"Did she know who you really were?"

Kyle shook his head. "But I made the mistake of asking if she could swim, and she couldn't, which didn't come as a surprise. Women aren't allowed to do much of anything except household tasks."

"Swim? Why was that important?"

"SEALs come and go by sea."

"You're telling me you swam into Libya. From where?"

He chuckled at the incredulous inflection in her voice. His arm was still around her, and he gave her a hug before answering. "Remember the inflatable we used to get out of the mangroves? I left on a helicopter off a Navy ship. They dropped us into the ocean. We inflated the boat and motored as close to shore as we dared. I swam the rest of the way alone while the team went back to the ship. SOP."

"Standard Operating Procedure. I had no idea."

"My question about swimming must have panicked Shalah. The next night when I went to take her food, she was gone. I didn't suspect she'd turned on me until the following morning, when the men I was supposedly teaching how to make bombs ambushed me. All of a sudden I was facing two dozen men with Uzi's. They damn near killed me."

She went stock-still. "Oh, my God. What did you do?"

He threw back his head and looked at the ceiling festooned with lacy wooden scrollwork. He still couldn't quite believe he'd gotten out alive.

"Training kicked in. I threw a flash-bang. You know, it makes a helluva lot of noise and has a blinding light. Then I started firing. They fired back, but I'm a better shot."

"They hit your leg."

"And my arm and my shoulder, but I still managed to make it to the wharf. I radioed the ship, but they couldn't send a team for me until dark. Then the inflatable hovered off shore until I could reach it."

The wispy lashes shadowing her cheeks flew up, and she

looked at him with wide, astonished eyes. "You're not making this up, are you?"

"No, Jen, I'm not." If anything, he was glossing over the worst parts, sparing her from knowing he'd looked death in the teeth several times during the longest day of his life.

"You had three bullet wounds and yet you still managed to swim out to the boat?"

Even now, he could feel the wine-dark sea, pulling at him, dragging him down with every stroke he took. He'd managed—by sheer strength of will—to swim the two miles out to where the SEAL team was waiting. He'd refused to allow himself to die like his father.

Alone in a foreign land.

"I made it," he responded, downplaying the inner strength it had taken. "But I couldn't climb into the inflatable. The guys had to haul me in like a big fish."

"I can't imagine surviving an ordeal like that. Where did you find the courage?" She sagged against him, shaking her head. "I could never—"

"No one knows what they're capable of until the situation faces them. We rise to the occasion. I had been highly trained, and I fell back on what I learned. It kept me alive. That's why I've told you to improve your shooting skills. In an antiterrorist unit, you never know when—"

"Hul-low!" called a voice out of the darkness.

Plotzy. He was dressed in Day-glo orange Bermudas, sandals with black socks, and a Margaritaville T-shirt. If Jimmy Buffet saw Plotzy, he would shoot him on sight, and there wasn't a jury on the planet who would convict Buffet.

"Have you all seen Thelma Mae?" Plotzy asked.

"No, we haven't," Kyle answered.

Plotzy pointed at Jennifer. "She said I was an alien in disguise."

"It's a pretty good disguise," Kyle said. "Had me fooled."

Plotzy smiled. "Right-o. I'm off to Clive's party."

Lucky Clive.

From inside the dark house, Thelma Mae had been listening to Kyle and Jennifer. She had to admit Kyle was a very impressive man. A straight-shooter, she thought, then tamped down the feelings that brought to the surface.

It wasn't that Chad was a liar . . . exactly. Her son had suffered tremendously during his youth. Because of her. A wellspring of guilt made her sigh. Chad couldn't be blamed for stretching the truth occasionally.

She'd asked Kyle about his family when she'd first interviewed him for a place at Thunder Island. He'd had his father to guide him until he was nearly grown. It had made all the difference in his personality.

Had she been able to raise Chad, things would have been different, she assured herself. But life hadn't been easy on Chad. He'd been adopted by cruel parents who had molded him in strange ways.

Chad could have invited her tonight, she thought wistfully, but it hadn't occurred to him because he automatically avoided parents after his terrible experience. She didn't blame him, but still, she hated being here in this dark, empty house with nothing to do but eavesdrop on Jennifer and Kyle.

Chapter 26

Jennifer tuned out Plotzy as he rambled on and on and on to Kyle about the party at Clive's. Her mind was what Kyle had told her.

He had tried to find her.

She had assumed his father was alive and would find a way of locating them, if he'd wished to do so. But Kyle's father had died, and his circumstances had been nearly as terrible as her own. Maybe things had been worse for him, she decided. Kyle had a way of downplaying risky situations.

Just like his father.

And she was exactly like her mother. As much as she had loved her mother and mourned her death, Jennifer had to concede that her mother had been very self-centered. She had been so obsessed with Vince Parker that she couldn't accept the love of a decent, caring man, Hiram Whitmore. Even more upsetting, Jennifer's mother had killed herself just when Jennifer had needed her the most.

In many ways, she had the same failings as her mother.

Jennifer had never seriously stopped to consider that something terrible might have befallen Kyle. True, she had been in a traumatic situation herself, but she should have known Kyle wouldn't abandon her.

The warmth of his arm encircling her, his hand resting casually on her shoulder had been comforting a few moments ago. But now, taking a close look at herself, Jennifer felt ashamed and unworthy of his attention.

"Catch you later," Kyle said as Plotzy trotted off.

"Right-o."

"Let's take a minute to enjoy the beautiful moon and the stars." He gently rocked the swing back and forth. "Then let's talk about us and the future."

The future.

Those words brought forth a dull ache that she knew was her conscience scolding her. A part of her did want a future with this man, but how could she expect a future unless she was totally honest about the past?

She opened her mouth to tell him everything, but a twinge in her chest reminded her of the past. Of the pain.

The words did not want to come out. She sat there, lulled by the rhythmic movement of the swing and the softness of the balmy air and the comforting sturdiness of Kyle's warm body next to hers. She should have been happy, yet she wasn't and never would be until she told him the entire story.

"Jen, is something wrong?" His eyes probed to her very soul. "Is it Chad?"

Oh, Lordy. He actually thought she gave two hoots about that jerk. "No, I don't care about him. I don't know how I could have thought he was actually going to marry me. Even if he had, I never would be happy with him."

His whole face spread into a smile that made her feel even more disgusted with herself. *Tell him! Open up your mouth and say the words.*

Looking into his eyes, she tried to gather strength, but

it didn't work. If anything, she was less inclined to dig up a past full of hurtful memories still capable of tormenting.

"Something's wrong, Jen. I can feel it."

"I like the way you call me Jen," she hedged. "It's not babyish like Jenny or as serious as Jennifer." She leaned slightly into him, tilting her face up for a kiss.

He pressed his lips to hers, caressing her mouth more than kissing it. She curled her arms around his shoulders and kissed him back, letting him know how much she was enjoying this.

He pulled away, his expression darkening with some unreadable emotion. "Jen, level with me. What's going on in that head of yours?"

I can't bring myself to talk about it, she wanted to scream. Just thinking about it hurt too much. She found herself standing up, saying, "I need to be alone for awhile. I've made too many mistakes in my life to rush into . . ."

"Into what?"

She realized he hadn't actually asked her to do anything. He hadn't declared his intentions, or even said how he felt about her. She was leaping to conclusions by thinking he was committing himself. It was the same type of thinking that led to her disastrous relationship with Chad Roberts.

"I don't want to be involved in anything but my career right now. It's all that's important to me."

"Bullshit!" He shot to his feet and towered over her. "I'm the one, the only one for you. Sooner or later, you're going to admit it."

She ducked around him. "Come on, Sadie. Let's do your business and go to bed."

"Take your time, Jen. You know we belong together. We always have."

His bittersweet words echoing in her ears, she walked Sadie into the sea grass. They did belong together. She'd known it from the very first time he'd kissed her all those long years ago.

She had tried to hate him, but even then in some little corner of her heart she never had stopped loving him. How did he feel? He hadn't come right out and said he loved her. No. He'd insisted he was "the one" for her.

What did he mean?

All she had to do was turn around and call to him, but she couldn't. If he rejected her, Jennifer wasn't sure what she would do. If he actually came out and said he loved her, how would she respond?

Like phoenix rising from the ashes of the past, an unbidden memory returned. She saw her stepfather's two best bloodhounds at the edge of the pond. She'd raced up—and looked—before Hiram could shield her. The little girl was floating face down.

In her head she heard herself scream. *"Dear God, no! Why didn't they call us sooner?"*

She was still screaming half an hour later when old Doc Golden arrived and gave her an injection. Did she really want to risk another emotional upheaval by discussing something that still had the power to destroy her emotional equilibrium?

Almost as important, could she trust herself? She had been positive she loved Chad and wanted to marry him. Be cautious, warned an inner voice. Go slow.

When she returned to the porch, Kyle was still there, leaning one shoulder against a post, watching her. She climbed the two steps, then waited for Sadie to limp up. She braved a quick look at Kyle.

"I'll carry Sadie to your room." The emerging bristle on his jaw was as stiff as his voice.

"I'd appreciate it."

They went into the empty house and took the back stairs to Jennifer's room. She rushed ahead, unlocked the door, and turned on the light. Kyle wasn't far behind, and he deposited Sadie on her rug.

Kyle gazed at Jennifer for a long moment. The air in

the room was fraught with tension and the undercurrent of something she couldn't name. He seemed to be on the verge of saying something, but instead he turned and left.

"You did the right thing," she mumbled to herself as she locked the door. "Think carefully before you do anything you may regret."

Kyle all but kicked open the door to his room. What in hell was wrong with Jennifer? Just when he thought he was on solid ground, she yanked the rug out from under him.

He pulled off his shoes, asking himself, "If she isn't upset about Chad, what in hell is bothering her?"

One shoe hit the wall that he shared with Jennifer, but he didn't give a damn. Let her wonder. She had him upside down. Wondering.

He threw himself across the bed, rolled over and stared at the wide blades of the ceiling fan rotating over his head. Jennifer had asked him about those years when they'd been separated, and he had been candid. He'd told her the truth.

Okay, okay. It was the bare outline of what had happened. He hadn't confessed what a gut-wrenching experience Libya had been because he hadn't wanted to worry her.

He'd tried to spare her and succeeded in alienating her instead. What did he expect? He'd never had anything more than a sexual relationship with a woman.

Jennifer was different and she always had been. When he saw himself with her, he imagined a world he had never known, a place where a happy family lived together. A happy family, he thought.

What a concept.

Not that he believed in all that Freudian crap, but it was possible his subconscious was speaking to him. He'd never known much about his mother except she had turned her back on him, walking away and leaving a helpless baby in the care of a career military man.

Not that his father had done anything wrong. Vincent Parker had tried his best, but a mother's love was different. Aw, hell. Maybe it wasn't. What did he know? Still, he'd missed . . . something.

And he wanted that elusive "something" for his children.

Children? The concept frightened him in a way that nothing in his antiterrorism experience ever had. Until this very moment, he'd never given much consideration to being a father.

Danger and adventure had given him such a rush that he'd never stopped to think about a normal life. Now, he seemed—strangely enough—ready to accept the responsibilities of being a father.

He couldn't imagine any woman except Jennifer as the mother of his children. This revelation disturbed him because it altered his concept of his life and the future. He'd lived for the adrenaline high that danger brought.

A stable life with a woman he loved was a new idea, but it wasn't difficult for him to accept it. He'd been redefining himself since the incident in Libya had damn near killed him. He wanted to settle down, he realized with a certain degree of amazement.

When had that happened? When had he stopped living for the thrill of danger?

He crossed his arms behind his head and critically examined the situation. It was clear to him that Jennifer had been hurt when he hadn't found her despite the fact that he'd been going through hell himself.

The wound was much deeper than seemed reasonable to him. His sixth sense kicked in, telling him it was more than just the end of their relationship that was bothering Jennifer. Her unwillingness to talk about it indicated a dark, subterranean undercurrent, shaped by events in a past he knew nothing about.

"Okay, buddy," he whispered to himself. "Where do we go from here?"

Waiting seemed to be his only option. For damn sure, he couldn't make her talk until she was ready.

Mentally reviewing their conversations, searching for a clue to Jennifer's problem, he drifted off to sleep. A boisterous laugh awakened him, and he levered himself up on one elbow. More masculine laughter followed by a fit of giggles. Apparently the gang had returned from the party and were soused.

He waited for Thelma Mae to come thundering out of her room to reprimand them, but the laughter faded as doors opened and banged shut, and people returned to their rooms.

Kyle stripped down to his underwear, then carefully stowed his dirty clothes in the hamper. Some habits die hard, he thought. He had automatically gotten ready for bed without turning on the light. SEALs regularly practiced in the dark because they needed eyes of a cat for night maneuvers.

"Those days are over," he said out loud and flicked on the bathroom light.

He reached for his toothbrush, then squeezed a liberal amount of toothpaste on it. He took a close look at the label: Tartar Control Crest. Christ! He was already becoming an average Joe. Next thing he knew, he'd be flossing every night.

He brushed his teeth, then turned off the light. Crossing the room barefoot, a slight creak caught his attention. Jennifer's door. He'd lain awake enough nights already, listening for her to come home.

He went to bed and told himself not to wonder where she was going at this hour of the night. What time was it anyway? His Breitling glowed in the dark, and a quick check told him it was after midnight. He'd slept for several hours.

Had Jennifer been able to sleep, or was something still bothering her? His curiosity got the best of him, and he rose. She often went for a late night swim. From the shadows on his balcony, he looked out at the beach.

The moon was hidden by a dark cloud with wispy trailers. He spotted a woman at the beach, but there wasn't enough light to be certain it was Jennifer. Who else could it be?

He forced himself to go back to bed. There wasn't any point in trying to get Jennifer to talk until she was ready. He lay down and picked up the sound of voices. It was faint, but from their tones, he knew it was an argument. The noise stopped as suddenly as it had begun.

Unable to fall asleep, Kyle continued to listen. The only sound was the whirring hum of the ceiling fan overhead. He waited and waited with all the patience he'd learned on SEAL missions—not moving just listening—hyper-alert for any unusual sound.

He wanted to know Jennifer was safe in her own bed, not wandering alone on the beach in the middle of the night. Another creaking sound made him sit up in bed. It was a different sound than Jennifer's door, and it was farther away.

He lay down and told himself to get some rest. It had been too many nights with too little sleep. He dozed, half listening for Jennifer's door.

He sat bolt upright and looked around his room. It was still dark but the faint rosy-gray light of another dawn in Key West was appearing on the horizon. A noise had awakened him, but he couldn't identify the sound.

It was a dim echo in his brain like a half-remembered dream. He wasn't sure that he hadn't imagined it. The sound could have been part of a dream.

Pinpricks of sweat peppered the back of his neck, and he was slightly breathless, the way he often was when he dreamed about nearly dying in Libya. Aw, hell. That's what had made him wake up so suddenly.

He hadn't been troubled by those nightmares for months, he thought as he crossed the room and walked out onto the balcony to cool off. Telling Jennifer about Libya had brought back memories he would do better to forget.

He leaned against the railing and gazed out at the dark sea. Off to the side of the lawn, something caught his eye. A woman had collapsed on the lawn.

"Jennifer?"

No, not Jennifer. Relief hit him like a blow to the gut.

It was Thelma Mae, and she was crying.

That was what had awakened him, he decided as he hurried into the room and pulled on a clean pair of khaki shorts. Not bothering with a shirt or shoes, he rushed downstairs. The lawn beneath his feet was moist with dew, and there was a heaviness in the air, signaling an oncoming shower.

"What's wrong?" Kyle asked, dropping down beside the older woman.

"My boy! My boy!" she cried, the words garbled by tears and frantic gulping for air. "My son's been killed!"

Chapter 27

Kyle touched Thelma Mae's shoulder. Upon seeing him, her soft sobs became keening wails. From inside Thunder Island, lights popped on, and people rushed to the windows calling out, "What's wrong?"

Kyle gently shook Thelma Mae's shoulder. "Tell me what happened."

Thelma Mae's sobs only escalated with each question. Now she was hysterical, doubled over on the grass and pounding the ground with her fists as she cried. Jesus! This had to be damn serious. Thelma Mae, the epitome of cool and control, had fractured into a thousand pieces.

"What's going on?"

Tyler had appeared, asking the question. Beside him stood Plotzy and Raven, anxious expressions on their faces. Kyle looked at them, shrugging his shoulders. Other guests ran out of the house, heading their way in various states of dress, but he didn't see Jennifer.

Kyle told Thelma Mae, "We can't help you unless we know what's going on."

Thelma Mae threw her head back, gasping for air, but she made no attempt to answer the question. Instead, she seemed to be asking heaven, "Why? Why? Why?"

Lisa and Chuck rushed up. "What's going on?"

Kyle shook his head. "I'm not sure. An accident, I think. She said something about her son being killed."

"Impossible! She doesn't have any children. Do you, Thelma Mae?"

Kyle noticed Plotzy had said this from a safe distance. Thelma Mae was now pulling up chunks of grass and hurling them toward the beach as she sobbed.

Raven ventured up to Kyle's side, saying, "Thelma Mae, do you have a child?"

"M-m-my boy, Ch-chad."

"Chad Roberts?"

Lisa's voice was indignant, almost outraged. Kyle had to admit this was a stretch. No two people seemed less likely to be related than blond, blue-eyed Chad and dark-eyed Thelma Mae with her gloss black hair.

"She's lost it," Lisa said in a low voice to her brother. "Sometimes people go like that. They just snap."

"No," Kyle said, "something's happened."

He looked around at the small group, most of them in night clothes, hair tousled. There were a couple of new faces, tourists he didn't know who must have arrived just that evening. The regulars were all there except for Jennifer and Chad.

He asked, "Has anybody seen Chad?"

The instant he uttered the name, Thelma Mae wailed even louder. She'd stopped throwing grass now and was clawing at the dirt with her bare fingers. Raven tried to pull her upright, but the older woman shoved her away.

"Let's call a doctor," suggested Tyler.

"Right-o. I'll call Dr. Martens."

"Plotzy, you dummy. Dr. Martens are shoes," Chuck said.

"Let's call an ambulance," Tyler said.

"Tell them it's a psycho case," Lisa said. "They may want to bring a straight jacket."

"Oh, no," cried Raven. "She needs a doctor. That's all."

Kyle wasn't so certain. He had zero experience with grief-stricken women, but this seemed to be much too intense to be normal. It might be some type of psychotic episode.

Raven touched Thelma Mae's shoulder. "If we can't help you, we're going to have to call an ambulance to take you to the hospital."

Thelma Mae's sobs became quieter, and she stopped clawing the ground. Tears were still coursing down her cheeks, but she managed to speak.

"Ch-ch-chad . . . my baby." Thelma Mae stood up and walked toward the water.

"See, I told you she was ready for the funny farm," Lisa said. "Chad would have told me if Thelma Mae was his mother."

"Right-o. She never mentioned it to me, and we've been friends for years."

"What's Thelma Mae doing?" Raven asked.

She was standing in the water, the foaming surf covering her shoes. Her arms were outstretched as if she were reaching for someone.

"Oh, for God's sake," Lisa protested with a disgusted huff. "Let's call nine-one-one."

As much as he resented Lisa's callous attitude, he thought she might be right. They needed professional help.

"Tyler, watch Thelma Mae. Don't let her do anything foolish," Kyle said, taking charge.

"Like what?" Plotzy asked.

"Like hurt someone or herself, you idiot," Lisa said.

"Lisa, you call nine-one-one," Kyle said. "Chuck, come with me. We'll check Chad's room and see if he can help."

"What's Chad's room number?" Chuck asked his sister.

Lisa shrugged. "I don't know. He always comes to my room."

Kyle asked, "Does anyone know which room is Chad's?"

"We could ask Thelma Mae," suggested Plotzy.

"Sure, Plotzy." Lisa rolled her eyes. "Great idea."

"Chad's staying in the widow's waiting room."

Kyle recognized Jennifer's voice as she walked up to them. Even in the hazy light, he could see she'd been crying. "Jen, what's wrong?"

"Why are you crying?" asked Lisa.

"Did Chad make you cry?" Plotzy wanted to know.

Jennifer didn't answer. Her eyes were on Kyle as if she expected something from him. He rushed over to her and put his arm around her, pulling her close to his side. She leaned against him in a way that signaled she needed him.

"I'm all right," she said, her voice ragged from crying. "I was just thinking about my mother . . . and things."

"Did something happen to your mother?" Raven asked.

"She died years ago," Kyle told everyone.

"Have you seen Chad?" Chuck asked as if Jennifer's tears weren't important.

Kyle hugged her closer, asking, "You okay?"

She looked up at him, her eyes misty. "I'm fine now." She turned toward Chuck. "I haven't seen Chad since sunset at Mallory Dock, but I know his room is up there." She pointed to the widow's waiting room behind the widow's walk on top of Thunder Island.

"There's nothing up there," insisted Plotzy. "It's a false room. Thelma Mae told me all about it."

Lisa flounced over to Jennifer. "Chad's staying up there? I don't *think* so. He would have told me."

"It's a secret room," Jennifer said, ignoring the jealousy in Lisa's voice. To Kyle, she said, "Come on. I'll show you."

They started toward the house, the group following, and Kyle looked over his shoulder at Thelma Mae. She was still standing in the surf, deep sobs racking her body as she silently cried. Tyler was with her, talking to her, but they were too far away to hear what he was saying.

Jennifer led them inside and up the stairs to the second floor landing where a watercolor of the Donkey Milk House hung on the high-gloss paneling. The owner of the meticulously restored mansion was a friend of Trevor's, and Kyle had attended a party there. He'd admired the painting each time he'd walked by, but he hadn't paid much attention to the slightly larger grove in the paneling near the watercolor.

Jennifer put the palm of her hand next to the painting and pressed. The paneling popped open, revealing a very narrow staircase. At the top of the dark stairs, light seeped out from under a door.

"I'll be damned. There *is* a room up there," Chuck said.

"Chad's room?" Lisa asked Jennifer, and she nodded.

"Why would Thelma Mae lie about the room?" Raven asked.

What else was she hiding? Kyle wondered.

"If the light's on in that room, why didn't we see it from the beach?" Raven wanted to know.

"Good question," Chuck said as he winked at her.

"You're pretty smart for a fan dancer," Lisa added.

"There's special paint on the windows." Jennifer looked up at him as she talked. Her eyes were still puffy and red, but her voice no longer sounded teary. "Even if the lights are on, you can't see them from outside."

"Are we going to stand here talking this to death, or is someone going to see if Chad is up there?" asked Tyler.

"I thought you were with Thelma Mae," Kyle said.

"Plotzy took over. He knows her better."

"Great, just great." Kyle stepped forward, disgusted.

Plotzy was worth next to nothing in situations like this. "I'll check on Chad. Everyone else stay here."

"Why?" Lisa asked.

"In case it's a crime scene."

"Don't you think you're being a little dramatic?" Chuck asked.

"I sure as hell hope so." But inside he had a hinkie feeling about this. Thelma Mae had flipped out. There had to be a reason why.

Near the top of the dark stairs, almost hidden in the shadows, he spotted something on the floor. He bent down to pick it up, then stopped, reminding himself of crime scene protocol. He looked closer. It was a small, white cocktail napkin with TI in one corner. A Thunder Island cocktail napkin.

He kept going, calling out, "Chad, Chad," as he approached the door. No answer. He knocked, then waited.

"Is he there?" yelled Chuck from the bottom of the stairs.

"I don't know." Kyle tried the doorknob and found it was unlocked. He swung it open. "Chad?"

His SEAL training kicked in and he quickly scanned the room to see what he was up against.

A broken glass on the floor.

Droplets of blood.

A double bed that no one had slept in. A cell phone on the nightstand. A Tiffany style lamp. A pair of cutoff shorts thrown or dropped on the highly polished wood floor.

Barefoot, he stepped into the small room and craned his neck to look into the adjacent bathroom. No one was in there. He took another step, taking care to avoid stepping on broken glass and saw flesh.

The heel of a bare foot was partially concealed by the dust ruffle on the bed. Aw, shit! Kyle inched forward, his height giving him an advantage. He could see over the bed at this angle, when most people couldn't have.

Chad Roberts was sprawled across the floor on the far side of the bed, a knife in his chest.

Kyle backed out of the room, trying to put his feet exactly where they'd been to preserve the crime scene. Jesus! No wonder Thelma Mae had gone bonkers.

Jennifer could tell by the way Kyle carefully descended the stairs that something was terribly wrong. The others were asking questions, but she didn't add to the confusion.

"Call the police," Kyle said as he neared the group. "Chad's been murdered."

"Is he dead?" Plotzy had appeared on the stairs behind them.

"No, he's still alive." Chuck's voice dripped sarcasm.

Lisa had collapsed against her brother, her fist shoved against her mouth to stifle a scream of disbelief. Jennifer tried to feel something but couldn't. She'd been out on the beach, reliving the past, and thinking about her future. She'd cried so hard and so long as she had finally exorcised the demons who had possessed her emotionally all this time.

She had nothing left to give.

Of course, she didn't want Chad to die, but the gut-wrenching emotion Lisa was experiencing or the quiet tears Raven was shedding, didn't seem right for her.

"We were going to be married," Lisa said as the tears began to fall.

Jennifer caught Raven's eye. The brunette was standing beside Chuck, tears tumbling down her cheeks, but Chuck had his arm around his sister. Raven shook her head just enough to ruffle her long hair and let Jennifer know she understood. Chad had conned yet another woman.

Kyle took charge, closing the concealed panel and telling the group, "Let's all wait downstairs for the police."

"Police?" Plotzy questioned, wide-eyed. "We're one street beyond Old Town's boundary. Call the sheriff. We're in his, his"—Plotzy turned to Tyler—"his what?"

"Jurisdiction. We're in the sheriff's jurisdiction."

From the search for Holly Block, Jennifer remembered Sheriff Prichett, the redneck who despised her. An inexplicable feeling of dread waltzed down her spine.

They trailed along behind Kyle down the stairs and into the large drawing room where guests gathered. It was a room filled with comfortable wicker furniture, but everyone sat on the edge of their seats while Kyle made the call, and they waited for the sheriff to arrive.

Kyle hung up and came over to sit beside her. "You okay?" he whispered. When she nodded, he asked, "Why were you so upset?"

"I'll explain later. It has nothing to do with this. It's about us."

He squeezed her hand and smiled. Her heart did a lazy backflip. She'd spent half the night walking the shoreline, thinking about her life, and finally coming to a decision about her future. She knew what she wanted—finally.

But did she and Kyle want the same thing?

"Help! Help!" a guest she didn't know rushed into the room, waving her arms and screaming. "I think she's dead."

Everyone jumped up asking, "Who?"

"The lady who runs this place."

They all ran out of the house to the beach where they'd last seen Thelma Mae. Her prone body was on the shore just beyond the surf. Two of the hotel guests were with her. From the looks of his clothes, one of the men had gone into the water to get her.

"W-we tried to save her but—but we couldn't."

Kyle kneeled beside the lifeless form and tried CPR. Jennifer waited with the others, silently wondering how all of this fit together. It was obvious Thelma Mae had ended her life by drowning.

Finally, Kyle rocked back on his heels and shook his head. "It's no use."

Plotzy stumbled forward, wailing, "Thelma Mae said she just wanted to avoid the curse. I knew she couldn't swim, but I let her go into the water anyway. Avoiding the curse is so important, you know."

"You said the curse strikes at sundown," Raven pointed out. "This is sunrise."

Plotzy turned red and shrugged. "I was confused."

To say Plotzy was intellectually challenged would be an understatement, Jennifer decided. Either that or he was a terrific actor.

Chapter 28

Jennifer couldn't help saying, "Plotzy, how could you leave Thelma Mae alone? You saw how upset she was."

"How was I to know?" Plotzy whined.

Jennifer turned her back on the whole scene, sickened by the dreadful sight. What a waste! She hadn't known Thelma Mae well and Jennifer had thought the woman was odd, but to end her life this way was beyond depressing.

She gazed up at the widow's walk and the secret room. What had gone on up there to drive a woman to suicide?

Behind her Plotzy said, "She told me the whole story."

Jennifer spun around as Raven said, "Really?" with a fair amount of disbelief.

"Yes. Chad was her son. She'd given him up for adoption at birth. He tracked her down about four years ago."

Everyone had gathered around Plotzy, listening intently. In the distance the wail of police sirens pierced the dawn air.

"Why didn't she tell anyone this?" Kyle asked.

"I didn't think to ask her that."

Jennifer doubted the story. Plotzy lived in some sort of twilight world halfway between fantasy and reality. Considering the state Thelma Mae had been in when they'd last seen her, Jennifer couldn't imagine the woman having much of a conversation with anyone let alone Plotzy.

Still, what if he was telling the truth? Biting her lip, she looked away to hide the ache in her heart. Giving up a child was the most emotionally distressing decision a woman could face. She tried to imagine what it would be like to wonder about your child for years, then find him late in life. Losing him again would be devastating.

"Why didn't she tell people he was her son?" Raven wanted to know.

"*That* I asked," Plotzy replied, obviously pleased with himself. "Chad wouldn't let her. He was afraid the drug lords would kill her if they knew she was his mother."

This was the same explanation Chad had given her for not making their engagement public. She couldn't tell what Kyle was thinking, but Raven seemed skeptical. It sounded like Chad's pat excuse.

"What's going on?" yelled someone from the terrace.

Jennifer turned and saw Sheriff Prichett and two of his deputies. They spotted Thelma Mae's body and hurried down to the beach.

"There's another body upstairs," Chuck said.

Lisa was quick to add, "This one's suicide. The other one's murder."

The beefy sheriff came to a halt near them. "Son of a bitch!" His hominy and grits accent made it sound like *Sum' bitch.* He turned to one of his deputies. "Git on the horn and roust the boys."

Jennifer listened as Kyle explained what had happened. She hadn't heard the details concerning the broken glass and the napkin on the staircase.

"Sheriff," she said when Kyle finished, "I have an idea."

The sheriff's steely gaze shifted to her. Judging from his

expression, she decided he hadn't realized she was among the group gathered on the beach. And she was about as welcome as a blizzard in Key West.

"My bloodhound's upstairs." She couldn't resist adding, "You remember Sadie, don't you?"

The sheriff let loose with something that sounded suspiciously like a snort. "Yeah, I remember."

Despite his honeyed drawl, the sheriff's tone indicated he was still fried about losing face. Jennifer ignored his attitude. "Sadie could sniff the napkin on the stairs and lead you right to whoever dropped it."

"Then you'd have the killer," Raven said.

The sheriff took his sweet time, considering his options or something, then nodded. Jennifer raced ahead of the group to get Sadie.

The deputies were hanging yellow and black crime scene tape along the stairs, cordoning off the upper floor of the guest house. She told them what she was doing, and they allowed her to go to her room with a deputy to accompany her.

"Sadie, girl," she said as she came through the door. "We have work to do." She started to open the closet where she kept Sadie's lead and choke chain, but the deputy stopped her. "I have to get Sadie's things or she won't be able to work."

He nodded, and she opened the door, then pulled Sadie's choke chain off the hook. Hearing the noise, Sadie clumsily lurched to her feet, tail whipping the air. Jennifer slipped the chain around her neck. Back in the hall, Sheriff Prichett and Kyle were waiting for her along with the deputies.

"Evver'un's dunstars." *Everyone's downstairs.*

The sheriff's gruff tone told her *evver'un* was a suspect at this point. Jennifer decided on the spot the sheriff was in over his head. There weren't many homicides in Key West. How many cases had the sheriff solved?

"I'll show you the napkin," Kyle said as he stood near the open panel that led to the secret room.

He pointed to a small cocktail size napkin barely visible at the top of the stairs. Wearing crime scene booties, one of the deputies went up the stairs and placed the napkin in an evidence bag.

"Sadie will need to take a whiff—"

Sheriff Prichett cut her off. "I know all 'bout these dawgs."

The deputy with the bagged napkin had rejoined them on the landing. He looked to the sheriff for instructions, and his boss told him to let the "dawg" sniff inside the bag. He leaned down, and Sadie stuck her nose into the opened bag.

"Seek, Sadie, seek," Jennifer told her, then turned to Kyle. "She'll need help with the stairs."

They were halfway between the first and second floor. Depending on what her keen sense of smell told her, Sadie would opt to go up to one of the bedrooms on the second level, or she would go downstairs where the residents were gathered and where the other bedrooms were located.

Sadie circled, her nose twitching in the air, and banged her cast against the stair railing. Sheriff Prichett gave his deputies one of those man-to-man looks that said this was a waste of his valuable time.

"How do we know the killer dropped the napkin?" asked one of the deputies.

"We don't," she replied professionally despite the obnoxious sheriff's attitude, "but we already know Chad's scent isn't on it strongly enough for Sadie to lead us upstairs to Chad."

Sadie was pointing up the stairs, her head bobbing in the air as she sniffed. Kyle stood nearby, waiting to help Sadie. The dog was standing in one spot, but she kept turning to sniff over her shoulder, then swiveling around to smell the air coming from the second floor.

Jennifer told the group. "Sadie has detected the same smell that's on the napkin. The person may recently have been upstairs on the second floor or may live downstairs. She's evaluating the scents to decide which is the freshest and strongest."

"The dawg's sump'm else," said the sheriff with a smirk.

"Last year at the National Police Academy's Extreme Bloodhound Trials, Sadie finished first," Kyle told them.

The sheriff grunted, but the deputies had the good sense to look impressed. Sadie turned, bumped into the sheriff's leg with her cast, then lurched toward the stairs going down.

"Here, girl," Kyle said. "Let me help."

He scooped up the dog and carried her to the bottom of the stairs. The deputies followed Jennifer down. Behind them lumbered Sheriff Prichett. Sadie was circling in the figure eight pattern she'd been taught. The dog whined and looked over her shoulder at Jennifer.

"She's locked on to the scent," Jennifer said as she took the leash from Kyle.

Excited, Sadie lunged forward, almost tripping over her cast.

"Whoa, girl. Slow down." Jennifer jerked on the choke chain.

"She's heading toward the great room where everyone is supposed to be waiting," Kyle said.

"The killer is one of us?" Jennifer said before she could stop herself. To be professional, she should keep her mouth shut and let Sadie do her job. Jennifer assumed Chad's death was related to his drug work.

Sadie lurched into the great room, pulling Jennifer behind her. The people gathered were the same group that had been on the beach earlier. They looked startled to see the bloodhound charging at them.

"What's going on?" Chuck asked.

Before Jennifer could answer, Sadie staggered across the

room. She lurched to a halt in front of Lisa. Sadie threw back her head and bayed loud enough to be heard in Miami.

Lisa jumped up. "Help! The crazy dog is going to bite me."

"Tale her ta shuddup," bellowed the sheriff. *Tell her to shut up.*

Sadie kept howling, thoroughly pleased with herself. Jennifer looked at Kyle, who had moved up beside her, then said, "Sadie, quiet," as she petted her dog.

Chuck rose from a nearby sofa where he'd been with Raven to stand by his sister. Plotzy was sitting cross-legged on the floor. He put his hands together and closed his eyes. Presumably he was praying.

Jennifer turned to Sheriff Prichett. "Sadie bays because it's the way she gets rewarded for her work."

"What do you mean?" Tyler asked.

Jennifer kept looking at the sheriff. "The scent on the napkin is Lisa's."

The sheriff stood there, obviously not knowing how to proceed.

One of the deputies, who should have known better, waved the plastic bag with the cocktail napkin even though evidence shouldn't be shown to a suspect. This was not a crack homicide team.

"Of course, that's my napkin. I had a glass of wine on the terrace with Chad after Trevor's party. I didn't finish mine. Chad took it with him, and he must have picked up the napkin at the same time."

"A-ah," the sheriff said, "That'z sump'm."

That's something? Check it out, Jennifer said under her breath.

Lisa was one step ahead of her. "Look in the book for Lisa, if you don't believe me."

"Book?" asked one of the deputies.

Plotzy's head came up from his prayer. "The honor book we all sign for our drinks. It's outside on the bar."

"Check it out," Sheriff Prichett told a deputy.

Kyle spoke up. "Use gloves. You may want to dust the bar for Chad's prints."

The deputy shuffled off, and Lisa cast a quick sideways glance at her brother. He immediately spoke up.

"After Lisa left Chad, she came to my room. We were together until we heard Thelma Mae down on the beach crying," Chuck told the sheriff.

Jennifer quickly looked at Raven. The brunette's expression didn't register any shock. Somehow Jennifer had assumed Raven would have spent the night in Chuck's bed and would know if he was lying.

An oddly primitive warning sounded in her brain. Her eyes shifted to Tyler. The handsome man's face was closed, his eyes expressionless, as if he was guarding a secret.

"She's telling the truth," announced the deputy, walking back into the room. "Her name is the last one in the book. She signed for one glass of chardonnay."

Sheriff Prichett rocked back on his heels, arms crossed across his chest and regarded the group with narrowed eyes. "This joint's a crime scene. Evver'un stay put. No un goez to their rooms."

"May we go outside?" Raven asked.

The sheriff thought about it for a moment, then nodded. "Stay off the beach."

Kyle led Jennifer out the door, and Sadie hobbled along beside them. They walked out into the pool area where they found chaises. Jennifer sat down, then took off Sadie's choke chain to let the dog know she was no longer expected to work.

"What do you think?" she asked Kyle as she stroked Sadie's head.

"Gut reaction. The twins are covering for each other.

How else do you account for Lisa's scent being on the napkin and not Chad's?"

"That can be explained. Sadie picks up numerous scents, but she's trained to follow the strongest scent. Chad may have touched the napkin. Lisa left more scent on it. That's not uncommon. There are no oil or sweat glands in our hands.

"People wouldn't leave fingerprints except that they touch their hair or face or some other part of their body and pick up a substance, which leaves a print. I read a study that shows women are three times as likely to fiddle with their hair or touch their faces than men. That could account for why Sadie went directly for Lisa rather than head up the stairs to where Chad is."

Kyle looked at her for a moment. The sun had crept over the horizon, its early morning light stealing through the trees surrounding the pool. The golden-pink glow made him look healthy, yet his face was drawn, tired. She could only imagine how she looked after her crying jag.

"Okay, so there's an explanation," he said. "What do you think?"

"I'm not sure. It's possible Lisa covered her tracks. We were all standing at the bottom of the stairs when you went up. Tyler asked what the white thing was at the top of the stairs. Raven said it looked like Kleenex. No one said anything else about it."

"Did Lisa or Chuck leave the group? Could they have had time to sign the book and make it appear that she'd had a drink?"

"No, not while you were up there, but one of them could have done it while we were working with Sadie."

"U-u-um." Kyle nodded. "There's something strange going on, and I'm not sure if Prichett can figure it out."

"That's what I was thinking."

"But he'll be hard pressed to solve the case. There's

one thing everyone in Key West dreads. Crime. They won't want people thinking a killer is on the loose in paradise."

She leaned back on the chaise and studied the mirrorlike surface of the swimming pool and let one hand drop down to touch Sadie's back. The bloodhound was on her side, the leg with the cast outstretched.

"Jen," Kyle said quietly from the chaise next to hers. He wasn't stretching out. He was sitting, facing her, arms resting on his knees. His eyes captured hers, intense green and calculating. "Why were you so upset earlier? What made you cry?"

Chapter 29

Jennifer intended to tell Kyle the whole truth about the past. She'd walked the beach for half the night, thinking about it, agonizing over what had happened. Tears had fallen, the way she knew they would, accompanying them was the bleak agony of despair that comes when someone you love with all your heart dies . . . unexpectedly.

But now, with Thelma Mae's apparent suicide and Chad's killer still on the loose, it didn't seem as if it were the appropriate time to discuss her problems. An inner voice, the one she usually tuned out, delivered a message. *You're going into a denial mode again. Not talking about it won't make it go away.*

She sat up and swung around, facing him, careful not to hit Sadie with her feet. Knees touching, she gazed across the short space into his eyes.

"My mother's death was hard on me for several reasons," she began. "I was in a strange place, a farm outside of Macon, Georgia. The man my mother had married so hastily didn't give a hoot about me, and I knew it. I was baggage who came with my mother. With her gone, I was absolutely terrified about what would become of me."

She paused, bracing herself for the rest of the story, and Kyle said, "I know how you felt. I recall arriving at my cousin's house with the social worker. I'd never met my second cousin and barely remembered Dad mentioning her. Then there I was at her door. I questioned if she would want me. As it turned out, she didn't."

There was a ring in his voice that sounded achingly familiar. She knew he'd endured unimaginable hardships during those years when their parents' deaths had separated them. What had happened to her didn't mean he hadn't suffered as well.

"Go on," he eagerly prompted when she didn't continue.

"I was frightened," she confessed, "although there was no reason to be. Hiram Whitmore was a very special man. When he died, I found a quote from Louis L'Amour in his wallet: 'Sometimes the most important things in a man's life are the ones he talks about least.' "

Kyle thought for a moment, then said, "That fit my father, too. He adored your mother, but he couldn't quite bring himself to say how he felt."

"Then it was too late for words."

Kyle nodded. "You're right. At a certain point, it's too late for words."

Jennifer nodded. In her heart, she knew how she felt, but was it too late for words, too late to express the sadness she struggled to forget.

"Jen? You were telling me about your stepfather," prompted Kyle.

She inhaled a stabilizing breath, looked directly into his eyes, then continued, "The night before my mother took her life, she came to my room. I don't know how she'd missed it for so long, but she'd finally noticed . . . I was pregnant."

The words hung in the early-morning air as incomprehensible as a foreign language. For a moment, Kyle didn't say anything, but his eyes suddenly darkened with emotion. "My baby?" he whispered in a hoarse voice.

All Jennifer could do was nod. In her mind's eye, she saw their little girl. Laughing green eyes. A captivating smile. The most precious child in the whole world.

Kyle sprang to his feet, then sat on the chaise beside her. He hugged her close, not saying anything as he rested his forehead against hers. "Jenny, oh, God, I never knew." He threw back his head and raked his hand through his dark hair so roughly that strands pulled loose from the thong at the nape of his neck. "I thought we'd been careful."

She drew into herself, looking at him, yet seeing their little girl when she gazed into those same green eyes. Her lower lip began to tremble, and it was all she could do to keep herself from crying. She bit down on her lip until it hurt to steady herself.

"We weren't careful enough," she heard herself whisper. "Mom confronted me, and I admitted you were the father."

"Oh, Jenny, I wish I could have been there to help."

"There wasn't anything you could have done. The minute I uttered your name, mother backed away from me, shaking her head. She adored you and couldn't believe you and I had . . . you know."

"I should have known better. We were too young to be having sex."

She shrugged. "We were just kids. Babies having babies was what my stepfather said."

"We were in love." His hoarse whisper broke the silence. "I'm still in love with you, Jenny. I've never stopped loving you."

Some part of her still loved him, too. He would always have a place in her heart, but she had experienced another, different kind of love, a profound, all-encompassing type of love that still gripped her.

His words hung between them like a dark shroud. She hadn't meant to burden him with guilt or recrimination, but she didn't know what to say. There was so much more to tell, yet she couldn't make herself say the words.

"You told your mother this just before she killed herself, so you blame yourself for her death, right?"

"Not entirely." She glanced up at the morning sun glinting through the trees and tried to be totally honest. "My mother left a note saying she couldn't live without your father, never mentioning my pregnancy. I had to break the news to Hiram myself."

"What did your stepfather say?" Kyle asked, slipping his arm around her again.

"He was shocked, of course, but he was a very good man. He was so supportive." A flash of wild grief ripped through her, remembering the taciturn man who'd stood by her side when she had no one else. "I kept hoping you and your father would come."

"Oh, Jenny," he breathed the words into the hair covering her ear as he hugged her close, "nothing on earth would have kept me away had I known where to find you. My dad would have done anything to help you, but he was already gone."

Her sense of loss was too deep for tears, too terrible to express. She gazed into the green eyes that had haunted her for all of her adult life: the eyes of the father and the eyes of his child.

He tipped her face up with the palm of his large hand, then kissed the tip of her nose. "Jenny, you gave up our baby, didn't you?"

She pulled back, closing her eyes and reliving the pain. Her throat seemed to close up and her tongue felt too thick to speak.

"It's okay," he said gently when she didn't answer. "No

wonder you doused me with that pitcher of margaritas. You had to go through the birth and adoption alone."

Her disappointment in him became a heavy, painful knot in her chest. "How could you possibly think I would give up our baby? I couldn't allow my baby to go to some family who might divorce or might mistreat her. People told me that it would be better, but I didn't believe them."

He covered his eyes with his hand, then moaned. "Oh, Jen, what can I say?"

She lifted her shoulders in a halfhearted shrug. What could anyone say now that Hiram Whitmore was gone? Her stepfather had been there for her, and no one else but Hiram could truly appreciate the grief that still weighed her down.

Kyle studied her intently for a long moment, then asked, "What became of our child?"

"Chloe. Our baby was a little girl and I named her Chloe." She didn't add that the baby had been born with blue eyes, which later became hauntingly familiar green eyes. "I kept her, and took her home to Hiram's farm outside Macon, Georgia."

"Where is she now?" he asked, his voice raw with emotion.

Her lower lip trembled as she returned his gaze. All she could force herself to say was, "Chloe died."

He threw back his head and looked up at the morning sky for a moment. "How? Did she become ill, or what?"

"No. Chloe was a healthy baby, and so cute." A long-forgotten image popped into her mind. Chloe trying to walk, holding on to the rump of one of the bloodhounds her stepfather raised. She took a tumble and the dog turned around and licked the little girl's face. Chloe had giggled with delight. "You can't imagine how precious Chloe was."

"Jen, what happened to her?"

Guilt raced through her bloodstream like a powerful

narcotic. How could she admit what she had done? But Kyle's unwavering gaze told her that now was the time to confess.

"I brought Chloe home and learned to take care of her from a neighbor lady. My stepfather did what he could, but he'd never had children."

"Aw, hell. I wish I could have been there."

She didn't know what to say. If Kyle had been with her, things might have been different, but he hadn't been at her side. She had been the one responsible for what had happened.

"You have no idea how much I loved Chloe. No matter what happened to me, she was worth it." She looked away, remembering the hurt yet shunting it aside. "How do you think the other students at school felt about an unwed mother?"

He exhaled in one long sigh, his head pitching forward and releasing more hair from the thong at the nape of his neck. When his head came up again, he gazed at her for a moment, then said, "They were cruel to you."

"Yes, but I didn't care. All I wanted to do was graduate so I could go on to college."

"With a baby?"

"Of course. I planned to move to Atlanta, attend college part time while I worked to support us."

His green eyes pierced the distance between them, expecting nothing less than the whole truth. "Jen, tell me what happened to Chloe. You've gotten sidetracked."

She'd put it off as long as she could. "I was finishing my senior year, and Chloe was staying with a neighbor down the road. This arrangement worked for us because I was gone all day, and Mrs. Littleton watched her grandson as well as Chloe.

"I would come back each afternoon, pick up Chloe and walk back to the farm, then prepare dinner. Hiram would drift in later and join us. He adored Chloe. To see him, you would have thought he was her grandfather."

"What happened?" he asked again.

"One day I came to the Littletons' to pick up Chloe, and they told me Chloe had wandered away, but they thought she was nearby. Instead of calling my stepfather to bring one of his man trailers, I rushed out to find her and lost valuable time." Guilt ate at her insides, burning like a corrosive acid. "If only I had called Hiram immediately, Chloe would be alive today."

"Jen, don't blame yourself," he said, his voice gentle. "Every mother would have done the same thing."

"But I wasn't every mother. I'd watched Hiram train the bloodhounds. I'd even gone on several searches with him. I knew how crucial it is to get the dogs to the scene. Time is everything. The first hour a person is missing is called the Golden Hour because the scent trail is still fresh, and you have the best chance of finding them." She threw up her hands. "I blew it. By the time Hiram arrived with his best bloodhound, Chloe had been gone for over two hours. We searched the area and came to the ravine that fills up and becomes a pond in wet years."

"Oh, Jen, no, no."

"My stepfather reached the pond first, then I came up behind him."

A shadow of alarm crossed Kyle's face, and he reached out to touch her shoulder. He clasped it with his large hand and squeezed, expressing his sympathy.

"There was Chloe floating, face down." She heard her own voice break. "I knew she was dead, but I flung myself into the water. I pulled Chloe to shore and tried to revive her, but i-it was too late."

"Aw, hell, Jenny," he said, pulling her close. "I'm so sorry I wasn't there with you. I can't imagine . . ."

"Until then I had no idea that lost children gravitate to water. The very water they love so much kills them."

"Jenny," he muttered, his voice cracking. "What you must have gone through. I'm so sorry, honey."

"I was a total basket case. I don't remember much. Hiram took care of the funeral. I stood there while the earth was being shoveled on top of the little white coffin, but it seemed surreal. If Hiram hadn't been holding me, I would have jumped in with Chloe." As she spoke, her voice dropped until she was barely whispering.

She pulled away, fighting back the tears. Unspoken pain glimmered in his eyes as he brushed away a tear she didn't know had fallen. The smooth pad of his thumb rubbed the droplet away. It was a simple gesture, but one that seemed infinitely tender.

"I wish I'd been there to help you, Jenny."

"Chloe was the most wonderful thing that has ever happened to me."

"I wish I could have known her."

"She had your green eyes, and her hair was light like mine." Swallowing the sob rising in her throat, she went on. "She was a smart, happy child."

He gathered her in his arms and held her snugly against his chest. Gazing into her eyes, he said, "I meant what I said. I love you. I always have." He touched his lips to her forehead. "I know there will never be another Chloe, but I want to marry you and have a family."

She parted her lips to tell him that she was *never ever* going to have another child, but he kept talking.

"I've always wanted a big family. Three, maybe four kids. I think I'll be a good father." He flashed her an adorable grin. "So, what do you say? Will you marry me?"

She started to explain why she couldn't marry him. Sheriff Prichett came crashing through the bushes into the pool area followed by one of his deputies, cutting her off before she'd begun.

"Tol' ya they'd be tagether." *Told you they'd be together.* The sheriff rocked back on his heels, saying to Jennifer, "Well, missy, looks like you're the prime suspect."

Chapter 30

Kyle jumped up, still shaken by what Jennifer had told him, and confronted the sheriff. "What in hell are you talking about?"

Jennifer leaped up, too, saying, "I didn't kill Chad Roberts. Why would I?"

"He dumped you," the deputy responded. "If you couldn't have him, you didn't want anyone else to have him."

"That's ridiculous," Jennifer said. All the color had leeched from her face and there was a lingering sadness in her eyes from telling Kyle about Chloe.

"We found a rifle in your room."

"I checked it out from the firing range at the base. I planned to go into the mangroves and see if I could shoot a poisonous snake."

"What does the gun have to do with it? Roberts was stabbed." Kyle turned away from the deputy to Prichett, who hadn't said much. But he had a dangerous lopsided smile on his face. Kyle knew the sheriff was dying to pin the murder on Jennifer.

"I didn't kill Chad," she repeated.

"Killing him upset you," the deputy said to her. "Evver'un told us you were cryin'."

"*Everyone* was right. I had been crying, but not about Chad."

"Are you going to charge her or just harass her?" Kyle asked, becoming more uneasy by the second. "If you're going to charge her, you'd better read her the Miranda. Then I'll call a lawyer."

"Hold your horses. We're just gatherin' the facts." The sheriff turned to Jennifer, his eyes hooded like those of a hawk. "Mind if I look at your hands?"

Jennifer held out her hands. There was a small cut on one finger. Kyle knew where the sheriff was going with this. There had been a drop of blood beside the broken glass. Evidently Chad didn't have a cut on his hand, so the blood on the floor wasn't his.

Kyle held out his hands. He had a small scratch on his thumb. "I'll bet most everyone here has a nick or a cut on their hands. We spent the day helping with hurricane damage at a house being restored on Angela Street."

He didn't mention that Jennifer had not been with the group at Trevor's house. Jennifer didn't offer any explanation for the cut.

"Several others have cuts," the deputy conceded.

"Where were you between ten o'clock and say five A.M.?"

She hesitated a moment, then answered, "I was walking on the beach by myself."

"I was alone, too," Kyle added, trying to distract the sheriff.

"Don't that beat all," the deputy said. "Only those twins have an alibi. I'd thought, you know, in a place like this that more of you all would be shacked up together."

"Let's git back inside," the sheriff said.

They followed the sheriff down the path and into the house, Sadie lumbering along behind them. Jennifer slowed down and motioned for him to drop back, too.

"Kyle," she whispered, her pretty face etched with worry, "my fingerprints are in Chad's room."

Aw, shit! No alibi. A cut on her hand. A rifle in her room. Circumstantial evidence, but incriminating nonetheless. A spasm in his gut tightened into a cold knot of fear.

"How'd that happen?"

"Chad invited me up to his room the night he came home," she replied, a quaver in her voice. He held the door for her, and they walked into the house. "That's when he dumped me as the sheriff said."

"Why would he have you up, yet not ask Lisa?"

Jennifer leveled very blue, very troubled eyes on him. "Maybe he did. Sadie went straight for Lisa, and I sensed she was lying."

The group was again gathered in the great room. The sun was so bright that someone had angled the shutters down so the golden light spilled across the polished floor. It had always been a room filled with laughter, the place guests relaxed, but from the tight expressions, no one was happy today.

The room faced the front of the house, and through an open window came the sound of voices. Lots of voices.

"What's going on out there?" he asked.

"The press is camped out on the front lawn," Chuck told him.

He should have guessed. Thunder Island was Key West's most popular guest house, and Thelma Mae Horton had been one of the best known local residents. Murder at Thunder Island would be big news. The death of a DEA agent would rate attention from the national media as well.

Just what Jennifer did not need. Prichett would be hard-pressed to solve the case quickly. If only she hadn't gone up to Chad's room. Her prints along with the other circumstantial evidence could be enough to arrest her.

A man in a white jumpsuit with "coroner" stenciled across the back in bold red letters pulled the sheriff aside. Prichett told the deputy to take over.

"Here's what's going to happen," the deputy informed the group. "We've already made a preliminary search of your rooms. Next we'll conduct an in-depth search. We're going to take you one at a time to your rooms. Get what you absolutely have to have."

"You mean we're not going to be staying here?" asked Raven.

"No. The whole place is a crime scene. We'll log out as possible evidence anything you must take like your purse."

"Where will we go?" Lisa asked.

"We could go up the street to Bahama Bob's Clothing Optional Guest House," said Plotzy.

Plotzy without clothes. Scary.

"We need to know exactly where everyone is staying. All of you are still suspects."

"Why?" Chuck wanted to know. "I have an alibi, so does my sister."

How convenient. Kyle couldn't resist saying, "Maybe you both did it."

Lisa glared at him. "Very funny."

The sheriff returned to the group. "Is there anything you might have forgotten to tell us? Any little thing might break the case."

Tyler raised his hand. "I've known both the dead people for years."

Really? The night Chad arrived, neither man acted as if he knew the other. What was the big secret?

Tyler continued, "I used to come to Thunder Island when I was a child. That's how I first met Thelma Mae Horton. One night my mother had too much to drink, which wasn't unusual for her, and she told Thelma Mae about becoming pregnant when she was a teenager. She put the child up for adoption, and never got over it. Thelma Mae confessed she'd done the same thing. They became friendly and she told my mother all about the son she'd given up. She was still very, very upset about it."

Next to him, Kyle felt Jennifer stiffen and knew what she was thinking. He hated the way she'd suffered, losing Chloe so tragically, but she had done the right thing by keeping their baby. Their baby. He still couldn't get over it.

He'd never seen the little girl, but just hearing about her caused a hollow ache in his chest. He could only imagine how terrible Jennifer felt. What an extraordinary void there would be in your life when you lost a child.

"Iz there a point to this?" asked the sheriff.

Tyler nodded, looking very guiltily around at the others. "I met Chad Roberts in Bogotá when I was working for a coffee exporting firm. We hit it off. One night I told him about my mother, and I happened to mention Thelma Mae. We agreed women were nutty about their kids. They never got over losing one."

Kyle reached over and took Jennifer's hand. Her fingers were cool as he laced them between his and gave her a reassuring squeeze.

"Chad got this brilliant idea. He decided to pose as Thelma Mae's long lost son. He figured she was rich and she'd leave him all her money."

"You're making this up," insisted Lisa. "Chad would never do such a thing."

"Don't be so sure." Raven fluffed her long hair with one hand. "He was a con artist."

"He kept it secret," Tyler told them, "so his parents wouldn't find out. He comes from a real nice family in Iowa. Nice but poor. Chad hated being poor."

"Maybe Thelma Mae found out the truth and killed him."

This brilliant thought from Plotzy. Didn't he remember Thelma Mae sobbing because her "son" was dead?

"I saw how rattled Thelma Mae was over Chad's death," Tyler said. "She didn't know the truth until I told her."

"Oh, my God," Jennifer said. "You told her when she was so upset."

"I thought it would bring her out of it."

What a guy. So sensitive.

"Maybe that's why she killed herself," suggested Chuck. "She couldn't take the truth."

"I've heard enough," Prichett said. "This isn't helping us find the killer."

"Now you know how deceitful Chad was. If you check into his background, you might discover the motive for the killing." Kyle wasn't sure this would add anything, but it would buy him some time. He might just need the additional time to clear Jennifer by finding the real killer.

Puffed up with importance, the sheriff stepped out front to hold a press conference. The deputy took Plotzy upstairs to gather his things.

"The sheriff seems to think you're the number one suspect, Jennifer," Lisa said, a calculating edge to her voice.

Raven spoke up. "Lisa told him that Chad left you for her. I said Chad had thrown me over, too, and we'd talked about it. I said you weren't angry, but he didn't pay any attention."

Aw, hell. Raven had just confirmed his suspicions. Not that he had any doubt Prichett would try to hang this on Jennifer if he could. An intellectual brain trust, the sheriff wasn't. He'd take the easy way out rather than take a beating in the media for not making an arrest.

"Then they found the rifle in your room. It looks bad," Tyler said.

"It's a sharpshooter's rifle. I have to be able to hit the head of a snake, if I'm going to be useful on an S&R team.

If I planned to shoot someone at close range, I'd use a handgun."

Kyle led Jennifer away, saying, "You don't have to explain yourself to them."

"Where are we going?"

"I'm calling Trevor. He'll let us stay at Half Moon Bay until this case is solved." This he said loudly enough for the group to hear. When they were down the hall by the telephone, he told Jen, "I have a plan. Pretend we're going to Trevor's to stay. We'll go out to the base and get some special equipment I have."

"I'm nervous," she admitted, and he put his arm around her. "They'll arrest me the minute they run the fingerprints in Chad's room through the police computer."

"We're going to solve the case before they can run the prints. I plan to double back here and go up to Chad's room as soon as the sheriff's men leave. With luck, there'll be a bit of blood still left on the floor."

"You're going to run a field DNA test."

He hugged her. "Great minds think alike."

"What good will it do? We can't get DNA samples from everyone."

"Why not? As long as we have access to the house, we can go in each room and get a hair out of their hairbrush or off a pillow and compare it to the results we get with the blood."

She nodded, saying, "The first thing we'll learn is if Lisa is lying. The DNA test will tell us if the blood is a man or a woman's. I'm betting Lisa's blood."

"I'm suspicious of Tyler. Want to bet he wasn't working for a coffee firm in Bogotá? Or if he was, he was involved in drug trafficking on the side. I—"

"Your turn," called the deputy, interrupting them.

Kyle stayed downstairs with Sadie, telling Jennifer he would call Trevor, then pack up the dog's kibble and bowl. He made the call, getting Trevor's machine. He went into the mud room where Jennifer fed Sadie. He picked up Sadie's things and walked out to the back porch to wait his turn to go to his room.

Sitting on the swing, Sadie at his feet, Kyle tried to concentrate on Chad's murder, but his mind kept replaying his conversation with Jennifer. He'd been a father and he hadn't even known it.

What might have been.

The cruelest words in the English language, he decided. If only he had known. If only he could have been with Jennifer. Chloe might have lived.

He tried to imagine what their little girl had been like. A young Jennifer, he decided. Smart and fun-loving and as cute as the devil.

Even though he hadn't known Chloe, the same dull ache seeped through him, the way it had when his father had died. He hadn't seen their child, had never held her in his arms. Knowing she'd lived and he'd never had the chance to hear her say "Daddy" hurt much more than he expected.

He wanted to marry Jennifer and have a family. No child would ever replace Chloe and nothing could change the way Jenny had suffered, but he believed they would be happy together. They'd make great parents.

Jennifer followed the deputy upstairs, apprehension coursing through her. She hadn't killed Chad, but someone was guilty. There should be enough evidence in his room to implicate the real killer, but she couldn't be certain.

They passed the open panel to the secret room on their way upstairs. She saw several men at the top of the landing, but she couldn't tell just what they were doing.

"Have they removed the body?"

The deputy nodded. "Yes."

She wanted to ask if they'd dusted for prints yet, but she didn't dare. She went into her room and packed a few things while the deputy watched. Inside her closet was the rifle she'd planned to take into the mangroves. They knew it was there, but they hadn't seized it as evidence.

Yet.

Chapter 31

Carrying her things in a small duffel, Jennifer went downstairs. She was looking for Kyle and Sadie, when she ran into Raven in the kitchen. Since their talk on the beach, Jennifer felt a special bond with Raven. The former fan dancer had tried to help by telling the sheriff that Chad didn't mean anything to Jennifer.

"Where are you going to stay?" Raven asked.

"Kyle arranged for us to stay with Trevor." Jennifer remembered that Kyle wanted everyone to think they were going directly to Trevor's home. "We're on our way to Sunset Key now. Where are you going?"

"Right next door to Weller's Guest House. They have vacancies because of the hurricane. Chuck doesn't think we'll be there very long. He says Thunder Island will reopen right away."

"You and Chuck patched things up?"

Raven broke into a wide, open smile. "Yesterday we went to Trent Jewelers and picked out a diamond. It should be ready this afternoon."

"You're getting married." She looked down and saw a small cut on the tip of Raven's ring finger.

"Yes. It's going to be a big, formal wedding." Raven's joy was almost infectious.

Jennifer glanced around the kitchen where Thelma Mae had spent countless hours. Her death seemed so sad, so unnecessary. After hearing about the child Thelma Mae had given up, Jennifer knew how terribly the woman had suffered. Losing a child was extremely difficult, something you never got over.

Kyle wanted to marry her. Jennifer wished she could be thrilled and anxious to plan a wedding. But like Thelma Mae, Jennifer couldn't forget her child. She wasn't getting married and having any more children. She couldn't put herself through that again.

Jennifer forced herself to focus on getting any helpful information she could. "How does Lisa feel about it?"

Raven's smile vanished. "Lisa is Lisa. She and Chuck are *so* close. But she was okay with it because she was going to marry Chad. Now . . ." She shrugged as if to say who knows?

"Do you think Chad would have married Lisa? It was just a line with him."

"Lisa believed him. I tried to tell her, but she insisted, she was different."

"I guess we'll never know." Jennifer tried to think how to delicately put her next question. "I'm a little surprised Lisa and Chuck were together last night. I thought he would have been with you."

Raven's gaze shifted to one side, then flashed back to Jennifer with an unmistakable spark of anger. "Don't try to pin Chad's murder on Chuck. He's a good man. If he said he was with Lisa, then he was with his sister."

"That doesn't seem odd to you? Why would they be together in the middle of the night?"

"Sometimes Lisa can't sleep. She dreams she still has

leukemia and needs a bone marrow transplant again. Chuck is the only family she has. He donated his bone marrow to save her. He understands what she went through."

Raven flounced out of the kitchen, saying, "Maybe the sheriff was right about you being the killer. You sure are trying hard to blame Chuck."

She hadn't blamed Chuck, Jennifer thought. She'd merely asked a question. Obviously, this was a sore subject. Despite being engaged to Chuck, Raven had not spent the night in his bed. She wasn't positive she bought the nightmare story.

Kyle opened the locker where he kept his special equipment, most of it experimental, and took out the laptop computer.

"I thought we were running a DNA test," said Jennifer.

"We are, but it'll be hours probably before we can get into the house. While we're waiting, let's do a little checking on Tyler Langley."

"Good idea. Right, Sadie?" She petted the bloodhound as Kyle pulled out several other pieces of equipment and loaded them into a military-style backpack.

"I think I paid too much attention to Sadie," Jen told him.

"What do you mean?" he asked over his shoulder. He was trying to hurry without appearing desperate and worrying her more. It wouldn't be long before the authorities matched Jennifer's fingerprints with those in Chad's room.

"I've read a lot of the research on crime. Women tend to shoot or poison the people they kill. Knives are rarely a weapon of choice especially with a man like Chad. He was big and fit. He could fend off any woman."

"Unless she took him by surprise."

"Think of the crime scene. A broken glass with blood

next to it. That doesn't sound like anyone crept up on him."

Kyle zipped up the pack, saying, "Maybe, maybe not. We're assuming the two things are connected. It's possible that the glass had been broken earlier. Then hours later, someone took Chad by surprise."

Jennifer shook her head, sending her blond hair fluttering across her shoulders. "No way. Chad was too anal. He would have cleaned up the glass and the blood immediately."

Her observation upset him more than he was willing to concede. He'd realized Jennifer had slept with Chad and must have known him intimately. Still, he didn't like it one bit. He padlocked the storage locker and turned to go.

"I know what you're thinking."

Was it written on his forehead? He'd never thought of himself as jealous or possessive, but when it came to Jennifer, his feelings became surprisingly intense.

"You think I'm a total idiot for getting involved with Chad Roberts." She bit down on her lower lip, the way she often did when she was upset. "You're right. If I'd taken my time and really gotten to know him, I would never have fallen for him."

She blamed herself for too much, he thought. She felt guilty over her mother's suicide and outright blamed herself for Chloe's death. Now she was coming down hard on herself over Chad.

He slipped his arm around her, saying, "That wasn't what I was thinking at all. I was jealous of the time Chad had spent with you." He wrapped his arms around her midriff and kissed her, then forced himself to let her go. They didn't have any time to waste. "Women fell for Chad. Lots of them. Don't go blaming yourself or thinking you were stupid. He was a pathological liar, and like most pathological liars, he was damn good at it."

"True." She nodded, knowing he was right, but she still blamed herself for being such a fool.

He studied her a moment, then asked, "How did you cut your finger?"

She gazed down at the small cut on her index finger. "I don't know. I didn't realize I had a cut until the sheriff asked to see my hands." She thought a moment. "I might have cut it when I climbed to the rocks at the edge of the beach. I sat on top of them and thought things out. I was so upset that I wouldn't have noticed a small cut."

"That's probably what happened."

Kyle might agree with her, but she doubted the sheriff would accept this explanation. "Raven has a cut on her finger."

"Like I told the sheriff, most all of us do. Helping out at Trevor's caused a lot of us to get small cuts or scrapes."

"Jennifer! There you are. One of the men told me you were here."

They turned and saw Mike Dowd walking up to them. Dowd was wearing his off duty uniform: khaki shorts and an olive polo shirt. Kyle hoped Dowd didn't ask what was in the backpack. None of the equipment was supposed to leave the base.

"I've got some great news," Mike told Jennifer. "I told the rest of the Miami-Dade S&R, but I couldn't find you. Your team has received a federal grant, the first of its kind. They're going to spend a bloody fortune training all of you. Then when you come back home, you'll be a crack team ready to train other groups."

The fine hairs across the back of Kyle's neck stood at attention. "Back home?"

"Yeah, the team will spend eighteen months at top anti-terrorist schools and camps around the world. After you certify them, Kyle, they're off to Israel. No one's better at antiterrorism than the Israelis, right?"

Kyle managed to nod. The ecstatic expression on Jennifer's face told him all he needed to know. She'd leap at this chance, and he couldn't blame her. They'd have to wait to be married.

Hey, maybe not. They could get married before she went away. He didn't like the idea of her training with a bunch of men without a ring on her finger. Guys would be hitting on her right and left.

"After Israel, they're sending you to Saudi, then to Munich. The police in Munich are the best civilian force in the world," Dowd told her. "After the Olympic massacre, they got serious about terrorists. They were way ahead of everyone else. You'll spend some time at New Scotland Yard, where they developed programs to combat the IRA."

"It sounds like a great opportunity," Jennifer said, excitement punctuating every syllable. She turned to Kyle. "Now, if I can just pass the marksmanship test. I'm getting better, but . . ."

She rolled her eyes heavenward. It was all he could do not to grab her and kiss her until she said she would rather stay with him than spend her time training abroad.

"The team finishes up in Japan, where they've done a lot with chemical and biological terrorism after that saran gas attack in the subway. Then you and your bloodhound," he pointed at Sadie, who was sitting on her haunches, waiting for them, "are going to spend six months in Kesseldorf."

"Kesseldorf! Oh, my God!" She leaned down and petted Sadie. "The big time, girl."

"What in hell is Kesseldorf?"

Mike opened his mouth to answer, but Jennifer was quicker. "That's where they train the best dogs. A Kesseldorf dog is worth seventy-five thousand dollars, maybe more. They train them and sell the dogs to police departments all over the world."

Aw, shit. She'd be tied up for two years. Two long, miserable years. Even if they were married, they'd be apart most of the time.

"I'm outta here," Dowd said. "I have a golf game."

Dowd left and Kyle stood there while Jennifer cooed to Sadie, telling the dog what a challenge Kesseldorf was going to be. Didn't he mean anything to her?

"We'd better leave," he said.

"We're lucky Mike didn't ask what you have in the pack," Jen said as they left the building.

"Damn lucky."

"You don't sound happy. Aren't you excited for me? This is such an opportunity."

"It's great." He forced enthusiasm into his voice. "Don't worry about the marksmanship course. We'll have you ready."

Unless you're in jail, added an inner voice. He decided to put off discussing their relationship. There'd be time for that when they'd found the real killer. Still, he couldn't help being bothered by her attitude.

"You don't know how important training at Kesseldorf is to me," she said quietly as he opened the car door for her.

He opened the back door and helped Sadie get in. He put his backpack in the trunk and took out the police scanner, then closed the lid. Inside the car, he attached the device to the dashboard and turned it on. A blast of static shot out of the machine. He adjusted the volume, listening to the police dispatcher. He fiddled with the dial until he was on the sheriff's department channel.

Turning the key in the ignition, he said, "You started to tell me why Kesseldorf is so important."

He shot a glance at her as he drove away. The solemn expression on her face and the chilling look in her eyes alarmed him. Uh-oh.

"After Chloe drowned, I wanted to die. I wouldn't eat. I wouldn't talk. My stepfather didn't know what to do. I suppose I needed professional counseling, but we were poor and lived out in the country.

"One of his bloodhound bitches had a litter but her milk ran dry. There were seven pups who constantly needed to be fed. He marched me out to the barn, showed me the puppies, and told me they were my responsibility. If I didn't take care of them, they would die.

"At first, I just sat there, feeling sorry for myself, refusing to help. He left me alone with them. I couldn't let helpless little puppies—all ears at that stage—starve to death. With no one to help me, I couldn't take a break or sleep. In saving them, I saved myself."

"Oh, Jenny, I wish I'd been there."

"After that I threw myself into working with bloodhounds, training them to track, schooling others to be mantrailers. For a time, the only talking I did was to the dogs. Hiram was patient with me; he wasn't much of a talker anyway. Gradually, I pulled out of my depressed state.

"I've never gotten over Chloe's death, but I no longer think about killing myself. I have my stepfather to thank. Through his contacts, I worked at a kennel to help put myself through Georgia State. Before coming to Miami, I worked the Atlanta airport with a team of dogs who checked luggage for drugs."

"Dogs are special to you," he said. "They're more than a career."

He drove along, slowed by cars full of tourists who were gawking at Key West's unique buildings. While Jenny had been talking, he'd kept an ear tuned to the scanner to see if the sheriff was looking for Jennifer. He wasn't certain what any of this had to do with Kesseldorf, but with when Jennifer opened up, she took her time and told you the whole story. He wouldn't have it any other way.

"Yes, dogs are special," she said as she reached over the back of the seat to pet Sadie. "They remind me of a very special man. Hiram Whitmore adopted me, and in his quiet manner, loved me as if I'd been his own flesh and blood. My mother's death, the pregnancy, then Chloe drowning were blows that came one after the other. I don't know what would have become of me if it weren't for him."

Nothing in her tone suggested she blamed him for not being there for her, but he couldn't help being upset with himself. It had never occurred to him that she was pregnant. While she'd been suffering, he'd acted out, deliberately behaving badly and getting himself into trouble because he was mad at the world over his father's death.

"Four years ago, Hiram was diagnosed with cancer. I gave up my job in Atlanta and went home to take care of him."

He shuddered inwardly, thinking she had experienced so much pain for someone so young. With a dull ache of foreboding, he decided her past life had changed her in ways he was only beginning to discover.

"He lingered a year, suffering terribly," she said. "By then I knew how much I loved him, and I realized how lonely his life must have been. We talked a lot. He told me the happiest years of his life were after I came to live with him. He loved me so much. My real father—wherever he is—couldn't have loved me more or helped me when I needed him."

Kyle spotted a parking place and pulled into it. He shut off the engine and turned to Jennifer. "Jenny, I'm sorry. I wish—"

"Don't be sorry. I'm just trying to explain why I want to go to Kesseldorf. Hiram had nothing to pass on to me except his ability to work with bloodhounds. I've always dreamed that one day I could start a kennel of my own. Not just any kennel, but a first-rate one where I could train dogs for S&R and police work. Kesseldorf is the best training facility in the world. Attending classes there would put me among the elite of trainers and handlers."

"What about the antiterrorist work?" His voice sounded weak even to himself. He could see how important this was to her, and he had no idea if he fit into her plans.

"I'll stay with the team for a while. Between Kesseldorf and my antiterrorist training, I'll have the best credentials imaginable. My dogs will be worth a fortune."

"Jenny, I—"

"Listen!" She turned up the volume on the scanner.

"Attention! Attention! This is an All Points Bulletin. Wanted for arrest for murder: Jennifer Anne Whitmore. Five feet four inches tall. Blond hair. Blue eyes. The subject is considered armed and dangerous."

Chapter 32

"Oh, my God!" cried Jennifer. "What am I going to do?"

Kyle's large hands cupped her face, and he looked directly into her eyes. "*We*, not you—*we*. *We're* in this together, and *we* have a plan."

She'd been alone so long, with no one to count on but her stepfather. Now she faced another crisis, and she had no idea where to turn. She had to trust Kyle to help her.

They listened in silence as the APB was again repeated this time with more information. They knew so much! She'd been seen last with Kyle Parker. They had descriptions of both their cars. And Sadie.

She reached for the door handle.

Kyle grabbed her hand. "What in hell are you doing?"

"Leaving you. Please take care of Sadie."

"I said we're in this together. I meant it."

"Think again. If you help me now, you'll be charged with aiding and abetting a fugitive. It'll ruin your career if nothing else."

"To hell with my career," he said in his deep voice. "I love you. I'm not bailing out on you. Not now, not ever."

The expression on his face was so galvanizing it sent a tremor through her. She knew he meant every word.

He pulled her roughly to him, looked directly into her eyes, then said, "I love you, Jenny. Repeat after me: We're in this *together.*"

She hesitated a moment, then found herself saying, "We're in this together."

He let go of her and turned down the volume on the police scanner. "I have an idea. Since it's Sunday, no one will be working at the house Trevor is restoring. There's a garage where we can hide the car. We'll use the house until it's dark, then we can sneak into Thunder Island."

He started the car, and she scrunched down low in her seat, hoping no one would recognize her. "We're still going to start by checking on Tyler Langley?"

"Yes. If he really worked in Colombia, then the CIA has a file on him."

They were only blocks from Trevor's house on Angela Street. They drove there without seeing any of the sheriff's deputies or police. The single car garage was a narrow building that dated back to Model-T days. They parked the car, then closed the garage door.

"Anybody here?" Kyle yelled as he went into the back door of the house.

The only response was the hollow echo of his voice in the empty building. Sadie hobbled in with them, her cast clack-clacking on the wooden floor. They set up a makeshift table by using a sawhorse and set up the computer on top of it.

Sitting on spools of electrical wire, they linked-up to the satellite to access the computer in the Pentagon. As Kyle tapped on the keys, she watched him and wondered how she was going to deal with him.

She loved Kyle; she always had. He'd given her the most

precious gift of all—Chloe. Even though her young life had ended so tragically, Jennifer still treasured every second they'd spent together.

She knew Kyle expected more of her than she could possibly give. He deserved someone who shared his dream of a big family. Kyle had been an only child. She vividly recalled their discussions when they'd been young and in love. He'd been lonely; he wanted his children to have lots of brothers and sisters.

Kyle turned to her while he waited for the computer to verify his identity. "Let's hope Tyler Langley is his real name."

"The way my luck's going, I'm not betting on a thing."

"I'm verified." He punched the keyboard with a vengeance. "Let's check the CIA database first. Too bad we don't know his middle name, in case there's more than one Tyler Langley."

Waiting, she bent down to pet Sadie. The dog nuzzled her hand.

"Son of a bitch! I think *our* luck has just changed." He covered enough of the screen with his big hand so she couldn't read it. "They have Tyler. What do you think he really does for a living?"

"I give up."

He winked at her. "Since you're so cute, I'm not going to torture you by making you guess." He kissed the tip of her nose. "He's a special agent with the FBI."

"No!" She slapped her bare thigh. "He doesn't seem like the type. He callously told Thelma Mae the truth, then she killed herself. Or do you think he made that up?"

"Why would he?"

Kyle took his hand off the screen, and she closely inspected Tyler's picture and the information about him. "He's with the computer fraud division. Along with techies at AOL, Tyler cracked the Melissa Computer Virus case that screwed up everyone's e-mail. What do you suppose he's investigating at Thunder Island?"

"Who says he's investigating anything? It could be a vacation."

"Can't we get into the FBI database and see?"

He reached down and squeezed her knee. "Great minds think alike."

This time it wasn't so easy. It took over half an hour to ferret through the FBI files.

"Okay, here it is." Kyle pointed to the screen. "He's investigating an on-line fraud case. Who uses a computer at Thunder Island? Not Plotzy."

"Chuck does. He day trades stocks." She thought a moment. "Lisa may use her brother's computer, but I've never heard her mention it. Raven doesn't have a computer. She claims she's roadkill on the information superhighway."

She thought a moment, then added, "Why didn't Tyler explain what he was doing to the sheriff? Then Sheriff Prichett would have investigated more thoroughly."

"I don't know, but I'm going to ask him."

"Ask Tyler?" she said as he shut down the computer. "We don't even know where he is."

Kyle's half smile assured her that he was cunning like a fox. "I'll call the sheriff and pretend I'm an advance person with a big television network. I'll say Peter Jennings wants to interview him and some of the other Thunder Island residents, but I don't know how to contact the others."

To Jennifer's amazement, Kyle didn't even have to speak directly with Sheriff Prichett. Those two magic words "national television" got him the information.

"Tyler is staying at the Banyan Resort over on Whitehead Street. I'm going over there and talk to him."

"What if someone spots you?"

"Trevor keeps work clothes upstairs. I'll change my shirt and cover my hair with a baseball cap."

He was so tall, so distinctive looking that she worried it wouldn't work. He'll go to jail for helping you, whispered a warning voice in her head. But she knew she couldn't stop him. He was every bit as stubborn as she was, maybe more.

"Stay right here," he told her when he reappeared wearing a blue denim shirt splattered with paint, and a Marlin's ball cap. "It may take a while. If something should happen to me, I'll get word to you. Whatever you do, don't leave. Promise?"

He headed for the door, but she couldn't let him go without saying something. She ran after him. "Kyle, I know you're taking an enormous risk for me. Th-thank you."

"When you love someone, you help them any way you can."

Kyle walked into the Parrot Bar, pulled off his shades, and squinted into the darkness. The woman at the desk of the Banyan House had said Tyler had gone to a nearby bar to watch the soccer match on the big screen. He spotted Tyler at a corner table, drinking a beer.

Tyler saw him and motioned him over. Aw, hell. So much for a good disguise.

His eyes adjusting to the darkness, Kyle quickly scanned the room. No law enforcement officers in sight. He wouldn't have expected them to be here on the fringe of Bahama Village unless there was trouble in the bar. But the last thing he needed was for the cops to pick him up. He couldn't do Jennifer any good in jail.

"What's happening?" Tyler asked as Kyle sat down opposite him at the small table.

"You know there's a warrant out for Jennifer's arrest."

"Yeah, too bad. She doesn't seem like the type to—"

"She didn't kill him. The sheriff's just too lazy to investigate until he finds the real killer."

Tyler kicked back the rest of his beer. "A good defense lawyer can get her off. No sweat."

Kyle nearly vaulted out of his chair, but he reminded himself that starting a fight was a sure way to have the bartender call the cops. He calmly reached across the table, grabbed Tyler's hand, and in one quick twist nearly wrenched his arm from the socket.

"Look, you son of a bitch! This is a woman's life that we're talking about. Do you want me announcing on the six o'clock news that an FBI agent was staying at the scene of the crime and failed to identify himself to the authorities?"

Even in the bar's dim light, Kyle could see the color and the animation had drained from Tyler's face. Kyle let go of the man's hand, and Tyler rubbed his shoulder, glaring at him.

"I told the sheriff that I was with the FBI."

Kyle bluffed. "But you didn't say you were here on business, did you?"

"How in hell do you know—"

"It doesn't matter. All I care about is seeing that Jennifer Whitmore isn't convicted of a murder she didn't commit."

"My investigation has nothing to do with the crime."

"How do you know until you talk it over with someone?"

Beads of sweat peppered Tyler's upper lip, and Kyle knew he was still smarting from the little twist he'd given Tyler's arm. Hell. He should have gone the whole nine yards—the way the Afghani rebels did—and bent Tyler's arm until it broke at the elbow. Backwards.

"You're to blame for Thelma Mae's death. Do you want to take responsibility for ruining Jennifer's life? If she's arrested—"

"Hasn't she turned herself in?"

"I wouldn't know. I haven't seen her in some time," he hedged. "But I'm warning you, I'll get you—when you least expect it—if anything happens to Jennifer."

"Okay, okay." Tyler pulled a few bills out of his pocket and threw them on the table. "Let's get out of here."

Outside, the afternoon sunlight nearly blinded him, and Kyle pulled on his shades. He quickly checked the nearby area and didn't see any police. They walked along Whitehead Street into Bahama Village.

The village marked the division between the tourist area and the darker side of Key West. Rows of shotgun houses crammed between Cuban shops and Bahamian restaurants, the village was home to an ethnic mix of colorful people. But it was the kind of area where tourists didn't venture.

Kyle had found the village was like a Caribbean island, and he enjoyed wandering the streets and back alleys. He was accustomed to danger, and whatever trouble could be found in Bahama Village was nothing compared to places he'd been.

They stopped and sat on the wall in front of a Cuban club that hadn't yet opened. The blistering tropical sun beat down on the palms shading the area. The denim shirt Kyle had borrowed was too hot for this weather. A trickle of sweat dribbled down the back of his spine.

"Were you telling the truth about knowing Thelma Mae for years?" Kyle asked.

Tyler's expression was somber. "Yes. Nothing I told the group was a lie. I omitted here and there—"

"Where?"

Tyler gazed at him a moment before answering. "What I said about my mother and Thelma Mae was the whole truth. My mother obsessed, and I mean obsessed, about the baby she gave up for adoption. It's all I heard when I was growing up.

"It didn't seem to matter that she had my father and me as well as my older sister, Mother kept thinking of the child she'd put up for adoption long before my father came along."

"Okay, so?"

"So my mother died. She drank herself to death. I was fifteen at the time, almost grown, but her death haunted me. I kept wondering about my half brother."

"Chad," he guessed.

"That's right. I used my FBI connections to track him down."

"I get the picture."

"I told Chad who I was and we hit it off. At first, I was really impressed with my half brother. We made plans to vacation together, and I told him about Thunder Island. I must have mentioned Thelma Mae."

"Aw, shit. Come on. You told Chad all about Thelma Mae. Didn't you?"

Tyler frowned. "Yes, I did because I didn't want him to think our mother was any different than other mothers who'd given up babies. I had no idea Chad paid much attention until my next visit to Key West."

"Let me guess. Thelma Mae's long lost son has reappeared."

"Exactly. From then on, everything I learned about my brother made me want to deny I knew him."

The bitterness in Tyler's voice stopped him short. He tried to imagine what Tyler had felt and how he might have reacted. Could Cain have killed Abel?

"Chad was after Thelma Mae's money. He was a good actor, who could pretend he didn't give a hoot about money, but money was everything to him. That's why he wanted to marry Lisa. She was loaded."

"Was?"

"Chuck lost most of their fortune speculating on stocks on the Internet."

Something about the way Tyler answered made Kyle think the guy was holding back something.

"Did Chad know this?"

"Yeah," Tyler conceded. "I told him."

The way you told Thelma Mae the truth. What a guy!

"How did Chad feel about it?" Kyle asked.

"He didn't give a damn," Tyler responded, shaking his head. "He'd met some rich woman in South America. He'd planned to unload Lisa way before I told him that she was flat broke."

"You didn't tell this to the sheriff?" Kyle barely resisted the urge to punch his lights out. Only the thought that the jerk might be useful in helping Jennifer stopped him.

"Yes. I told him, but didn't mention I was related to Chad. Why complicate matters? But I did say that Chad had told me that he was finally going to marry someone. He was going to break it off with Lisa just the way he'd broken it off with"—Tyler shrugged—"who knows how many women."

"When did Chad tell you all this?"

"At the barbecue in Truman Annex."

"What time was it?"

"Early in the evening. Yeah. It was eightish, I think."

"Didn't Sheriff Prichett think that gave Lisa a motive to kill? Crimes of passion are typical."

Tyler shook his head. "I told the sheriff, but I also told him that Chad planned to string Lisa along for a few days. From what Chad told me, she was a pretty hot number. He wasn't going to blow her off until just before he left."

Kyle wasn't certain what to make of this except that the sheriff wasn't looking for the real killer. Prichett would rather pin the murder on Jennifer.

"Why didn't Chad have women up in the secret room?"

"As far as I know, he did. Back when he had a thing going with Raven, she used to go up there. I'd go up there, too. It wasn't any big deal except to Thelma Mae.

"She was a little weird. She kept the room secret and told everyone what they saw from the outside was just a facade. She used to go up there to get away from the guests. Then Chad came along and she gave the room to him.

That way whenever he decided to pop into town, he always had a place to stay.''

''What did you really say that made Thelma Mae walk into the ocean?''

Tyler threw back his head and stared up at the palms fluttering in the light breeze. He exhaled, lowered his head and looked at Kyle.

''I thought I was helping her by telling her the truth, but she wigged out. She didn't believe me. She wanted Chad to be her long lost son so badly that she wouldn't listen to the truth. She screamed at me and told me never to come back to Thunder Island. That's why I left her with Plotzy.''

The guy seemed genuinely sorry. Okay, so he wasn't the most sensitive man in Key West, but he did regret what had happened to Thelma Mae. Now that he thought about it, Tyler seemed more upset about her death than Chad's murder.

''Who do you think killed your brother?''

''He was killed with his own knife. He always kept it in his pocket except when he was in his room. He'd put it on the nightstand. I don't think the murder was premeditated. I think Chad had an argument with Plotzy and he grabbed the knife.''

''Plotzy?'' Kyle nearly fell off the wall. ''You think Plotzy murdered your brother?''

Chapter 33

Jennifer jumped up at the sound of someone coming through the rear door of the home Trevor was restoring. She rushed toward the back of the house, expecting Kyle, then stopped dead in her tracks.

"Oh, my God!"

If Sadie hadn't been beating the air with her tail, it would have taken Jennifer a full minute to recognize Kyle. He'd cut his gloss-black hair ruthlessly short, and he was wearing tailored white Bermudas and a black tank top that gloved his powerful torso. He'd applied lotion to his tanned skin and it glistened even in the unlit room. Around his neck was a gold chain as thick as a rope.

"What do you think?" he asked. "Is this a good disguise, or what?"

"Or what. You look . . ."

"Gay?"

"Yes. If I didn't know—"

"Hey, this is Key West. Gays everywhere. The cops won't look twice at me." He held up a bag. "Here's a disguise for you. A brown wig, and''—he hesitated a moment—''a maternity dress and a toss pillow to go under it.''

She grabbed the bag, shutting Chloe out of her mind. ''Been there; done that. I can waddle like any woman does near term. Tell me what happened while I put these on.''

She stripped down to her underwear while Kyle filled her in on what Tyler had told him. ''Why would Plotzy kill Chad? That's assuming Plotzy could get it together long enough to stab anyone.''

''Chad had conned him out of a lot of money by convincing Plotzy that he could corner the aquatic vegetable market.''

Jennifer was laughing so hard she could barely secure the small toss pillow around her midriff with the belt Kyle had brought. ''What are aquatic veggies?''

''How the hell would I know?'' Kyle replied with a smile.

She pulled the maternity dress over her head, asking, ''Did Tyler know whose prints were on the knife?''

''The sheriff told him it was wiped clean.''

''Great, just great.''

''One other thing. Didn't Raven say she'd never been up in the secret room?''

Jennifer fluffed the short, springy curls on the wig. ''Yes, and so did Plotzy.''

''Tyler didn't know for certain if Plotzy had been up there, but he knew Raven went to Chad's room when they'd been together.''

''Why would she lie about it?''

''Beats me.''

She stuffed her hair up under the wig, then asked, ''How do I look?''

The featherlike laugh lines around his green eyes crinkled. ''Beautiful. But no one's going to recognize you.''

''What are we going to do about Sadie?''

On cue, the dog whined when she heard her name. She

gazed up adoringly at Kyle, her tail swishing through the air.

"She's a dead give-away."

"I already fed her. I put water in a pan I found. I don't like leaving her, but I guess we don't have any choice."

Unwilling to risk having someone spot the car, Kyle walked and Jennifer waddled at his side over to Thunder Island. A gay man and a pregnant woman. A few men looked at Kyle like he was a piece of meat, but he ignored them.

They didn't attract any special attention even though Kyle had to tote his military issue backpack with his equipment. He let it hang off one shoulder in a casual way that wouldn't suggest it contained anything of value.

"There's a police car," Jennifer said, her voice shaking with nerves.

"Keep walking. Look up at me and laugh like you're having fun."

Jennifer did what she was told, and he couldn't help thinking how great she looked. Pregnant. One day they were going to have a family, a big family. He hadn't realized how much he wanted children until he'd discovered he had fathered a little girl.

"They didn't even slow down and take a second look," Jennifer said, interrupting his thoughts.

While they walked, they discussed the facts they had and the clues, but were no closer to narrowing the possible list of suspects when they turned down the lane toward Thunder Island. Ahead, they saw the mansion wreathed in yellow and black crime scene tape, but there wasn't a sheriff's car anywhere around. The droves of media with their vans and cameras were gone as well.

"Are we just going to walk up?" Jennifer asked. "What if there's a deputy guarding the place that we can't see?"

"I don't think they'd leave anyone without a squad car. Let's casually wander up the path, then duck into the bushes separating Thunder Island from Weller's Guest House. You'll hide out by the pool while I check the house."

"Almost everyone from Thunder Island is staying at Weller's," commented Jennifer. "Except for Tyler who's across town. Most of the suspects are right next door."

"I wouldn't rule out Tyler Langley. Just because he's an FBI agent doesn't mean he couldn't have killed Chad."

"What motive would he have?"

"Hell, I don't know. Remember Cain and Abel. Tyler did not like his brother at all."

They walked up the footpath without meeting anyone, which wasn't surprising. Most of the people who used the path came from Thunder Island. The guests at Weller's took the shortcut along the shore to walk to the main street.

They slipped between the bushes that grew tall and wild between the two guest houses. From Weller's pool came the raucous sounds of laughter and splashing water. The late afternoon sun cast long shadows, and the scent of decaying leaves rose from the damp soil. Kyle held back a branch and motioned for Jennifer to step out of the brush onto Thunder Island's grounds.

They were in the pool area now, and he quickly glanced around. Towels were flung over a few chaises, and soda cans were on the tables. Thelma Mae would never have allowed the clutter, but she was no longer around. The place appeared deserted.

"Stay right here. If someone comes, duck into the bushes."

He left his backpack with Jennifer and gave her a quick peck on the cheek, then went to see if the sheriff was smart enough to leave a guard to prevent anyone from tampering with the scene. As he moved stealthily from room to room, finding no one, he thought about Jennifer.

This case was one hell of a mess. If they couldn't match the DNA, he didn't know if there would be enough time to unravel the mystery before Jennifer was arrested.

He loved her so damn much, he actually experienced physical pain when he thought of her in jail. She was a complex woman, not easy to know. He wondered if she let anyone really get close to her. Because of the past, it was clear she protected herself with an emotional shield.

Changing her attitude was going to take time and a lot of love. But how in hell could he get through to her if she disappeared from his life for two whole years?

"Prichett didn't post a guard," he told Jennifer when he'd finished searching and returned to the pool. He picked up his heavy backpack. "Let's see if they left enough blood on the floor for us to work with."

All the shutters were closed inside the house and the shadowy staircase was darker than usual, making it difficult to see even though the sun hadn't set. They didn't dare open the shutters in case someone noticed and called the police. Kyle took a small flashlight out of his backpack.

"I've got a great flashlight in my room," Jennifer told him.

"Good. We'll use your desk. The last thing we want to do is spend too much time in Chad's room and mess up the crime scene." He didn't want to worry her more than she already was, but if she was arrested, Kyle was going to make certain the FBI became involved. They would send out their own men to recheck the crime scene.

The house seemed eerily quiet, and they found themselves tiptoeing up the stairs. They passed the landing with the panel leading to the secret room. Tape was all over it, crisscrossed from top to bottom.

"We'll have to be very careful or they'll know someone tampered with the crime scene," he said, his voice low.

"I have an idea. I'll run down to the kitchen and get plastic bags to put over our hands and feet. Plastic doesn't leave trace fibers, right?"

"Right. I'll be in your room setting up the machine."

By the time she returned, he had the DNA field test kit ready to use.

She walked through the door, saying, "I'm small. Maybe I should be the one to go up there."

He took the plastic bags from her. "No. I saw exactly where the wine glass broke. I know exactly where to look."

"What can I do?" she asked as he shoved his feet into plastic bags the maids used to line wastepaper baskets.

"Get me some tape, so I don't trip over these damn things and break my neck."

She opened the door to her closet. "Look! They left the rifle."

Kyle glanced up. "Prichett's damn sloppy."

She brought out a roll of tape from a basket in the closet and helped secure the bags on his hands and feet.

"Take the police scanner out of my pack while I'm gone," he told her. "Let's see what they're up to."

The narrow stairs leading to the secret room were pitch dark and slippery as hell. Kyle used his flashlight to guide him. The doorjamb looked gritty from having been dusted for fingerprints.

He eased into the room and quickly flashed his light around while looking up and down in the zigzag pattern he'd been taught for recon missions with the SEALs. Sloppy did not describe the sheriff's work. Bits of glass were still scattered on the floor and someone had spilled something on the bed cover. He was too highly trained not to have noticed the spot the night he found the body.

Most of the drop of blood was still there, although it appeared someone had *attempted* to retrieve a sample. The stupid bags on his hands made him fumble while trying to pull the knife he'd taken out of his pack and placed in his pocket. He yanked it out and pressed on it and the deadly blade flipped out.

He crouched down and used the tip of the knife to scrape up the dried blood without scratching the floor. Kyle kept the knife in one hand, the flashlight in the other and went downstairs. Jennifer was waiting for him on the other side of the tape.

"Take this." He wiggled the knife through the tape cobwebbing the door.

He dropped to his knees and slithered under the tape on his belly. He surged to his feet, then bent down and reattached the single piece of tape he'd undone near the bottom of the floor.

"I can't believe you got under there. I couldn't."

"SEALs are trained to get in and out of tight spots." He took the knife from her. "Let's see what we've got."

They hurried back to her room, and Kyle yanked off the plastic bags while Jennifer prepared the slide. The static-filled scanner caught his attention.

"Anything new?"

"No. They just keep repeating the same APB. They've stopped a couple of people, but, of course, they haven't found me."

He was about to suggest turning on the television and finding out what CNN had to say, then decided against it. Jennifer was anxious enough without seeing her picture flashed across the screen as a murder suspect.

He retrieved the knife he'd placed blade up on the nightstand. She handed him the slide and he smeared the dried blood on it. Inwardly saying a prayer, he put it in the machine.

"What's your guess?" he asked. "Man or woman?"

"Woman," she replied without hesitation. "Caucasian."

"White? That's a given, considering the suspects."

The machine whirred, then out came a piece of paper. He read it: "Male Caucasian."

"Well, that eliminates Raven and Lisa. I'm stunned. My money was on Lisa." She looked at the small strip of paper. "What else does it tell? Can we rule out anyone else?"

"Not unless we knew their blood types. This man's is O negative. It's not very common. The rest of the info is technical."

"What good is the machine, if that's all it does?"

She was cute when she was mad, he thought, then decided this wasn't anger. It was Jenny's way of expressing her unspoken fear. She'd been hoping for a miracle. He should have warned her not to expect too much.

"This machine is a prototype. Most of the time you don't need to know more than the terrorist's race and sex. What the machine excels at is DNA matches. If you find a suspect, you'll know in less than a minute if you've found the right person."

"I see," she said, calmer now. "We should split up and gather samples, correct?"

"Yes, blood's the best but it's harder to find. Look on the pillow for hair samples. Use the tweezers to pick up one of them. Look for a hair with the follicle intact, if possible."

"Why?"

"That's next easiest to read. Too many people bleach or color their hair. It strips the shaft. You can get a read, but it's not as reliable." He picked up a handful of small plastic bags off the bed. "I'll do Tyler's. You check Chuck's room. Do you know where it is?"

"Sure. I know where Chuck and Plotzy's rooms are, but not Tyler's. He's probably across the house in the wing where Thelma Mae put the short-term guests. It should be listed in the guest register at the front desk."

"I'll find out, then search Tyler's room. You get a sample from Chuck. If these two are negative, we'll get a DNA sample from Plotzy's room. I think he's a long shot and we haven't time to waste."

Kyle raced down the stairs, something niggling at the back of his mind, though he wasn't certain what it was. He located the guest book. Tyler had been assigned a room at the far end of the other wing.

The room was locked. Kyle was tempted to use the knife he'd put back in his pocket to pick the lock, but decided against it. He might leave telltale scratches on the dark wood.

"Aw, shit," he cursed as he rushed down the hall and out onto the verandah that wrapped around Thunder Island.

The breeze was blowing toward him, carrying with it the sounds of cocktail chatter from Weller's Guest House. It was nearing summer and the days were longer now. Cocktail time lasted several hours. He imagined the killer sipping a drink, confident he'd tricked the sheriff.

"Come on, baby," he whispered as he tried the window in Tyler's room.

The first was locked, but the second one was open a crack. He slid his hand between the window and the sill, then pushed up, and it lifted without making a sound. Inside, shadows darkened the small room.

A swish of his flashlight revealed a room that looked as if no one had been there in days. He opened the closet door, but nothing was inside. Noticing the bed was made, he wondered if Tyler was anal enough to have made the bed that morning after they had discovered Chad's body.

He threw back the sheets and trained his flashlight on the linen. Not a single hair on either pillow or the sheets. He bent down and sniffed the pillow, inhaling deeply.

Aw, hell.

He recognized the clean, fresh scent. Linens were changed daily at Thunder Island. Tyler had not slept in his bed last night.

Interesting.

He hurried into the bathroom and risked turning on the light. None of the usual toiletries or personal items were there—certainly not the hairbrush or comb he'd been hoping to find. That left the shower and the toilet.

The sheriff's deputies had turned the maids away this morning. Even if Tyler hadn't spent the night in his bed, he must have showered and gone to the bathroom since the room had last been cleaned.

He inspected the shower thoroughly and couldn't find a single hair. Mentally crossing his fingers, he checked the toilet.

Nothing.

Then he spotted a wiry hair just under the rim. "Son of a bitch," he said out loud. Using the tweezers, he bagged it.

Jennifer was waiting for him in her room. "What took you so long? I had time to get a hair sample from Plotzy's room. I'm running it right now."

"It was hard to get anything on Tyler."

The machine whirred and spit out an inch of tape: *Sample does not match.*

"Okay, I never thought it was Plotzy," Kyle told her.

"Let's run Tyler next. I've got a funny feeling about this case. Something's bothering me, but I'm not quite sure what it is." He used the tweezers to remove the hair from the plastic bag.

"Yuck! Is that what I think it is?" she asked.

"It's a pubic hair and I'm damn lucky to have found it." He carefully placed it on the slide she was holding in front of him.

He put his arm around her as they waited. In the distance, they heard the wail of a police siren. Her whole body went stock still. The sound moved closer and closer.

Hugging her to his side, he said, "It'll be okay. I'll do whatever it takes to clear you."

She gazed up at him with diamond-bright eyes. "How can I thank you?"

Let me love you the way you deserve to be loved. Forget the past. Give us a chance.

"The siren stopped," she cried. "They're not coming to Thunder Island."

The machine purred and out came another small piece of paper. Kyle grabbed it and tipped it so he could read it.

"Sample does not match."

The spark of hope extinguished, something churned in the pit of his stomach. He did not like the way this was going. Too much was at stake.

"That leaves Chuck." She sounded as depressed as he felt. "He doesn't have a motive."

"That we know about." This time he prepared the slide for her while she removed a small piece of toilet paper from a plastic bag. "What's that?"

"Chuck must have cut himself shaving. You said blood was best. I have a hair sample, too, if you—"

"No. Blood is better. Clamp down on the center of the sample. I'll use my tweezers to pull away the extra paper. That way it'll fit onto the slide."

As he removed the excess paper, he said, "You know, even if this sample comes up negative, there are several possible explanations. I was relying on how hyper Thelma Mae was about cleanliness. It's possible the hair I found came from a previous guest, and the maid missed it when she cleaned the toilet. It didn't appear as if Tyler spent much time in the room. His bed hadn't been slept in."

"Really? Where was he last night when Chad was murdered?"

"Damned if I know."

He put the sample into the machine. "Then there's always the possibility that an outsider killed Chad. Then the DNA will never match."

She nodded slowly, her eyes on the machine. It didn't take a rocket scientist to know she was silently praying. He put his arm around her, and they waited, seconds ticking by like hours as the machine analyzed the DNA. At last the tape rolled out of the machine.

He had trouble bringing himself to read it.

Looking down, he saw: *Sample matches.*

Chapter 34

Jennifer spun around to Kyle, not believing the reading he'd gotten from the DNA Field Test. "Are you sure Chuck's blood sample matches the one of the person who broke the wineglass? That's hard to believe."

Kyle stared down at the printout. "The computer doesn't lie."

"What could be his motive?"

"Hey, the sleaze-master was marrying Chuck's sister. Maybe he was pissed off enough to kill the guy."

"It's possible," she said, slowly accepting the machine's verdict. "Whatever the reason, we can't prove anything, can we?"

Kyle hesitated a moment too long, then replied, "In court, we could duplicate these results—"

"In court? That would mean I'd rot in jail for months, maybe—"

"Jenny, Jenny." He put both hands on her shoulders and leveled his intense green eyes on hers. "I have an idea. Chuck and Lisa are staying next door. I'm going over there and talk to them."

She waited for him to add something. When he didn't, a dark undertow from the past weighed her down. How could she ever have thought she was going to be successful? She might have dreamed of Kesseldorf and a kennel of her own. But fate had been lurking all these years, slowly punishing her for the death of her daughter, but waiting to exact the ultimate revenge.

She sank down into the chair beside the desk and stared straight ahead at the closed plantation shutters. The slats resembled bars . . . prison bars, she thought.

Kyle shook her arm. "Jen, listen to me. Here's what we're going to do. I've got a great new piece of equipment. It's a tiny microphone that can be concealed easily without all the wire and tape the police now have to use."

She wondered how this was going to help her.

"It sends a signal to this transmitter, which records the entire conversation. I'm going to talk to the twins. Lisa must be in on it too. I know I can trip them up, and get them to confess."

"Why would they?" She heard her own voice sounding impossibly world-weary and drained of the will to fight.

He pulled something out of his pack, then lowered himself onto the bed beside her. For a moment there was no sound in the room except the slow whoosh of the ceiling fan. He swept her, weightless, into his arms and held her close.

The solid thump of his heart against hers should have been reassuring, but it only reminded her of how alone she'd been, and how alone she was going to be. In prison.

"I'm going to bluff them into thinking Chad tape recorded their conversation the night he was killed. All the while, we'll be using this guy"—he held up the tiny microphone that looked like a black button—"to record their reaction."

"You're wasting your time," she said flatly.

"I'll tell them the police sent the blood sample to a special FBI lab, and they IDed it as Chuck's. I'll say I got the info through my SEAL connections, and the sheriff hasn't gotten the report yet. That should shake them."

She doubted it could work. There was something strange about the twins, and something cold and calculating about Lisa. Even a man as smart as Kyle wasn't likely to trick them into telling the truth.

He stood up and took something out of his backpack. "Look, I've got to hurry. I want to catch them while they're still sipping cocktails around the pool at Weller's. Let me show you how to work this. I want you to listen to the conversation and record every word. All I'll have will be the hidden microphone. You'll be the important person using this laser recorder."

"Laser recorder?"

In the palm of his hand, he held a device the size of a paperback book. "It's voice activated. In the old days, if we wanted to hide a tape, we turned it on and it ran and ran and ran. Imagine the miles of blank tape."

Again, he showed her the minuscule microphone in the palm of his hand. "This baby transmits sound to a recorder that can be as far away as half a mile. I've put this switch on, so you can listen."

"I have a thought," she said, an idea forming. "Is the recorder portable? Can I take it with me?"

"Sure. It's battery operated. Where are you going with it?"

"While you're talking to Lisa and Chuck, I'm going to search their rooms. Maybe I can find something that will help us."

"Good thinking."

He rummaged through his pack, then handed her a wristwatch. "In case you find something, we need to be able to communicate. Press here." He showed her a small tab at the side of the watch. "My Breitling will vibrate. I'll know you have something to tell me. It may take me a minute to get to a place where I can talk to you, so be patient."

"Then what do I do?"

"Hold the watch up to your ear to listen. Press on this button and keep it down while you talk, just like you would a two-way radio."

"Okay. I get it. My watch talks to your watch." She strapped it on her wrist. Obviously it had been designed for the military. It was so big it hung on her like a bangle bracelet.

"Like my watch, your watch will vibrate, if I need to talk to you."

His steady gaze was riveted on her face. For a long moment, he didn't say a word. Finally, he spoke and his voice cracked with emotion.

"I'm going to come through for you, Jenny. This time I'm not going to let you down."

"Kyle, don't—"

He smothered the words with a quick, searing kiss.

"Listen to the recorder and buzz me if you find anything important."

Before she could say another word, he left her room. She slipped the laser recorder into the deep pocket of the ridiculous maternity dress she was wearing. The pillow strapped to her midriff was scratchy and unbearably hot. She unhooked the belt holding it in place and dumped it on the bed.

Using her flashlight, she ventured up the dark hallway to Chuck's room. He'd left it unlocked and she tiptoed inside. There wasn't much of interest in his closet except for a suitcase filled with computer printouts of stock he'd traded on the Internet.

On the small writing desk found in every room, she discovered a laptop computer and more printouts, these more recent. There might be a clue in them, but she didn't know enough about stocks or Internet trading to decipher them.

She glanced down at her own watch and saw nearly half an hour had passed. How was he doing? she wondered. Evidently, he wasn't talking to Lisa and Chuck because he hadn't activated the microphone.

She closed the door to Chuck's room and hoped she would have better luck with Lisa's room. Halfway down the hall, a burst of noise made her jump. Kyle had turned on his microphone and the device in her pocket was picking up the transmission.

There was some background chatter, then Raven's voice came through. "I don't know why Lisa can't let Chuck have a life of his own."

Listening, Jennifer walked down the hall and let herself into Lisa's room.

"Things will be better after you're married," she heard Kyle tell Raven. "Lisa will get used to having you around."

Jennifer flashed the light around the room. What a mess! Clothes flung everywhere as if Lisa had tried on a multitude of outfits before deciding which to wear. She opened the closet and found it was so crammed with clothes that it would take her months to search through everything.

Common sense said anything of importance would be in one of her multitude of purses or in the desk. Fashion magazines were heaped on the desk, but it appeared to be easier to search.

She half listened to Kyle as he consoled Raven and rifled through the desk. Lisa's bank account was overdrawn. There were overdue notices from Visa, MasterCard, and Discover. American Express had revoked her card.

In the bottom drawer, she found an accordion file

stuffed with bills and other medical records. She was ferreting through the sheets of reports when the watch dangling on her wrist began to shake. Kyle was trying to reach her. She realized she'd been so absorbed with the file that she hadn't realized voices were no longer coming from the recorder.

Turning the confounded watch around, she fumbled with it until she found the correct button. "Kyle?"

"Yeah, babe. I'm here."

"What's happening?"

"Tension and a shitload of it." There was a slight pause and she thought the watch had malfunctioned. Then Kyle said, "Sorry about the cussing. I'm frustrated. I can *feel* something's going on, but I don't know what it is."

She kept flipping through the file, scanning the medical documents. Lisa had made notes on some of them.

"Did anyone ask about me?" she wanted to know.

"Sure. The minute I walked in they asked about you. I said I hadn't seen you since this morning."

She read a questionnaire from the American Cancer Society that Lisa had filled out but never sent in.

"Did you find anything in Chuck's room?"

"Not really," she replied, quickly reading the form. "He trades a lot of stock. It would take time to go through it all, and we'd need someone with more expertise than I have to figure it out. It appears that Lisa's broke. She has bills galore and enough overdue notices to paper the Taj Mahal."

"Okay, I'm going to get Chuck to take a walk on the beach with me. When I have him alone, I'm going to pull the bit about the secret recorder in Chad's room, then I'm going to lay the DNA data on him."

"Good luck," she said into the watch. "You be careful."

She replaced the questionnaire in the file, then looked at the next paper. Something in her brain clicked. She reread the one page inquiry from the American Cancer Society.

"O negative," she said out loud, then read the document more closely. "That's it!"

She twirled the watch around, pressed the button, and waited for Kyle to call her. Seconds passed. Nothing. She hit the button again, in case it wasn't working.

"Be patient," she whispered to herself. "He's probably talking to someone and can't get away."

Minutes dragged by, then he finally answered. "Jen, what's wrong?"

"Nothing. I figured out who really killed Chad. Sadie didn't make a mistake. It was Lisa, not her brother."

"Jenny, the DNA—"

"Listen to me! I just read a questionnaire from the American Cancer Society. Lisa had a bone marrow transplant from Chuck. She's producing his blood now, right?"

"I guess," he replied, but he didn't sound so sure.

"She was AB positive before chemotherapy for leukemia. It destroyed her blood cells. Then Chuck donated his bone marrow, and her system started producing his blood. She became O negative. Don't you see? They both have the exact same blood because it's Chuck's blood."

"Jesus H. Christ! I ask you, what are the chances of something like this?"

"The test kit came up with a match because it compared blood to blood where the DNA is Chuck's. If I'd used a hair sample, it wouldn't have matched."

"Jennifer, you're good, really good."

"Trust women's intuition. I sensed Lisa was lying when she said she was with Chuck the night of the murder. Chad must have told Lisa that he wasn't going to marry her, and she killed him."

She thought a moment, then added, "There's one other thing. Didn't Tyler tell you Chuck lost a ton of money day trading?"

"That's right."

"Lisa seems to be broke. Money could have figured into the murder somehow. Chad might have let Lisa know he was after her money."

"I'm going to get Lisa out on the beach alone and see if I can bluff the truth out of her."

Suddenly, her throat worked hard, sliding up and down as she tried to speak. "Darling, be careful. Lisa's killed once with a knife. It's pretty gutsy for a woman to attack a big man like Chad that way. I don't want anything to happen to you."

"Don't worry about me, Jen. I've been in tighter spots. Listen to the recorder. With luck, we'll crack this case yet."

"Bye," she said with a terrible sense of foreboding.

Hell hath no fury like a woman scorned. Or cornered.

She rushed back to her room and searched through Kyle's backpack for a gun. Criminy! All he had was a smart gun. The Colt wouldn't respond to her voice.

Remembering the sharpshooter's rifle with the scope in the closet, she grabbed it.

From the recorder, she heard Kyle talking to Lisa. He was chatting her up, and saying he needed to talk to her privately.

Jennifer ran down the stairs, the rifle in one hand. It was nearly dark. The sun had set but its light lingered in the sky. It was tricky to shoot at dusk; the light played tricks on the eyes.

She rushed out the side door, through the garden and into the pool area, assuring herself that she wasn't going to have to use the rifle. She just wanted to be nearby should Kyle need her.

She plunged into the thicket of brambly bushes separating Thunder Island from Weller's Guest House. As she moved along, she could hear people talking, but she couldn't see them through the thick growth. From the sound of the conversation, Lisa and Kyle were walking on the beach.

Jennifer shouldered her way through the brush until she came to the end of the foliage. She hung back just enough to conceal herself, then peered through the branches and saw Kyle with Lisa at the far side of the beach.

Chapter 35

Jennifer was too far up the deserted beach to see Lisa and Kyle's faces, but the tiny bug Kyle put in his pocket transmitted their conversation.

"I can prove you killed Chad," Kyle said.

Jennifer quickly raised the rifle. By looking through its scope she could watch Lisa. Darkness was falling quickly, but there was enough light to see the smug smile on Lisa's face.

She lowered the rifle, and listened to Lisa. "I didn't kill him. I have an alibi, remember?"

"The blood next to the broken glass is yours."

"That's ridiculous. They haven't tested the blood."

"I tested the blood with a DNA field test kit the military uses. It's yours. No question about it."

"I don't have to stand here and listen to these wild accusations. You can't prove a thing."

"Yes, I can. Your medical records show you were AB positive until you had the bone marrow transplant. Now you're O negative like your brother because his bone marrow is now yours and it produces the same blood—his blood."

There was a moment of silence. The only sound coming from the hidden microphone was the surf pounding the shore.

"You're making this up," Lisa said, but she didn't sound as confident as before.

Jennifer knew they'd nailed the killer. The trick would be getting Lisa to admit what she'd done. Then they would need more evidence. She doubted this recording could be used in court, but it would be a start. If the case was investigated properly, she would be cleared, and Lisa would be indicted.

Kyle kept at Lisa. "A friend has removed Chuck's computer and all his records. We'll be able to prove—"

"What friend?"

"A close friend."

She could hear the smile in his voice, and she couldn't resist raising the rifle to take a look at them. The shadows were deeper now, but she could just make out Kyle's stern expression. He was amazingly convincing.

Out of the corner of her eye, she caught movement. She turned, the scope in place and saw Chuck racing across the sand. The breeze flapped his shirt, and she saw he had a gun tucked into the waistband at the small of his back.

"Oh, my God," she said outloud.

She waited, listening and praying Kyle could take care of himself even though he wasn't armed. The last thing she wanted to do was take a risky shot at twilight.

"What's going on?" Chuck's voice was breathless.

"I can prove your sister killed Chad Roberts," Kyle said.

"Yeah, sure. We were together when he was killed."

"He says a friend took your computer and all your records," Lisa told her brother.

There was something odd in Lisa's voice, and Jennifer

knew she was trying to tell her brother something. Or warn him.

Chuck barked a laugh, then said, "Bullshit. Pure bullshit. You know, Parker, when you waltzed into Weller's in that outfit, I knew you were up to something. I just ran over to Thunder Island to check my room. My computer's there, and so are all my records."

Lisa screamed at Kyle, "You lying sack of shit!"

"Lisa, get a grip," her brother said.

"Chuck, he knows too much."

The premonition Jennifer had felt morphed into bone-chilling fear. Chuck had a gun, and no one was around. The light was dying so quickly that she didn't have a prayer of firing an accurate shot.

Lisa kept talking. "He knows we're the same blood type because of the bone marrow transplant."

"Shut up, you idiot!"

"My friend took the information to the FBI," Kyle said.

"Give me a break!" Chuck said. "Do you think I'm going to fall for that?"

"It's true."

"He knows too much," Lisa repeated. "Way too much."

Jennifer raised the rifle again and peered through the scope into the near darkness.

"He's too smart for his own good," Chuck agreed as he pulled the gun on Kyle. "He's a dead man."

"Question," Kyle said, his voice amazingly calm. "Which one of you actually stabbed Chad?"

The group was far enough away from Weller's that a shot from a revolver would be muffled by the surf. Kyle couldn't possibly know she was nearby. He was just trying to get the conversation recorded to prove her innocence.

I'm going to come through for you, Jenny. This time I'm not going to let you down.

She swallowed back the sob rising in her throat as she recalled his words. Her arm shaking, she lowered the rifle.

He loved her, truly loved her, and he was set to give his life to make up to her for not being around when she had needed him.

She didn't blame him for what had happened. Chloe had been the result of their affair, and the baby had become the most important thing in her life. Kyle shouldn't blame himself for anything. She was the one who had failed Chloe.

"Who do you think killed the cocky prick?" Chuck asked Kyle.

"Checking blood only, you both have the same DNA. I'm sure the lab that the sheriff sent the sample to will—"

"You're stalling, Parker," Chuck said. "But since you think you're so smart, you'll like knowing the sheriff said he has enough evidence to convict Jennifer. He doesn't need to run a DNA check that might take months."

Sheriff Prichett didn't need to look at the blood beside the broken glass at the murder scene? Her arms turned to Jell-O. What kind of sheriff so easily dismissed physical evidence?

A man who hates you, her logical brain answered.

"Do you suppose Jennifer's around here somewhere?" asked Lisa.

Jennifer pulled back into the bushes.

"Nah, I just heard she was arrested at Papa Joe's bar," her brother replied.

Arrested? Jennifer pitied the poor tourist who must have been caught without proper ID and mistakenly identified as Jennifer Whitmore.

Kyle said, "Chuck, you killed Chad because he took you for a lot of money."

No, Kyle! Lisa killed Chad—not Chuck.

Jennifer lifted the rifle again. Through the scope, she viewed the threesome down the beach. The way Kyle was standing, she didn't have a clear shot. With her luck, if she fired, she would kill the wrong man.

"Chad fucked us big-time. He conned us into investing everything we had in some crazy Internet stock that bombed. I investigated and discovered the money went into an account in the Caymans. Know whose account?"

"Chad's?"

"Right. The stupid prick thought I wouldn't find out he was behind it."

"I went up to Chad's to try to get some of our money back," Lisa explained. "He laughed in my face. That's when I slammed the wineglass down on the table and broke it."

"I was outside the door on the stairs." Chuck's voice came through the microphone with startling vehemence. "I was inside and on Chad in a heartbeat."

"Just what I thought," Kyle said.

"That's it, Kyle, keep them talking," Jennifer whispered to herself.

"A classic love triangle," Kyle continued. "Chad and two women."

"Lisa never loved that prick." Chuck's voice was bitter. "We love each other. We've been together our whole lives."

"What about Raven?" Kyle asked.

Move over, Jennifer silently pleaded with Kyle. The light was almost nonexistent now. In another few minutes, she wouldn't be able to take a shot. Good or bad.

"Raven's father is richer than sin," Lisa informed Kyle.

Really? What on earth was she doing fan dancing, Jennifer wondered.

"Chuck's going to marry her, then she'll meet with an accident." Lisa laughed.

"That's a little cold, isn't it?" Kyle shifted to one side.

"Cold?" Chuck aimed his gun.

"It's now or never," Jennifer told herself with a silent prayer that all her time on the firing range would pay off when it counted the most. She sighted Chuck between the cross hairs and squeezed the trigger.

The kick knocked her backward. She staggered, her dress catching on a branch, then she stood upright, her eyes closed.

"Please, God. Spare Kyle."

Ear-piercing screams split the air. Jennifer opened her eyes and saw Kyle standing in the distance. She dropped to her knees, unable to keep the sobs from coming.

"Jenny, it's okay, honey." Kyle gathered Jennifer in his arms. She clung to him, crying even harder.

"I-I was so w-worried," she told him between sobs. "I-I thought they were going to kill you."

He kissed her moist cheek, touched she cared this deeply about him. He loved her so much, it frightened him. Maybe there was a chance for them after all.

"I knew you were hiding here. I saw you right away."

"H-how? I-I thought I was hidden."

"You were," he replied, "but I wouldn't have made it through SEAL training if I couldn't spot movement in the bushes."

"Did I kill Chuck?"

"No, but you damn near blew off his arm."

"Really? I was aiming for his gun."

He brushed a kiss across her forehead. "You saved my life. I guess I'll have to certify your marksmanship."

"Don't joke!"

Kyle looked up the beach. The paramedics were loading Chuck onto a stretcher. Seconds after the shot was fired, a couple had come out from Weller's. Kyle had used their cell phone.

"Come on, Jen. The police will want to interview you."

"The sheriff might—"

"Don't worry. I called the chief of police and explained

the problem. He's contacted the FBI. Since Chad was using an offshore bank to defraud people, the Feds can investigate this case."

It took hours at the police station for each of them to be interviewed. Just as they were leaving, the FBI arrived, and they had to go through the whole process again. A little after midnight, they walked out the double doors into the balmy night air. The sound of reggae music drifted toward them from a bar on Duval Street. Along with it came the early summer scent of night blooming jasmine.

Kyle smiled inwardly. The sense of relief he felt defied words. Not even when he'd been in Libya, hiding out and praying he didn't bleed to death before he could swim out to the SEAL boat, had he been so frightened. Fear had damn near paralyzed him so that he couldn't have helped Jennifer. In the end, she'd saved him.

He slipped his arm around her as they walked up the street. She'd pulled off the cheap wig he'd bought in Bahama Village, but she hadn't combed her hair. It was tousled and sexy as hell.

"Trevor wants us to stay with him at Half Moon Bay," he told her, thinking she was strangely silent. Undoubtedly she was exhausted from the ordeal. "Let's go over to Sunset Pier and catch the water shuttle to Sunset Key."

"There are only two days left in the antiterrorist course," she said out of the blue. "Then I'll leave for Israel."

Be understanding, he told himself. This is a great opportunity for Jennifer. More important, the Kesseldorf part would fulfill her dream. They were passing a sidewalk café that had closed. He guided her to a table.

"Let's sit down a minute."

Without a word, she took a chair, and he sat next to her, scooting his chair close. The only light came from the moon filtering through a palm. It was much darker here than he would have liked.

"Jen," he began, then found he didn't know what to say exactly. Hell, he'd never been good at stuff like this. He knew what he felt, but he didn't know how to express it. He gazed into the blue eyes he loved so much and blurted out, "What about us?"

For a painfully long moment, she looked away, then she faced him. "I love you, and I have since I was a young girl. Tonight when I had to fire the rifle to save you, I realized I will *never* love anyone else."

Her words, spoken in a heartfelt, soft voice, were the most touching he'd ever heard spoken. He'd felt she loved him, but listening to her actually say the words meant so much more than he had ever expected.

"Jenny, you don't know how much I wanted to hear you say that. We're going to get married and raise a big family. I know you miss Chloe, and nothing will ever be quite the same without her, but you'll love our children, too. I know how important this training program is to you. We can work it out. Let's get married now, and I'll—"

"No. I can't marry you."

"Why, Jen? You said how much you love me."

She dropped her eyes before his questioning gaze. "I meant every word. I love you with all my heart, but I can't marry you. Children. A big family. I want them for you. I can't think of anyone who would be a better father. I'm a lousy mother. I don't want any more children. Period. End of discussion."

The truth hit him. Jenny still blamed herself for their daughter's death. He should have realized this and approached the subject differently.

"Jen, I know how much you loved Chloe. What happened could have happened to any mother. You—"

"I knew better. If I had called my stepfather to bring a dog, Chloe would be with us today."

With *us*. The words sounded so sweet to him. She was finally thinking in terms of "us." He took her hand and squeezed it gently to reassure her.

"Jen, think about it. If mothers called S&R every time a child wandered out of a yard, we would have to have dozens of teams per city instead of one."

Her chin hitched up a notch. "It was a rural area that backed up to the wilderness. I . . ." She stood up, planted her hands on her hips, then continued, "I'm never having another child."

He believed her, realizing she'd thought about this for years. How could he change her mind? Kyle wondered. He must have hesitated a second too long.

"There's no way I'd marry you. You deserve someone who will love you and give you the family you want."

Before he could stand up, she had vanished into the tropical night.

Kyle watched the last of the Miami-Dade County Antiterrorist Task Force complete the field test. He signed the man's certificate and handed it to him.

"What about Jennifer Whitmore?" asked one of the other men.

"I've signed her certificate," Kyle said, keeping his tone neutral. "After all she's been through, she needs her rest."

To tell the truth he had no idea where Jennifer was. She hadn't shown up for the final days of training. A dead weight in his chest, he had signed the paper certifying she had passed the course and vouching for her superior marksmanship.

He'd searched the town for her, but no one knew where she'd gone. The team was scheduled to leave on a military flight for Israel that evening. He was betting she would be on the plane.

Kyle hung around the firing range, testing a new gun

that could fire at varying speeds, depending on if it was necessary to kill someone or merely stun them. It was an interesting weapon, which was still in the test phase, but he found it hard to concentrate.

His mind was on Jennifer.

He was on the tarmac as the team boarded the plane for the flight to Israel. Jennifer walked up with Sadie at her side. The dog furiously wagged her tail and hopped up and down, overjoyed to see him. Jennifer smiled, a neutral half smile that she might have given a stranger.

"Good luck, Jen." The words came out with a slight rasp. "I'm here if you need me."

Jennifer stopped in front of him, her blue eyes serious. "Forget me, Kyle. Find someone who will give you what you deserve. It isn't me."

He bent down to kiss her, but she turned away. "I love you, Jenny. I always have. I always will. Look into your heart and forgive yourself. Then you'll be able to love me."

She boarded the plane without looking back.

Epilogue

Eighteen months later

Kyle stood on Thunder Island's back terrace and thought about the long, lonely months that had passed since he'd last seen Jennifer. Chuck and Lisa Wilson had been convicted of murder. Justice in America being what it was, their convictions were on appeal. Raven had disappeared, last seen dancing in a topless bar in South Beach. Plotzy had moved to Jo'Mama's Clothing Optional Guest House where he bathed in the nude every evening at sunset to ward off "the curse."

Sheriff Prichett had not survived the scandal surrounding his botched investigation of Chad's murder. The public who adored Teflon presidents and Oval Office scandals had drawn the line at plotting against a woman who had rescued a lost child. Prichett lost his office to a gay man who ran on a "green is the only hope for earth" platform.

"What about you?" Kyle asked the stars. He stared up

at the night sky, thinking how lonely he'd been since the last time he'd seen Jennifer.

He'd left the Navy's antiterrorist program and joined his friend Sam Halford's security company that specialized in corporate accounts. Within six months, Kyle had become a partner. The money that flowed from a private business had been astounding.

Still, neither success nor money could replace Jennifer.

He spoke to her once every few months—when he could catch her somewhere—and knew she was thrilled with her job. There didn't seem to be any way to repair their relationship, but he'd be damned if he would give up on her so easily.

Unexpectedly, she'd called and said she needed to see him. They'd arranged to meet at Thunder Island where they could have some privacy. She was scheduled to be on a military transport plane that was flying into Key West. It had been delayed in Puerto Rico, so he'd come here to wait.

"Why does she want to see me?" he wondered out loud.

She'd called from London where she'd been training with New Scotland Yard's Antiterrorist team to say she needed to talk to him. From the sound of her voice, this wasn't going to be good news. Each time he'd spoken with Jenny, she'd seemed more and more distant.

"She's slipped into another world," he whispered to himself. "You can't bring her back. She has to decide for herself that she wants to share her life with you."

He turned and walked across the unmowed grass to the main house. It had been in probate, the court unable to locate any heirs, since Thelma Mae's death. He opened the back door near the bar area where guests had gathered each evening. He could almost hear the voices of yesterday chattering in the dusk.

Almost.

He twisted the knob, then shouldered the door open.

Dust motes fluttered in the last rays of the setting sun. The house smelled dank and moldy. Deserted.

Eerily quiet.

Remnants of the crime scene tape dangled from the banister as he walked up to Jennifer's room. He raised his hand, feeling the dust accumulating beneath his fingers as he touched the rail. At the landing, he paused.

Someone had closed the door to the secret room.

He took one step, then another, then another until he came to a stop at Jennifer's door. The knob was cold beneath his hand as he twisted it, and the door creaked open. Inside dark shadows cloaked the room and adjacent bathroom.

Kyle threw himself across the bed face down. His nose against the unmade sheets, he inhaled deeper and deeper and deeper. With the air came the faint scent of Jennifer's perfume.

"Aw, Jenny, give our love a chance."

Again, he sniffed at the sheets that had remained on Jennifer's bed for months. Once more, Jenny's unique scent filled his lungs, his heart. Jennifer was coming home.

At last.

Kyle scooted upright and looked around the dark room. What could he say to change her mind about their relationship? He'd had months to come up with something, but he hadn't been able to think of anything that he hadn't already told her.

He lay on Jennifer's bed wondering what he could possibly do, when he heard a noise downstairs. He vaulted to his feet, his SEAL training still kicking-in. Scanning the shadowy room, he realized no one had gotten the drop on him.

He descended the stairs, thinking he was imagining sounds from the past when Thunder Island had been a hive of noise and activity. At the bottom of the shadowy staircase stood a solitary figure.

"Jenny? Is that you?"

"Who else were you expecting in this tomb?" she called from the bottom of the stairs.

"I knew your flight was delayed." He raced down the stairs, squinting, trying to see her in the shadowy darkness. He made out her petite form clad in white shorts and navy shirt. "I wasn't sure when you would arrive."

"The Navy transport just landed."

Resisting the urge to kiss her, he guided her out the door onto the verandah. "Let's sit here," he said when they came to the swing.

Jennifer smiled over her shoulder as she sat down and the swing creaked. She'd cut her hair into a chin length bob that had just a hint of a natural wave to it. Otherwise, she looked exactly the way he'd remembered her.

Bright blue eyes. Sexy smile.

His Jenny.

An image seared into his brain from his youth.

"I've been thinking . . . a lot," she said.

Uh-oh.

"Before you say anything," he told her. "I want you to know nothing's changed for me."

"Everything's changed for me," she told him, her voice low. "I've spent months in antiterrorist training. I've seen unimaginable horror. Land mines. Maimed children. People living for years in tent cities."

He nodded slowly, afraid to say a word.

"What do you mean when you say nothing has changed?" she asked.

"I still love you. I understand how you feel after losing Chloe. Even if we don't have children, I want to marry you." He looked at her, trying to communicate with his eyes, how deeply he loved her. "I love you enough to forget having children."

She gazed up at him and shook her head. "I love you too much to allow you to make such a sacrifice."

Fear tightened in his chest. This was the same argument she'd thrown at him before, and he still didn't have an answer. She *had* to forgive herself. "Jenny, please—"

"I asked you to meet me for a reason," she said, cutting him off.

He nodded slowly, wondering where this was going. And not liking what his gut instinct told him. Time and experience had toughened Jennifer. Her career was going to take the place of a family.

"I've spent a good deal of time in Bosnia. You can't imagine how those children have suffered. Every time I saw a child who had been ripped apart—by senseless acts of terrorism—I remembered Chloe.

"A senseless mistake on my part caused her to lose her life. What the children over there are enduring is something entirely different. Seeing them and thinking about the meaning of life and the joy that can come from a child . . ." She paused and gazed up at him.

He held his breath, afraid to allow himself to hope.

"I'm willing to risk having another baby . . . babies. I'll do my level best to be a good mother, I promise."

It took a full second for her words to sink in. As it did a wellspring of tenderness and happiness surged through him. Thank you, God.

"You won't be sorry, Jenny. We were meant to be together. We knew it years ago. We're older, but in our hearts nothing has changed. I love you so much more than you can imagine."

Tears glistened in her blue eyes, making them even brighter. "Thank you for waiting."

"I'd wait forever, if that's what it took."

He pulled her into his arms, hardly able to comprehend her change of heart. He kissed the top of her head, then whispered, "What about Kesseldorf?"

"You're more important than learning how to train dogs. Sadie's still in London working with New Scotland

Yard. When she finishes next week, I plan to bring her home."

"Jen, where is home?"

She shrugged. "Wherever you are."

"I'm in Miami, remember? I'm a partner in a private security firm now."

"Is there a problem? I can go back to my S&R unit with Sadie."

"Not at all," he assured her. "I just don't want you to give up Kesseldorf for me. I want to get married, then I'll go over there and wait while you and Sadie train with the Germans."

"Really?" She gazed up at him, smiling. "You'd do that for me?"

"Sure. I know how important it is to you."

The smoldering flame he saw in her eyes startled him. Jenny slid her arms around his neck. He didn't need any more encouragement. He kissed her, the soft curves of her body molding against his chest.

She pulled back, whispering, "While we're in Germany, we can work on having a family, right?"

He nodded, lowering his head to kiss her again. He felt the sooner they started a family, the more likely Jenny would be to forgive herself completely and put the past behind her.

"I can't think of anything I'd rather do," he said with a chuckle. "I love you, Jenny. We're going to be great parents."

Sixteen Months Later: Coral Gables, Florida

Jennifer sat up in the chaise lounge and watched Kyle playing in the shallow end of the pool with the twins. Sadie paced the side watching the gleeful giggling and splashing with a wary eye. Jennifer shared the dog's concern.

Although Kyle was cautious to a fault and had both Andrew and Brianna in lifejackets, a thought always hovered in her mind.

Something might happen.

She'd gotten pregnant immediately, probably before they'd arrived in Germany. During the sophisticated canine training program, they'd learned she was carrying twins. She'd tried her best not to worry, and it had worked.

Until the nurses had handed her a little boy, then a little girl.

"Jenny," Kyle called from the pool as he towed the seven-month-old twins in a circle, "relax and sit back. I'm right here and the star of Kesseldorf canine school is keeping watch."

She lay back and closed her eyes, letting the warm Florida sun wash over her. Kyle was right. She had to back off and let her children enjoy life, or she'd stifle their emotional growth.

Her family was happy here in the gracious old home that Kyle had bought upon their return from Germany. It was large, big enough for more children, and she wanted a larger family. Kyle had proven to be a remarkable father.

When she opened her eyes again, she realized she must have drifted off. The pool area was deserted. A quick glance at her watch told her that Kyle put the twins down for a nap. Naturally, Sadie had gone with them.

Her first impulse was to jump up and run to the nursery to see if they were okay, but she made herself stay put. Kyle was perfectly capable—more capable actually—of getting the twins to take a nap. She waited, not as anxious as she usually was, until Kyle came out.

"With any luck, we'll have a couple of hours to ourselves." He flopped onto the chaise next to hers. "And I thought antiterrorist work was exhausting."

She reached across the small space separating the two

recliners and touched his bare torso. "Thank you for being so patient with me."

He took her hand and planted a kiss in the center of her palm. "You're getting better. You're not as frantic as you were when they were born. Don't put too much pressure on yourself. I'm here, and fathers worry, too. I'm watching over them all the time."

"I know. That's why I love you so much." She hadn't realized how terribly alone she'd been until after she'd married Kyle. His love and understanding filled in a void that she hadn't realized was there.

"I love you," he replied, his voice pitched low, "more now than I did before. You've shown me how great it feels to be part of a real family. Exhausting sometimes, but fulfilling."

"You know, I was thinking. Maybe the twins need a brother or a sister. While they're napping we might give it a try if you're not too tired."

"Come on, Jenny. You know me better than that."

He hopped over to her lounge, and she gazed into his intense green eyes. Desire smoldered in their depths, but there was something else in them as well.

Love.

And tenderness. And understanding. She loved him more than words could possibly express, so she didn't try. Instead she put her arms around him and pulled him to her.